UNCLE ABERRANT'S COMPENDIUM OF COSMIC DELIGHTS

JASON PETERS   DANIEL KURLAND

ASHTON MACAULAY   VANESSA KRAUSS

M.T. ROBERTS   NICK DORSEY   EMMA JUN

BEN MARINER   CHRIS WOOLSEY

ABERRANT LITERATURE

for the weirdos

CONTENTS

WELCOME, FRIENDS!

Hey there, kiddos! It's your new best bud Uncle Aberrant here, comin' to you live from the depths of Hell or possibly somewhere along the Equator; it's always so hard to tell. Thanks for visiting me here in the underworld! I was getting super lonely and BORED AS HERE watching these idiots toil away at ironic punishments under the ever-watchful eye of The Big Guy. You know who I'm talking about. Steve. Steve's a bastard. You hear me, Steve?!

So, no offense, but what brings you here? Don't get me wrong, I like the company, but I'm pretty sure it's my day off, or at least that's what I've been telling people. It's just—I'm sorry, what? You bought a book? Whoop-de-Crap, what do I care? Oh, you bought MY book?! Woah, nutso! Sorry about that! I mean, don't get me wrong, I'm super stoked, I just didn't even realize it had gone on sale. Wild. I've gotta talk to my agent. I wonder how old Harry's doing? He was the last person I spoke to before I died in that freak elephant stampede. Live by the circus, die by the circus, am I right?

I guess since you're here, I may as well give you a quick run-down on what the haps be. As mentioned, my name is Uncle Aberrant and no, I won't tell you my first name so don't ask! If you got a problem with that, just assume my mother named me Uncle and go about your day, which is a stupid way to live but whatever, you do you. Sorry, I just get kinda testy when people jump up my ass about arbitrary crap. I mean, what's in a name, anyway? I guarantee you it doesn't translate to "he who carries the sun in a basket of mélange" or some cool shit like that.

What were we talking about again? Right, the book! Okay, this one is called Compendium of Cosmic Delights, a kick-ass name that gums up your throat like peanut butter licked off of a playing card. It's a collection of short fiction tales inspired by traditional cosmic horror and given a zany twist, kind of like Rod Serling meets M. Night Shyamalan on acid, which is a reference that will definitely stand the test of time. It's from a collection of oddball writers, none of whom are famous, but all of whom are insanely talented—emphasis on insane. Kind of like me if I knew how to write, but, hey, get a couple IPAs in me and I'll rant your ear off for days. You can also let me introduce your book, that works, too.

Throughout the following twelve stories, I'll be dropping in to give quick intros, ostensibly so you can be prepared for what you're about to read but mostly because I like the attention. Every story in here is as unique and deranged as I am, which is absolutely saying something. So, kick back, relax, indulge in your favorite beverage or hardcore narcotic (or a nice spot of tea, it's all good!), and get ready to enjoy the twelve twisted, maniacal tales presented right here in:

1

So, you actually decided to stick around, eh? Far be it for me to judge, I'm all about that strange and I love an audience! The fact that you're still here in the underworld with me fills my cold, blackened heart with an intense tingling sensation that's almost certainly a stroke. And hey, since you're obviously looking for a weird-ass time, let's get into it!

Our first story features a drifter ambling through an alternate dimension at the behest of an unknown figure. Kind of like how I'm constantly being peppered with inane requests from The Big Guy despite the fact he never shows his face around the office. You wash the blood out of the Iron Maiden, Steve! Seriously, what's the point? It's just going to get filled with gore again. It reminds me of people that make their bed every day; what the Here is wrong with you all?!

The drifter's name is Ezekiel and the world he traverses seems as though it could be ours, except for the impossibly colored skies and, of course, all the demons and magic and such. Other than that, it's spot-on! Like looking out a space window toward Earth. *sigh* I miss that place. The drugs were on par with the people, which is to say inconsistent at best. But plentiful! And cheap.

There's also a guy that pops up later in the story that I'm pretty sure I partied with. It was at that Andy Warhol shindig I "accidentally" wandered into. If so, he owes me sixty dollars and I have every intention of collecting. Also, he should definitely get tested.

This story blends the Old West with the Old Gods in the most delicious of ways. Now while I consider the many fantastic, torturous weapons available at my disposal (I already told you, I'm not cleaning the Iron Maiden out, Steve!), please enjoy An Incident at Fort Merilee.

AN INCIDENT AT FORT MERILEE

JASON PETERS

R ed and purple ribbons coalesced beside a domineering moon over land that would one day be known as Los Angeles, California. Ezekiel's emerald-colored boots kicked up black sand illuminated by lunar light as soft wind caused his dark violet duster to ripple and sway. Matching chaps covered saffron-colored jeans below a black blouse, while his loosely hanging belt—stained verdant to match his shoes—concealed no weapon or holster.

Ezekiel stopped, cocked his head down and to the side as if listening to a voice riding the breeze. He caressed the wide brim of his black hat during a long and silent moment, then produced a curt, agreeable nod and changed his trajectory due southeast.

Night gave way to daybreak as the drifter came upon the object of his pursuit. The town was named Fort Merilee and possessed a sunny ambiance that matched its namesake's phonetic quality. Ezekiel considered that, as with most of the cities he visited, there was likely a less-than-savory underbelly that coursed throughout. Still, he had to admit that even from a relative distance and despite the early-morning hour, this developing community vibrated with commerce and activity.

The rising sun burned the sky fuchsia and revealed an imposing six-foot wall that encircled the city's entrance. Behind this, the local foothills provided a beautiful, elevated backdrop scattered with modest, newly built homes. Ezekiel approached the expansive opening that allowed entry to the city. He expected guards high atop the outposts and was surprised to find them unmanned. Without breaking stride, he soon found himself upon the main boulevard, where numerous stores beheld themselves to tourists and locals alike.

It was early in the day; accordingly, the streets were not packed with crowds as they would be later. Ezekiel noted the absence of significant religious structures and ruled out a Catholic or Mormon population. This was beneficial, as they often complicated his pursuits.

As he stood surveying the area, a fly landed on his unkempt beard, which rested somewhere between five o'clock and Thursday. He flicked the insect with a swift motion, felt the slight crack of hexapodous exoskeleton against his fingernail. The stretch of road looked to be roughly a quarter mile long. It featured a row of businesses on one side that ranged from banks to drug stores to mailing posts to restaurants. Several nondescript buildings Ezekiel rightly assumed to be brothels posed as saloons.

With a relaxed motion, Ezekiel lifted the black hat from his head. He ran his fingers through shaggy hair that cascaded to his shoulders when a distinguished-looking gentleman flanked his vision. The man was all tailcoat and cane, with a monocle secure in his breast pocket that brandished a pronounced fragrance of stature. He spoke with an accent that split the difference between Old English and The Old West, calling from several dozen feet away as he approached the drifter.

"My dear boy! I say, my dear boy! I do not believe I've had the pleasure of your acquaintance here before." He came to a halt with his cane sturdy in one hand, lifted his free arm openly as if presenting a circus attraction. "As mayor of this fine settlement, allow me to be the first to say, 'Welcome to Fort Merilee!'"

"Nice place." Ezekiel was never a man for many words.

The aristocrat responded, his pinched glabella communicating as much as his words. "A bit of an understatement if I do say so myself. Why, my town represents the richest, most vibrant offerings any city has to offer! Whatever your pleasure, whatever it is you seek, you'll be hard-pressed to find more exquisite goods than those presented here, yes indeed."

Ezekiel's face reflected his lack of awe. "When do the stores open?"

The man stood back, raised his eyebrows with a growing smile. "Well, well, it looks like we have a consumer here among us! We welcome your kind with open arms, my boy. Come, come, see here." He put an arm around Ezekiel and ushered him down the boulevard. "Every store you see before you has been personally approved by the Board of Commerce. A city must have standards, my boy, and standards of commerce are no matter to be taken lightly, no. Business makes the world go 'round, as you will no doubt affirm here shortly. Of course, should you find yourself lacking for coin, we can always put you to work in any number of various capacities. You seem like you would perform strongly in the pursuit of bounties." The man stopped, turned to face Ezekiel eye-to-eye. "Can I interest you in any such opportunity? All rewards are split fifty-fifty between us. A fair proposition, yes, very fair indeed."

Ezekiel smiled, bowed his head politely. "Much obliged, but I've got other matters to tend to."

The mayor gave a subtle wince of disappointment, turned to continue escorting Ezekiel down the road. "Not to worry, my good boy, I've an immeasurable number of such people at my disposal."

"I'm certain you do."

The man stopped, again turned to Ezekiel. "Where have my manners departed? I have failed to properly introduce myself, a most grievous of sins indeed."

"I can think of a few worse."

"J. Alfred Farthington the Third, Esquire. Pleased to make your acquaintance." He extended a hand, and Ezekiel received it in kind.

"Pleasure's mine, sir."

"And your name?"

"Most call my Ezekiel."

"And what do the others call you?"

"There is only one who calls me by another name."

An awkward silence persisted.

"Well, never you mind about that, Ezekiel. Of greater concern is that you have arrived at our fair marketplace rather early. Few of our proprietors open before noon, as most of our businesses stay open well into the night; that's when the action *really* gets going, my boy. Have you ever partaken of a striptease from a woman born south of the border? It really is a sight to behold. The elegance, the sophistication, the raw sexuality; it's all there and really quite invigorating to a man's…spirit, if you catch my drift."

"Subtle but understood."

Farthington smiled in a way that felt practiced, as though he had taken great offense to a relatively innocuous comment. "Say, you look like a man that enjoys a stiff drink."

"I've been known to indulge."

"Well, as fortune would have it, we have found ourselves precisely before Miss May's Fine Lagers and Ales. Perhaps you would find a brief visit an acceptable way to pass the dull moments before the marketplace opens?"

Ezekiel considered the proposition. "I do believe you're right about that."

"Most excellent!" Farthington twiddled his fingers against one another in an excited manner. "I shall leave you to your devices. The bright red double doors on your left will take you where you're looking to go." He grabbed his cane and gave it a forceful tap on the ground. "Enjoy your time in my vibrant town! Perhaps we shall see one another again this evening."

Ezekiel nodded in subtle agreement. "Something tells me we will."

THE DRIFTER EZEKIEL sat with his head hung low over the bar while he drank brown and bitter ale. His hat's brim acted as a shield from potential chit-chat with patrons and barmaids alike. He wondered if the woman before him was the titular Miss May, then wondered how many others wondered the same.

Something interrupted his thoughts, and he again cocked his head in a way that indicated concentration and intent. "Yeah, I know. Why the hell else would we be here?" He spoke in a subtle whisper, hoping nobody in the establishment would notice. "You're not wrong. Already I can tell these people deserve it as much as anybody. But I'm sick of you stringing me along. After every stop, the criteria changes. I'm tired of it. I don't deserve this."

The heavyset barmaid that may or may not have been Miss May walked past Ezekiel. He peeked past the brim of his hat and gave her a forced smile with no teeth. She eyed him with suspicion as she continued down the bar toward another patron.

"Just stop moving the goalposts, alright? When I'm done, you release me. Simple as that." After some time, Ezekiel sighed in exasperation. His shoulders drooped as if giving up a fight in which they never had any chance of victory. "With every fiber of whatever soul I have left, I hate you."

SEVEN BEERS and three hours later, maybe/maybe-not Miss May addressed the defeated-looking cowboy. "You got some sort of tolerance there, mister. You ain't so much as swayed the entire time you been sittin' down."

"Years of drinking will do that to a man."

"I'll say. You ain't even been slurrin' while you're sitting here talkin' to yerself."

Reflexively, Ezekiel smiled, genuine this time. "You heard that?"

"Not so much as could just sort of tell. The way yer body was all hustlin' and jerkin' around, it was either that, or you was playin' with yourself, and I ain't never seen yer pants down none."

"You're a perceptive lady."

"All barkeeps are."

Ezekiel looked away from the woman and down at the bar, melancholy etched onto his face. "Say...I don't suppose you'd be willing to take the day off here now, would ya?"

The lady that may or may not have been Miss May chuckled. "No, I don't suppose I would."

Ezekiel nodded, knowing the answer to the question before he asked. "Yeah...I didn't suppose so." He knocked his closed fist twice against the bar, then stood. "Should you happen to change your mind after the sun goes down…that wouldn't be a bad idea."

She regarded him with a squint that spoke to myriad emotions and calculations being processed at once. "I'll keep that in mind, mister."

"You take care, ma'am." Ezekiel tipped his black hat in her direction, then dropped money on the table before he exited the saloon.

THE STREETS WERE JUST as Farthington described them, packed with all sorts of people looking to spend money on various items and activities. Along the quarter-mile stretch of cobblestone road that approximated Foothill Boulevard, vendors advertised their wares and services. Little space existed between each building save enough to access certain technological infrastructures such as telephone and electricity cables; this maximized the number of commercial opportunities within the town.

Horse-drawn carriages escorted the city's wealthy and elite; beggars ignored them in favor of ordinary folk who were more generous with their money. Ezekiel walked among the rabble, which seemed to include a higher percentage of locals than expected, given the familiar geniality they displayed toward vendors.

With so many people pressing against him, he reflexively positioned his arm and shoulder out to protect the object hidden in his duster's inside pocket. A petite, middle-aged lady appeared before him, holding what seemed to be an acrylic vase. However, such material was almost impossible to acquire except in the most technologically advanced cities, typically identifiable by the presence of an established, accredited university, of which this city had none. Clearly, as far as the town of Fort Merilee was considered, education came second to profits. That suited them just fine.

"Hey there, handsome!" The lady flashed a grin featuring numerous gold and silver teeth. "You look like someone who likes to impress the ladies, am I right?" Ezekiel failed to answer, kept moving. The lady donned an air of indignation. "Listen here, it's rude to ignore your elders, son; now answer the question. Do you like to impress the ladies or not?"

"Sure," Ezekiel answered, continuing forward.

"A man of few words, huh?" She was unimpressed. Unlike Ezekiel, who admired the skill with which this lady walked backward. She kept the vase continuously displayed while avoiding contact with those around her; it was clear she had rehearsed his act thousands of times before. "Well, if you gift this here vase to a gal of your choosing, ain't no female alive that wouldn't drop her panties for ya in a heartbeat!"

"Not interested, lady."

Great offense crossed the woman's face. "And why not, huh? You too good for my wares? Think ole Jezebel's gonna sell you faulty product? How dare you! Not once in my life have I ever sold somebody somethin' wasn't genuine." The emphatic and unprompted nature of her claim made Ezekiel believe otherwise.

"Okay, Jezebel. You have yourself a nice day now." Ezekiel politely tipped the brim of his hat in her direction.

"Plebian." The woman returned to her post in a huff, then immediately dropped the frown and approached another potential mark with a smile.

With the crowd's din in full swing, Ezekiel felt comfortable engaging in one of the clandestine conversations he so carefully and desperately hid from others and spoke into his coat. "Why do we always have to go through this ridiculous song and dance? Why not just get it over with?" A young couple noticed him and looked his way in confusion. He pretended to be embarrassed, manufacturing a sheepish grin, but in truth, he didn't much care about the opinions of others. He hadn't always been of such disposition, but his experiences since the day he made that particularly fateful decision had worn him down.

Again, he felt at the object inside his breast pocket. He sighed and shook his head in disapproval when he was approached by another vendor, this time selling foul-smelling meat. "Hey there, fella, you ever get a taste of real-life boar's rump? Best meat in the west, lemme tell ya. Here, help yourself to a free sample, then you come on into my restaurant, and we'll fix you up a nice meal proper!" The corpulent chef picked up a strip of meat and attempted to shove it in Ezekiel's mouth. The drifter smacked the man's hand away, prompting him to spill his tray to the ground. "Now, what the hell'd you go and that for! That meat costs me money, ingrate!"

"Well, maybe you should have better sense than jamming assorted proteins down a man's gullet against his wishes."

The chef's face contorted, seething with anger and resentment. "How dare you? Do you know who I am? I'm *Mister* Gavelston. Of *Gavelston Meats*! Yeah, that's right! The hell you think you are throwing my product to the ground like that?!"

From the corner of his eye, Ezekiel saw the lady Jezebel re-appear. "Hey Gavelston, is this asshole giving you trouble?!"

"Damn right, he is!"

"Sunnuvabitch was mouthy as shit with me, too. Matter of fact...I don't even think he's here to buy!" She shouted this at the top of her lungs while pointing an accusatory finger at Ezekiel, prompting a collective gasp from the entirety of the marketplace. From patrons to vendors, everyone froze, shocked, then turned to Ezekiel with questioning, accusatory eyes.

With the crowd silent and still, J. Alfred Farthington the Third parted the sea of people and approached Ezekiel. "My boy. My dear, sweet boy. Is this true? Tell me it isn't so! I had such high hopes for you. You've the air of a man of discriminating taste, the type of man welcomed here by every vendor and businessperson alike." Ezekiel remained silent, unsure of the correct response to this increasingly volatile situation.

"Gavelston?!" Farthington demanded.

"Yes, good sir?"

"Are you hereby making a formal inquiry into the charge of Lack of Legitimate Commercial Interests?"

"Yes, formally! The accused shall brandish his wallet or coin purse as dictated by Ordinance C.716!"

With a sigh, Farthington turned to Ezekiel. "You've heard the man. By order of the town charter, you are required to procure the currency with which you intend to engage in commercial activity. Posthaste."

Ezekiel reached into both pockets of his saffron-colored jeans but soon realized he had spent all his money at Maybe-Miss May's. He gulped before addressing Farthington. "It would appear I spent the last of my coin on ale." A suspicious murmur carried across the crowd.

"Lies!" Gavelston shouted.

"Treasonous!" Jezebel called out. "The poor degenerate wishes to deceive us!"

Farthington bellowed out across the boulevard. "Then we shall call upon Miss May to settle this matter. Miss May! Oh, Miss May! Attend the position at once!"

A husky voice called out over the crowd. "I'm 'ere, sir, I'm comin'!" Within moments, the woman that served Ezekiel appeared, answering the question he had considered since first stepping foot in the establishment.

Farthington addressed her formally. "Do you recognize this man?"

She looked Ezekiel up and down, slowly, carefully. He flashed a recognizing smile when her eyes met his. "Nope, ne'er seen this man before in me life." Ezekiel's face dropped.

"See?!" Jezebel implored. "Dirty tricks from a dirty trickster!"

Gavelston chimed in. "Dirty tricks from a dirty trickster! Dirty tricks from a dirty trickster!" It only took a few seconds for the call to become a full-blown chant. All around him, the chorus grew. Beads of sweat trickled down his forehead, and he could sense the crowd beginning to mobilize. "Dirty tricks from a dirty trickster! Dirty tricks from a dirty trickster!"

Then, that look of concentration as Ezekiel cocked his head down and to the side. As the throng encroached upon him, he quickly gave an affirmative head nod and lifted his chin to address the oncoming horde. "Enough!" The force with which he spoke was enough to halt the mob. He paused to ensure he had the people's attention, that their advance would not continue. Upon feeling assured in both regards, he continued.

"Ladies and Gentlemen, forgive my lack of formal introduction." He spoke with a charismatic blend of humility and confidence that rivaled the best of public speakers. "My name is Ezekiel Goodfellow, and I admit that I have not come here in search of purchase." The din of the crowd returned, all harsh whispers and scowling brows. "However, it is the case that I have something in my possession, an object the likes of which none of you have ever seen!" Again, a commotion, but this sound was anew, infused with curiosity and interest. "This object is so magnificent, so wonderful, so tantalizingly curious, that to gaze upon it is to marvel at the very nature of existence! To question the reality of life itself! To fundamentally change the concept of space and time as you know it!"

As Ezekiel expected, attitudes shifted. People were now actively curious, relishing the idea of what this mysterious object could be as they attempted random guesses to dissect the enigma.

"Is it a clock that slows down time?"

"How about an invincibility cape?"

"What if it's a self-propelling passenger vehicle of some kind?"

"Don't be stupid, that's just science fiction!"

"I bet it's an animal that feeds off of its own waste!"

"Ewww, gross!"

"Okay, but you'd never have to clean up after the hogs again!"

"I don't wanna eat bacon that's eaten the shit of other bacon!"

"That's an oversimplification, and you know it!"

Ezekiel felt compelled to interject. "Fellows, fellows, please. To disclose the object right now would be to rob each and every one of you of the thrill of anticipation, that most noble of emotions. That is why we shall hold an auction this evening at dusk, right here in this very town!"

Again, the throng erupted in commotion. Farthington returned the attention to himself by way of loud proclamation. "Yes, yes, of course, my boy! A most ostentatious act indeed! Splendid, just splendid!" J. Alfred clasped his hands together around his cane. The smile on his face couldn't be wider without tearing the flesh at the corners of his mouth. "I've been running this city for longer than I can remember, and this is by far the most unnecessary and superfluous act I've seen in my tenure! How glorious for you to bestow this gift upon us! Yes, an auction! A public auction! Let it be known that tonight at dusk, the activities shall commence!"

The crowd erupted in enthusiastic applause as people surrounded Ezekiel and clapped him on the shoulders; he resented the resultant handprints left on his dark violet duster. Farthington continued, addressing both Ezekiel and the crowd. "And let us hope that this object you've procured is worth its weight in said anticipation! We would all hate very much to be let down by this most curious revelation. Why, I don't think we'd be able to live with such a person should he let us down like that." J. Alfred maintained direct eye contact with Ezekiel as he spoke the last line; the threat was effectively received. "Until dusk!" He lifted his arms and cane as the mob cheered in exultation for the coming festivities.

THE TOWN CENTER had been decorated in a manner befitting the excitement surrounding the evening's events. It featured an assortment of brightly colored ribbons and banners that hung about the walls of the vast, circular enclosure. Numerous strings of small incandescent light bulbs met above a podium set atop a grand stage and flared outward over the gathering masses that swelled the main entrance.

The sun had begun its slow descent towards the opposite hemisphere, bringing about the customary streams of red and purple starlight that battled the moon for attention every night. Ezekiel stood off to the side of the main stage that looked out across the crowd, watching the people shuffle in and assemble, noticing how eagerly everyone seemed to anticipate the night's events. He again felt for the object in his breast pocket, shook his head upon confirmation of its presence. "This will likely be our biggest haul in some time. I expect to be remunerated accordingly. No more tricks. I mean it." Again, he appeared to listen intently to his surroundings before shaking his head and speaking through gritted teeth. "I said. No. More. Tricks." Ezekiel's patience was being severely tested. He spent several long moments observing the Town Center's cobblestone construction; it provided an almost medieval ambiance. The night's crowd could be responsible for a record-setting sum the likes of which Ezekiel had yet to see.

But of course, he and his partner were never in it for the money.

It was then that J. Alfred Farthington approached, his cane rapping across the stones. "Ezekiel, my boy! What a delight! I must say that this turnout is exceeding even my lofty expectations. Three cheers for spectacle, eh, my boy?!"

"Here, here." Ezekiel's delivery couldn't have been more deadpan.

"Now, your certain this object of yours is prepared to impress? As I mentioned, this level of turnout is only going to inspire a furor should you fail to deliver on your promise."

"I'm certain. Hasn't failed me yet."

"Splendid, splendid..." Something about the tone of Ezekiel's remark caused Farthington unease, but he couldn't immediately identify the offense. His thinking was interrupted by the proclamation of a large bell that rang seven times, indicating the festivities were set to begin. With a shake of his head as if clearing away a mental fog, his expression returned to the generous, overly enthusiastic smile that stood as arguably the most valuable part of his public persona.

Townspeople continued to trickle in despite the packed courtyard; there was little room to accommodate additional bodies. Farthington walked up shallow steps beside the stage and strode theatrically to the podium placed front and center. "Good ladies and gentlemen, locals and tourists alike, allow me to humbly and officially welcome you to Fort Merilee!" He raised his hands and cane, and the audience responded with an appropriately exaggerated level of applause. The audience seemed determined to enjoy a spectacle and, in turn, would be delivered one.

J. Alfred spoke with a sense of enticing mystery that quickly drew the crowd in. "Tonight, we have been promised a strange and exotic artifact, the likes of which none of us has seen before. Indeed, if the stories are to be believed, what we witness here in just a few short moments could upend the very fabric of reality as we know it!" Again, excited murmurs snaked through the crowd. "Now, upon revelation of this most exciting financial prospect, our local appraiser Lord Alex Winterbottom," he turned a hand offstage toward an elderly, bespectacled gentleman, "will determine an acceptable starting price in which to begin the bidding." The audience applauded, less out of due respect and more because they had been incited to by a showman. "Now, without further ado, allow me to introduce the man currently in ownership of this incredible artifact, the drifter known as Ezekiel Goodfellow!"

A spotlight flashed on with a loud, mechanical roar and quickly found Ezekiel. The crowd went silent, allowing the buzz of the enlarged incandescent to carry across the courtyard. The sound seemed to reflect Ezekiel's mind at that moment; he couldn't tell whether that was comforting or disconcerting. As he looked across the crowd, he raised a hand above his face to shield his eyes from the spotlight. "So many people..." he whispered to himself. J. Alfred began to nervously fidget and twitter. "Well, now, my boy, let's not keep the good people of this fair city waiting. After all, we've commerce to tend to." While he held his smile, the stern glare into Ezekiel's eyes spoke of a different emotion entirely.

With a heavy sigh, Ezekiel patted the object in his breast pocket and took the stage. Upon reaching the podium, he looked out among the massive sea of people and immediately grew light-headed. He gripped both sides of the platform, hoping he appeared as though deep in thought but mostly trying not to collapse.

After a fit that lasted no more than a few agonizingly long seconds, his presence of mind returned, and the spell quickly dissipated. Back to sorts, he took a deep breath and addressed the audience, trying hard to match the good-natured theatrics displayed by J. Alfred Farthington. "Good people of Fort Merilee, I thank you for this most gracious of receptions." It always surprised Ezekiel how quickly the ease of public speaking returned the moment he graced the stage. "It is true that I bring before you today an object of most stunning construction, an object the likes of which no other exists across the land. This is not hyperbole but rather a statement of fact. Should anyone claim otherwise after seeing it, bring me proof, and I shall see to it that you are awarded seventy dollars. *That* is how certain I am."

The townspeople gasped. Even Farthington sputtered at the assertion. "Seventy dollars, my boy?! An outrageous sum, even for this most prosperous of trading communities!"

"Again, this is to indicate my level of conviction regarding the uniqueness and scarcity of the object I am about to reveal."

J. Alfred considered this severely, then relaxed his face to a smile. "Very well. Again, your penchant for ostentatious display proves unparalleled. Please, continue, for I am so enjoying the show."

"Very well." The drifter Ezekiel stepped back from the front of the stage, his emerald boots clacking across the polished wood. His dark violet coat swayed in a breeze that cooled his skin, warm as it was from the spotlight and the anticipation of the reveal. He reached for his breast pocket, drawing his coat out ever so slightly before letting it go and lifting that same hand to the brim of his hat. "Ladies and gentle-men...it's been a pleasure." He returned his hand inside the breast pocket of his coat, then pulled out a tiny, smoothly polished human skull with various colored jewels adorning the crown.

Immediately, a wave of disappointment washed over the crowd.

"A miniature skull?! That's the big reveal?!"

"Whoop-dee-shit, I've got three of those at home, and it didn't cost me a wooden nickel!"

"You seriously wasted our time for this?!"

"You're useless!"

"You're nothing!"

"Asshole!"

"Shyster!"

"I want my seventy dollars!"

"Boo, this man! Booooooo!"

The chorus of displeasure swelled many times over when Ezekiel made to quiet the raucous audience. "People, people, relax! Of course, there is nothing special about a regular old human skull, even one as small as this. Why, even these jewels aren't enough to distinguish it to the level that I have promised you. But there is a secret about this skull that has yet to be revealed!" The townspeople, willing to entertain Ezekiel's suggestion, allowed their indignation to be silenced for the moment. "Observe!"

Ezekiel returned to the front and center of the stage and placed the skull to stare outwardly at the vast throng of people; the spotlight generated a hot spot on its forehead. Ezekiel backed away, and for an incredibly long, silent moment, there was nary a sound to be heard anywhere, save for the buzz of the oversized incandescent bulb.

Then, before the audience, the skull quickly grew to average size and spoke. "Whaaaaaaaaaat's uuuuuuuuuuup, biiiiiiii-itchesssssssssssss!" It possessed a nasally, high-pitched voice with a bit of New York thrown in for good measure. The townspeople, in accordance, looked at each other, confused.

"What the hell is this, some sort of parlor trick?" someone called out.

"Natch, bud!" the skull answered enthusiastically. "You are lookin' at a true original, live and in the flesh! Well, in the bone, I suppose."

A small child expressed his confusion through a series of grunts, then cried in disappointment. Other children cried as well, though mostly out of fear.

"Awww, c'mon, kids, no need for the waterworks. Tell me, what do stupid children from this era enjoy? You guys have television here yet?"

"What's television?" someone asked.

"Fantastic, nevermind! Tell ya what, here's a yellow elephant riding a unicycle, that ought to shut you idiots up!" The skull then uttered a mantra of uninterpretable words that sounded like an unholy combination of Arabic and German. "Klaatu Barada Nikto!" There was a brief flash of light on stage. Suddenly, as promised, a yellow elephant appeared. It balanced itself precariously on a unicycle while holding an umbrella in its trunk. Most of the adults cleared the area in a panic as the children rushed to the front of the stage excitedly, giant smiles on their faces. "Doesn't that just obliterate your tiny little pea brains?!" the skull enthused. The elephant balanced itself on its hind legs and traversed the stage while the children marveled in delight, giggling enthusiastically. The skull opened its mouth to produce circus music that carried across the courtyard at ear-splitting volume. Most adults pressed their hands to their ears in exaggerated displays Ezekiel found unnecessary. Still, they had a lot to take in, psychologically speaking. Besides, the children loved it; nothing but ear-to-ear grins all around.

This continued for some time when the skull noticed that many of the adult townspeople had successfully and appropriately fled the Town Center and its abrasive soundwaves and incomprehensible visuals. The skull closed its mouth, and the music immediately ceased. The elephant promptly vanished into thin air and left behind a cartoonish cloud of smoke. "Easy there, fellas and lady-fellas! You didn't think I'd leave you guys out, did ya? Check this, yo!" The skull rocked back and forth on its jaw, picking up speed until it had enough momentum to launch itself into the air. It somersaulted itself to a height of no less than a dozen feet and tumbled over itself, airborne. Adults and children alike stared with gaped jaws, save for Ezekiel; he had seen this act more than once. "I wonder who it's going to be this time?" he asked out loud to no one in particular.

The skull remained suspended in the air, continuing to roll faster and faster as the audience became entranced through no magic save that which it used to perform. Then, the skull crashed down to the stage and opened its jaws wide to produce a cartoonish flash of smoke. It slowly dissipated to reveal famed 1990's saxophonist Kenny G. performing his most famous ballad, Songbird, which everyone knows by melody but not by name.

The children quickly became disinterested, with many indicating as much by way of stink-face. However, the adults were intrigued by the soothing melody that now entranced and beckoned them. Slowly, the adults crowded the front of the stage, with many that had previously left returning to rejoice in the heavenly, foreign sounds. By the second chorus, Kenny had the adults in the metaphorical palm of his metaphorical hand. Almost instantly, the Town Center was packed again, a thousand lame adults swaying to the soothing sounds of a song that would one day appear on KOST 103.5 FM.

It was easy to forget this instrument was foreign to the people of Fort Merilee, but that didn't stop Ezekiel from judging them all the same. Then, in an instant, the skull closed its mouth, and the music and Kenny ceased to exist. The audience seemed disappointed that the experience was over but pleased that it had occurred in the first place. Ezekiel joined the skull, and the two looked across the sea of people in silence. He picked it up and displayed it for the crowd with one hand flat and the other open behind. This act, coupled with Kenny's recent appearance, reminded him of Vanna White and Wheel of Fortune, which in turn made him nostalgic for the 1990s. He wondered if they would ever get the privilege of returning to that era he quite enjoyed. "Probably not," he said to himself sadly.

"Hey, Johnson, I don't know where you drifted off to but get your ass back here! We've got a job to do." Ezekiel hated it when the skull used his real name, as it reminded him of a life far removed from his own.

"Right." Ezekiel inhaled deeply and addressed the audience. "With this display, you should all now understand the power of this artifact and the immense value it undoubtedly possesses. Whether collector or trader, it stands to reason that only the most powerful and elite of persons should stand to inherit such a possession." He looked to J. Alfred, who was himself astonished. "Mr. Farthington. With your permission, I shall ask Mr. Winterbottom to assess an official valuation to be deemed acceptable as a starting bid."

Farthington wiped at his brow with a silk handkerchief and waved Ezekiel on. "Yes, yes, of course, posthaste. Let us not dally any further with this most marvelous of wonders. Mr. Winterbottom, if you will." He raised his hand to the elderly man, who nodded his head in subtle affirmation and walked across the stage with incredible difficulty. Eventually, he reached Ezekiel and proceeded to examine the skull thoroughly and with precision. After many long minutes, he snapped the skull's jaw shut, satisfied, and indicated a nod to J. Alfred, then turned to Ezekiel and whispered a sum in his ear. Ezekiel received the information without reaction, nodding in affirmation, then relayed that figure to the audience. "The bidding shall commence at one hundred and fifty dollars!"

Immediately, an uproar buoyed across the throng.

"One hundred and fifty dollars?! That's outrageous!"

"There's nary more than a dozen men alive could afford such a sum!"

"Certainly, none of them are here right now!"

"That's more than even Farthington could procure!"

A stunned, silent gasp washed over the crowd. Slowly, the people all looked to J. Alfred as the spotlight followed suit. Farthington fidgeted, then righted himself and spoke. "My good people, do not be so offended by the assertion. Yes, one hundred and fifty dollars is a vast fortune, even for me! I do believe I could gather the money if necessary, but admittedly it would most certainly wipe me out."

"What can I say?" the skull enthused. "I'm a bad-ass, boss-ass bitch, and I know it! Y'all ain't never seen nothin' like this before, so it's put-up-or-shut-up time in Skull Town, ya feel me?!"

The townspeople looked at each other, confused.

"I don't think they feel you," Ezekiel said to the skull before addressing the audience. "Allow me to interpret. What he means to say is that he is one-of-a-kind. You could comb the most remote deserts of the most exotic lands and still not come across a creation of his exact design. He is as precious as the most brilliant of metals; rarer than that, to be truthful."

Confusion made way to understanding and agreement among the crowd. They looked to J. Alfred for some level of advice on the matter. With the spotlight still trained on his person, he stacked both hands atop the ball of his cane and rested his chin there, deep in thought. The audience remained silent for the long minutes this process entailed until, with a triumphant snort, J. Alfred Farthington stomped his cane against the ground and promptly stood.

"Citizens and visitors of Fort Merilee, while it is true that a great many opinions exist regarding our fine town, can we all not agree that such commerce-minded ways make perfect sense to each of us?" The townspeople nodded in approval. A few clapped. "And as proper business-minded folk with an appropriately developed understanding of commercial interests, it's safe to declare that we all appreciate the importance of influential marketing, isn't that correct?" Again, the townspeople's heads bobbed in agreement, with more joining in the applause. "As businessmen and women of the highest intellect, it is imperative that we recognize a once-in-a-lifetime opportunity when it approaches us. It is most certain that such an occasion presents itself here and now. To not determine an imminent solution would be to engage in amateurism and peasantry. We are far better than that!"

"Here, here!" the crowd exulted.

J. Alfred continued. "What we shall do is impose a new duty, effective immediately."

The crowd erupted in displeasure.

"Fascist!"

"Communist!"

"Cuck!"

Farthington held up his hands to silence the crowd. "Relax, ladies and gentlemen, relax. Do not forget that I am your commerce president. When it comes to our economy, I alone can fix it. Do not think I would ever impose such a burden on honest, hard-working businesspersons as yourselves, no! This duty is for the workers, those black sheep of society we would happily abolish from the face of our planet was it not for the necessity of their labor. That is why we will be instituting an additional tax on sales immediately! Your profits are yours to keep, my brothers and sisters."

The crowd exploded in applause, roaring its approval.

"Here, here!"

"J. Alfred Farthington is a genius!"

"This is why we elected him!"

"He was never elected, actually!"

"Shut up, socialist!"

Farthington leaned his weight against his cane and smiled. He looked to Mr. Winterbottom, who stared intently at one particular spot on the ground. This was a common act that some regarded as evidence of a keen supernatural ability; others determined it to merely indicate senility. "Good Mr. Winterbottom! Prepare the documents to make this official within our charter! And begin contacting the newspapers to run stories on this remarkable new achievement of ours: the possession of a rare and previously undiscovered artifact!"

As Mr. Winterbottom slowly turned, Ezekiel approached J. Alfred. "Mr. Farthington, to seal this arrangement, you need only to shake my hand. We have seen that you are in the process of gathering the necessary cash via your many vehicles of liquidity. But understand that a handshake is not just a handshake, not here or anywhere. It is a sacred, binding agreement the likes of which you cannot take back. So, I ask you: are you certain you wish to engage in this purchase? Will you shake my hand in agreement on behalf of you and your entire town?" Ezekiel extended his hand to the wealthily dressed man. J. Alfred considered the proposition for less than half a second before eagerly receiving it. "Yes, my boy, yes! A thousand times, yes!"

Ezekiel sighed, heavy and forlorn. "Very well. The deed is done. The skull is yours."

The skull bounced around excitedly on stage. "Oh boy, oh boy, oh boy! That's right, I'm yours, ba-baaaaaaaaaaaaaaay! And everything that comes along with me!" The skull trotted out to center stage and began the incantation as he had at so many Town Centers before. "Kunda, Estrata, Montose, Conda! Kunda, Estrata, Montose, Conda! Kunda, Estrata, Montose, Conda!" At this, red and purple streams of starlight splintered, separating into new groupings and patterns. Yellow energy swirled around green particles that interlaced with purple luminescence in a grand display of light across a perfectly darkened skyscape. The moon stood steadfast and strong through it all, refusing to budge.

Streams of color surrounded one another to create a vortex of vibrant power that was as beautiful and breathtaking as it was dangerous. With the audience's attention held rapt on the swirling energy, few noticed the skull as it underwent a transformation of its own, growing ever larger as the colored jewels around its crown detached. They traversed the skull's circumference at various degrees, like particles encircling a nucleus in constant motion. It grew to over twenty feet in diameter as colors wailed about at incredible speeds. Accordingly, people fled in terror. Screams and mayhem announced their presence. This was the part the skull always relished most, as it indicated a job finally and well accomplished.

The jewels surrounding the skull reached terminal velocity, transfixing any and all who happened to gaze upon them; given the ostentatiousness of the display, this was everyone. More than a thousand people stood in the Town Center, frozen, eyes transfixed on the enormous skull and its dazzlingly colorful vortex.

"Y'ALL BITCHES WANTED A SHOW!" the skull screamed, insanity dominating his character. "WELL, HERE YA GO, STRAIGHT OUT OF PRIME TIME, YOU IGNORANT FUCKS! BWAAAAAAAAAAAAAAAAAAHHHHHHHHHHHHHH!!!" A low-pitched, violent, throaty scream cast itself across the land like an explosion of energy, bringing violence and death to all who stood within its path. This, again, was everyone.

The resultant carnage was horrendous. The energy produced from the skull brought a gruesome death related to each person's innermost fears.

A man who was deathly afraid of fire burst into flames, his skin charring and cauterizing its own wounds, pieces of flesh and bone exposed to the elements. His blood coagulated like sugar on a frying pan. It remained stuck to his skin in defiance of gravity's supposed laws.

A woman afraid of drowning found herself melting into a literal pile of goo, all puss, blood, and urine collecting into a small, babbling puddle. Others who had not yet suffered their fates repeatedly stepped into the viscera, sending splashes of what was once a woman across the cobblestone floor.

A claustrophobic man found himself immobile when an unseen force compressed his body like an invisible, four-sided compactor. His bones snapped as he was fashioned into a square-like proportion. Yelling followed. His shoulders splintered, and his ribcage shattered, which caused his inner organs to slosh around. As his screams grew more forceful, he found himself asphyxiating when his heart became lodged in the bottom of his own esophagus. It is still unclear which act precisely caused his death, but it's safe to assume that all of this played a factor.

A small child whose biggest fear was being left alone was, in turn, left alone, unharmed, one of the few survivors of the onslaught. It is unclear whether this was due to an act of kindness or a flaw in the system.

When all was said and done, the Town Center was nothing but cobblestone and red viscera, punctuated by a few bloody, shivering, crying children. The vortex quickly dissipated as the sky returned to normal, red and purple starshine doing its best to remain alongside the moon without disturbing it.

The skull had returned to average size. Next to it stood Ezekiel, who stared at the few remaining children in sorrow. He wished to his own personal savior that he had not made the decision that led to him being enslaved by this skull, a mere tool used to do its bidding. But alas, as everyone knows, there is no changing the past.

THE DRIFTER EZEKIEL trudged across the desert. The colors of the night sky danced beside the moon as his emerald boots kicked up wisps of black sand. The skull hopped alongside him, leaving a uniquely patterned trail in the dunes. An eerie pinkish-red glow emitted from the remnants of Fort Merilee behind them.

"So, are we calling that an even thousand?" Ezekiel asked.

"Sounds fair to me," the skull replied. "What does that leave you with?"

"Another 6,482 left to go."

"Damn, son, that was a good one for ya, wasn't it?! Straight like ten percent of your quota just like, BAM, you know?!"

"I do." Ezekiel looked up to the moon as if for some level of assistance he knew it could not provide.

"Hey, dude, I know you're not always super stoked to be with me out here, but I gotta say, traveling through time and space just isn't the same without you. I mean, I've had a lot of different creatures on these sorts of travels, and I don't know what it is about you, but I feel like I do my best work when you're around. I mean, Kenny G? Did you see that shit? C'mon, that was righteous!"

"I have to admit, it was pretty inspired." Ezekiel kicked at the sand beneath him.

"C'mon, man, cheer up. What is it that's *really* bothering you?"

"Aside from being enslaved… it's just…those kids. I keep seeing the looks on their faces, all shivering and cold and frightened. It loops through my mind over and over."

"Psh, that?! Are you serious?! C'mon, man! Kids are just tiny, stupid adults. Leave 'em alone, and they become the same adults you don't have any problem killing."

"I never said I don't have a problem with it."

"Whatever, the insinuation was understood."

The two walked in silence under the rays of moonshine and colored starlight that illuminated the vast black dunes around them.

"I just…" Ezekiel hesitated.

"You just what?"

"I just don't understand why you have to be such a bastard all the time."

The skull stopped and smiled as much as a skull can before turning to Ezekiel. "Because, bro! I'm the fuckin' Devil!"

Woah, can you believe that ending? The Big Guy at it again! I swear, he just doesn't stop. And for as much fun as that was, we're just getting started!

Our next story takes the crazy and amps it up to thirteen. I know, I know, volume is only supposed to go as high as eleven, but you should be starting to figure out that I'm kind of into pushing matters to extremes. Like, you should have seen Motley Crue when those chaps first hit the streets. Bunch of pansies, I tell ya. Then I got a hold of 'em and showed them the ways of fine blow and street prostitutes. They've never looked back since! And in case you're wondering, yeah, Tommy Lee absolutely made a deal with The Big Guy to get stacked like that.

Ray Primus is our protagonist, and he's a teenage kid who loves television and hates summer camp. But that doesn't stop his totally uncool parents from putting him in a totally uncool program called Camp Clear Skies, which I'm pretty sure is where Vince Neil got clean after I was through with him. (Man, if you don't listen to 80's metal, these references must just be flying over your head, in which case, why are you still here and not listening to Kickstart My Heart?!)

Needless to say, some weird stuff happens to Ray and then even weirder stuff happens to Ray until the whole thing is whipped together into one giant, weird-flavored smoothie that hits hard and goes down easy. The entire matter gets insanely twisty-turny, and I'm not just talking about the plot! You'll have to read on to see what I mean. (Enticed, much?)

Now while I try to remember which band members still owe me from all the drugs I gave them on consignment, please enjoy Obedient Plant.

OBEDIENT PLANT

DANIEL KURLAND

The sky is amber and viridian, but it doesn't matter to Ray Primus because he's stuck in summer camp.

Ray Primus looks at all the joyful campers around him relishing a day of plant identification. He swears this is supposed to be a punishment. What else could it be? Some meager attempt to move him outside his comfort zone and broaden his horizons? Ray's horizons are plenty broad. Sometimes he even pees sitting down. No, this is punishment. Ray Primus nods to himself in conviction, as if the act makes his beliefs more accurate.

Culver's root. Blue vervain. New England aster. Ray lifelessly identifies the foliage he passes.

Ray has never expressed any interest in going away to summer camp. His pallid complexion is proof enough that he and sunlight aren't on a first-name basis. Ray Primus thrives indoors. His parents not only know this but have supported such habits for these fifteen years of his life. Ray is no Thomas Magnum. Hell, he's not even on the same level as either of the Simon brothers from *Simon & Simon*—well, maybe A.J.

But Ray can still read between the lines. He knows his abandonment at Camp Clear Skies directly results from poor freshman-year grades and that many other teenagers are here for the exact opposite reason. Still, he understands the complicated and passive-aggressive ways in which his parents operate.

Camp Clear Skies offers plenty of programs that aren't available at any other summer camps, but that's not what attracted Ray's parents to the package. Camp Clear Skies is the only summer camp within Essex County, Massachusetts that operates from June 5th to June 12th. These may seem arbitrary dates to most, but it's a stretch on the calendar that Ray's anticipated for an entire year. *The Man with Two Brains, Trading Places,* and the new James Bond film, *Octopussy,* all come out during this window, not to mention the final seasons of *Taxi* and *Cheers.* Missing these films is like being without oxygen as far as Ray is concerned. His entrapment at Camp Clear Skies guarantees that he'll be clueless about this summer's cultural touchstones.

Love can often be weaponized in a much more powerful way than hate, and it's only because Ray's parents love him so much that they can devise such a camouflaged form of torture. Most disaffected parents would have just grounded Ray or created some arbitrary obstacle that begins to evaporate the minute it's established. Neglectful parents can't test their children in the same ways as good guardians. It's impossible.

Ray has learned that high standards can be worse than no standards. Ray's parents once removed his door after failing a history exam to ensure he was studying to the level of their approval. Ray chuckles because his father drilling out hinges is a relatively tame example of what his parents could do to him.

Ray has an overachieving nature like his parents and, in that sense, was disappointed in his grades, too. He could do better. But he also knows when it's wise to take shortcuts. His ninth-grade marks aren't going to hold him back in life.

Ray notices two young campers pass him by as shimmering, iridescent bubbles follow their trail of jubilation. Both of their Camp Clear Skies shirts are decked out in kaleidoscope patterns of purple and blue tie-dye. Ray's shirt remains its original, drab grey.

Ray better examines his attire and thinks about how the name Camp Clear Skies sounds more like a rehab center than a summer camp. Ray earnestly considers if he'd rather be in a clinic instead of his current situation and ultimately decides there are likely better television privileges at a rehab center.

Ray admits that most of New York City's heavy pollution hasn't reached Essex County. He looks at the blue sky and the wisps of clouds that decorate it before his gaze returns to the ground, where he feigns the identification of leaves. Ray decides ten seconds of sky is enough before it loses its novelty.

Switchgrass. Wild bergamot. Great blue lobelia. Somewhere, Ray's parents are getting swept up in unexplainable joy.

The back of Ray's hand stings lightly. He realizes that a tiny droplet of blood is streaming down and figures he must have nicked it on one of the plants he passed. Ray brings his hand to suck at the wound when he sees two teenage counselors making out against a tree. A bitter and metallic taste briefly fills Ray's mouth as he watches the two counselors get deeper into each other's faces. Ray's older brother, Nathan, teased that camp would be a great place to lose his virginity, that it was always overflowing with raging hormones. Ray knows that his brother was joking — he hasn't even had his first real kiss yet — but he can't help but fantasize every time a female camper runs past him in shorts.

Ray has never felt a true bond with anyone before and doesn't expect Camp Clear Skies to become the setting for some lurid story. However, maybe he can exchange phone numbers with someone local. Perhaps some spur-of-the-moment summer romance isn't a completely absurd idea.

Lanceleaf coreopsis. Foxglove beardtongue. Obedient plant. Ray laughs at the name "obedient plant" and how he wouldn't be surprised if this were his parents' nickname for Nathan, the golden child.

Ray quickly flips through a robust nature pamphlet — xeroxed and stapled with manic disregard — to see if there's a local plant called Golden Child but finds only a Blackeyed Susan. Ray resents his brother's perfectionist nature, but he's happy he's more of an Obedient Plant than a Blackeyed Susan.

Ray goes to place a lazy checkmark against the corresponding image when he realizes that the flowers in front of him aren't quite the same. They are the standard tubular shape featuring purple and white coloring, but there is also more to them. Sunlight hits the alien plant at an odd angle, and Ray swears that he can see the entire spectrum of the rainbow reflected at him, fractals of honeycombed oranges and blues that quickly shimmer into greens and yellows.

The plant appears to blink at Ray. Once, then two more times in quick succession. Ray leans in for a closer look when the flower is suddenly snatched out of sight. A female camper skips by into the distance, roots in hand, while she sings some rhyme that sounds like a foreign language.

It's only a few seconds until the female camper is out of sight. Her dark raven hair chaotically bounces against the bright foliage as she tucks the flower under her right ear. She continues on her journey, utterly unaware of the impression she's left on Ray. He notices the sky has darkened and is now full of stars. He's not sure how much time has passed and whether he lost track during his fascination with the flower or the girl who took it. For fun, Ray attempts to use the North Star as a compass to get back to his cabin.

He quickly gives up. The stars aren't where they are supposed to be.

THE NEXT DAY the entirety of Camp Clear Skies cools off at the lake. Ray is excluded from this activity because his hand has worsened and turned a sickly shade of yellow. He doesn't think it'd be good to get the thing wet and risk further infection, and the counselors agree. Camp Clear Skies doesn't have much to offer Ray in terms of alternatives, so instead, he just sits by the dock and watches everyone else enjoy the water. Campers fling themselves off the pier with stylish backflips and garish cannonballs that cause heavy splashes and heavier laughs. Ray watches someone in a canoe negotiate some mild waves, and he recognizes that it's the female camper from yesterday that plucked the Not-Obedient Plant. The teenage girl elegantly steers the canoe, and Ray considers joining her in this activity but ultimately decides against it since it's all handwork.

The laughter on the docks is loud when Ray hears muffled sobs cut through the merriment. A camper stands off by the cabin. Her body shakes as she cries. Ray can't make out what she's saying through her tears, but it sounds something like, "Where would she go?"

Ray is about to offer help when a counselor comes out of the cabin and pulls her inside. The distraught camper appears to resist, but it all happens too fast for Ray to be sure. He does know that he hears her moan, "She was my best friend," as she gets taken inside.

Ray never sees either of them return, even after swimming transitions to arts and crafts. Admittedly, though, Ray's distracted by the identity of the attractive and mysterious girl he continues to see.

The outrageous craft everyone is tasked with involves mastery over the application of googly eyes to pinecones, of which it's crucial to not forget the secret ingredient: glue. Ray examines the pile of pinecones in front of him and notes they all feature a strange white color and smooth exterior. It doesn't look like they have been painted. It's as if they're somehow made of bone. Ray curiously snaps off the end of a branch and sees a powdery brown substance inside that looks enough like bone marrow that Ray yelps and drops the pinecone. Two tables over, Ray notices the raven-haired girl laugh at him. Ray's surprised to see her sitting by herself and wonders if she's a disaffected lone wolf just like him. He assesses his craft supplies and realizes that all his googly eyes have multiple pupils. That will do. Ray gets up with his defective googly eyes and approaches the camper.

"Do you have any extra googly eyes? All of mine are weirdsville," says Ray as he shakes some of his multi-pupiled eyes.

"I do, but you know you really shouldn't call them that."

"Googly eyes? What's wrong with—"

"*Jiggly* eyes," the camper says in an instructive tone. "The Googly family are victims of a tragedy, and they've been turned into a punchline. Sara Googly, a three-month-old infant, swallowed and choked on a *jiggly* eye. The company couldn't afford to pay the lawsuit settlement, and rather than declare bankruptcy, they decided to continue operations and send all profits to the Googly family."

Ray stares at the female camper, dumbfounded. She continues. "Jiggly eyes started to unofficially call themselves googly eyes as a tribute to the family, but the grieving Googlys hated the association. The company tried to backpedal to jiggly eyes, but at that point, the damage was already done."

Sara leans back in satisfaction, then quickly erupts in laughter.

"None of that's true, is it?" asks Ray.

"Not even a little bit. Sara, by the way. No 'h.' Not Googly. There is no Sara Googly. Well, there might be, just not one with any morbid connection to googly eyes."

Ray's eyes widen. "I'm Ray. Ray Primus. Uh, also no 'h.'"

Ray and Sara's introduction is immediately cut short when a counselor blows a brass whistle that alerts Camp Clear Skies to return to their cabins and prepare for something very special by the campfire.

Forced team morale isn't Ray's favorite way to spend time, but the soothing nature of a good campfire is hard to deny. A raging fire is already well underway when Ray and the rest of the campers take the field. Standing on two pieces of firewood with their faces cast in shadows are a male and female counselor with wide eyes that smile at the crowd even when their mouths remain thin, horizontal lines. Ray thinks they might be the two he saw making out yesterday, but with the way the shadows dance across their features, it's impossible to tell. Both counselors carry guitars and start to strum a background rhythm.

"Hello there, everyone," booms the male counselor intensely. "I'm Counselor Hathaway, and I'd like to formally give you all a Camp Clear Skies welcome!"

Counselor Hathaway waves his hand across the crowd, and before he can continue, the female counselor jumps in.

"And *I'm* Counselor Chambers, and *I'd* like to formally give you all a Camp Clear Skies welcome!"

Counselor Chambers waves her hand across the crowd in the opposite direction as both of their guitars crescendo.

"And we'd *both* really, really, *really* like to tell you why this place is so important to us," the two counselors say in unison.

Ray anticipates the typically lame lyrics that, for some reason, must circulate through every unimaginative summer camp. He is not disappointed when Counselor Hathaway and Counselor Chambers open their mouths.

We love to camp. We love to play.
We love to swim and craft all day.
Camp Clear Skies is the place to be.
In this camp, we're one big family.
So praise above to Camp Clear Skies,
Where we'll camp so hard, it will be our demise.

THE TWO CAMP counselors work through these lyrics in a call-and-response fashion with the campers. Their enthusiasm is so intense that the cheerful words sound more like a threat than a lesson in morale. Ray rolls his eyes. He recites the creed in an exaggerated manner that nearly puts Counselor Hathaway and Counselor Chambers' performances to shame. Ray catches Sara snicker at his mock camp spirit. He didn't realize she was this close to him. That snicker is encouraging, though. Is she as jaded as Ray? Does she lament being stuck in this camp? Would she rather be laughing at Steve Martin's increased comedic abilities due to having two brains? If this were a Sarah with an "h", then Ray would say it's impossible, but this is a no-"h" Sara that Ray's dealing with.

The flames of the fire illuminate and cast shadows across Sara's face. When stray cinders blow towards her, she embraces the warmth rather than shy away. She combs her pitch-black hair behind her ears, and Ray is thankful that he's not some cartoon wolf because his heart would be bursting several feet out of his chest over this staggering act of beauty. In a momentary burst of elucidation, Ray inspects the rest of himself to ensure that nothing else on his body might be sticking out before he bridges the few feet between him and Sara.

We love to camp. We love to play.
We love to swim and craft all day.

Ray and Sara communicate through boilerplate camp song pabulum, but their eyes and expressions manage to break the ice and make this meaningless nonsense feel like a conversation. Ray's inner monologue turns into a spinning Rolodex of witty asides that he can say to Sara once the camp songs come to an end — *"That song was fire!"*, *"Didn't Guns N' Roses originally do that one?"* — but they're all so dreadful and complex that he's grateful for the sing-a-long. Sara's hand grazes against Ray's, and after a few clumsy gestures, she casually holds his hand in her own. At this point, if Ray actually were a cartoon wolf, his heart would straight up explode.

So praise above to Camp Clear Skies,
Where we'll camp so hard, it will be our demise.

Ray is astounded at how much confidence these five interlocked fingers can infuse into his body. He and Sara sing together in loud, dorky voices free of shame and full of youth. Ray catches himself tapping his foot to the rhythm, and for a brief moment, he kind of maybe sort of enjoys camp and doesn't care that he's missing one of the final episodes of *Taxi*. Somehow, Sara's clammy hand is more satisfying than a dozen Christopher Lloyds and Andy Kaufmans combined.

A tremor of pain ripples through Ray's left arm. He then realizes that Sara is — and has been — holding his gross, wounded hand. She must not have noticed in the dark, but every micro-gesture that Sara makes causes fireworks of agony to erupt in Ray's body like embers in the fire before them.

Ray hides his pain through manic singing. He focuses on the crackling flames of the campfire, the swirling crimson and sienna that grows and combusts as hungry flames swarm and consume. Smoke trickles upward, littered with sparks that give the campfire contour and dimension. Ray feels his face grow hot. His eyes sting from the fumes that blow toward him, yet he can't direct them away from the flame.

There's something in there.

Ray knows it's a crazy thought, but the more he focuses, the clearer he recognizes the flickering, macabre image in the fire. Ray sees a face. Not a human face, but one with dozens of eyes and chomping mandibles. The flames feed this image as its eyes and claws continue to grow. The fire hisses. The beast within knows that he has been seen.

Between the fire and the throbbing pain in his hand, Ray is so lost that he doesn't question Counselor Hathaway and Counselor Chambers' changes to the lyrics of their friendly chant.

Ulyaoth y'hah, nglui lw'nafh ph'grah'n orr'eagl ilyaa y-sgn'wahl gotha,
Orr'e y'hah nglui uaaahyar k'yarnak.

THE SURREAL WORDS gradually become natural to the many campers thanks to the phonetic call-and-response rhythm that Hathaway and Chambers use to work through the material. After a few recitals of the chorus—or what Ray has to assume is the chorus—the campers freely sing along without any help. Dozens of transfixed teenagers turn guttural anomalies and punishing tongue twisters into an empowering ballad with no end.

Ph'nglui mglw'nafh Chattur'gha R'lyeh wgah'nagl fhtagn.
F'ya ee, mg ep Chattur'gha goka sgn'wahl ngmg,
Orr'e goka 'bthnk fm'latgh ftaghu y-ebunma.

A BUZZING BEGINS to fill Ray's ears, and he can't tell if it's a byproduct of the strange music that surrounds him or not. He looks to Sara's flame-licked face and hopes that one well-timed snicker or act of sarcasm from her will untie the knots in his stomach. Instead, all Ray sees is the residual, pulsating image of the face in the fire burned into his rods and cones. Sara sways her head to the music, but the flame creature's mandibles flap at Ray while many eyes blink in disturbing succession. Sara sings on, and Ray joins her.

THE FIRE MORPHS into mounds of lumpy mashed potatoes with rivulets of gray gravy. Apparently, it's morning. Ray moves the pallid, food-like substance before him as if doing so may cause it to disappear. Ray doesn't expect Michelin Star dining at Camp Clear Skies, but the cuisine has helped him appreciate how much he likes food. *Real* food.

Ray has noticed that he's been losing track of time, and he's unsure if it's from the lack of nourishment or the repeated nightmares that keep him awake. Ray's hand sends another signal flare through his body, and he puts down the spoon in defeat. The wound doesn't just throb; upsetting, mauve-colored pus leaks out of it sporadically. Sharp purple lines cascade up his arm, and a distinct heat exudes from the wound that makes Ray sick to his stomach. Ray's plan was to talk to the nurse about all of this because his hand looks like a special effect and he feels awful, but he hopes to first cross paths with Sara during breakfast.

Ray doesn't spot Sara even though the mess hall is particularly sparse this morning. About a third of the camp is present, if that, and the majority are covered in strange, iridescent rashes. Ray is too preoccupied with his own hand to notice the prevalent skin ailment until a male camper yells at him, his entire face covered by the shimmering rash. He's asking Ray (and anyone else he can find) if he's seen his missing sister. These shiny spots are on most people in the mess hall, and Ray quickly scans himself to ensure he's not afflicted by the same abnormalities. He supposes that a monster hand is enough to worry about without adding a rainbow rash on top.

A trio of people adorned in rashes runs out of the infirmary as Ray knocks on the door and enters. A mousy, blue-eyed nurse who doesn't look like she could be that far out of college looks Ray over.

"Sorry, Nurse Nurgle doesn't do nose jobs."

"Excuse me?" Ray stammers.

"I'm just having some fun because there's nothing wrong with you. Are you just trying to get out of the water balloon fight or something?"

As if on cue, Ray hears the loud *splaaat* of a water balloon connecting with someone's body. He turns his attention to the window and watches the aquatic bombs explode upon contact with the campers as he tries to get through to the nurse.

"My hand," squeaks Ray. "Shouldn't we do something about it?"

"I saw your hand when you came in. It just looks like a bad case of allergies to me. I can bandage it up if that will make you feel better, but something like that should really get some air to breathe."

Ray's focus is shattered when he sees Sara run past the infirmary windows. Sara cautiously pulls back her arm as she prepares to hurl a water balloon, and Ray can see that her hands have the same iridescent rash. She appears to be otherwise unscathed. Sara screams and drops her water balloon, which bursts at her feet when another wobbly projectile makes a surprise collision with the side of her face. Water runs down Sara as she laughs and runs out of Ray's view, preparing for her next attack.

The nurse continues to talk to Ray about allergies, which Ray uses as an opportunity to get an answer to a different question.

"Is that what's going on with that shiny rash everyone has? I want to be sure to avoid—"

"I've really got a busy day that I've got to get on top of, kid," says Nurse Nurgle in a stern voice. "Good luck with the nose job."

Ray's trip to the infirmary causes him to miss the water balloon fight, but he's fortunately out in time to make it to archery. Archery is the only area where Ray's universal disinterest in summer camp wavers, the one silver lining. Ray isn't a huge comic book reader, but he appreciates that several superheroes are simply people good with a bow and arrow who aren't afraid to take some risks with fashion. Robin Hood overturns a corrupt monarchy without much more than a bow and arrow. John Rambo even understands that certain situations require precision and subtlety over the brute power of an automatic weapon. Ray hopes he'll wind up a natural, but it also seems so ridiculous that he didn't even share this thought with Nathan after he pitched him the high fantasy of losing his virginity.

Camp Clear Skies' archery field has a dozen traditional bullseye targets spread across a cramped space of about 150 feet. There's a brush area beyond the bullseyes that would allow for a more expansive range, but it's clear that nobody wants to take on the extra maintenance.

The camper at the target beside Ray is sitting as he furiously writes a letter. Counselor Hathaway either doesn't notice the camper's lack of participation or doesn't care and seems more focused on the tight hand gestures he performs while he looks up at the sky. Ray watches this solo secret handshake long enough to see that it has about five distinct movements before it repeats itself. Ray turns to the neighboring camper, who becomes aware of his attention. He briefly stops his writing, only to resume as he speaks.

"You can take my arrows if you want. I doubt I'll get around to using them."

"That's kind of you, but let me at least fire off my own first and see if I'm worthy of a bonus round."

The determined camper lifelessly shrugs as he continues to write. He tilts his head in the direction of his quiver and arrows.

"A lot of family members to touch base with?" Ray asks, half-joking as he gestures towards the letter.

It looks like the camper isn't going to respond for the longest time, but when Ray turns his back, the kid mutters under his breath. "Somebody needs to know what's going on here."

Ray takes a second to examine the bow and arrow, then loads the weapon in a dramatic fashion. Ray observes that the archery equipment isn't state-of-the-art, but he's surprised to see that it's in better shape than most other equipment at Camp Clear Skies. Ray pulls back his left arm and keeps it straight as the bow becomes increasingly taut. A dozen campers are launching arrows, all focused on their individual targets, yet Ray can't help but put on a show. He doesn't know when he'll be wielding this weapon again, if ever, so Ray — figuratively and literally — takes his shot. He fires the arrow at his target, but not before he bellows, "God didn't make Rambo. I made him!"

Ray doesn't get the opportunity to see if anyone hears or cares about his mediocre Colonel Trautman impression because he's temporarily blinded. During the apex of the shot, the stress ruptures the wound on Ray's hand, which squirts a fine rope of discharge into his eye. Ray is suddenly glad that Sara isn't present, nor does he think she'd have picked up on the *Rambo* reference.

Ray repeatedly blinks to clear his vision and wash out his eye. When he wipes at his face, he sees a lilac secretion left behind on his hand, not unlike the color of the Obedient Plant, *Physostegia Virginiana*. A purple spot grows beneath the bandages and culminates in a distressing yellow hue around the borders. Ray attempts to readjust and tighten his bandages, but the slightest of disturbances triggers avalanches of pain that have Ray decide to ignore his left hand as if it's a phantom limb. Ray notices that the purple vines on his arms now reach up to the sleeves of his Camp Clear Skies tee shirt.

Ray's never picked up a bow and arrow before, and his hand is in terrible condition, but he's still genuinely shocked when his first attempt at archery results in an arrow landing far beyond its target. John Rambo makes it look so easy, and he's riddled with PTSD. Ray Primus' life is no *First Blood.* Hell, it's not even "First Scrape." The most significant trauma Ray faced was when *M*A*S*H** ended this year. He still gets emotional when he flips past CBS.

Ray heads off in the direction of his poor aim, beyond the perimeter of the archery field. Ray sees no sign of his arrow and wonders how it could have gone this far. Ray continues his search as he ponders how much a single arrow costs and if Camp Clear Skies is even aware of their arrow total to notice if one were to go missing. The sun temporarily blinds Ray and ignites a jackhammer behind his eyes. He turns his gaze back to the ground.

The sky looks *mostly* normal today, which Ray supposes is a good thing. It's currently more of a violet color, but one could still trick themselves into thinking it's a shade of blue. The sporadic patches of pink are harder to explain, as is the occasional *click-click-clicking* that sounds like the sky is eating something.

Ray's arrow is still nowhere in sight as he combs through yet more nature to find three puddles of mud that bubble violently. Ray inches closer and realizes the substance is not mud but something dark and viscous that looks more like tar. Thick black bubbles rise, then pop as they leave the surface. Ray watches an animal pull itself out of the muck.

At first, Ray thinks it's a frog, but he can see that it has wings by its side that spasm and unsuccessfully flap. The not-frog sputters as it tries to shed the thick sludge from its body. More tar drips away, and Ray notices that the creature's prominent front legs are bent into claws like a praying mantis. The clumsy performance lasts only a few seconds before the frog-mantis races towards Ray with a shrill chirping sound. Ray watches the unreal abomination stumble toward him. He wants to scream, but his throat won't work. The tar monster reaches Ray, and without thinking, he stomps down on it with the total weight of his body. A grotesque pop harmonizes with further chirping until Ray grinds his heel into the earth. The noises stop.

Not a second after Ray has killed this nightmare chimera, Ray sees another hobble out of the murky tar. Then a second. And a third. Within moments, half a dozen tar beasts gallop clumsily toward Ray until he stomps on all of them like he's crushing grapes at some Satanic vineyard. Ray feels the wet crunch under his feet as the creatures swat at his ankles with stray appendages.

After the last frog-mantis becomes black mush on the ground, Ray realizes he has been screaming. Ray has no interest in learning what these things are and runs back to the archery field once the opportunity presents itself. His lost arrow suddenly seems less important. *Let them have it*, thinks Ray.

Ray begins to panic when he sees some bushes behind him rustle. He turns to run. Ray starts to run faster when he hears the frog-mantis' chirping sound, and just when it looks like something is about to emerge from the bushes, he collides with Counselor Hathaway and sees stars.

"Jesus, kid. It's archery, not football," Hathaway remarks from the ground. "Where's the fire?"

"They're out there!" screams Ray. "Those things are out there!"

Counselor Hathaway's gaze hardens on Ray. "There's nothing out there," he assures calmly. "What would be out there?"

Ray points to his shoes, then notices the black filth is also halfway to his knees. "Look at this stuff. There are wings and all sorts of stuff stuck to my feet and—"

"Forget about your feet. Look at your hand."

An unhealthy discharge runs out of Ray's bandages. Fuchsia punctuates it like a bullseye.

"Yeah, that's right," Hathaway sneers while rubbing at similarly colored stains on his Camp Clear Skies shirt. "You got some of that stuff on me during your winning touchdown. Get back to the infirmary and deal with that, so you're not getting gross fluid all over half the camp."

As soon as Counselor Hathaway points out the severity of Ray's wound, he begins to feel considerably dizzier. He even needs to stop to catch his breath on the short way to the infirmary. It's amazing how the brain operates, how awareness is so crucial. That cartoon coyote doesn't fall to his doom until he realizes he's run off the end of the cliff. Ray's balance is still off, but he picks up his pace when he hears a garbled "*sssubmittt*" out of his left hand. Ray tells himself it's just the pain, another of the brain's beautiful tricks. But he doesn't slow down.

In the infirmary, Ray is greeted by a different nurse than before. She refuses to admit this is the case. "I'm the only healthcare worker this camp's got, honey." She chides Ray with a hollow expression.

This nurse claims to be Nurse Nurgle, just as the last one did, but Ray's not so delirious that he can't tell they're entirely different people. This Nurse Nurgle is easily ten years older and has long scars that run down both arms. New Nurgle's tanned skin causes these scars to pop out like searching worms every time she reaches out to him.

She seems indifferent not only to Ray but to his wound. She keeps her back to him as she meticulously combs through different drugs until she finally turns around. New Nurgle sticks out a bony arm and presents Ray with a paper cup filled with purple pills of different shades.

"For infection," New Nurgle proudly croaks.

"I didn't have to take pills last—"

"For infection," she repeats and pushes the paper cup into Ray's chest.

Ray understands just how disoriented he is when the nurse's gesture knocks him backward. He needs to deal with his hand.

"But what are they? What's in them?" Ray woozily mumbles.

"Camp cheer," responds Nurgle without hesitation, as if she's gotten used to the question.

Ray's hand and head throb. Clusters of light impair his vision when he turns back to the door, only for New Nurgle to walk over and close it.

"I can't let you leave until I've seen you take the medicine, honey. What kind of nurse would I be otherwise?"

The pounding in Ray grows more intense. New Nurgle plasters her face with an overly cheerful smile as though she can tell he's in pain.

"Camp cheer," New Nurgle reiterates without breaking her smile somehow. "Submit."

New Nurgle smiles at Ray, and the corners of her mouth continue to stretch to inhuman proportions. Almost as if this is part of Ray's ultimatum, that this devil's grin will subside if he just takes his medicine. New Nurgle's shaky hand holds out the tiny paper cup with its purple spectrum of pills while the corners of her smile inch past the tops of her ears.

Ray can't take it anymore. He grabs the cup of "camp cheer" and swallows. No chaser. He doesn't trust the water.

SARA RUNS through the woods of Camp Clear Skies as Ray chases after her. He follows the illuminating glow that Sara exudes as the world around them grows darker. Soon, Ray can't see anything, not even what's immediately in front of him. Sara's light gets farther away and becomes a dim hum that is swallowed by the deafening roars behind. Ray can't see them — he can't see anything — but he feels the presence of malevolent forces close the distance. He feels an evil, angry energy that doesn't just want to consume him but erase his entire existence and remake him in its own twisted image.

The glow of Sara is now completely gone. Ray hurdles himself forward into the black abyss until his joints pop and his muscles scream. He knows he can't stop. His body moves ahead when Ray feels his arms grabbed by ropey tendrils. More invasive tentacles wrap around his body, constrict his neck, and fill his throat. His screams only allow the dark creature to burrow deeper.

As Ray's body is yanked backward, he jolts upward in his cabin bed, face-to-face with Sara. Sara holds Ray's arms as she shakes any remaining sleep out of his body.

"He was going to attack you."

Sara motions towards Counselor Hathaway, who is unconscious on the floor. His body fidgets. Beside a shovel on the ground, Ray sees a scalpel several feet from Hathaway's body. The blood on the blade indicates this was Sara's weapon.

"We have to go," Sara firmly states. "He's already moving."

Still thrown by all of this, Ray nods his head and winces from the pain. He looks at his hand to find it's worse than ever. The poisonous vines have reached Ray's neck and are beginning to show on his left leg. At the same time, Ray realizes that Sara's iridescent, splotchy rashes are now all over her face and shoulders. The limited light catches Sara's markings, and Ray thinks she looks like a dragonfly's wing. Ray absolutely means this as a compliment and is still stunned by Sara's face, but he doesn't share the stilted praise with her. Instead, Sara smiles, and the dimples on her face set off a whole new and spectacular light show.

"I haven't seen you in two days. I thought they already got you."

Ray remains entranced by Sara's rashes but still hears what she's said. "Wait. What are you talking about? I've been asleep for two days?"

A low groan escapes Counselor Hathaway as one of his heavy arms rubs the goose egg that's started to grow on his head.

Ray continues. "No. When did we—"

"Now," interrupts Sara.

Sara and Ray stampede out of the cabin, where he's surprised to be greeted by the darkness of night. They can see and hear a massive campfire sing-along in the distance, and Ray looks above as he powers ahead with Sara.

The sky is something that's increasingly bothered Ray during his time at Camp Clear Skies. He's now positive the name he used to associate with a rehab center is more of a taunting threat. Ray's avoided the sky as much as possible because it only continues to show him the accepted tenets of this universe are as fluid as anything else.

The collection of stars above is unavoidable, different than the last time he got a good look at the sky—no, the gaping maw of uncertainty that *used* to be the sky. The stars somehow seem aggressive. Angry. A cluster directly above Ray and Sara eschews Ursa Major in favor of Manticore Major as it swarms with seething stars.

Or maybe Ray's completely off. He's the first to admit that he really doesn't know much about astronomy, and perhaps this *is* what Ursa Major is supposed to look like. Or it could even be an entirely different constellation because how many constellations could Ray actually name? Four? Five?

Ursa Minor. Orion. Aries...

Ray runs constellations and grade school planetary trivia to distract himself from absolutely everything that's going on. Simultaneous screams echo and bleed out of cabins around Camp Clear Skies, a massacre in stereoscopic sound where there's not a bad seat in the house.

The cries put the wealth of horror films Ray's seen to shame. Nathan once told Ray that some of the grislier slasher films use actual audio recordings of murders for their screams. Ray never believed this could be true and was surprised that someone with instincts like Nathan would fall for such an urban legend.

More pained yells rattle the air, and Ray's now positive that his brother was full of shit. Ray knows he'll never be able to forget these sounds, that they'll haunt him for the rest of his life. He thinks back to the scalpel on the floor of his cabin and shudders. His screams would've undoubtedly been added to this death chorus if Sara hadn't intervened.

"Thank you," Ray pants out.

"You already said that," says Sara.

"I know, but just, thank you."

Ray and Sara get closer to the campfire, quickly turning back in terror. They see it's not Camp Clear Skies reciting songs but a group of individuals in black robes lost in scripture.

Ph'nglui mglw'nafh Chattur'gha R'lyeh wgah'nagl fhtagn.
Ulyaoth hlirgh Yoggoth y-nilgh'ri n'gha,
Mantorok shogg mg y'hah n'gha r'luh chtenff sgn'wahl y-gnaiih

THE GROUP'S chants become louder. Ray sees four severed heads placed around the campfire, which get tossed into the flames one by one. The last screams from the cabins are heard as a figure in a purple robe steps forward.

"At last, enough blood of the pure and unsoiled has been spilled. We summon you, Chattur'gha! We summon you, Ulyaoth!"

The rest of the group responds in unison. "We summon you, Chattur'gha! We summon you, Ulyaoth!"

The flames of the campfire shoot up. A deafening crack is heard as the sky shimmers and breaks open. The atmosphere overlaps itself, and Ray has to look away because the image is too confounding.

Sara covers her ears as a thunderous *chit-chit-chitter* emanates from the cracks in the sky. The shadows of impossible creatures push their way through. Ray huddles around Sara as the sky flickers like a television channel losing its signal. Several robed members throw themselves into the fire in celebration. Others experience severe convulsions and are reduced to fleshy puddles, as though they've shaken all the bones out of their bodies.

Sara looks up at Ray, her eyes wet and her face trembling in fear. He's shaking just as hard. Ray wants to make her feel better and take away this pain. He wants to say the perfect thing.

Instead, he kisses her.

Ray kisses Sara, and she kisses him back. It's clumsy and hungry and cautious in the way that many first kisses are, but it temporarily makes Ray and Sara feel normal and forget that the world is crumbling apart around them. They continue to kiss, and Ray tries to reciprocate Sara's ferocity until he realizes it's not her tongue. Or it's at least not *just* her tongue.

Ray tries to pull away from the kiss but feels his mouth sink deeper into Sara's. The two form a writhing pink seal. Ray's tongue negotiates its space and makes contact with something in Sara's mouth. He feels Sara grip his back to gain leverage but then emits a low moan into their shared mouth hole when her fingers sink into his shoulders. Ray's body adjusts to this displacement of organs while, out of the corner of his eye, he sees an assortment of organs push out of his chest. As they drip down his body, Ray thinks he sees his heart among the dispelled viscera and chuckles into his shared mouth hole. Maybe he's not that different from a cartoon wolf, after all. Besides, it doesn't matter. He still has her heart. Ray doesn't need to feel so possessive over such arbitrary things as vital organs or a circulatory system. He and Sara are one now.

Ray feels other parts of his body — his knees, maybe? — suction themselves to Sara. Soon, limbs slide through each other like heated metal skewers through marshmallows. More of their body fuses together and awkwardly figures out its new shape as a human s'more. This new Ray/Sara mass buckles under its weight and falls to the ground as its three arms of contrasting length unsuccessfully attempt to shoulder the fall. Ray's vision is a murky cloud, and he can't tell if the entire camp has fallen victim to this same fate or if he and Sara are simply lucky. Obtrusive, scared thoughts pound through Ray's head.

You think we're lucky?

All of this is just as foreign to Ray as to Sara, but he immediately knows that these are her thoughts. What's left of their brains is likely some messy cocktail of their respective lobes. The writhing Ray/Sara globule attempts further movement, only to stop after more of its body folds in on itself.

New protrusions absorb others. Ray considers that maybe they'll never stop transforming and that this is a new form of evolution.

Maybe there's a creature of beauty on the other end of this haunted alchemy that may—

No. This isn't beauty. This is nothing. Less than nothing.

This is everything, but that's okay. There's plenty of time for Ray/Sara to work this out and find their rhythm. Already acclimating to his new existence, Ray knows far better than to think such thoughts anymore. It'd be rude to the partner that shares this body with him. They're a unit now. Body, mind, and soul.

The sky rains down chaos while a cacophony of chants reverberates through the camp. The Ray/Sara hybrid gloms forward, and Ray can't help but work the muscles that used to be associated with his face into a disturbing but genuine smile.

Maybe camp's not so bad, after all.

III

Oh man, what an ending, amirite? I mean, there's crazy, and then there's just absolute insanity; that clearly crossed the threshold. Certifiable, man. And listen, I know what you're thinking right now, "Uncle Abs, seriously, you couldn't possibly keep this up for a whole book," and my response to that is, "HOW DARE YOU QUESTION ME?!"

ahem Sorry for yelling like that. I just really don't appreciate being doubted. Like, I wouldn't flaunt it if I done didn't have it, so don't you worry, buttercup, just let me steer this tempestuous vessel, and we'll careen into the stable by daybreak, ya dig? (if not, just nod and say you do, it's easier this way)

The third story in our collection is another wild one that leans into the creepy side of the pillow; the dark side of the linens, if you will (and I know you will!) It features a farm that allows people to have an entire damn appendage replaced, which is not at all the type of business that anyone would accuse of being nefarious. Seriously, I always used to tell people that I could get them whatever they needed, but a fresh, new arm? That would've tested even the likes of me. And I'm pretty sure that if I could've gotten an arm, someone from Motley Crue would've asked me for one. They did some serious damage to their bodies, partying like that.

Also, why stop at arms? I know some obscenely wealthy people who would gladly pay to enhance significantly less impressive appendages. You know what I'm talking about! (Toes. I'm talking about toes. Some people have seriously unattractive toes, don't you think? Psh, whatever. Quentin Tarantino gets me.)

Now, I'm going to take some time to consider various appendage-related business ideas. In the meantime, please enjoy The Arm Farm.

THE ARM FARM

ASHTON MACAULAY

A BARN IN THE MIDDLE OF NOWHERE

The stuttering rumble of the engine cut clear across the open fields that passed on either side. Chris looked longingly out through the passenger window, wishing he were the one doing ninety on a back-country road. He could almost feel the stick in his right hand. Hell, he could almost feel a lot of things in his right hand.

Years. It had been years since Chris could drive himself anywhere. A memory of his last drive in a cherry-red Mustang before deployment made him wince. *God, I miss that.* The car slowed as Megan made a left turn onto a long drive. A crude sign read, 'Art's Arm Farm.' Fields of low plants stretched out on either side for what felt like miles. Chris lifted his head and looked over the dash to see a massive farmhouse in the distance. The red paint with white trim was fresh enough that the building could have been plucked from a child's playset. "You sure this is the place famous for feats of bioengineering?"

"Didn't you see the sign?" Megan was kind but firm. She had pushed for them to come out in the first place.

Chris looked down at the stump of his right arm, then back to the barn. "What the hell is an arm farm, anyway?"

"I'm certain it's just a gimmick. Below that simple exterior, there's probably a sprawling, well-funded lab. The farm aesthetic is meant to put people like you at ease." She smiled and squeezed his arm with her free hand. "They certainly know their clientele."

"There's the reminder that I married a psychologist."

Megan rolled her eyes. "You know I keep work and life separate. Besides, I'm out of your price range."

"Right." Ordinarily, Chris might have laughed at the joke, but the farm kept him ill at ease. His eyes were drawn to short-stalked plants wrapped in opaque plastic bags. "What do you suppose he's growing here?"

She put a spooky warble in her voice. "It's the arms."

"Bet it's beans. Boring old beans for a boring old farm. A waste of a perfectly good Saturday."

"Yes, that's what's ruining this Saturday."

Chris ignored the implication. "Looks like they've got pests, too." He motioned to the plastic bags. "Man can't even keep beans alive. What's he supposed to do for me?"

Megan nodded. "Yes, Chris, everyone in this car is well aware of your agricultural expertise." She pulled up to a series of parking spaces. A hand-painted banner draped over the side of the barn read 'Art's Arm Farm' in childlike lettering.

"Think people forget where they're going? Out in the middle of nowhere, and he still needs a second sign...." The letters were crude and thick. Chris didn't like them.

The air conditioner eked out a final blast of cool air as Megan cut the ignition. She turned to Chris with searching eyes. "Remember, we're just here to see what he has to offer, that's it."

Chris rested his head on the window, feeling the heat seep through from the midday sun. Soon, the car would be a sweatbox, and he'd need to get out or ask Megan to take them back. That would be admitting defeat.

She continued. "If you don't like what he has to offer, we'll leave, simple as that."

"Simple as that?" He mumbled the words, feeling rooted to his chair.

"I keep my word." Megan smiled, the exhaustion in the gesture plain to see.

"Alright, fine. I'll give him fifteen minutes." Chris opened the car door to a blast of rolling heat. His first thought was that it smelled wrong; farms were supposed to smell like manure, crops, and sweat. The classic smell of fertilizer was still there, but something clean and fresh was mixed with it. "You smell that?"

Megan opened her door and wrinkled her nose. "Yeah. Is that…" She gave the air another whiff. "Baby powder?"

Chris sniffed the air again and nodded. A tingling pain at the base of his spine ran straight up his back. "I think that might be it." That wasn't entirely right, though. The farm didn't smell like baby powder; it simply smelled like baby.

Megan shrugged. "Beats pig shit. Maybe he's trying to appeal to city folk like us?"

"Yeah, maybe. I guess it doesn't smell bad." No, not bad, just wrong. Chris looked up. A broad set of sliding doors hung open, revealing flashing lights inside. 'ENTER HERE' was painted above in the same haphazard lettering. "Think we're supposed to go in there?" he asked, joking through the unease.

"Now there's the brain I fell in love with. After you." Megan made a sweeping gesture with her hand.

"Sure, send the cripple into the mysterious barn." Even as a joke, Chris didn't like using the term. After returning from service, he had trained doubly hard to make his left arm worth a damn. He took pride in that; a solider that couldn't defend themselves was lost. He could do just about anything besides operate his beloved car.

Chris walked to the open door while pushing the strange knot in his stomach away and was immediately assaulted by peculiar music. The discordant notes sounded like a car crash. He went to clamp his head in pain, but before his hands could reach his ears, the beat morphed into a familiar disco song. "What the hell?"

"Something wrong?" If Megan heard the noise, she wasn't showing it.

"Did you hear that?"

"Come on. I know you don't love disco, but it's not that bad."

Chris felt the sound in his bones, shook his head. Had it been disco the whole time? He supposed it wasn't out of the ballpark. There were still nights he heard sniper fire for miles. He took a deep breath and walked through the barn door.

Bright fluorescent lights ran the length of the ceiling and shone down in stark rows. Metal tables covered in medical equipment glistened in a neat line beneath them. Chris stood still in the entryway and was suddenly confronted by a fit of irrational anger. He wondered if the engineer responsible for creating the weapon that blew off his hand worked in a lab like this one. Almost in answer, a small man danced into view at the end of the long tables. If he noticed his guests, he made no sign of it, moving to the strange beat and twirling between rows of equipment while sporting a long wizard's beard and a technicolor lab coat. Coke bottle glasses rested on the brim of his nose, magnifying his closed eyes.

Chris backed away slowly. *What's threatening about an old man dancing?* He couldn't answer the question; he just knew he needed to leave. "Megan, I don't like—"

The man stopped and opened his eyes. His face flushed with embarrassment as he scuttled to pick up a remote from a nearby table. With a flick of his wrist, the music was gone. "Sorry about that!" he called from the other end of the barn. His voice was worn and old but full of forced joy. "I didn't think we would have any guests today." As he bustled toward Megan and Chris, he ran his hands lovingly over the lab equipment. "It seems I never have time to enjoy a good dance anymore."

"We're happy to come back another time," offered Chris. Megan stepped behind him and put a hand on his shoulder.

"Nonsense, my boy!" The man walked up and put out his hand. Chris recoiled slightly, trying to hide his stump. "No need for that," the old man explained, then switched hands. Chris took it and felt the man's feeble grip beneath his. "Strong hand. I like that. What's your name?"

"It's Chris." Despite himself, the near comical appearance of the man helped him relax. Nothing was threatening about a tiny eccentric man in a lab coat. As usual, Chris was jumping at shadows.

"Well, Chris, my name's Art. We're going to get you all sorted out."

THE SALES PITCH

Art led Chris and Megan to the middle of the barn, passing high stacks of jumbled mechanical equipment along the way. Some pieces sat idly by, as though they hadn't been used in generations, while others hummed along, performing unknown tasks. At the building's center, the tables spiraled out in all directions, creating a maze of potential scientific catastrophes. Unbothered, Art walked with confidence, clearly aware of some unbeknownst order through all the chaos.

"I started this project around five years ago now. You wouldn't believe the progress we've made since those early days." He gazed at the machines fondly.

Chris struggled to comprehend what he was looking at. While many of the contraptions were actively engaged in tasks, he failed to see any connecting threads to prosthetics. "Do you actually use all of this?"

Art chuckled. "Certainly not. One of those mechanical friends is working to make me an omelet, but it never gets the consistency right. I suppose we can't succeed at everything we try." The thought of a lackluster omelet brought a genuinely dark pallor to Art's face. "Lucky for you, you're not here for my breakfast special. You're here about the arms!" His bright demeanor returned in a flash.

"Just the one." Chris held up his stump and tried to give a friendly laugh.

Art nodded and turned to a flat wooden table covered in measuring tape and paint swatches. "Well, don't you worry, Chris. Like I said, we're going to get you fixed up." Art reached out for Chris's arm and, almost as an afterthought, asked: "Do you mind?"

Chris did mind, but he could feel Megan behind him. He owed it to her to try. "Not at all." He held out what remained of his arm.

Art took the stump in his hand with practiced care, ran his fingers along the edge, reached into his pocket, and pulled out a tape recorder. It was oversized, as though it might have been a relic from one of the great wars. "Right arm is severed just above the elbow. Neat job sewing it up, probably decent nerve connectivity." He set the tape recorder down and picked up the paint swatches. Art muttered and flipped through several shades of pink and beige, holding each against Chris's skin for comparison. "Pigmentation is white, probably three or three-quarters. Light freckling on the remaining limb, customer choice for matching." Art paused and looked up expectantly.

"I'm sorry, what?"

"You've got some sun damage on your remaining arm leading to a light freckling. Is that something you'd want to have matched?"

"That's something you can do?"

"Wouldn't be a very good arm farm if we couldn't."

"I like his freckles," said Megan with a short giggle.

"They are quite endearing, aren't they? I'm sorry, where are my manners? I don't think I caught your name." Art set his supplies down and held his hand out to Megan.

"I'm Megan, the one who dragged him here."

Art laughed. "Well, you wouldn't be the first. Don't you worry about those freckles; I'll keep them safe and sound." He shook her hand and returned his attention to Chris. "Time flies when you're having fun, right?"

The creak of an old board on the other side of the barn made Chris twitch. "Right."

"Hesitation is natural." Art ducked down behind a towering pile of metal implements. Crashes and clanks filled the space as various tools were tossed aside. Eventually, Art came up with a bastardized version of a tire pressure gauge. He pressed the cool metal to Chris's good arm. "Excellent muscle density, very firm. Getting used to a new arm is always tricky, but if this one is any indication, it's going to a delightful home."

"Thanks, I guess?" Chris looked to Megan, trying to find some modicum of support in his discomfort. However, she was perfectly at home in the oddity of it all and was even smiling.

Art clicked the tape recorder off and slid it into his pocket. "You should be proud. You've got quite a robust remaining limb."

"Thank you." A hot flush crept up Chris's face. It was a strange compliment, to say the least, but it still filled him with pride.

"I think you're going to like what I have to show you. Why don't we go see some samples?"

"Sure, why not?" The rapid nature of Art's process made it hard to believe any of it could be real. Was it all some kind of a joke? If it was, why was no one laughing? Still, the childlike possibility that it wasn't drove Chris forward.

Art bounded through the labyrinth of lab benches, spouting facts every few seconds that Chris could hardly listen to. They passed by tables of increasingly bizarre oddities that grew more disjointed with each passing step. A menacing tower that looked to be made entirely of wire and spinning blades loomed over them. Chris stepped past it and felt the machine's menace. As they made their way deeper into the barn, the tables possessed something familiar. Rows of clay pots and loose soil were arranged beneath blazing grow lights.

Chris clung to the mundane, tried to ground himself. The feeling didn't last long. What little normalcy he found evaporated when they came to a set of tables covered in fleshy pods. They hung from steel rods, with black cables that ran around their edges and hummed with electricity. A small grow light behind each sack illuminated a lumpy shape within.

Through the opaque liquid, Chris saw movement. Something curled and uncurled in a primal rhythm. Despite his distance, he felt a heartbeat thumping, vibrating the air, so loud that his ears rang.

A voice shattered the calm like a rogue cannonball. "It's all a bit strange, isn't it?" Art's beady eyes looked up at him. The man stood less than a foot away. Chris wasn't sure how long he had been there; too long not to be noticed. He was used to the patient stares he now received, which were the same directed at him during PTSD flare-ups. The ringing in his ear grew louder. *Tinnitus, nothing more.* "Yes, quite," he managed through gritted teeth.

Megan came in for the save. "What are they?"

Chris pressed all of his love for her into one look. She always had his back.

Art clucked his tongue. "It'll make a lot more sense when you see the fields, but if you must know, they're incubation chambers. Testing different strains before they go in the dirt. A necessary step in the process."

Chris watched as the liquid in the pod shifted. A black tentacle whipped out of the darkness and traced the outline of the enclosure.

Art was unphased. "Let's keep moving."

Chris watched the tentacle curve into a tight spiral. Shivers ran across his arm and prickled it with goose flesh. Even in the empty air where his right arm would have been, he felt his hairs stand on end. He wondered why the others failed to react. *They don't see it.* Chris blinked, and the tentacle retreated into the center of the pod. "Yeah, some fresh air sounds nice."

"Ah, I get it. This old barn gets stuffy during the day." Art's tone bubbled with excitement. "I keep it mostly sealed so the air conditioner doesn't run itself to death. Really quite a thing, getting an old barn like this completely airtight." He motioned for them to follow as he bounded toward the side door.

Chris followed on leaden feet. He looked at Megan but saw no discomfort there. As if sensing him, she whispered, "Alright, it's a little weird, but let's see what they have."

A little weird was putting it mildly. Chris felt as though he had stepped into a world where gravity pulled objects into the sky. The barn had a charged, constrictive atmosphere, like a balloon so close to popping that its rubber is entirely white. "Right. I'll just be happy to get outside." He took a deep breath and put one foot in front of the other until he had caught up to their host.

"Started this business about five years back," Art called as he threw open the barn's side door. Warm light streamed through and painted a bright yellow rectangle on the dusty floor. "Back then, it was one lab table and a small pot for growing the prototypes. Look at it now."

Chris approached the barn door and felt the heat radiate from outside. He stepped into the sunlight and savored the sweltering sensation on his skin. In front of them, rows of strange stalks covered in plastic stretched out toward the edge of a distant cornfield. Chris took comfort in the small slice of mundane, however far away.

Art stepped back and shut the barn door with a loud crash that echoed across the field. "It is a beautiful day for it." He moved forward, hands on his hips, proud of his creation.

The smell of newborn baby was back, overwhelming in its power. "What exactly is it you're growing out here?" Chris knew the answer. The thought of it brought a cold, unsettled dread to the pit of his stomach.

"Didn't you read the sign, son?" Art laughed. "You're here looking for a new arm. Well, here's my stock."

Confusion raced through Chris's brain. He had known the answer to his own question, but even still, his heart raced.

Megan shifted nervously. "Sorry, it's all just a little—"

"Much?" asked Art. "Yes, alright, come here and let's sate your curiosity, shall we?" He bent down to a bag at his feet. Chris wanted to shout at him, to tell him to leave it where it was, but Art was a man on a mission. With a practiced flourish, he swept the plastic bag off and revealed a five-fingered hand reaching out of the dirt. It was pale and perfectly human. As the sun touched its fingers, they opened and closed reflexively.

Megan stepped back. Chris felt sick. The farm was spinning.

"Ah yes, sometimes they move like that, don't worry. It's actually a good thing. Shows the reflexes are working as they should." Art smiled weakly.

"The sign is literal." Megan coughed, trying to regain her balance.

Art chuckled heartily. "Of course, it is!"

Despite himself, Chris laughed. "You literally grow arms." Hearing the words come out of his own mouth was disorienting.

"Indeed, I do." Art beamed. "Now, let's take a look at my measurements and see if we can get you fixed up with a suitable replacement."

THE FARM

Each step in the fields reverberated with a sense of illusion. Chris was no longer sure whether this was a dream, nightmare, or panic attack.

The bags crinkled as a light breeze blew through, and he wondered if it was the wind or the hands themselves moving beneath the plastic covers. *How does someone do something like this?* Art seemed genuine enough, but Chris thought of the pod. He could still feel the tentacle moving, the pulsing of the creature's heart. When something seemed too good to be true, it often was. Chris had learned this lesson more times than he wanted to count.

"Now, let me check my notes." Art pulled out the tape recorder and pushed play. Chris wasn't listening; he was looking out across the fields. How could he look anywhere else? Megan grabbed his hand and squeezed, ran her soft fingers across his. Ordinarily, it would have made him feel calm; now, he just thought of fingers that reached for the sky in a desperate attempt to feel the breeze.

Chris gave Megan a weak smile, dropped her hand, and stepped out of reach. A primal sense told him he needed to stay alert. *That's called paranoia.* His therapist's words echoed through Chris's head, and he shook them away. *It's only paranoia if you're wrong.*

"Ah, yes…white, three or a four for pigment, some freckling…" Art bent down to inspect a plastic sheet pinned to a wood post. "That's going to be row fifteen. Not too far of a walk." He strode forward and motioned for them to follow. "Step careful now, and if you can help it, don't touch the bags." Chris didn't have to be told twice. All he could think about was an arm grabbing at his ankles like he was in some Sixties horror movie.

The whole field was watching him. Sure, the hands didn't have eyes, but he could feel them following his movement, shifting imperceptibly to track his steps. He remembered the sound from the barn, a cacophony loud enough to rattle his bones. Had it actually been disco music?

"How many prosthetics are you growing here?" Megan's voice held a tentative note that she pushed past. Questions were an effective way to ground otherwise intangible situations; at least, that's what the research said.

Chris thought about employing mental tactics of his own; God knows he had plenty from years of therapy. *Maybe try a deep breathing exercise to center yourself in the present moment.* Instead, he ran through the time it would take them to get to the car at a dead run. Art wasn't carrying a weapon, but they were on a farm, which meant a rifle probably wasn't far away. It wouldn't be a long sprint, but they would make it. So long as the car started, they could be out of range by the time Art got his third shot off.

Art continued. He either didn't notice or chose to ignore Chris's silence. "I think we're up to about two hundred, and that's not counting the incubators. Right now, we've placed about fifty. The results have been extraordinary. Full rehabilitation in a matter of weeks." The pride was evident in his voice.

Megan smiled. "That's incredible."

"You should see their expression after everything gets fitted." Art stopped at a row of crops with a plastic number fifteen posted beside them. "Ah yes, here we go." He stepped between two lines of plastic bags to examine the small tags beneath them. "Ok, I like to go with a best-of-three methodology." Art unceremoniously whipped off the plastic to reveal three human arms that extended toward the sun. Their flesh met the dirt just below the elbow.

Chris winced. Sunlight reflected off their pink fingernails, causing the tips of the hands to glow in the midday heat. Despite his discomfort, Chris couldn't help but marvel at them. They were the best prosthetics he had ever seen. He looked down at the stump of his right arm and wondered what it would feel like.

He felt his hand running over his beloved car's stick shift, still warm from the midday heat. As he looked down at uncalloused fingers and pale skin, he could feel what it would be like to pluck his guitar for the first time in years. Elation ran through him in a wave and chased away his misgivings. *What if this is the real deal? What if it was simply garden-variety paranoia?* Embarrassment flushed hot in his face. After a few deep breaths that brought the smell of soil and the odd scent the hands gave off, he considered that he had never seen anything so strange. The truly bizarre nature of his situation brought about humor and perspective. "That can be my arm?" The words felt clunky and stupid but also tinged with excitement.

"Yes, Chris, that can be your arm." Art beamed up at him, his eyes full of light and joy. "There it is. That look right there is why I do it."

Chris laughed, a hysterical noise in the quiet field. He crouched down, putting his good hand on his knee as he took stock of the situation. "They're incredible."

Art squatted next to him. "I know this can all seem a bit much but trust me, when you get this bad boy attached in a few months..." He whistled. "You'll forget you ever had any misgivings to begin with."

Was I that obvious? "They certainly do have a disarming effect."

Art gave a hearty belly laugh. "Now, there it is! A sense of humor poking out from beneath it all. I like that. Now, we've got an important piece of business to deal with."

"What's that?"

"Well, you have to tell me which one you like, of course!" He slapped Chris on the shoulder. "Go on, take a closer look, don't be shy."

Chris approached nervously. He bent low to each of the arms and noticed their skin looked soft and fresh, at odds with the summer sun. The irony of unworked hands being tilled in a field gave the situation dark levity. At first glance, the arms all looked similar, but as he inspected further, he noticed myriad intricacies. Much like snowflakes, tiny variations made all the difference in the world. Knuckle size, finger length; all things he had never thought of before. But now, he noticed.

Eventually, he came to settle on the middle stalk. He held his hand up for comparison; it would never be a complete match, but it was close enough. Shifting to put his stump next to the stalk, Chris tried to imagine what it would be like. A smile crept over his face. The government would have a hell of a time understanding the difference in his fingerprints.

Art grinned. "I think we have a winner."

"I think I agree." Chris blinked back tears, sudden and surprising. *Straighten up.* With the niceties out of the way, this was now a business negotiation.

Art shuffled to the arm and put a tag around a fingertip. It read 'RESERVED FOR CUSTOMER' in the same blocky lettering as the sign out front. He then replaced the opaque bags around them. "Don't worry, we'll leave it out in the sun a little each day to get the right pigmentation and get started on those freckles. Baby steps."

"Thank you." The dreamlike quality of the farm returned.

"Look at that, he's stunned speechless." Megan wrapped her arms around Chris. "Told you this was a good idea."

Art smiled at them both. "Well, now that we've got the part I like out of the way, it's time for the ugly bit. We've got to discuss payment, insurance, all the stuff that makes my skin crawl." He shivered. "Why don't we head on over to my office, and we can iron out the details."

"Of course." Chris put his good arm around Megan, barely able to stop himself from shouting his gratitude. "You're running a business, after all. How much are we talking?"

A high-pitched screech cut across the farm. Adrenaline leaped into Chris's veins, evaporating the calm. "What the hell was that?" *Forty seconds to the car, five seconds to start it, thirty seconds to the road.*

A flicker of annoyance and anger crossed Art's face. "It's the goddamned buzzard hawks trying to get at the fields again. I'll handle it and meet you both back at the barn. Take the front door."

Before Chris had time to say anything else, Art ran across the field toward the barn. "Don't you dare!" he yelled, waving his hands like a madman.

When Art was out of earshot, Chris let out a long breath he didn't know he'd been holding. "That didn't sound like a buzzard hawk." He watched Art cut across the field, surprised at the man's speed.

There was a hint of fear in Megan's eyes, however slight. "What else could it be?"

Chris looked out at the field of bags. His stomach churned. "If something feels too good to be true, it probably is. This is too good to be true, Megan."

"Oh, Chris, come—"

"No. I did what I agreed to. Something is wrong here, and we're getting the hell out." His words were clipped, bordering on anger. *I'm sorry.* Saying it out loud would undermine the urgency, but he saw the hurt in Megan's eyes. She didn't have to tell him he was acting irrationally. *Run, you need to run.*

Megan looked at Art as he entered the barn. "But he's such a nice man."

Fear constricted Chris's throat. He recognized the feeling as the moment before a fight. "I'm sorry, Megan, but we need to go. I don't know what it is, but we can't be here. Let's go, straight to the car. At a walk, but don't stop."

She sighed, then nodded.

The vehicle wasn't nearly as far as it had been in Chris's mind, and he said a silent thank you. Even though it felt like fight or flight, the heavy shroud of shame clung to his shoulders. The threat felt very real, but he knew once they were out, it would seem silly. That was how mental illness worked. He looked to the barn and then back to the field. *This isn't your PTSD. Walk faster.*

As if to answer his thoughts, Megan ran a firm hand along his back, working at the tension.

"I'm sorry, Megan, I—"

Another screech cut across the farm. A man burst into the sunlight from behind the barn, completely naked, his shaved head glinting. Chris's eyes immediately fell on his missing arm. Blood ran down the man's back in rivulets, smeared across his pale skin. "Help me!" He staggered toward them. "Please. This place isn't right!"

A shot rang out, and a puff of red mist exploded between the naked man's eyes. He brought a hand up to the neat hole in his forehead, confused, then fell forward into the field of plastic bags.

TOO GOOD TO BE TRUE

Chris watched as the man's blood hung in the air. Sunlight caught red droplets on their fall to earth, projecting vivid swatches of red to match the barn. His heart pounded. "Megan, get to the car, get it started." Old instincts took over. This wasn't a day trip; it was a combat zone.

"I'm not going to—"

"Get to the car, get it started, and if I'm not there in five minutes, go get help." Chris wasn't exactly sure what to do with those five minutes, but there was no simple getaway. The naked man in the field had been shot at some distance square in the head, which meant that Art had range on his side and was a halfway decent marksman. The parked car would be out of any direct line of sight. If they tried to drive out the way they had come, at least one of them would be injured or killed. Art had to be dealt with.

Megan's eyes were wide, but her words were calm. "If you're not back in five minutes, I'm going to say the nastiest shit at your funeral."

He smiled at her. "I'll be back in four."

Silently, Megan moved toward the car, keeping low to the ground while Chris ran to the side of the barn. He hunkered behind a set of hay bales. Adrenaline charged through him and dulled any sense of logic. Through deep breaths, Chris tried to bring his brain to focus.

Art stomped out from between the double doors, his good humor gone. Dark circles ringed his eyes as if he suddenly hadn't slept in days. A rifle hung loosely at his side, long and smooth with a bulky, rectangular sight.

Chris looked at the weapon, confused. As with the farm, there was something off; the gun was unlike anything he had ever seen. Sure, the component parts of a rifle were there, but slightly disjointed, like someone's interpretation of a rifle instead of the genuine item. He tensed behind the bale and waited for Art to turn back.

Art never did.

Instead, he walked to where the dead man lay in the hot sun and kicked the corpse. "Shit." Art ran a hand through his beard and mustered his friendliest salesman tone. "Look, I'm sorry you all had to see that, but I assure you this is nothing out of the ordinary." The twitches in his posture said otherwise.

Nothing out of the ordinary? Chris took the opportunity to sneak into the barn through the open doors. Without a weapon of his own, he needed the element of surprise. He moved quickly, trying to pick his way through the mess of equipment, looking for something that could be used as a weapon, when a rush of cool air met him and sent prickles up his skin.

Unlike before, the barn was silent. The machinery had stopped running, leaving nothing but the low hum of the fluorescent lights. Chris crouched down, listening to determine whether he'd been followed. A muted 'thunk' broke the silence.

A black tentacle whipped around within a fleshy pod before him. It prodded incessantly at its squishy enclosure. With each movement, Chris felt cold dread slide over him. "Stop that," he hissed, hoping it would do something. The appendage ignored him, striking again and creating a seam in the pod. *No, no, no.* Chris didn't know what the creature was, but he sure didn't want it out.

The tentacle continued its assault and widened the small gap. A sharp, slimy point wiggled its way through the opening, where it tasted air for the first time. It moved unnaturally, jerking from side to side like a compass struggling to find north. Chris froze as the childlike notion of holding still to avoid detection took over. The tentacle extended slowly and grew to over a foot long. A foul, black substance that coated it dripped silently to the floor.

Chris held his breath. In a flash, the tentacle struck out toward him. The wriggling mass caressed the air just a few feet from his face.

Art's shuffling footsteps pierced the air and echoed through the eerie silence. "Chris, you in here? Look, I'm sorry you had to see that." His voice rode the razor's edge between friendship and menace. "Maybe you come out, and we can have a talk about discounts. Everyone gets to leave here happy." Art continued further into the barn.

Chris knew a lie when he heard one. But the longer he waited, the closer the tentacle got. A second appendage split from the first and attempted to pry itself from the fleshy prison. *You need to move, now. Freezing is what gets people killed.* Chris didn't know if that applied to creepy aliens in psychotic barns, but it wasn't like there were other options. He did his best to put the creature from his mind and scanned the room.

Heading back toward the barn door was suicide. Art stood blocking the entrance, his finger around the rifle's trigger. "Come on, Chris. There's nowhere for you to go in here." A hint of frustration rose in Art's voice. "It's not too late for us to talk through this."

Chris took a deep breath and left cover, moving at a low crouch, the rows of silent machinery able to shield him from Art's view. Mostly.

Art sniffed at the air. "Oh, come on, Chris, let's not do this." He shuffled toward the incubators, where he found a creature desperately trying to follow its prey. "What the hell are you doing out? Did you see something that spooked you?"

Chris made his way to a table covered in surgical instruments. Using Art's momentary distraction, he stood and picked up a long scalpel. Against a rifle, it wouldn't be much, but if he could get close, it might just do the trick.

"You know you need to stay in there. Was it that big man Chris you saw?" Art cooed at the creature. A response came in the form of a high-pitched, warbling chitter. Chris dropped the scalpel and clapped a hand to his ear out of reflex.

The sound of metal hitting the concrete floor was loud enough that, within seconds, the deafening report of the rifle filled the barn. A beaker too close to Chris's hiding spot exploded in a shower of glass; Chris winced at his own stupidity and picked up the scalpel. Sitting still wasn't an option. He tensed and took off between the tables, hoping to get some distance before Art could get another shot off.

"I told you not to do that!" Art yelled, racking the rifle. Chris refused to offer any precious energy as a response; every fiber of his being was dedicated to putting one foot in front of the other. Instinctively, he slid beneath another table and moved to the adjacent row. At that exact moment, Art fired again. The bullet ripped through the metal table above Chris and left a sizeable hole as it buried itself in the concrete floor. Shrapnel stung as it struck the back of Chris's neck.

He tried to stay focused. Time moved slowly, every heaving breath a marathon. *There is a way out of this.* He looked ahead to a staircase that sloped into a tunnel and out toward the field. There was some chance it led to a basement, where Chris would find himself trapped, but remaining above ground wasn't an option. He looked at the scalpel and hoped that whatever lay below would allow him to close the distance between himself and Art.

Chris picked up his speed and slid across the floor toward metal steps. Momentum carried him down, but he managed to stop himself before he fell all the way. From above, Art shouted. "I'm trying to make this quick, Chris! Why couldn't you just take the damn arm?"

Chris couldn't tell for sure, but it sounded like Art was moving further away. *He didn't see me.* Carefully, he made his way further down the stairs. A slimy substance coated the metal and threatened to send him slipping with each step. At the foot of the stairs, a long concrete hallway stretched to a dark room in the distance. A blue light pulsed at the end of the corridor.

Upstairs, Art fired another shot. A great clatter shook the ceiling as machinery fell. Chris stepped off the stairs and into the tunnel. Dread rose in his throat despite numbing adrenaline. In the same instant, the lights turned red, and an alarm claxon blared. Chris looked to his feet, where he was greeted by the infrared sensor he had just tripped.

OLDER AND WISER

The sound of Art descending the stairs was immediate. Chris took off down the hallway, where red lights flashed, leaving him in fleeting moments of shadow. His legs were rubber. Each breath burned his lungs. Yet he continued. *You are not going to die beneath some Podunk barn in the middle of nowhere.* He had to laugh; there really wasn't anything Podunk about the barn at all. Without the hand-painted exterior, it could have been easily mistaken for a secret military base. Before he had time to sort through the implication, Art called from behind.

"Chris, trust me. At this point, the bullet would be kinder!" His voice came in ragged wheezes, sounding genuine for the first time all day.

"Cut the bullshit, Art!" Chris wrapped his fingers around the scalpel and hoped there was cover ahead. The corridor was empty, offering a straight shot for Art. But it wouldn't stay that way forever. Ahead, the pulsing blue light grew brighter. It radiated static energy, lifting the hairs on Chris's arm. He treated it like a guide. The tunnel's end was his only slim chance of survival.

He couldn't hear Art's footsteps above the constant blare of the alarm, but he assumed he was still in pursuit. The tunnel sloped outward, and the flashing lights grew further away. A heavy gloom settled over the path as it transitioned to a metal catwalk. Chris didn't realize until he looked down that the ground had fallen away into a dark abyss. Short flashes of blue light blossomed in the darkness. *Anyone and anything that ends up down there never comes back.* Chris wasn't sure why he thought that, but a needling sense in the back of his mind told him it was true.

He continued running, dismayed by the catwalk that extended before him. The air grew noticeably cold, and a fine mist hung all around. Blue light pulsed above, illuminating large sacks that hung from the ceiling at varying heights. As he made his way further in, he saw small staircases and ladders that led to certain of the pods. Ahead, the catwalk continued indefinitely.

A bolt of lightning revealed the pit below. It was devoid of sound as electricity arched across the expanse. Chris waited for a clap of thunder that never came, and somehow that was worse. The light showed a series of catwalks above while something massive moved in the gloom below. Nausea turned in his stomach, and he grabbed the railing for stability. Not far ahead, the path split into a four-way junction. To the right, stairs spiraled upward. Chris mustered what little energy he possessed and ran toward them.

Up was out. At least, he hoped. The stairs would put challenging terrain between him and Art; every second he could delay his pursuer was another second he stayed alive. As he ascended, he could see the slimy surfaces of the hanging pods in fine detail. They appeared to be the same material as the incubators he had seen upstairs and substantially bigger. The transparent fluid inside revealed large, pale objects suspended within. Chris counted himself lucky that no black tentacles tried to break free.

He rounded the top of the stairs and stepped onto another long catwalk. Pods hung in rows on either side of him, shrouded in white mist, when a shadow shifted within one of them. Chris's eyes darted to the hazy enclosure and fixed on it. Once more, he felt the urge to turn around, but his feet continued forward. *I know what's in there; I just need to see it.* With each step, the mist surrounding the pod cleared. At first, his mind couldn't make sense of it. *A tangle of flesh suspended in liquid with an appendage reaching toward the sky.* He looked at it, then saw its face through the haze.

It was a woman, shriveled and withered like a rotten apple. Her long hair flowed out in a cloud behind her while one of her legs kicked weakly. Her right arm reached up toward the top of the pod, where a tight metal cylinder wrapped around her forearm, holding it in place. A long tube ran from her mouth and nose through the pod and into the gloom below.

Chris leaned in, not quite able to piece together what he was seeing. "What the—"

The woman's eyes blinked open, glassy and dead from long years spent submerged. Her free hand shot out toward him. Chris recoiled in shock and nearly fell over the railing behind him. "What the fuck, what the fuck?" He sank to a seated position and locked eyes with the woman. A horrible static hiss filled his ears and underscored the true silence of the room surrounding him.

"I told you, you weren't supposed to see any of this." Art approached from the stairs, his words a sensory bombardment in such a quiet space.

Chris moved the scalpel out of Art's view, drew a deep breath, and steadied his hand. "What the hell is going on here?"

"Well, that's a question that would have been better asked upstairs, don't you think?"

Chris needed to run, but his body wouldn't let him. He was rooted to the spot. The time to fight was approaching, but every second he could delay brought him an advantage. "What's in the pit?"

Art let out a long breath between clenched teeth. "You know what's in the pit."

Lightning flashed above the catwalk, revealing the twisting, writhing shadows below. Chris's mind hovered on the edge of understanding. Static filled his ears, wiped away the boundaries of thought, and sanded down the corners of his mind. Time moved at a snail's pace, apart from his conversation with Art.

"Suffice it to say, it's big and old. Older than either of us by a measure. Wiser too, if you'd bother to listen."

The black barrel of Art's rifle was pointed firmly at Chris's head. One twitch, and none of it would matter. All the same, Chris found it hard to keep his attention on the immediate danger with the omnipresent static in his ears. There were whispers in the moments between; an ancient language, maybe? *No. You need to stay alert; you can make it out of here. Keep him talking.* "I can hear it, trying to talk to me."

Art's smile returned. "Yes, I suppose you would. There's a reason we chose you, Chris."

Chris tensed his legs, ready to move at the slightest drop in Art's concentration. There was no margin for error, but with guns, there rarely was. "What the hell is that thing?" The words came out more strained than he liked; each syllable was more challenging to pronounce than the last.

"I already told you, it's big and old. But what you really want to know is where it came from. Hell, I want to know that, too." Art sighed. "But, Chris, as you would have learned, there are some things that are simply beyond us. Five years ago, when that thing came here, I learned something. There's bliss in serving a higher power." He looked at the pod lovingly. "I know it's a bit much to take in, but when you've really felt its mind, you'll feel differently." A hardness crept into his voice. "I just wish you could have done that from the surface, living your happy life with your beautiful new arm."

Chris slowly rose to his feet. He realized just how short his time was.

Art paid him no attention. Instead, he moved to caress the pod's surface. "Before it came here, I was living off government subsidies. Barely enough to keep a roof over my head and food in my bowl. Now," he chuckled, "you wouldn't believe what people pay for a high-quality prosthetic."

Chris bit his lip. "And all the people down here?"

Art turned toward the pod. "Well, sacrifices have to be made in service of the greater good. I would think a soldier could understand that."

Chris seized the opportunity and charged. There were only a few feet between him and Art when a rifle barked from behind him. The cavern swallowed the sound whole as if it had never existed in the first place. Splinters of agony shot out from Chris's shoulder. Bones broke, and warmth flooded the side of his body. *How did he do that?*

"Oh, Chris. We've had a few disappointments, but this one hurt more than most."

Chris tried to continue, but shock set in quickly. Each step grew more lumbered than the last. The world swayed as a voice came from behind. "Careful now; you don't want to fall in." Chris fell to his knees, coming dangerously close to the catwalk's edge. A lightning bolt illuminated a churning maw of teeth and hundreds of eyes that stared at him from the darkness below. Fear, pure and distilled, sent rigid electricity through his limbs. He turned back toward the voice and felt the sluggish pace of near-death wash over him.

Megan stood on the catwalk, a rifle loosely held in her arms. A thin trail of smoke rose from the barrel. "There just had to be a runner, today of all days." There was genuine disappointment in her voice.

"Very disappointing," repeated Art. "But you know how *she* likes to toy with them."

A new pain crept into Chris's throat as he stared up at Megan. "Why?" The cavern grew darker. His vision narrowed.

"You were never supposed to see all this, Chris. Your purpose wasn't to understand; it was to serve." There was genuine pity in her voice. "We could have been happy."

Chris's equilibrium gave way, and he fell onto the metal grating. There was no pain as his face struck the surface, only a dull sensation that something was very wrong. Lightning flashed and became muddled memories of light as all reason faded from the world. He floated in the dark. *What a strange place to die.*

A WARM BREEZE caressed the bare tips of Chris's fingers. Beautiful calm spread over him as the sun baked his skin, reminding him of lost summers spent in the open air. The smell of freshly cut grass and recently tilled earth filled the air and brought a much-needed sense of safety and familiarity. He clung to them like a child's blanket.

When he moved his hand to block the bright sun, firm pressure around his forearm prevented it. *Must have fallen asleep.* He tried again and waited for the familiar pins and needles sensation of the limb waking. Instead, he felt cold rubber gripped tightly around his skin. His arm wouldn't budge.

Memories that felt like they could have been a hundred years old returned to him. An image of a massive barn spread out before him, ringed by fields of plastic bags. Blue light glowed from beneath the soil. Static, heavy static everywhere. He tried to move his arm again; nothing. He kicked his legs and found them surrounded by liquid. Desperation gripped him as he shook violently back and forth and tried to free himself. *Pods.* The single word was enough to fill him with a dread usually reserved for children's nightmares.

No, please, no. It had been a car accident, and the barn was simply a bad dream from too-strong painkillers. It wouldn't be the first time. *My arm is restrained so I don't injure myself anymore.* The thoughts were empty. They provided no relief. Eventually, he would have to open his eyes and accept the truth. As he took a deep breath, he noticed a tube attached to his mouth and the hollow sound that came with his inhale.

He opened his eyes. Murky liquid spread out across a field of hanging sacks. Pulsing blue light revealed two figures standing on a catwalk some feet away.

"It would be more comfortable in there if you stopped squirming around." Art's voice was calm and easy. Chris tried to reply with a stream of expletives, but the tube snaking out of his mouth caught the words before they could form. He shook his arm violently, which sent a spike of pain through his shoulder.

"I said stop that!" Art rapped on the side of the pod. "You'll waste another perfectly good arm."

Megan stepped into view and put a hand on Art's shoulder. "Maybe let me do the talking." Art grumbled something and stepped back reluctantly. "I really am sorry about this, Chris, but he's right. Struggling isn't going to help you. Your shoulder is barely hanging together as it is. It'll heal with time, but you need to stay still." She leaned toward the pod, looking into his eyes.

Years. Chris had spent years looking into those eyes. Clear, green pools. They were beautiful. A dull, aching pain grew in Chris's chest. Her gaze softened, and for a moment, Chris hoped that she would tell him everything was going to be alright, that the love they shared would save him.

"If you damage the arm, then you're no use to *her*." Megan's eyes flitted down to the cavern below. "I can't tell you what she does to those that get released, but I can tell you it's a hell of a lot worse than hanging in a medicated bubble."

Chris's heart sank.

"You just had to play the hero, didn't you? I suppose it was what you were bred to do." Electricity arched behind her, casting dark shadows over a familiar face. A far-off pod burst, leaving a naked man dangling from the ceiling by his wrist. Goo dripped off his feet to the chasm below as his air tube popped out. The man shrieked wildly; the sound pierced the low-level static that permeated the room.

Art stepped forward once more. "I think that's our cue to go." The naked man kicked and writhed while the restraint on his arm kept him firmly in place. Liquid dripped in slow, silent rivulets off his body.

Megan looked at the man and back to Chris. "Trust me, it's better if you don't see this. I'll give you something that will help." She pulled out a tablet and tapped quickly on the screen. Chilled liquid flowed down the tube in Chris's throat. In the distance, a black tentacle snaked out of the gloom and grazed the struggling man's feet. *She likes to toy with them.* He waited for terror to come but felt nothing. He tried to muster anger, alertness, anything, but felt only a blanket of calm. The pod was good; the pod was safe. He needed to stay there.

"Goodbye, Chris." Megan offered a small wave.

The sorrow at her minimal gesture was dulled, as was the world. None of it mattered. Chris watched dispassionately as Art and Megan strode down the catwalk and out of sight. The tentacle reached up toward the man's legs, grabbed hold of his bony midriff, and yanked. The man's arm separated at the restraining cuff, which sent a gout of blood spraying. Screams slowly faded into silence as the man was pulled down into the darkness. A final flash of lightning illuminated the churning fate that waited below the gloom. The creature below released a deep, sonorous cry that reverberated through Chris's pod. He was surprised to find that he didn't care. The light faded from the world around him once more. He was exhausted.

Why fight it?

IV

Ho, ho, ho, and a bottle of FUN! I mean, I've heard of stories "hanging around" until the end, but that was something extra, wouldn't you say? I hope I never learn agriculture from that guy. I bet he'd charge an arm and a leg for his services. (where's Ed McMahon when you need him?! Oh, right, dead.)

The crazy train keeps chugging along with our next story, which features arguably the single cutest entity I've ever allowed myself to be associated with. It's this little ball of fluff with big Bambi eyes; I know, TERRIFYING, right? Just the thought of something so vomit-inducingly adorable makes me want to gouge my eyes out with a Freddy Kreuger claw.

I will say, though, that the way the little beast can eat is awe-inspiring. It reminds me of how I used to inhale pizza back in the day when I had a digestive tract. You can't imagine how hard it is to process dairy when you don't have a digestive tract. And then these assholes try to make some crap-equivalent for sensitive stomachs, and of all ingredients, it involves cauliflower crust. Can you imagine? CAULIFLOWER!

ON PIZZA! And they have the gall to still call it edible. For shame. I mean, science can grow a functioning human ear on the back of a rodent, and you're telling me this is the best we can do for pizza alternatives? Despicable.

Great, now all this talk about food has made me hungry, and I don't even have any cash left over from the racetrack yesterday. *sigh* I'm such a degenerate. Oh, well. Looks like it's time to take a trip to the company break room, where someone's brown bag is about to get seriously pilfered. So, while I rummage through the communal fridge for some yummy food (that most certainly doesn't involve CAULIFLOWER!), you crazy cats enjoy Cuddles, Devourer of Worlds.

CUDDLES, DEVOURER OF WORLDS

VANESSA KRAUSS

J ane was wrenched from her college application by the piercing death cries of a tortured animal. The neighborhood cats had caught a baby rabbit. It wasn't the first time.

"Meep! Meep! Meep!"

She charged from the dining room to the patio door, where she saw three of the neighbors' cats —Tabbycoat, Mambalad, and Whispers— paw at a speck of quivering fluff.

"Bad cats. Shoo! Leave it alone!" Jane ran to the trio of tormentors while flailing her arms and yelling. The tabby hissed, unwilling to give up his prize, whereas the Persian and ginger tabby fled over the backyard fence, fully aware they were outmatched. "Get! Scat!" Tabbycoat refused to budge. He glowered over his catch and yowled at her. Jane kicked at the air. "Go!" The cat got the message and scaled the nearby birch tree. His disapproving gaze leered at Jane from behind a grouping of leaves.

"Jerk."

Jane stood braced over the baby bunny and made it clear who owned the yard and the creatures within. The cat gave up and took off across a branch, crossed over the cedar fence, and jumped into the Cullins' backyard. Peace was restored until the next time Tabbycoat and his band of meowing marauders returned to plunder native wildlife.

"You poor thing," murmured Jane. She leaned over to scoop up the bunny but stopped suddenly and retracted her hand. Such a queer appearance. Wild rabbits typically had speckled brown coats. This shaking ball of fuzz was pastel-pink with shimmering iridescent edges. It was missing ears, and Jane's first thought was that the cats bit them off. "Shh, shh, it's okay," she whispered as she cradled the creature. "There, there. You'll be fine. I've got you."

The critter nestled into the palm of her hand as Jane's chestnut brown gaze met large cerulean blue eyes.

"Well, aren't you a cutie."

"Mreem." It fluttered its dense eyelashes, a picture of helpless, sweet cluelessness. The creature was surprisingly calm, despite all that it went through. Still, it could try to escape. She covered it with her fingers.

"Let me get you inside and see if you're hurt. Okay?"

The girl found a box and placed the maybe-a-rabbit in it. Once it was safely contained, she fished through the pantry for a suitable first-aid kit. "Bet that little snot, Isaac, spray painted it and left it for the cats to get. If I see him…ooh, he's going to get it," she muttered.

The bright red first-aid bag was next to a box of kitty litter, a must-have for spills. Jane returned to the dining room with the medical equipment in hand, prepared to clean whatever injuries the rabbit had sustained. The little animal was quiet but awake. It was hard to ignore its saucer eyes following her as she went to work.

"Okay, little guy. I'm going to check to see if you're hurt. Nothing scary." Talking out loud soothed Jane—the animal seemed indifferent to it. She handled the critter gently and parted its hair while she examined for any sign of injury. It made no fuss; very un-rabbit-like.

The animal had no tail and no feet. Jane also never found any ears. It was a literal ball of fluff with two big eyes and a mouth. As she combed through the silky fur, she realized the pink color went down to the roots. The teenager held it away from her face and assessed what it could be.

It was not a rabbit. Nor a chinchilla. It was warm and soft, possibly a mammal, but she had never seen a creature like it before.

"What are you?"

"Meep," the fluff squeaked. It was adorable, for sure.

"Aww!" Jane swooned. "Well, it doesn't look like the cats had time to hurt you, whatever you are. Should still call Dr. Nelson. He'll know what to do."

Jane looked back to the kitchen and the open pantry. There was bird seed, alfalfa, kitten formula, tins of cat food, kibble, and even some dried insect larva for the occasional skink. She went through her mental checklist of what else was in the house when luxurious softness interrupted her thoughts.

"Mrrm-wrrm-rrr!" The pink pom-pom had bounced to her pale, freckled shoulder, nuzzled into her neck, and purred.

Jane's cheeks flushed. Cuteness overload. She had to get it together. Chin up, chest out, cell phone in sight. Priorities.

"Need to figure out what you eat."

Dr. Nelson's number was near the top of her call list. Jane dialed the number and was greeted by a receptionist. "Dr. Nelson's Exotics Animal Care, Tracy speaking. Good afternoon, Jane. Got another patient for us?" Jane called so often that her number was etched into Tracy's memory.

"Yep. Don't know what this one is, though. Can I get Dr. Nelson to examine it?"

"Something you don't recognize?" Tracy sounded puzzled. Jane had seen enough of suburban Austin's fauna that Tracy considered her an expert.

"Yeah. Must be rare." Jane peered through her auburn locks at the creature nuzzled into her neck. "Pink. Round. Fluffy. Big blue eyes. Not sure if it's an omnivore or herbivore."

"Interesting. Unfortunately, Dr. Nelson is at a conference for the next two weeks. We're only taking emergency cases. Have you tried placing food in front of it and seeing what it likes?"

"I guess I can give that a try."

"Give us a call in two weeks, and we'll make sure it's taken care of."

"Thank you."

Jane put down the phone. The fluffball remained snuggled up to her. "You're quite a cuddler, aren't you?" The pink critter blinked.

"Cuddles. Because you're cute and cuddly. I think that will work until we find out what you are. Should figure out what you want to eat, too." She eyed the contents of her pantry. Plenty of options.

Cuddles' dinner was an assortment of fruit, vegetables, nuts, and cooked chicken, alongside every type of pet food Jane had on hand. She placed Cuddles on the dining room table in front of the smorgasbord and gave it a choice to eat what it fancied most.

The powderpuff bounced, letting out a joyful "Mee!" before digging in. It moved left to right, eating whatever was closest to it, then progressing down the line until the end.

Jane watched in astonishment as Cuddles mowed through kale, strawberries, liver pâté, and crunchy seed mix. It then bum-shuffled itself back to where it began and finished off some mealworms. Jane had to intervene when Cuddles started sucking on a plate.

"That's not food." She pulled the dish from its mouth. Not a crumb was left. "Looks like you'll eat anything." Jane stared hard at a sparkly-eyed and unaware Cuddles. "Or you're a porker and going to be really sick in the morning." For emphasis, she poked the pink critter below its mouth. "All that food you ate has to go somewhere." Where, exactly, was up for debate.

Jane cordoned part of the dining room and lay down newspaper, puppy pads, and open boxes of sawdust. She was busy setting up a litter box when her mom came home.

"Jane, I'm home!" Her voice echoed through the two-story dwelling.

"Hey, Mom!"

Jane's mom crossed to the adjoining living room. A Southern belle fifty-five years young. She stood and watched her daughter, arms folded.

"Oh, no, not another one. What did you rescue this time?" She gave a long sigh and then moved in for a closer inspection. Jane was quiet as she let her mother examine Cuddles. "What is it?"

Jane's mom hovered over the shimmery pink ball of cotton candy fluff. Her head bandied back and forth, uncertain. Cuddles looked up, blinking its beautiful blue peepers.

"That's Cuddles," Jane explained. "Dr. Nelson is out at a conference, so I'll be its guardian for the next two weeks."

"Ooo-kaaay…" The older woman's tone was wary. "Two weeks is a long time. You know how your father feels about that."

Jane shrugged. Nothing she could do.

Her mother sighed. "Same rules as always. Feed and clean up after it. And don't forget to work on your veterinary college applications."

"Yep. Got it all covered."

"Good." Her mother's law was established. Everything was above board.

THE FOLLOWING MORNING, Jane trudged downstairs, uneager to discover what the combination of rabbit, cat, lizard, and bird food had done to the creature's bowels—and hopefully not the hardwood floors. She entered the dining room to find Cuddles dozing in a cat bed with the litter box and puppy pads unsoiled.

Jane reasoned that perhaps it was toilet trained. She stepped into the pen with a leash in one hand and a dog collar in the other. A wad of waste bags was stuffed in her denim pockets.

"Morning, Cuddles. I should take you for a walk."

Jane easily leashed the complacent creature and left the house. It soon became apparent that whatever Cuddles was doing, it wasn't walking. Instead, it scooted across the sidewalk at a decent pace. Morning dog walkers stopped to stare at Jane and the strange thing tied to the end of a dog leash. Jane ignored them and continued down the street.

"Okay, Cuddles. Do your business, and then we can have breakfast." Cuddles had stopped to appreciate the Cullins' immaculate rose bushes. The sound of yapping interrupted the peaceful moment.

"Yip-yip-yip-yip!"

Jane looked down to find Daisy the Chihuahua at her feet. At the end of her leash was her equally irritating owner, Mr. Dickens.

The scrawny, balding man glared at Jane overtop his square glasses.

His wrinkled face furrowed as he honed in on the object of Daisy's derision. "What is that?" His hooked nose pointed at the cute creature while Daisy continued to yip. The dog's leash strained as she inched closer to the animal under Jane's care.

"A rare species," Jane stated. "Can you get Daisy under control?" Jane tried to pull Cuddles away, but it would not budge.

Then, Cuddles solved the problem for them. There was a yelp, and Daisy was gone. Her leash was left hanging from Cuddles' mouth.

Mr. Dickens yelled, first at Jane and then at Cuddles. "My dog! Get it to spit her out! Spit her out!"

The collar around Jane's furry critter snapped, and she was left with no recourse but to get down on her knees and pry the Chihuahua out of Cuddles' mouth. "Come on. Spit her out. Spit her out, Cuddles." Jane pointed to the sidewalk, hoping a saliva-covered Chihuahua would end up in its place. In response, the creature batted its eyelids, sweet, adorable, and newly doubled in size thanks to the canine snack.

"Mree?" The creature fluttered its pink eyelids again. Order not heeded. Jane opted for the alternate approach and used her hands to pry open Cuddles' mouth. Inside, there was nothing. Jane expected to see a terrified Chihuahua but found only a dark, toothless void that permeated warmth. She turned the pink creature to Mr. Dickens, its mouth still agape as they peered into the pit of Cuddles' stomach.

"D-D-Daisy. My Daisy..." Mr. Dickens' body trembled, his face ashen. He stumbled backward onto the curb, crawling until he had thought enough to stand. Hurriedly, the man fled across the street to his house and slammed the front door.

"Maybe we should go home," Jane whispered.

"ALL THAT FOOD—AND Daisy—has to come out eventually." Jane let Cuddles into the yard multiple times a day, where she kept a casual watch in case the cats attacked. Not that they would anymore; Cuddles had reached the size of a Golden Retriever.

"Where's the poop?" Jane searched through the bushes and tall grass that surrounded the perimeter. There had to be poop; it's not like Cuddles could bury it. The phenomenal growth could be rationally explained. Maybe Cuddles was a baby animal. But an animal couldn't avoid defecation and be healthy. It had to poop!

"Okay, buster. Where are you hiding the goods?" Jane dead-stared the creature into submission. "Are you burying it? Spraying it?" Cuddles gave her no answer and instead blinked. "Is it liquid? Is that why I'm not seeing it? You must have a butt. You do have a butt, right?"

"Mrrm?"

"I can't imagine the cats would eat your poop. Don't think coyotes would either. I've seen what you eat." Jane glanced around the yard, surprisingly unscathed. Cuddles, eater of all things except the back-yard. Perhaps it ate its own poop?

"I'm going to find out what you did with your turds. I'm on to you. You can't keep this up forever, Cuddles. I'm a master of sniffing out doo-doo." Jane leered at the creature with a grin. Detective Shitlock was on the case. There will be poop.

Jane busied herself with the bird feeders. Depending on the season, she typically had to replenish stocks every two days. Yet, all the bird feeders were presently full. She took out the mix and rolled it over in her hands. It didn't smell rotten.

Jane nibbled on a peanut. Whatever was good for her was suitable for the birds, and the nut tasted fine. Then, she whipped around, caught in fear by the startled yowl of Tabbycoat. Jane turned her attention from the fence to the trees to the yard. She found no cat, only Cuddles sitting where she had left it.

"You okay, Cuddles?" The pink fluffball sat turned away from her. Fear rose as she ran to check on it and stumbled upon a crime in progress. Hanging out of Cuddles' mouth was the limp form of a tabby's tail. Jane stared, unable to turn away as she watched Cuddles' meal, served al dente, slip into its mouth, fur and all.

Cuddles ate Daisy, and now it had eaten Tabbycoat. Had it also eaten all the birds? Was that why the bird feeders were still full? Jane looked from the adorable, possible apex predator to the many feeders that surrounded her home.

A distant knock at the door, followed by a manic ringing of the doorbell, called her away. Jane swung the door open to a verbal assault. "There she is! That's her! She's the one with the monster who ate my Daisy!"

Mr. Dickens huffed and puffed at the threshold. Two sheriffs were in attendance. In one of their hands was a piece of paper.

"Ma'am," began the stern-faced man with the name Sterling written on his badge. "We have been informed that an animal under your care has killed the pet belonging to Mr. Dickens. We want to see the animal." The seizure order was tossed at her. Without invitation, the group of men marched through her family's home.

The fat sheriff carrying a net barked, "Where's the animal?"

Jane waved reluctantly toward the back of the house. "Out in the yard." She shuffled behind the men. Mr. Dickens skipped along, fueled by a giddy vengeance.

"I see it! I see it. It's there in the backyard!"

So what if Cuddles had eaten that dog? Daisy was a menace to people and pets alike, all because she had a terrible owner. Mr. Dickens was a bad person. Because of him, Cuddles would be seized, and Jane would be marked as a dangerous pet owner on her permanent record. She'd never get into veterinary school, and Cuddles would be put down.

The three men surrounded Cuddles. Jane stood to the side and brushed away her anguish.

"I'm sorry, Cuddles." This was not what she wanted.

"Mreem?" Cuddles' eyes went from man to man to man; three beasts against one modest, mostly defenseless creature.

"This *thing* ate my Daisy. I want you to take it, cage it, and kill it." Mr. Dickens jabbed his finger towards Cuddles, consumed by mania. He would avenge his dog, and Cuddles would die, but not before mocking the pink critter. "Hahahaha! You hear that?! This is what you get for eating my dog!" Mr. Dickens was right in Cuddles' face. He prodded it between the eyes. "Good riddance, you piece of sh—"

Cuddles' maw went high. The top loomed over Mr. Dickens' head and cast an ominous shadow before it consumed him whole. One lone foot stuck out. It writhed and twitched before the ankle was gone, along with everything else. All that remained of Mr. Dickens was a black patent shoe.

"Holy Jesus Christ!" screamed Fat Sheriff as he dropped the net.

Sterling, clearly the smart one, grabbed his gun. "S-s-stay back, and we won't shoot!" he stammered as the weapon shook in his hands.

Jane was too stunned to react. Cuddles inched closer to the two sheriffs as Fat Sheriff radioed for help. "Backup. We need backup. We've got a…" the sheriff paused and struggled to describe the true horror before him. "The owner is armed, and we're pinned down."

Blatant lie. Jane called him out on it. "Hey! That's not true!"

Sheriff Sterling and his pistol were focused on Cuddles. "I said, '*Stay back!*'" Sterling screamed at the pink ball as it leered at him. Two shots were fired.

Cuddles didn't flinch but edged closer as its mouth stretched wide. All Sterling saw was a massive void before he was eaten. The imposing pink ball turned to Fat Sheriff. Despite Fat Sheriff being fat, he made a good act of running for his life and beelined to the backyard gate at record speed.

A moment of chaos turned eerily quiet, punctuated by a rustle of leaves. Jane was trying to process what had transpired. Cuddles ate two people, and whatever went in never came out. They were dead.

A fluffball the size of a sub-compact car shuffled over. Jane couldn't flee. Her feet were rooted to the ground, paralyzed with fear. The bottomless pit of a creature got closer and closer. She shut her eyes and anticipated the inevitable when a silky caress passed across her cheek.

"Mrrm-wrrm-rrr." The familiar purr. Jane peered through her eyelashes at the monster she called Cuddles. It lived up to its given name.

"Guess you're not going to eat me?" Jane swept a hand between its eyes and down to its mouth, the most dangerous part of its body. There were no bullet holes or gunpowder burns. Just clean, voluminous fur. The dead sheriff and his shaky hands must have missed. "You wanted to protect me, didn't you?"

"Mrrm."

She traced her fingers through the dense fur, wondering what was next, where this would go, what would happen to Cuddles. The sheriff had radioed for help—the Texas kind. It was upon them within a minute in a cavalcade of sirens, whirling lights, and screeching tires. Jane could hear rugged soles pound on pavement as the officers readied themselves outside her home.

A man's voice blared across a megaphone. "This is the Police Department. Drop your weapons and come out with your hands up!"

Jane shouted from behind her fluffy defensive shield. "I'm not armed! We don't own guns!" She did not want to leave the yard and risk a shower of gunfire.

"You have one minute to come out, or we'll shoot!"

If Jane remained still, she was dead. She stepped towards the gate when Cuddles sped ahead and blocked Jane from proceeding.

Jane protested. "Let me go. They'll shoot us otherwise." She pushed against Cuddles. Try as she might, it wouldn't budge. "You need to move." Instead, Cuddles skittered toward the gate. "Not that way!"

Cuddles wriggled through the gate and broke the posts with its girth. The eight law enforcement members took a step back, startled by what came to greet them. Cuddles had no weapons or hands to wield them with. The true terror of the creature was the void in the middle of its face. It expanded wider and wider as it moved towards the cluster of people.

"Shoot it! Shoot it!"

A hail of bullets followed. Jane covered her ears. It was the Fourth of July, full of explosions. Red and blue lights flashed against a soundscape of cheers.

No, wait, those were screams. Lots of screams. Blood-curdling cries and shrieks of despair. Of people devoured.

The noises ceased, and suburbia returned to normal. Jane treaded to the front yard to witness the massacre but found the crime scene had vanished along with the officers and their vehicles. All that remained was a rotund ball of pink fluff the height of a school bus.

Jane gazed upwards at the immense mass that was Cuddles, motionless except for an iridescent pink coat that waved in the wind. The smell of charred metal carried across her nostrils. Discharged ammunition. With the amount of firepower thrown at it, maybe Cuddles was dead? Her lips were pursed, contemplative. She didn't know whether to express joy or grief. The cute little ball of defenseless fuzz went from almost being eaten by cats to devouring cars. She walked around to its other side.

"Mrrw." Cuddles hummed deeply as its giant blue orbs followed Jane. Definitely not dead. But there was no way that many armed officers could miss such as massive target. She parted its fur, peering through the plush fibers for any sign of injury.

Not a scratch. Cuddles was bulletproof. Jane patted the creature. "Guess you don't have much to worry about, do you?" Her eyes went wide in preemptive horror as more police sirens wailed in the distance.

"Meep! Meep! Meep!" Cuddles bleated and gave Jane gentle head butts.

"Hey. Quit that!"

Cuddles persisted. "Meep! Meep! Meep!"

"What do you want?" Jane tried to push it away when Cuddles dipped its body down. Jane faltered, then tumbled onto Cuddles' head. It rose to its full height, with Jane perched precariously on top of it. She gripped the long pink fur for stability. Sure, she had ridden horses before, but they weren't thirty-five feet high and ate people.

"Cuuuuudddlllllles..." Jane spoke its name disapprovingly as she watched the oncoming police vehicles from up on high. She noted them as potential victims. Cuddles shuddered towards the cars. "You don't have to do this. You could run away. Hide. They're not going to come after me." As Jane tried to reason with the giant, moving stomach, her own was in her throat. Cuddles slugged onward, oblivious, as Jane lurched forward with it.

Cruiser after police cruiser raced up the street, and behind them, an armored vehicle rumbled forth marked with the name 'Austin' across its side. Cuddles met this convoy at the intersection of the main boulevard and the street Jane lived on. These men and women in riot gear wielded automatic weapons and were ready to do battle. Jane wasn't. She hid in the shag of Cuddles' fur, where she wished it would be over soon.

The shouts and gunfire were muffled as they hit Cuddles' impenetrable gut. It consumed whole squads, five at a time. The forces were demolished in moments. Silence followed the calamity. Jane peered through the dense grass of pink fur to see they were gone. Vanished. Consumed. Eaten alive.

Jane's view atop Cuddles made it hard for her to discern her ride's height, but she was undoubtedly higher than before. Looking down gave her vertigo; instead, she focused on the horizon. She could see the rooftops and noted that a lot of people could stand to clean their gutters.

Cuddles slugged along the road, gaining momentum. Incoming cars saw a tunnel with no light at the other end. One after the other, they went in, forever lost to the darkness. Jane lifted her head, barely able to clear the dense fur and see the skyline of Austin in the distance.

Another police cruiser appeared alongside another armored vehicle. More cars, more traffic. Ahead of Jane and her mount, the highway loomed, a veritable feast for a creature that had no qualms with consuming all it encountered.

Jane could see a flicker of hope from her position above the great maw. The military had set up a defensive barrier of tanks across the multi-lane highway in a standoff against the pink puff of destruction. She crossed her fingers for their success.

While she couldn't hear the tanks' fire, she could feel the impact of their artillery as it hit Cuddles. Three ballistic shells caused the creature to stagger. The fourth and fifth failed to impede its progress. Jane peeked her head out and realized what a mistake the military was making.

Cuddles let the tanks shoot straight into its gullet. They were feeding it.

As Cuddles sped up, Jane buried herself deep in its coat where she would be protected from the wind. She watched through a small part as Cuddles covered a great distance in no time.

Cuddles supped on an extravagant meal courtesy of the American taxpayer, an expensive array of Humvees, personnel carriers, utility vehicles, and armored tanks. Second helpings were made of support squads. Cuddles veered towards a fast-food restaurant featuring a pair of golden arches but quickly turned away. Apparently, there was food even Cuddles wouldn't eat. The smile was wiped from her face when she saw the mall across the street. In it were a food court and a buffet of people.

The behemoth crossed the highway and headed for the shopping center. Jane could no longer hear cries from her elevation as people scurried about, infinitesimal in scale, no longer worth the effort for Cuddles to pick through and eat.

Cars were still on the menu, but only as appetizers.

The parking lot disappeared, and soon the shopping center did, too. Jane's head was spinning. The number of deceased. The massive amount of people perished in a single gulp. The slow-moving disaster continued unabated, as unstoppable as a hurricane, as deadly as a tornado. Jane scanned the skies for salvation and found a glimmer of promise: fighter planes. She hid in Cuddles' cornfield-high pastel plushness, eyes locked above. She could see the aircraft circle overhead as smoke escaped them. Seconds later, Jane was knocked to her side. A successful bombardment. Jane groaned and pushed herself upright. Being knocked over hurt.

Cuddles growled deeply. "Mrrm…" Something within the creature rose to the surface, and it wasn't its last meal. It approached Austin and its dense downtown full of corporate buildings and skyscrapers. Jane wondered if Cuddles was trying to hide among the larger structures. Her assumptions were quickly proven wrong as Cuddles' voracious appetite escalated to the extreme.

The creature charged toward the first office, a six-story brick building, and tore into it with gusto. A neighboring building received the same treatment, shredded to pieces. Brick and masonry flew everywhere. Cuddles was consuming a high-rise building when the next wave of aerial assaults began. The Air Force pilots came in low; the whine of their engines buzzed in Jane's ears. They swooped in with deafening thunder before they released their payload and spiraled away.

The other sound Jane noticed was that of Cuddles' growling. It hadn't ceased since the first airstrike. Cuddles seemed to ignore the attacks and focused instead on eating as many structures as possible. Weird. Earlier it had chased its assailants.

Cuddles' fur stretched the height of sequoias, and its body was as tall as a skyscraper. Jane could see the horrified people on the fifty-eighth floor of The Independent. At least until the creature demolished it in a single mouthful.

Cuddles swelled further. Bye-bye, beautiful Austin.

A resolute, guttural vibration echoed from Cuddles' core. "Mrrm." It turned to confront the fighter planes, which were taken out in short order. It was hard to evade a mouth the width of several city blocks; fighter planes went in, and that was the end. Nothing left but chemtrails.

Jane stood, her arms looped around a long strand of fur. She witnessed the Colorado River wither to a snaking sliver in the distance. To be so high up where no one could harm her was liberating but also felt treacherous. There was no way to get down, no one to rescue her. She wondered if that was Cuddles' goal, some means to keep her away from planes that could rain missiles atop her head. Her hands shook as she thought about it.

Cuddles pivoted. With the early-afternoon sun to their right, Jane knew where it was headed.

Houston.

Jane's observations told her that Cuddles' fur grew proportionately with its body. The distance between her and the iridescent tips had remained unchanged. Either its meals were small, or there was a limit to what size Cuddles' species could attain. A silent prayer passed her lips. So she hoped. Her answer would come when they reached the Houston suburbs.

Cuddles followed the I-10, the grey seam that divided the Texas farmland. Jane was entirely removed from the world. The little specks below might have been houses or truck stops, while smaller particles were perhaps artillery steamrolled by the giant amorphous blob.

It didn't take long before Jane could see the Houston skyline. As she spied the world through Cuddles' pink fringe, her stomach sank. Ahead skyscrapers, stadiums, airports, and other enormous structures lay in wait. A buffet of metal, glass, brick, and concrete was about to get swallowed up by Cuddles' gaping crevasse.

Soon, whole city blocks were stripped bare. Weeping pipes were left to pump water into the basements of buildings raptured from existence. Cuddles posed among the desolation. Houston's center was gone.

The creature's attention turned to the glimmering bay. Jane's fingers dug deep into her enormous, furry support strand. The bay opened into the Gulf, exchanging water with the Atlantic Ocean at a colossal volume.

Divine intervention was all she could ask for, and it was delivered. A wave of light more brilliant than the sun flashed across Trinity Bay. It chased the clouds away, toppled buildings, and ignited structures. But not even the light of a thousand suns could penetrate Cuddles' darkened depths. Cuddles moved along unharmed.

Jane surveyed what she could of the wreckage behind her, her vision dominated by a billowing mushroom cloud that rose high into the stratosphere. Houston was gone, crushed, devoured, nuked. Cuddles and Jane were all that remained.

No one could stop Cuddles. It would be the death of everything.

Cuddles continued into the sea. Water rushed into its maw as it guzzled gallons in an unending vortex that spiraled into nothing. It drained the Gulf of Mexico and inhaled Cuba. She couldn't see anything after that.

Jane was lost in a dense forest of pink, each hair taller than the tallest trees. The iridescent tips stretched further and further away as the bleakness of space grew closer. She brushed her hands across her sleeveless arms, absent the telltale goosebumps.

Jane was fine, physically. Emotionally, it was hard to say. She bit her lip. If anything, she was tired. She fell onto her back to gaze at the sky, the colors transitioning from indigo to denim blue to dark navy before approaching black. But then, slowly, the colors reversed. Denim to indigo, cerulean, azure, and then sky, where it remained.

Cuddles must have shrunk!

Jane leaped to her feet. The apocalypse she had unwittingly unleashed on the world had ceased. "Oh, God." Jane threw her head into her hands and sobbed.

You are safe now. Do not fear.

Jane wasn't expecting God to answer. "God?" She peered through her fingers. There was no holy apparition.

Not God. The voice echoed through Jane's head.

"Cuddles?"

I am a Devourer of Worlds, one of countless flung into the vastness of space in hopes of landing on a hospitable world to begin the process anew. I thank you for saving me from the Kahats. Your generosity let me thrive and grow.

"B-but...what about Earth?"

What about the billions of people that lived there? The animals, the oceans, the beautiful blue jewel she called home? What happened to her house? What about her mom? She searched the pastel-pink forest surrounding her, desperate to find anything she recognized. There was only Cuddles. "What did you do to my home? My family? Cuddles, what did you do?" Jane's words quaked. She had to ask the questions despite the apparent answers. She needed to hear them for herself.

The old world is gone. Devoured whole. I am your world. Your planet.

No world and no Earth. Still an atmosphere, though. Above, the pale crescent sliver of the moon drifted a lonely traverse around the fuzzy pink sphere.

"What now?" Jane's voice was hollowed of enthusiasm. "What happens now?" Make the moon into a personal cookie? Eat the rest of the solar system? The thought that Jane had nurtured a black hole creature into existence sent a shudder of revulsion down her spine. She tore into her long locks and screeched. "What have I done?!" She had stopped the cats from killing an adorable terror she unwittingly unleashed on the world. "It's all my fault!"

A deep rumble emanated beneath Jane's feet, a purr of attempted reassurance. But Jane was beyond comfort. She glared down at the pink ground where she stood, a flea on a pastel orb that conversed with her.

Why do you cry over evil beings who exerted their influence, threatened you with harm, sent fire to incinerate you? You showed me a great kindness and deserved a great kindness in turn. You have been spared.

The winds hummed as the skyscraper strands thrummed. Jane brushed her arm across her eyes. She had been saved; however, she was stuck on a gobbling guzzler of a globe that posed a severe cosmic threat.

"So, what now?"

My friend, I will protect and sustain you as you have protected and sustained me. I shall share my breaths with you to breathe, my tears with you to drink, my flesh with you to feed. You will be safe on my surface for the rest of your days.

Jane spun around within an eternal forest of pink. This was her new life. She was alone save for the monster that murdered everyone.

"And what will you do?"

Little, for I am rooted in place around this star, tugged along as one of its many planets until the end of my days, when my body expires, or the star decays." Cuddles couldn't shuffle itself through space. Despite her fear and grief, Jane let out a massive sigh before it caught in her throat.

I have reached the point in my life cycle where I shall seed my progeny throughout the universe. Someday, may my children and their children's children be so fortunate as to find a generous spirit such as yours.

Jane gazed upon her palms, large enough to cradle a single entity of mass destruction. She clenched her fingers tightly. "Do you need to? Do you absolutely need to do this? Imagine if these were your children. Why do this to someone else?" Reason or empathy might work; it cared enough to protect Jane.

That is life.

Jane looked up to the sky, to the voice that echoed inside of her head. She despaired. Devourers of Worlds were inattentive parents. They reproduced asexually and flung their parasitic spawn off to the far reaches of space, where they hoped one would land on a welcoming planet so as to consume it.

The cats were smart. They would have been saviors. Whoever said cats were aloof and self-absorbed were liars and dog lovers. And also dead. Jane cursed herself, fists slamming into her thighs. Hopefully, the aliens would not make the same mistake she had.

Next time, let the cats eat the weird baby rabbit.

Thickey-boy Cuddles out here thirst-trapping it up! Is this just me? I'm just saying, she got curves, that's all. (She? He? It? Whatever, 10/10, would totally smash.)

Our next story brings the zaniness down a step while ratcheting the tension all the way up. It's about this girl Summer and her suspicious inter-actions with an older gentleman, Mr. Meab, which is just about as untrust-worthy a name as you could have. I mean, say it out loud...go on... SERIOUSLY, THAT'S AN ORDER! (Dammit. Sorry I'm being such an asshole today, I don't know where it comes from. Except to say that back on Earth, my father was a general contractor.)

This is one of those stories where right off the bat, you can tell there's something up with this Meab fella (again, that name!), but the mystery and excitement come from finding out just how messed up this dude actually is, which is what a lot of my ex-girlfriends would probably say about me.

It's also one of the few tales that's brave enough to examine the dangers of sharing a taxi with literally anyone. Now, you could argue this is likely not the author's intent, but then I'd be forced to call you names that insult your grandmother while insisting that we not make eye contact for the remainder of the book, and that just doesn't sound like fun for anyone.

So, while I sit here and think up new and creative ways to insult your extended family, please enjoy the next story in our collection, Summer.

SUMMER

MT ROBERTS

P ained by the limp in his left leg, Mr. Meab winced under the cold shadow of a high-rise. Despite his arthritis, he maintained a dull interest in the surrounding city. An incoherent crunch of electric guitars belted out of a used record store, where kids with baggy pants and low keychain wallets milled about smoking cigarettes. Their rabble, along with the smell of piss and monoxide in the cool pine air, told Mr. Meab all he needed to know—Seattle was in the midst of a new low amid the burgeoning rise of Generation X.

At a crosswalk, Meab waited for motorists, transfixed by the steam rising from a nearby manhole. He ran his tongue over his teeth and turned the corner, reluctant to kick his heels. There was a park near the old pergola he wanted to reach before sundown. Flexing knobby fingers under the handle of his leather valise, he shuffled ahead, cane clapping.

He turned the corner a few blocks down, where Occidental Square opened to him in a swath of red bricks and white bird droppings. Glaucous metal benches sat spaced apart beneath carefully manicured London planes. Eager to rest, Mr. Meab found the nearest vacant seat and eased himself onto its cold surface. He dragged his feet inward as dead leaves crackled beneath his orthopedic shoes. He watched a group of tourists take Polaroids before a totem pole as he brought his valise to his lap and opened it.

Pigeons hopped at his ankles as he scattered clumps of hair and an assortment of teeth over the ground. Passersby would crunch them into powder before long. He gave a resigned sigh, relishing the vapor this introduced into the air. A morose stillness settled over him as the sun's drowning light conveyed a tired glow, impressing an ancient weariness over the paper trash and faceless strangers around him. With the grace of a surgeon, Mr. Meab withdrew a small bundle from his valise and placed it behind him on the bench. It was oblong and wrapped in tin foil, about the length of a hammer. He then stood with a careful rise and stepped into the yellow cone of a warming street-lamp, tipping the brim of his hat beneath a dying, hollow afternoon.

SUMMER FREED herself from her office's revolving door and stood on the sidewalk. At five o'clock, it was already dark, and the rumble of cars and distant honking left her no desire to hail a taxi just yet. She spent half an hour walking to the end of Belltown before raising her hand. A yellow town car pulled up beside her and turned off its sign.

"Hey!"

An elderly man with a cane and leather briefcase shuffled past her and opened the rear door.

"Excuse me!" Summer yelled.

The old man turned to look at her from under the brim of a dirty Stetson.

"Yes?"

Summer took a deep breath. "Yeah, um, I think this one's mine? I just raised my hand."

"Oh. I see." The old man stepped away from the car door. "Please."

"Yeah, thanks!" Summer climbed in and looked at the driver fumbling with his meter. A surge of confused outrage played over her face as the old man scooted in beside her. She cleared her throat as her eyes connected with the driver through the rearview mirror. "Um, Forty-Fifth and Densmore, I guess."

Summer studied the old man from the corners of her eyes as the taxi creaked into the street. He smelled odd, the way a butcher or exterminator might. But there was an essence of cheap cologne, too. She grew aware of his features in the green tint of the dashboard lights. Like a mannequin bobbing up and down in the backseat, he was a specter.

Summer dared a glance at him.

"Are you from Seattle?" he asked beneath his broad hat, his voice soft, barely above a whisper.

"No." Summer shook her head. "I moved up from California about five months ago. Um, how about you?"

"Mm, I like to think I'm from here. But, no. I used to run a pediatric ward in Amarillo when I was…are you alright?"

Summer cracked her window, the old man's odor having grown a bit strong. "Oh, yeah," she said, "it's just a little stuffy in here."

The old man adjusted himself and leaned forward, leering at her. Summer could only make-out half of his face. His visible eye was a glistening, dark orb.

"My, you look quite young," he said. "When were you born?"

Summer tensed her hands in her lap. "April?"

The old man laughed and sat back, wiping his palm on his knee. Summer heard his skin rasp over the brown fabric of his pants. Rain fell as the taxi took a right onto Forty-Fifth.

"You can just pull over up here," Summer said to the driver. She began to dig through her purse when the old man laid his hand over hers.

"Oh no, I wouldn't think of it," he said. "Please. My treat."

Summer stared at his hand, large, ugly, and weightless. She disassociated and focused on her nails while the windshield wipers of the taxi grew louder. A great chill overtook her as if a tiny hair feathered the nape of her neck.

"If you insist," she said, forcing a smile.

"Oh, I do," the old man whispered. "It's not every day I share company with a beautiful young woman."

Summer opened the door, feeling the cold bite of rain plod her coat. "Well, thank you, mister…"

"Lincoln," the old man said. "Lincoln Meab."

"Well, thanks again, Lincoln. I hope you don't have too far to go."

"I live close enough, dear…and I'm sorry, what was your name again?"

Panicked, Summer blurted her full name, which Mr. Meab acknowledged. He savored the sound in his mouth. "Summer Tanzy. Yes. Well, goodnight."

"Goodnight." Summer shut the door, relieved to be away from the man. A few blocks down, she heard the wet hiss of the taxi turning around. As it passed, she noticed the back seat was empty. Alarmed, she peered across her shoulder to find a silhouetted couple approaching with what looked to be a dog. She hurried across the street to her apartment building and leaned against its glass door as she caught her breath. Rhythmic claps of a cane sounded from behind. Her heart pounded—was it him?

She quickly unlocked the main entrance to her building and darted inside the musty mailroom, where she shoved the door shut. Wet, cold, and panting, she stared out into the rainy night, watching in panic as cars passed.

AFTER ARRIVING HOME MUCH LATER than planned, Mr. Meab fumbled with his front door and reached inside to flip on the porch light. His eyes narrowed on a letter in his mail slot. He grabbed the white envelope through flared nostrils, shut the door behind him, and meandered toward his dark kitchen. Tossing his coat absentmindedly on the counter, he poured a glass of vodka and sat down at a small table, thumbing the envelope's loose flap. After a moment, he pulled the letter out.

We are sending you another package. You will receive it tomorrow morning at 7:00. Please adhere its contents to section Zn-9 and adjust your copy of the chart accordingly.

Mr. Meab moved to the living room and flicked the letter into his dormant fireplace. A year's worth lay piled within. He used to burn them, as instructed, but there was nothing further gained in pursuit of the Great Work, unlike when he was young, when he had been exposed to the desolate light of the stars and their distant, holy screams.

Mr. Meab rubbed his wrinkled forehead. If his display in the park had been found, it might all come to an end. They would surely send someone after him, but they would fail. No one knew how far he had been able to get on his own—the control he possessed.

Thoughts of the young woman Summer brought a grin to his lips. He thought it clever to follow her so soon after saying goodbye, to find out where she lived in the event she ignored his gift. This assured him a happy retirement. The Great Work, after all, was in service to a God rich in terrestrial pleasures; and oh, would his reward be grand.

Mr. Meab composed himself. Cleaning was the top priority, and he needed to prepare for the coming reprisal. Tired but filled with a lightness from thoughts of Summer, he grabbed his glass of vodka, went into the hallway, and unlocked the door to his basement. As always, rising fumes caressed him, disturbing his sinuses.

HAVING SHOWERED, Summer sat cross-legged on her couch, picking at a few bits of leftover chicken and rice from a date the other evening. The nightly news was on. A 'Breaking News' prompt flashed across the screen and the feed cut to a news anchor with a somber face.

> "—a gruesome sight was found earlier today in Occidental Park. Police are asking anyone with any information to please contact them. Warning, the story we're about to cover may be unsuitable for young audiences. We go live now to William Sero—"

Summer put her plate down and reached into her purse for a mint.

"—good evening. Police are unsure whether this recent discovery is linked to any missing women in the greater Seattle area but are not ruling out a possible connection to the Green River killings. Earlier this evening, a severed arm was found here in Occidental Park, wrapped in several layers of tin foil. More disturbing is that police have confirmed it does appear to be that of a child. When local SPD arrived on the scene, they discovered several teeth—"

Summer furrowed her brow as her fingers grazed an unfamiliar object at the bottom of her purse. She grabbed it and pulled her hand out, revealing a small human ear creased in the middle by a single dark staple—glazed and folded like a fortune cookie. She lurched off the couch and threw her hands out, mortified as the ear landed on the rug below the television.

SUMMER CAME in to work late the following day. Her desk was stacked with invoices. Groaning, she settled in while her computer booted up.

"Summer?"

She turned her head to see Mr. Richards lingering outside her cubicle. "Oh, good morning, sir."

"Morning…um, there's a…Detective Lyonson waiting for you in the meeting room. He's been here since nine. I told him you'd be in late on account of…well, you know."

"But I already talked with the police last night."

"Probably just following up on a few questions, Summer. I wouldn't worry too much. But, um, look…when you're done, would you mind putting in the order for lunch? We've got a big client coming this afternoon, and, well…thanks for coming in today, despite everything that happened." He tapped his fingers on the wall of her cubicle. "And if there's anything you need, my door is always open. I'm a good listener."

Summer killed her smile the moment Mr. Richards turned his back. Ringing phones and lagging printers only furthered her sense of displacement.

"Thanks for coming in?" she muttered. "Yeah, sure thing." Summer rolled her eyes. "Not much of a choice when you don't offer sick time...asshole."

THE MEETING ROOM was dull and gray when Summer entered. Its only light source was a row of windows that looked out to a neighboring building. Drops of rain freckled the glass. A large man in a navy blue suit stood at the far end of a long wooden table and crushed his cigarette into an ashtray. Smoke lapped his bloated face as he smiled.

"Ah, Ms.Tanzy," he said. "Sorry for the natural lighting. Heard those fluorescents can lead to seizures. You don't mind, do you?"

"Oh, not at all."

"Great, let's get started. I'm Detective Lyonson. You can call me Mike." He flashed another smile. "This should only take a few minutes. Please, have a seat."

Summer rolled out a chair and sat facing him, hands folded in her lap.

"I heard you had quite the night last night," Detective Lyonson said, taking out a notepad. He bent his face down and started writing. "I'm sorry for coming to your...place of employment. Tried calling you at home but then realized you'd probably already left for work."

"That's okay."

"Did you get any sleep?" The detective flipped a page and stared at her.

"No, not really."

"Well, me neither, if that helps." Detective Lyonson's pager went off; he clasped a big, muting hand to it.

"Now, the officers that came to your apartment last night said the man you rode home with went by Lincoln Meab, correct?"

"Yes."

"Alright...and at what time did you—"

"It belonged to him, didn't it?" Summer asked.

Detective Lyonson cocked an eyebrow and rubbed at his nose. "I'm sorry?"

"The ear the old man left in my purse. It was that kid's, wasn't it? The one whose arm they found in the park."

Detective Lyonson put his pen down and glared at the gloomy weather outside as he leaned back in his chair. He loosened his tie and released a long, drawn-out breath. "Afraid we don't know that just yet. It's possible, but...it's a little too early to tell." His pager went off again. "Jesus Christ," he muttered.

"Why would he do it?" Summer whispered, almost to herself. "What reason could anyone have to do something like that?"

"You mean killing a kid?" Detective Lyonson sat up. "Or leaving body parts in a public space?"

Summer seemed caught off guard by her own question. "Both, I guess."

"Well, we're not sure if anyone's actually dead," Detective Lyonson said. "People can survive just fine without an arm or teeth. But if I'm to be honest, I think maybe whoever did it wants to get caught. Furthermore... this Lincoln Meab? He may not even be the person we're looking for."

"Wait, is he at least in custody?" Summer tensed, incredulous.

"We have him, we have him...don't worry. We just don't have any evidence against him."

"That ear doesn't count? Haven't you searched his home? I know he's got to have something in his house, right? Or wherever he lives...right?"

"Warrant's under process, Ms. Tanzy. Truth be told, that's kind of why I'm here. It would greatly expedite the process if you were to pick him out of a lineup."

"Oh...um, I can talk to my boss and see if I can leave for a few—"

"No. It can wait. We have Mr. Meab for another nineteen hours, and he hasn't called for a lawyer. But do you think you could meet me downstairs after work? I'll pick you up myself. Can't imagine you'd be too keen on taking another taxi."

Summer gave an involuntary laugh, her pent-up nerves ebbing. "That would be great," she said. "Thank you, Detective."

"Mike. Please."

She smiled. "Thank you, Mike."

As he got up to leave, Detective Lyonson peered at her, his head cocked. "Could you maybe just not tell anyone about this? Confidential, you know."

Summer nodded with too much vigor, eager to please the detective. "I won't say a word."

FIVE O'CLOCK ARRIVED, and Summer waived to her co-workers on her way to the elevators. She waited by a fake fern for one of the double doors to open and take her down to the lobby.

Outside, she scanned the rows of blaring headlights locked in early evening traffic and saw a few cars parked illegally near the curb, their yellow hazards flashing. Taking a quick breath, she popped her umbrella and squinted through the darkness and the rain, ultimately disappointed by the detective's absence.

At thirty minutes past the hour, Summer stepped into a phone booth down the street and flipped through a dingy copy of the Yellow Pages. She dropped a nickel into the coin slot and dialed the number to the downtown police precinct. A bus roared past. She put a finger in her ear.

"Hello? Yes, hi—yes, hi, may I speak with Detective Lyonson? Oh… Detective…Lyonson? Oh…um, Summer Tanzy. Yes, I called last night about an incident that took place—oh, that's strange. Do I have the right department? Oh…well, no, wait, wait, please. He said he would pick me up from—okay…well…no, no, he didn't give me a card, but —okay."

Summer was placed on hold. Generic jazz cackled in the earpiece before she hung up. Cold, annoyed, and confused, she left the booth and walked back to her office building.

"Summer! Ms. Tanzy!" Detective Lyonson yelled at her from down the way. He approached her with his large hands fanned in apology.

"Today has just been hell. I'm so sorry. When I found out what time it was—"

"I was beginning to worry," Summer called to him, relieved. "I even rang the station!"

Detective Lyonson paused mid-step. "You did?"

Summer walked closer to him. "Yeah. It was weird. The department I called seemed confused when I asked for you. I'm sure I just wasn't heard right. Sounded like there was a lot of noise at the station, and then—"

Detective Lyonson nodded and grinned. "Yep, that'll do it! Place is always bustling. I'm from the Tacoma department, anyway. Temporary transfer in lieu of this recent, nasty business. You ready to go?"

They rounded the corner, where the detective led them to a brown Plymouth Acclaim. Not quite what she expected. Summer got in, hesitant. Detective Lyonson eased himself behind the wheel and turned the ignition. A news update blared on the radio.

"—other news, two Seattle police officers were found shot this morning near—"

Detective Lyonson switched it off with a laugh. "So, have you eaten anything?"

An uneasy feeling washed over Summer. "Not since lunch."

The inside of the car struck her as strange then. It seemed messy for a detective, and even if it was a private-marked car, it should have had a police radio. His was a standard one; beneath it, a mess of crumpled napkins and condiment packets lay stuffed inside a nook meant for a tape deck.

The detective lit a cigarette and let smoke fill the car. Summer wondered why he kept the window up, why he suddenly possessed an air of rudeness.

"What'd you have?" he asked, cigarette between his lips.

"What?"

"For lunch. What'd you have?"

That uneasy feeling sunk into her stomach. "A salad."

"Mm. Did you take a shit today?"

Summer gave a brittle snicker. "What?"

"Did you take a shit today?"

Uncomfortable, Summer shifted away from him. "That's really not funny, Mike."

"I wasn't trying to be funny, Summer. I just want to know if you're going to make a mess when I kill you."

Summer's throat constricted. Her head buzzed. In a dry, raspy voice, she whispered, "You're not really a detective, are you?"

Lyonson cackled. "Not the kind you're thinking of."

Summer reached for her door handle and found it was locked. Her lever to the roll-down window was missing as well.

"You're not leaving," Lyonson said.

"Are you...are you the Green River Killer?"

"No."

"Where are you taking me?"

"Told you," Lyonson mumbled, "we're off to see Lincoln Meab."

The car came to a stop at a red light. Summer banged on her window and screamed at a group of people on the sidewalk. Lost in the rainy moan of traffic, her actions went unnoticed.

"Hey!" Lyonson grabbed her by the wrist. "You want me to knock you out? Stop that."

"Leave me the fuck alone!" Summer clawed at him and scratched his face.

Lyonson grunted as he subdued her. "Can't do that, Summer. You're...bound now."

"Bound?" Summer yanked her arm free and rubbed her wrist, frowning.

The light turned green, and Lyonson accelerated. He massaged his reddening cheek. "You're bound to the Great Work that's been continued and is meant to continue. That's what you're bound to."

"What the fuck does that mean?"

Lyonson let out a bray of laughter and reached under his seat. He pulled out a plastic bottle and shook it. Looking at Summer, he slowed the car to a crawl. Without a word, Lyonson popped the bottle's cap and snagged a handful of napkins from the inlet of his missing tape deck.

"Hey, look at me."

Sniffling, Summer turned to him, scowling. A wad of bunched, wet napkins met her.

"...AND yes, I'll tell Reynolds when I see him. Yes. I got her. Yes. At Meab's now. No. I'll use the vat he has. Right. Because she called the station. No, because I caught up with the two officers before they had a chance to—yes. No. The new part for segment Zn-9 doesn't look to have been attached. Yes. We know where to—of course. Fire will do it."

Groggy, Summer craned her neck and peered around. She felt hungover, distantly aware of the cloth gag in her mouth. Everywhere she looked gleamed with the blur of a meteor. Blinking rapidly, she saw a small end table lit by a tall lamp and understood she was tied to a wooden dining chair adjacent to a dim hallway. Lyonson could be heard talking to someone on the phone in the other room. Summer tested her bindings as her throat gave an involuntary gurgle. The tiny hairs of her body stood erect when she realized there was a sudden silence, followed by an approaching footfall.

She was grabbed by the back of her chair and dragged down the hall over a rubescent carpet. The creak of an opening door fed her imagination unsavory scenarios. Summer struggled, gave up when Lyonson hit her. Without warning, she was pulled down a long flight of stairs through absolute darkness, each step a jolting thud on her spine. Chemical odors teased at her eyes and nose. She kept her gaze on the shrinking outline of the open doorway above her, vaguely aware of Lyonson's labored breathing as he brought them to a stop on an uneven surface.

"Now, be sure to look when it's time," Lyonson said. "Down here lies something truly amazing. Something only achieved by way of employing oneself with the Great Work, I'm told." The man licked his lips and left her in the pitch as he plowed up the stairs.

In time, her eyes acclimated to the low exposure. At the wall to her left, a high mound of dirt rose from an old cement floor, it's top covered by a flat steel hatch. Translucent liquid dribbled down the mound's sides and pooled around its base, gleaming with what looked like the night sky. Summer saw pin-pricked stars and mauve cloud clusters. Images of a galaxy leaked on the ground.

She noted the ceiling as tall for a basement and followed the run of its beams. The rest of the room evoked a dizzying sensation as her mind struggled with the indefinable dimensions of an unknown space. She found a grade of relief when a small red light blinked at her in the distance. Summer focused on it, letting her peripheral vision absorb what it could. An outline of something large and significant appeared as the red light warmed and cooled. Her first impression was of an upturned car, its undercarriage displayed in a complicated array of bent pipes and rounded implements. But the longer her eyes remained open, the more she realized the giant mass moved and swelled like a beached whale struggling to breathe.

The upper door swung open, followed by the click of a switch and the blinding flood of electric light. Summer squinted and heard the heavy footsteps of Lyonson as he descended the long staircase.

"Remember," he said, stopping behind her, "be sure you look."

Summer lifted her head and gradually widened her eyelids. Before her, in front of the mound, Mr. Meab sat slouched in a chair, lumped with contusions and dried blood. Like her, his arms were tied behind him, and his mouth was gagged.

"No, not there." Lyonson laughed. He grabbed her by the scalp and turned her face. At the room's dank back-end, a morass of curled arms and feet loomed before a row of soiled surgical carts, bulked together and suspended from the ceiling by an array of thick metal wires. Withered and stretched before her, a multicolored, waxen, ovular wad of conjoined limbs clattered like a drugged roach, as big as a Volkswagen bus. She groaned as she noticed several human heads belting its girth. Summer convulsed, shrieking through the cloth at her mouth. The abomination before her had the same sheen as the ear in her purse.

"Now, now, Ms. Tanzy," Lyonson whispered, leaning over her shoulder, "parts of this specimen are older than you and I put together. Show some reverence."

Summer watched as one of the small, hairless heads lolled amid the others and pushed them aside beneath a slanted eave of hands and draped elbows. The small head extended itself from the mass and tilted back, revealing a pale face with green eyes and a mouth stitched into a semi-permanent smile; patches of hair littered its skin, reaching out. Summer let another blood-curdling scream through her gag. The pale face's small mouth struggled to imitate her expression, tearing apart the ancient twine sewn through its lips.

Lyonson ensnared Summer's hair through his fingers and pulled her head back to look at him. "I'll say this, and I think you already know it, but you really are pretty. And goddamned lucky I got stuck dealing with you tonight instead of Reynolds." He grinned at her before letting go.

Whistling, Lyonson walked to Mr. Meab and removed the old man's gag. He patted him on the cheek and moved further into the room, past the enormous composite of twitching appendages. Lyonson grabbed a dirty hacksaw from one of the surgical benches and pivoted, looking at Summer.

"Have you ever heard of comet wine?" he asked, glaring beside the pulsating creature. "Well, these children—or pieces of them—are much the same." He brought the saw to his chest and played a finger along its toothy blade. "There's a body in space. An emissary that passes over once in a while." He pointed with the hacksaw to the squirming giant next to him. "Each part of this is composed of select individuals born under that passing emissary—some of what you're looking at stretches as far back as four hundred years ago. And yet, this particular paragon isn't even near completion. Our organization has much to do, and we can't afford even the slightest exposure!" Lyonson regarded his company with that of a prestigious breed of pet, its presence carrying a mark of repute. "Isn't that right, Lincoln?"

Mr. Meab squirmed in his chair as Lyonson approached. "Micheal," he said, "you're too young to understand, but the Great Work will never be completed. It's—"

Lyonson grabbed the back of Mr. Meab's chair, dragged him up the mound, and lifted the steel hatch onto its hinges. A vat of twinkling twilight bubbled within.

"I understand," Lyonson said, using the saw to cut away Mr.

Meab's bindings. "I understand you got tired of your role and wanted more. That you no longer care about the sacrifices and time and resources it took to get us this far—we will be joined come the next passage!"

"Micheal." Mr. Meab wheezed. "It will never accept us in our state. It is only the children that will get to go. And only by being together as one…"

"Stand up," Lyonson said, his face a rictus of rage. "Did you really think you weren't being watched? That you didn't have a place in all this? Know your station!"

Mr. Meab remained seated and gave Summer a curious grin. He smacked his bruised lips and winked at her.

"Goddamn traitor." Lyonson tugged at Mr. Meab's collar and threw him into the radiant liquid, pushing the hatch shut. Summer watched as Lyonson regained his composure from atop the mound, only to see him turn with a confused expression at the twang of wires being pulled beyond their load.

SUMMER WOKE ON THE FLOOR, covered in a light layer of dust freshly fallen from the ceiling. Several lights flickered. Inches away, a pale head with green eyes stared back at her, its tiny mouth spread in a grin. Above it, a noticeable depression was visible in a pallid patchwork of skin, a missing piece roughly the size of a child's arm. Summer wanted to scream until she drowned in her own noise, but the smothered yells of Lyonson beat her to it. The man's left arm protruded from under a chaotic curdle of limbs and slapped at the floor. A series of muffled beeps from his pager cut through the creature's heavy breathing. Summer, fully aware, recalled how just moments ago, every facet of the beast seemed to scowl as Lyonson slid off the mound and made for the stairs. At that moment, it emanated a dark, purple light that concussed the room and broke free of its harness.

Still tied to the chair, Summer shuffled across the cold cement and looked at the mound by the wall. Lyonson's hacksaw lay in the starlit puddle. She wormed toward it, writhing into the viscous liquid. Finessing her feet out of their heels, she stretched her toes through wet pantyhose and pushed against the floor for leverage. Maneuvering onto the mound, she splayed her bound hands for the saw, ignoring the pain of the chair pressing into her arm. She swiped the saw's edge, tried again, and cut herself. The liquid burned; a gross, boiling vapor wafted off her skin. Frantically, Summer kicked against the floor and gave herself enough hold to land on the saw. She grasped at the blade's handle and dragged it into her palm.

Half-muddled ideas formed inside her brain as she tore her bindings over the saw, thoughts of work and home. Eventually, she brought her hands to her face and flexed her fingers. Blood, sticky and scarlet, coated her forearms. The burn of fresh cuts mixed with the caustic liquid on her skin left her shaking. She tried to calm herself and backed onto the mound at an incline. The swollen creature continued to stare at her with its many adolescent faces and eyes, each emoting looks of joy, calm, or lust.

Summer struggled to her feet on unsteady legs. She cocked her head as she noticed an unfamiliar appendage connecting the creature's backside to the floor. It resembled an umbilical cord. Behind her, the steel hatch Lyonson closed on Mr. Meab shuddered ajar. A steaming, glistening hand reached out and grabbed at the moist dirt, fumbling for purchase. Mr. Meab pulled himself out of the mound and tumbled down into the twinkling liquid on the floor, where he crawled for the mass of limbs.

Sparks flared from his molten skin like tiny shooting stars. Summer looked on in disbelief, watching as the old man nuzzled against an outcrop of heads and hands. Mr. Meab positioned himself on his side and peered back at Summer.

"Oh," he said, "I wasn't going to let them get you, dear." He let a garbled laugh. "Fools thought they'd kill me...but I'm free now... they'll think me dead, and you and I can—"

Summer advanced and brought the saw down on his neck, then pushed the blade in to the hilt. Mr. Meab's face contracted in confusion before she yanked the saw back like the string of a lawnmower. Without waiting, Summer turned to clamor up the long steps out of the basement, ignoring the bellowing cries of Mr. Meab—the rumbling clack of the creature's limbs.

She soon found herself standing by a door with a wrinkled carpet. She wavered side to side as she felt the house shake. The hallway was empty. Vacancy permeated every cranny. She felt like a sullen, shuffling child, lost amid the silence.

Summer opened the door, letting the harsh light of the kitchen down the hall peak around her body. A child's bedroom was partially illuminated, displaying a pair of pink curtains that hung over a single barred window. Dolls rested in a neat procession along a low shelf. Above the green headboard of a twin bed, two plaques for Student of the Year hung in perfect aplomb. Tacked Polaroids curled from a corkboard near the window. Summer inspected them; a smiling girl with no legs sat in a wheelchair next to a middle-aged Mr. Meab. The girl's smile and green eyes seemed familiar.

Unsure, Summer sat on the bed and stared into a broken makeup mirror on the wall. Shattered from a crack in the bottom corner, she dismissed the battered woman looking back at her. Did she work around the office?

Fidgeting with her hair, Summer realized she was seeing herself and giggled. She began to count her many selves in the mirror but came to a forgettable sum and started over. Lost in her distorted reflections, she could not hear the front door as it swung open.

"Hey! Mike! It's Reynolds! Your pager dead or something? God, what I wouldn't have given to have your job last night!"

VI

What is it about Elder Gods that always make them so…gelatinous. You know what I mean? Like, you look at the classic Greek gods and they're all these beautiful Adonis' in skimpy loincloths that look like they're about to shoot late-night Skinemax porn (is that still a thing?), but then the moment you have a story that involves a god of a more Lovecraftian persuasion, they're just these enormous wads of indiscriminate limbs and flesh. That's not sexy. Shouldn't gods be sexy? The Greeks thought so. Maybe Lovecraft should have gotten out of New England once in a while.

Our next story features a protagonist who isn't a bad guy, just one who needs to involve himself in petty crime from time to time. You know, to make ends meet and such; not to hurt nobody. He also gets in deep with a certain vegetable from a certain place beyond our certain atmosphere (hint: it's space; that's why the story is called what it's called), and various shenanigans unfurl as a result. It's wackiness squared, and if you don't enjoy this one, you may just be averse to fun.

Speaking of space, when are we as a society going to start populating Mars? Has that shady dude from South Africa with all the rockets and satellites and child support payments made it happen yet? WHAT?! Well, color me shocked. I mean, I was confident that starting an entirely new chapter of civilization would be easier than purchasing that birdy-bird app. Man, it's too bad that guy wasn't around in 1983. He'd have made one hell of an 80s guy.

Now, in pure 80s fashion, I'm going to rummage through the boss's desk for some Columbian Disco Powder (that's right, Steve, we all know!) In the meantime, you all enjoy The Potato Out of Space.

THE POTATO OUT OF SPACE

NICK DORSEY

I t was cold as hell when I decided to rip off the Kansas City Outfit, the local chapter of a particular Italian-American subculture. I mean, I thought about it before. You work around those sorts of people, and your imagination goes in one direction or another. But imagining a thing is a far cry from doing it.

Anyway, the day I decided to get it done, freezing temperatures had come in from up north to make themselves comfortable. I was out there in my chef's whites and that old Kansas City Chiefs parka Vicky got me for Christmas a million years ago, hunched over the grill, thinking on what I was about to do before I immediately forced the thoughts out of my mind. Almost like I was a Zen monk, only without all the calm.

Wind slapped at the coals as they flared from grey to angry orange and billowed smoke into my face. But my eyeglasses stopped the worst of it, so I remained. The old Weber charcoal grill was a...what do you call it? An oasis. Missouri winters are nothing to talk down to. The grill was my own personal space heater on the sidewalk in front of Jino's Classic Italian Restaurant and Trattoria.

What a life I was living. One day at a time, man. That's what I kept telling myself. One day at a time, and today was the day. Maybe the rest of my days would be a little easier to manage after today. People gotta tell themselves something, you know? Gotta get through to Friday somehow.

I opened the butcher block paper and started loading the grill with grey links of sweet Italian in preparation for the lunch rush. The raw sausages were fat, blotchy things that hissed and crackled when they met the iron of the grill. I closed the lid and stepped a few feet away, making sure I wasn't under the awning fashioned after the Italian flag when I lit my cigarette. Frank said I couldn't smoke by the grill; it was important to follow little rules, especially if I was going to do what I thought I was going to do.

Still, it was cold as hell away from the grill. The tips of my fingers were already hard as river stones out in the wind, thanks to fingerless gloves. But I couldn't work the grill wearing full gloves. So there I was.

Gale was my first customer. It was like that two or three days a week. I wanted to tell her, hey, it's not healthy to eat that much sausage. She was already what my pops would have called a prosperous-looking woman. But she was one of the only regulars I liked, so I kept the health tips to myself.

The wind rippled the back of my old parka as I fixed her a paper tray. A charred sausage went on a bun loaded with peppers and onions and topped with mustard. She started to eat right there.

"You want to go sit?" I pointed to the tables inside.

"Nah. I been inside all morning."

That was fine. A few links were looking to burn, so I moved them to the cooler side of the grill and shut the lid. I lit another cigarette and stood with her while she ate. I asked her how her shift was.

"Slow. Usual. No weirdos." Gale worked the early morning shift at the Quick Trip gas station down the street. We traded stories now and then. Her eyes were bright blue, her cheeks red from the wind. A greasy slice of grilled onion curled out of the side of her mouth. She slurped it back. "You? Same old?"

"You know." I took a thoughtful drag of my cigarette and let smoke ooze from my nose. Getting some distance. Getting thoughtful.

Today was the day. That's what I kept telling myself.

THERE WERE lots of stories about Jino's. Rumors. Gossip, like. Cooks, veteran waiters, bartenders; they all knew the score.

Over the last fifty years, Jino's Classic Italian Restaurant and Trattoria had grown up some. It came into this world as a small butcher shop but was now a monster that occupied half a city block along Wornall Road on the south side of Kansas City. Jino Barra Senior, the founder, got the renovation money from the Kansas City Outfit.

Allegedly, that is.

Most of the place was a fine dining establishment; white tablecloths and candles, with somebody playing the mandolin on weekends. The Trattoria was a little cafe that served sandwiches and coffee and desserts. From eleven to two and again from four to six, Italian sausages were cooked on a charcoal grill outside. Old man Jino had started grilling them that way back in the Seventies, and it became something of a trademark. A quick meal for the working men.

When his son "Tiny" Jino wanted to take over, the old man would only hand over the keys on the condition that Tiny kept the sausages on the menu. Forever. Cheap, too. They were priced to move. Guess it was his way of giving back to the community that the Outfit spent so much time robbing and extorting.

Allegedly robbing and extorting. Everything's alleged with these guys.

While I was trying to bend her ear, pretending I was a decade or so past my prime, Rita the Hostess filled me in on the folks who used to run the grill. There was old man Jino, of course, but Tiny never grilled nothing in his whole life. For a while, it was Lawrence Ragusa until he went to jail for assault. Then it was Nicholas "No-no" Noto until he went to prison for money laundering and something called racketeering. Carlo Milazzo just disappeared one day. The ultimate no-call, no-show.

Stefano Enna? Wrapped up on a grand larceny indictment. Abel Bagero and Joey Trappani? They both worked the grill, and both were in prison now. Some coincidence, right?

So, there I was, a guy from the wrong side of Troost Avenue working the grill. I had to admit, it was a good job, even if I had to deal with people's little comments. But if all your co-workers had RAP sheets for assault and racketeering, you would learn to let certain remarks roll off your back. "Just jokes," the cooks would say. Like calling me eggplant as if I don't know what it means.

Still, it paid well. It was a good job, even if I had to kick a little tip money up to Frank every month to keep my parole officer happy. Even if I had to turn a blind eye to the boxes of assorted goods that appeared in the shed some evenings—just poof, and there they are.

Wait. Who am I trying to convert here? What the hell am I talking about? It was a shitty job. But, you know. I was a con. I had to take it all one day at a time.

That shed out in the alley was where I locked up the grill at night, next to all those mysterious boxes. Of course, I knew all that stuff was hotter than August. Usually, it was appliances, but it could've been liquor, maybe cigarettes. Stuff you figure is none of your business. But earlier this week, there was something different in there. A gunmetal grey case with a handle, sort of like a personal cooler. One just big enough to fit a lunch. But it was solid and new and had a gold lock.

The type of thing that might catch your eye.

Then, yesterday, I was reading the paper and saw an article about a robbery. A jewelry store in the Plaza had been hit. Rings, necklaces, bracelets, all that shit. None of those cubic zirconias or weak-ass scientist-made diamonds. Real rocks. So, I saw that article and thought about the gunmetal grey case. I can put two and two together just as well as anyone, can't I?

And that was that. If anybody was in a position to rip off the Outfit, it was me.

I SOLD out of sausages at a quarter to two and shut the grill down. The cafe was empty and warm. I got my free sandwich and went to the kitchen to eat. As I minded my own business in the corner, on my phone, reading some folk's Monday morning quarterback of last week's game, Frank waved me into the back office.

"Come see, Shawn," Frank said. "Come see." His hands moved at his neck, knotting a fat black tie. He was a fit guy. I'm not gonna say he was on steroids, but he could get ornery now and then. Always clean-shaven. Hair slicked back. He also had a wandering eye that would circle the room on its own, looking for god-knows-what. Rita the Hostess said it was from getting knocked around when he competed for Golden Gloves. Some of the cooks called him Fish-Eye Frank, but never to his face.

He could get ornery, you know?

Even with the eye, the guy knew how to dress. He was good with customers in the restaurant, too. I followed him to the office, reset my glasses on the bridge of my nose. Guess I was nervous. I had every right to be with what I was planning. Frank opened the door and let me go first. By the time I realized "Tiny" Jino Barra was sitting at Frank's desk, I was already positioned between the two.

Trapped, it felt like.

"You selling some sausages today?" Tiny asked.

"Yes, sir. Sold out." Yes, sir, please, and thank you. I could be respectable when I needed to be.

There was a crying sound like a dying animal as Frank pulled a metal chair from the wall and pushed it across the dark red tile. The chair bumped against my legs. He wasn't exactly offering me a seat so much as telling me to sit. I said thanks. What else do you say?

I did not like where this meeting was going at all. What could I have done wrong? I hadn't done anything yet...right? And it wasn't like these guys were psychic. I got myself a free sandwich and my portion of the family meal every day, but that was a perk of the job. That wasn't stealing. I wasn't rude to customers, even though they looked at me like I was dog crap on the bottom of their shoe half the time. I was good to the staff and tipped out generously.

I won't bullshit you. I was also six months out of Jackson County Prison for petty theft and possession of stolen goods. I sure as hell was planning on lifting those diamonds from the shed out back, fencing them, and never setting foot in Kansas City again. Neither on the

Missouri nor Kansas side. I'd be gone, even though the furthest I had been outside the city was the edge of Wyandotte County to sell off some acquired items. That was back in the old days.

Anyway, even with all that other stuff being true, at that moment, in that kitchen, I was basically an innocent man. Tiny held out a hand, and it was like he put the whole world on pause. He was older than Frank, the size and shape of a lump of granite. He was looking at me, then. Studying me.

"You done good work ever since you been here. And we been very good to you. Talking to your PO and so on," Tiny said, pointing. He wore a small ring with a small sapphire on his small finger, and the gem glinted. "I thought you could do me a favor."

"Uh," was all I could say. I tried to think of something else and just wound up straightening my glasses.

Frank cleared his throat, and I didn't jump out of my chair. Small victories. "No big deal," he said. "We just need you to do a little acting. We got the Christmas party coming up."

"You want me to play Santa Clause?"

Tiny Barra chuckled, the sound like a grunting pig. "C'mon. You're a little tan for Santa. But in Sicily, Santa doesn't have reindeer. He's got a little friend, Dominic the Donkey."

"Donkey?" I said.

Frank clapped his hands. The sound sent my ears ringing. "That's you, my friend. It's gonna be great. The kids are going to love it."

"Dominic the Donkey. Santa's helper. Everybody loves him. You'll see." Tiny sounded sure of that.

You ever found yourself in a donkey costume before? Me neither. Guess that's one of those once-in-a-lifetime events.

"Donkey. Uh. Sure," I said. Honestly, I was a little dazed. I thought that somehow, Frank knew about my plans. If it took me playing a donkey to get out of there, I would bray and snort with the best of them.

Tiny stood, and like a puppet, I stood with him. The old man pulled a fat roll of cash from his pocket. He took off the rubber band and peeled away a few hundred-dollar bills. He gave me a heavy handshake and said, "We'll get you the suit. It's got ears, a tail, a harness, everything. You're gonna be great."

I nodded. I mean, what the hell was happening?

All of a sudden, Frank was escorting me to the hallway. "Thanks, Shawn. I mean it," he said, grinning the whole time. Outside the office, he held his hand out and looked at me. Just that cock-eyed look. I knew what he wanted. A taste. What could I do? I handed over one of the bills. Frank pocketed it and went inside.

I took a moment to make sure I was still living and breathing. Could this have been a dream? Sure enough, from the hallway, I could hear them talking.

"The moolie as a donkey. Brilliant."

"We gotta get it on video."

Jesus. You believe that? I wasn't even barely out the door. It's a hard world. Sometimes, you gotta be hard yourself. But other times, you gotta make yourself small. So small they don't even notice you.

What a life I was living.

I finished my shift and even helped the waiters roll silverware. Real nice. Friendly. I cleaned my grill and brought it back to the shed. Nothing out of the ordinary at all. From time to time, my mind flew back into that office with Tiny Barra grunting his little piggy giggles. They wanted me to be a donkey. Damn.

What a life.

But not anymore. One day at a time, and today was the day. My shadow was huge, big-foot-sized as I walked out to the shed. It spread over the metal case. I could almost see the diamonds inside twinkling away in the black.

It was easy. I slid the grill aside, grabbed the gunmetal case, locked the shed, and left. Just like that. That's the thing about seizing your moment; not a lot to it, really. You just gotta work your nerve up to do the seizing.

The whole drive home, I had one eye on the thing. It was sitting in the passenger seat of my Avalon, begging me to open it. Like a girl who's all about you, and you're about her, and you both know it. Me and that case were made for one another. It was only after I had to slam on my brakes to avoid rear-ending a good-sized Dodge pick-up that I decided, hey, I better focus on the road.

I had a two-bedroom apartment that overlooked a spread of ware-houses and office parks. It was noisy during the day, dead at night. The spare bedroom was still full of Vicky's crap, even though she left me months ago for that asshole Devin.

Sometimes, life's got nothing but meanness to it, right?

Coming home early one evening, I opened the door to my apart-ment, walked down the hall, and saw the building's superintendent bucking away behind my wife on our living room couch. I had one jacket sleeve off, frozen in shock. Vicky's hair was still up in her leopard print head wrap. Devin was still wearing his grey work shirt. They never even knew they had an audience.

I didn't know what to do. Sweat started running down the middle of my back. My heart didn't beat any faster. Instead, it was like it had just stopped altogether. I thought I said something, but maybe I forgot. Either way, they didn't hear me.

I had to get somewhere else. Anywhere. I'm a man, and I've got my pride, and I've got anger when I need it. But right then? I had nothing. I took three steps backward and went through the first door I came to. It was the linen closet. That was fine.

I stood there with shelves digging into my back as my heart started beating again. Mile a minute. Loud, too. I was afraid they would hear it. The door to the closet hung crooked in its frame as a yellow rectangle of light cut through the black space before me. I caught my breath.

It got ugly with Vicky. She left in the end. We had been married for five years. Happy? I thought so. Who can tell? Then I spend eighteen months in Jackson County for selling stolen TVs, and everything goes to shit. That was only part of it, though. It was the way I was living. Never thinking about the future, not even thinking much about the past. Just worrying about how much money I could make that night by lifting this, moving that.

There, in the dark of the closet, I decided to finally do something. Take control of my life, you know? If I were a drunk, I would have called it hitting bottom; a sort of wake-up call right there in the linen closet. Something like finding Jesus, like somebody told me something so true it made the world set on its side. And that true thing hurt me because it made everything else a lie.

The life I was living wasn't the life I thought it was.

So I took it all one day at a time. Trying to plan my life the way I would plan a job. Thinking about it the way I would think about opening a lock. Taking my time. When I saw the bit about the diamonds, I finally realized my opportunity.

One day at a time. And today would be the day.

At the apartment, I sat the heavy metal case on the patio furniture I used for a kitchen table and found my kit. Dental picks, tweezers of various sizes, rakes, tension tools. Everything a man would need to bypass even the most stubborn of locks. I was never a gold-medal picker, but I did manage to get through some doors in my day. I'll tell you that for free.

The lock stood out a deep golden color against the grey of the case. There was even a little bit of scrollwork around the keyhole. Writing, like. Tiny looping patterns that seemed to almost be words, but none I knew. Delicate work, though. That had to mean whatever was inside was particularly valuable. Had to.

I turned on every light in the place and sat at the table. Within five minutes, the lock was impaled a dozen times over. Picks protruded every which way, but it was as tight as a drum. The next part took a little imagination. It was also the fun part.

I pulled my rake and stroked it into the lock. I had to feel around a bit; by sense of smell, almost. As I poked and prodded and found the tumblers, my mind saw how they would line up, and then I saw how the lock could open. Letting my glasses drop to the end of my nose, I worked a wafer rake into the keyhole and wiggled vigorously until I felt the tumblers give.

There it was. I rotated the lock. The mechanism slid home easy. The lid popped open. Smooth. Like we were made for one another.

I eased the lid back. Feeling good about it. Not rushing to pat myself on the back but feeling good. I pushed my glasses up my nose 'til I could feel my eyelashes against the lenses. Even with all the light,

I wasn't sure I could trust my eyes. The case wasn't full of glittering diamonds or emeralds, but it wasn't empty, either.

The thing in there was set into a foam cradle. It was round, maybe oval. Almost green, the color of a still-ripening banana, with scores of divots that looked like the eyes of a potato, only a pale lavender color. I pulled the thing out and held it up. It felt smooth and slightly rough at once, somewhat fibrous. Like a potato.

Fuck me.

I had stolen a goddamn potato.

The bottle of scotch on the kitchen counter called out to me. I poured a glass taller than usual. I had a right to, didn't I? I drank that down and cursed and poured another.

Sometimes, life's got nothing but meanness to it. I get the nerve to make a move against the Kansas City Outfit, and I come away with their goddamn produce order.

Goddamn fancy-ass potato.

Was this some kind of joke?

I walked laps around the table, drank, and cursed. Enough time passed that soon it was all just so damn funny. I sat there and giggled at the potato. All the nerves. All the planning. All the dreams of the life I could be living. And there I was. Funniest damn thing that ever happened to me, tell you the truth.

The only good thing about it was nobody knew I took the damn thing. So I had my life to fall back on, didn't I? And even if they found out, the Outfit wouldn't murder me over a potato.

Right?

I drank some more, and you know how that is. I got hungry. And I was furious at that potato. It had no right to be a damn potato. It was supposed to be diamonds. A necklace full of rare rubies or something.

The butcher knife whispered when I pulled it from the knife block. Funny how you remember certain things. It knocked against the table as I cut the potato. Once. Twice. The green and lavender flesh was faintly pale, lightly moist. I chopped without much skill. I worked that grill at the restaurant, but I never was no cook, to tell you the truth.

It browned nicely in the cast-iron pan Vicky forgot to take with her. I cooked it with eggs and bacon and red pepper and ate the whole damn thing with the rest of the scotch just to show it who was boss. How do you like that, you goddamn potato?

Bloated and drunk and satisfied with myself, I pushed away from the table, not thinking about the Kansas City Outside at all, not then. Instead, I was focused on staying upright. The room wobbled as I walked past the couch and stood at the window overlooking the warehouses. The dark outside was filled with stars. Beautiful, really. Then they dropped to Earth.

I took in a whisper of breath. Shooting stars. Crazy. They came one after the other. Then more; fat, flickering balls of white.

No, wait. Those weren't stars. It was snowing.

Like I said, I was pretty drunk. But it really was snowing, maybe a foot already. I liked my falling-star theory better than damn snow, though. I dropped into my ratty armchair and watched the sky fall.

DREAMS CAME varied and vivid and unfinished. I viewed my wife's adultery from a thousand angles at once in something like a fly's kaleidoscopic eye. A thousand Devins mounted a thousand Vickys on a thousand different couches that were all the same. Then, I was a kid stealing a pack of cigarettes from an older man waiting for the bus, but the old man was also me, and I ran after that little bastard. When the bus roared around the corner to flatten me into oblivion, I realized I was the bus driver, too. So I drove off somewhere. Where to? Well, to the same place I had driven to nearly every other day. Out of nowhere, I was at the grill outside Jino's Italian, cooking sausages. Only the links were all fat fingers, each sporting a sapphire ring exactly like Tiny Barra's ring. The gem shined at me through the smoke. Bright. Bright. Brighter than bright.

IN THE MORNING, I rose, zombie-like, to find the world outside was a wintery wasteland. Snow was still coming down, the world ashen in color. It looked like I felt. Used up. Cold. Hollow, sort of.

My stomach tightened, and I didn't feel so empty anymore. I had to use the toilet immediately. I'd leave this part out and preserve my pride, but it's kind of important.

The bathroom light was shockingly bright after spending so long in the dark. I dropped trou and tried to move my bowels. I strained but got no relief. Didn't even break wind. Whatever was in there sat in my gut like a chunk of stone. Right then, I knew something was wrong. I sat up straight and looked down. Should have been just belly leading all the way to my pride and joy but "should have" isn't necessarily what was.

Right then, my stomach was colonized by half a dozen growths, slightly fuzzy lumps colored pale green. The largest one was the size of my thumb. I twisted myself around to get a better look and saw the big one had its own fleshy lavender dimples. It looked more like a small tuber than anything.

Like a potato.

"Oh, shit," I said.

I left my pants pooled in front of the commode and went to the bathroom mirror. Delicately, I pulled the lump just to test it out. It hurt like I was being pinched, and it would not come free. It was part of me.

What can I say? I panicked. Where did I leave my phone? I turned the place upside down looking for it. Maybe I could do some research. See what was happening to me. Maybe it was nothing, right? I was clinging to that notion like dogshit on a tennis shoe.

But maybe that thing, that potato, had been in the metal case for a reason. Maybe it was contagious or something. Shit, maybe it was host to some sort of crazy virus that gave me those bumps. Like chickenpox except worse. Or maybe it gave me radiation poisoning or some lab-grown quick-cancer. The possibilities were endless. Either way, eating it was pure dumbassery.

I was running through every disease I had ever heard about when the front door opened and somebody came into the apartment. I walked into the hallway naked except for my shirt, Willie and Poor

Boys dangling free, and saw Vicky standing there. She wore a black pea coat with a purple scarf over her hair and was dusted with snow. Her shift on the admissions desk at Saint Luke's was over at seven. She looked tired, angry.

Even after all the shit she put me through, and in spite of my potentially having genetically engineered quick-cancer, she looked good. Even tired and angry. I got no defense on that front. I suppose I'm a glutton for punishment.

"What the hell are you doing?" she said, then looked to the ceiling as if the sight of me was repulsive. I didn't look my best, I'll give you that. She said, "I need to get my good shoes."

The velvet boots she wore were sopping wet. I stared at them. Vicky sighed and walked to the spare bedroom. When she came close, I said, "My stomach." Saying it was hard, like I was speaking with a mouth full of Jell-O.

She reeled. "Your breath smells like gasoline. Bet your stomach wouldn't hurt if you didn't sit up half the night drinking." She had a nursing degree, but her bedside manner was reserved for the hospital and never quite extended my way.

Pea coat flying behind her like a cape, Vicky disappeared into the spare bedroom, made as much noise as possible, and came out with her insulated black winter boots. I covered my frank and beans with one hand and the new growths on my stomach with the other before I gave her my best puppy-dog look. "Seriously. I feel funny."

Vicky stomped over to the patio table, grabbed something, and stomped back. "Probably got a headache because you're trying to see without your glasses again." She held my glasses out for me.

Thing was, that wasn't it. I could see just fine. I pressed my fingertips into the soft flesh just below my eyes to confirm that no, I wasn't wearing glasses. I've been nearsighted all my adult life. Can barely see past my nose without spectacles. Really.

But not right then.

"I can see okay," I said, and took the lenses. She didn't believe me, of course. Guess I had a hard time believing that, too.

Vicky rolled her eyes. "I can't deal with your drunk ass right now. I just came for my boots."

My tongue was working in a space that seemed too small to accomplish any meaningful work, but I tried to tell her what I had done. She opened the front door and slammed it behind her, never bothering to listen.

That was that. She left me.

Again.

I leaned against the hallway closet and breathed there. My stomach rumbled as if angry with me. Why had I eaten that damn thing? I couldn't have just thrown it away? Forgotten about it and found another way to make money? I was truly some special kind of idiot.

The front door opened again. She was coming back. Despite all she had done to me, I knew she wouldn't leave me in my hour of need. I fumbled with my glasses, trying to slip them back on just to make her happy, and said, "Vicky, listen. Something is really wrong."

That's as far as I got.

It wasn't Vicky. I slipped the glasses off and could see Frank Acerra just fine. The big restaurant manager and mobster was hunched over in a heavy grey overcoat, frowning deeply as if the whole apartment had pissed him off on some fundamental level. One eye seemed to float over the door frame. The other was locked on me.

Would it surprise you to know Frank had never stopped by my place before? Never came over to watch the Chiefs or anything? So this was new for everybody. And Frank Acerra wasn't the type of guy that took to new experiences well.

"Yeah. Something is really wrong, my friend." Frank kicked the door shut behind him. He sounded like he was a mile away.

I must have dropped my glasses because I heard them clatter on the floor. "What are you doing?" I said, offended-like because I wasn't on the clock yet. I figured that was the best way to go. Umbrage. Take the high ground. I just had to maintain my innocence a little longer. Get Frank out of there. Then I could deal with whatever was happening to my guts.

"Where's that fucking thing?" Frank said. He saw the grey box on the table, open. The foam cradle there, empty. "Oh, Mary, Mother of God."

"Wait a secom, mush a lait," I said, my words coming out twisted and thick. I held my jaw and tried to make it work right. "I gotta. I gotta."

When Frank pulled the gun, I shut up. Guns will do that to you. My mind raced and kept tripping over its own feet. I looked down and realized I was wearing a long-sleeved shirt and nothing else. Where were my pants?

The bathroom. Right. So much had happened since I was on the throne.

"Shawn," Frank said. "Hey, asshole." He knocked the butt of his gun on the kitchen counter. "Shawn, where's the brain?"

"Hunh?"

"The thing in the box. The brain. Where the hell is it?"

I let out a long, steadying breath. I focused on the words that swam to the front of my mind and spoke very slowly. "I ate it."

The words hung there for a moment.

Then Frank's words caught up with me.

Hold up. Hold up.

Brains?

"I ate brains?" I managed to say that right on the first try.

Frank snarled. "You ate the brain?" He went on to say more, but I was focused on holding myself up. Maybe it was the booze or the shock of being told I ate brains, but I felt higher than high. So stoned that I could fall asleep right there in the hallway.

I could.

Just drift.

Away.

A sharp pain in my cheek brought me back around.

Suddenly the big Italian was standing in front of me with his hand raised. "You need another one?"

I shook my head slowly.

My cheek stung from where Frank had slapped me.

I tried to focus.

Frank was in my apartment.

I had some sort of growth or quick-cancer on my gut.

Okay.

The man had just slapped me, but I remembered to take the high ground. I wasn't so far gone that I would have hit him, but I could be indignant. I was a man, after all. I still had my pride. "I'm'a get the grill," I said. "You make...make some sausages."

Seemed like a snappy little dig when I thought it up.

"Okay." Frank dug a knuckle into the side of his eye. "Here's what we're going to do." Under his watchful eye, it took only a minute for me to get into some pants and a jacket. No shoes. Frank said there wasn't time. The indignation was gone. I was just happy to have someone giving me direction.

Soon, the two of us were in Frank's Escalade, heading somewhere. I was driving, which was a terrible idea, honestly. Frank was in the passenger seat, but the mobster was nudging my shoulder every ten seconds, keeping me awake. "Hold those eyes open." Frank held his gun on one thigh. Ready.

I had my eyes open wider than wide but knew I couldn't keep it up. "I'm sick," I said. "Shouldn't be driving."

Frank made a sound and waved his free hand. "Eyes on the road."

Outside, the sky was the color of muddy snow even though the sun had risen. A color like that doesn't exactly keep you more alert. Just to hear the words aloud, I said, "My stomach hurts."

"I'll bet."

"What kind of potato was it?"

"No kind of potato."

"I don't want to go to Jino's."

"Too bad. You stole something that Tiny was holding for some important people. You gotta make things right. I can't believe you ate the damn thing. Tiny knows some weirdos, boy. Real goddamn nutjobs."

I ignored the "boy" remark.

Snow filled the world with static, as though reality's signal was being distorted the way they said solar rays could jack up FM radio. "Drive right," Frank said, sounding a little concerned.

"Doin' best," I muttered. And I was. I dug the heel of my hand into my eye to clear the gummy crust, causing bruise-like spots to bloom before me. It was grey outside, and I felt grey inside, and the next time my eyelids wanted to drop, I just gave in.

I shook in my seat like a man having a seizure. "Don't wanna take you to Jino's," I said. I leaned forward, and the hood of my Chiefs parka fell over my head. It was blissfully black.

"Hey! Christ!" Frank was far away but kept yelling at me. My hands dropped like iron lumps. I couldn't drive, couldn't raise my head at all. His body pushed against mine as he leaned into the driver's seat, trying to steer the truck on an icy road.

Black snow began to fall against the insides of my eyelids as the soft roar of the storm drowned Frank out completely. The snow shifted with a wind that was not wind, then the storm in my mind parted like spotted curtains to reveal deep, dark voids. This was not the dark of the insides of my eyelids. This was something else.

With idle amusement, I realized that my eyes were open. All the way open. I was looking out the windshield at the snow streaming by, and the storm was truly parted.

Strange folds opened.

A deep void yawned.

From the dark, they came.

Frank didn't see them, and that was fine.

But I did.

The occasional shuttered strip mall or abandoned gas station swooped by as we barreled on. Still, those yawning maws stayed in front of us. Something was moving in those dark, empty spaces that I could only see because my eyes were so out of focus. So unfocused that they were focused. Dark bits of night peeled off and flew towards us.

"Drive right!" Frank yelled and yanked the wheel. I could feel the ice and snow pulling the tires one way, then another, but I couldn't do a damn thing about it.

There were *things* out there.

When I was a boy, I would travel to Chicago with my father to visit Uncle Robbie. The big Lincoln took up two lanes of highway all by itself. The trip was long, so I would lean my head against the window and look outside and imagine wild horses running with us. Chasing the car or leaping billboards and motels or galloping all around the Lincoln, the sound of their hooves lost in the growling of the car's engine.

Now, something else was moving along with the vehicle. Many somethings. And the somethings I saw now weren't horses. They weren't running, either. They flew ahead of the car on shredded leather wings, with long pointed legs dangling from bodies hidden in shadow.

One of the beings swooped over the Escalade, close enough for its jagged leg to clack against the passenger window.

"*Dio Cane!*" Frank said.

I don't speak Italian, but I knew what the man meant.

The Escalade wobbled dangerously. Frank tried to correct, but the tires skidded against the ice-covered roads. The steering wheel bucked and jerked from side to side with a mind of its own. All-weather tires, my ass.

There was a curve in the road.

The guardrail was bright as Christmas in the Escalade's headlights.

I felt the impact a split second before the airbag exploded.

Time skipped ahead.

I didn't know how long I was out. I dreamed a little bit, then. Or maybe, continued to dream. Dark flowers, the kind that never grew in Mimaw's garden, bloomed. Their petals held cold, unblinking eyes.

A DOZEN tiny cuts cried out from all over my face when I pushed my head from the collapsing airbag. The horn sounded in a steady, dull whine. The air smelled of something burning amidst the chill. Glass was everywhere. Frank cursed next to me. But we were alive. If nothing else, the impact had sort of cleared my head. Not all car crashes are bad, I guess.

The world went dim as something with torn paper wings slammed onto the hood of the car. It blocked half the space where the windshield had been. Frank shrieked and raised his gun and fired, and the sound tried to shatter my eardrums. I don't think he hit anything, but it was hard to tell with my hands over my ears and my eyes shut tight.

There was a moment of calm then. After gunfire, everything seems calm. Frank said something more in Italian, and I said I didn't under-stand him on account of being deaf. On account of the gunshots.

Something thumped onto the hood of the car. Through the broken windshield roared frigid air and snow and something else. It chittered, rolled its black-shelled body into Frank, waved razored legs. Frank yelled and it became clear I wasn't deaf. I thought his yell sounded good, so I yelled too and clawed for my door handle. I collapsed out of the car and into the snow, vomiting eggs and green bile and what I hoped was potato.

Quick as I could, I pushed myself up. Suddenly, every one of my muscles constricted. I was standing on the side of the road. Jacket open. Barefoot. The car's front end was tangled hopelessly in a metal guard rail when the horn died, leaving only the sound of the wind and the winged nightmares surrounding us.

Frank struggled with the creature in the Escalade before it burst through the window, shrieking, leaving Frank hunkered down on the floorboards all folded up. Light reflected off his watery eyes, one staring at me while the other scanned the night sky. His voice was high and wet. "Don't let them get me," he said, covering his face with his hands. The cuffs of his jacket and shirt were shredded, the backs of his hands laced with weeping wounds as if from fending off tiny, sharp claws.

I backed away from the car, afraid of the man and whatever had happened to him. I wanted to run somewhere, anywhere.

"Oh, fuck all this," I said.

Beyond the guardrail, the land dropped into a steep valley that shouldn't have been. Instead of the low neighborhoods and spider-webbed power lines of Kansas City's south side, the valley held jagged towers of black and indigo stone. Flocks of those winged creatures flew overhead while other, stranger beings crawled and slithered below. They were horned and toothed and had too many legs, fighting among the shadows of mysterious towers and calling out a language that hurt my sinuses. The sky was angry, ruby-colored with no snowfall. The road failed to extend in either direction, as though lifted with the Escalade to another place entirely. Some nightmare place.

Somewhere Else.

I decided I was dreaming. It was too much. A dream. Nightmare. Whatever. I just had to wake up or wait it out. Heavy wings flapped around me, surrounding the Escalade, a pack of creatures arcing and cawing. One landed close by, and I got a good look. Wish I hadn't. Pale eyes looked out from a head tucked deep between ridged shoulder blades. I've never been a dinosaur guy, an enthusiast, but it looked like one of those flying dinosaurs. It had a shell consisting of broad, mismatched plates that looked like black samurai armor.

"Go away," I said. Worth a try. My voice echoed unnaturally.

The samurai's eyes remained wide and bright and unblinking as it hopped to me. Wings flapped to help it along. I held my hands out to ward it away, hoping I wouldn't have to strike the thing. The idea of touching it made my soul break out in gooseflesh.

My stomach burned an acidic, concrete-scouring burn. My elbows twisted inward, pushing into my torso, into the potato. It wasn't on purpose or nothing. I couldn't help it. A dozen tubers throbbed and jutted from my belly, swelling, pushing through my shirt like sprouting potatoes, fat and fleshy and full of tiny eyes.

I guess I didn't puke all the stuff up.

In the blink of an eye, the tubers budded and grew branches, vines. I cried, but there wasn't any pain, not really. Just pressure as the roots crawled, diving in and out, piercing my shirt and parka, sewing themselves into my flesh as they doubled back like cypress knees surfacing for air.

So this dream was incredibly vivid. That was fine. I imagined the flying samurai growing hips and breasts and turning into something out of Penthouse rather than a horror movie. If I was dreaming, Lord, let me dream right.

No. This was happening. Sometimes, life's got nothing but meanness to it.

The samurai cawed again. Maybe it figured I was weak or knew I was sick, that I would be easy prey. Its beak or muzzle cracked open and showed rows upon rows of broken teeth. It called once, a guttural hiss that was almost, "Spoon?" Then its jaw dropped, unhinged, and its dinosaur wings spread, and the samurai came at me with those gleaming claws. I raised a hand to knock it to the ground, but my arm went up and froze there. It wouldn't strike. It was petrified.

Then there was pain. Good, real pain, not some silly dream pain. Roots burst from my fingers. There was no blood. Fibrous tendrils spread like they were searching for water but instead found the samurai's yawning face. I didn't mean to do it. I didn't do anything, really. I was a spectator, weak and hunched and unable to control what protruded from my body. Tendrils snaked around the samurai, clamped its dinosaur wings tight to its body. Roots twisted like lengths of steel wire as its rigid, black skin bulged and cracked. Vibrant blue blood seeped out from that shattered armor. It screamed, and I felt it in my chest, in the pit of my stomach where the strange potato had taken root.

I was terrified of the tubers. Terrified of the screaming monster. Terrified of just about everything. I wanted to be gone, far from the dinosaur samurai and the quick-cancer potato. I wanted to be drunk on my kitchen floor, dreaming up all this madness. I wanted it with the deepest part of my soul. Even more than I wanted the Penthouse lady, I wanted out of that dream.

I figure some murky part of my mind must have worked at the problem while I was panicking. I don't know how the subconscious operates, or unconscious, or whatever, but part of us talks and walks and deals with the world as it is, and then there's another part. That keeps our lungs going. Keeps our hearts pumping. Makes little choices and changes every second without the other part worrying over it. Like how sometimes I find myself thinking about my troubles, and suddenly out of nowhere, I've got a cigarette in my mouth with half the thing smoked. I've even driven the entire way home from Jino's to the apartment and not really remembered the trip. Just been on autopilot, like. So, while most of what makes me "me" was scared shitless, that other, deeper part was working away with a diligence typically reserved for locks. Only instead of tumblers and so on, it was working out the potato. The flying dinosaur. The whole idea of Somewhere Else. Carefully. Delicately. Working. Near as I could figure, it found some hidden cylinder and poked and prodded and found the tumblers, saw how they would line up. Then my mind's eye saw how it could open. The potato, of course. And it did open, that potato.

It was that easy.

My newfound roots constricted around the samurai. It said again, "Spoon?" and it squeaked like a dog's chew toy, then burst in a shower of blue viscera and cracked carapace. My stomach turned and I thought I might vomit again, but I stood tall and sucked in air. Without warning, the flock of flying dinosaurs in armor was gone. The Escalade remained entangled in the guard rail, but the valley of jagged stone towers and monsters was absent, replaced by a latticework of snow-covered streets and familiar buildings.

I was awake. Or I had returned. Either way, I wasn't Somewhere Else, which was something to celebrate.

My stomach lumps congealed into one massive goiter, a potato to conquer all other potatoes. It pulsed softly. I dropped my hands and saw the roots retreat, burrowing into my flesh, becoming one with my veins, traveling deep into my body. A newly bulbous tuber grew out of my wrist like a fleshy watch.

What the hell was this? Dream or waking life?

I shivered in the cold, tried to tamp down my fear and shock. My bare feet were pale and freezing, but I barely noticed. The air filled with grey flurries once again.

Roots.

Potatoes.

Monsters.

Couldn't be. I was hallucinating. I must be sick. I looked in the Escalade, where Frank was huddled on top of the floorboards. I muttered, "I wish I hadn't eaten that damn thing."

Frank didn't say anything.

Leaning against the side of the Escalade, I willed away visions of potatoes invading my body, closing my eyelids. When I opened them, the tuber on my stomach was still there, pale and covered with lavender eyes. I had a momentary lapse in judgement and considered going to Vicky for help.

I could see how well that would go.

"I am become potato," I said to my reflection in the window of the

Escalade. Just to hear some words out loud, I guess. With great effort, I pulled myself into the driver's seat.

"Frank? Frank?" I said, but the man didn't answer.

Dream or reality, hallucination or whatever, something was seriously wrong with me. I had to admit that. Now with the dinosaur samurai gone along with those awful towers, it was easy to forget how real they had been. So I did my best to convince myself they weren't real.

If I had eaten a poisonous potato, I needed to know how toxic it was. Sitting there, I wrote myself into a small narrative. I was awake. This was real life. Maybe I could bring Frank back to the restaurant? Talk to somebody there. Tiny? Probably not. Better if it was a cook. Maybe one of the other Wiseguys that hung around the place?

Roots snaked out from my sleeves and wrapped around the steering wheel. That other part of my mind again, working on its own. Okay. I'd just have to embrace the strangeness for the time being.

A firm, fibrous creeper wrenched the car into reverse. I lost the Escalade's bumper to the guard rail but didn't care. As the tires slid over ice and caught, I threw it into drive, hunkered down against the freezing air, and drove.

To hell with it. I was going to Jino's after all.

I PARKED in the alley behind the restaurant. Tiny's Lexus was there, along with a few other cars. I just had to avoid the big man, that was all. I hefted my tumorous tuber out of the car, zipped up my torn parka in some attempt at modesty, and went in through the back.

It was warm in the kitchen of Jino's Classic Italian Restaurant and Trattoria. It was also empty. The lights were on, but it was too early for the cooks to prepare anything. Thin tendrils of root stuck out from beneath my hood like searching snakes. Snow melted and drained from my body, pooled at my feet. My toes looked like pale stone against the red tile. I had forgotten all about shoes.

"Hello?" I said.

There was some shuffling and small conversation from the dining area before Tiny entered, bull-headed and scowling, followed by a few men I recognized. Mike Infretto wore a knit cap, the kind with a little fluffy ball on top. Billy "The Razor" Rastelli was in a leather jacket. They were Outfit guys, friends of Franks. Not a good sign. Behind them were five men or women wearing forest green robes with black hoods.

That was different.

Guys in hoods? I thought I might have arrived in the middle of some sort of Klan meeting. I really didn't know what I could do about that.

"Oh, I don't want to interrupt," I said. Pretty weak. My parka covered the tuber, but it still looked like I had a newly formed potbelly. "I can do my prep work later."

"Stay," Tiny grumbled.

One of the hooded figures said, "Where's the brain?"

"Quiet. Where's Frank?" Tiny asked.

Too many questions at once. I gestured vaguely to the back door. "Frank's in the car."

Tiny raised a pinky, and the two Outfit guys left the way I entered. I leaned against the stainless-steel prep station. The kitchen pulsed slightly, the way it would if I had smoked a joint and stood up too quickly. I was starting to sweat, too. I really wanted to unzip the parka but knew that wouldn't be a good idea.

"You okay, Shawn?" Tiny lumbered over, taking me in with those calm, observant eyes. "You look sick, maybe."

"It's just allergies," I ventured. That wouldn't explain the cuts all over my face, but it was worth a shot.

"Where's the brain?" One of the hooded figures yelled, and the sound cut through me and struck a chord in my mind.

Then something really weird happened.

The shriek rippled brightly all around the kitchen. The man's yell was a wave of honey-colored air, crashing into me and turning back the way it came, flooding away from my legs. The strange tide washed over the men and women in the room, breaking against their shoulders. The honey-wave swirled in a whirlpool near the freezer, then splashed again and rippled out to the far corners of the room.

Instantly, my fear was gone. That wave was some shit.

I was filled with, I guess, "childlike wonder," is what you could call it. It was like seeing Christmas lights for the first time, or maybe fireworks. When I dipped my hands in the golden surf, the thinning waves caught and tugged my fingers.

Tiny slapped my hand away. He was right in front of me, and the waves were gone. It was just me and the kitchen and the fools in hoods and the big man. He said, "I got a question for you. You take anything from the shed?" When I didn't answer, he tapped my parka-covered stomach. I shivered and tried to step away, but he came at me. "Maybe you had a big turkey dinner last night? Or maybe you took something from me, and now you found some religion all of a sudden, and you're smuggling that thing back into my shop."

Game over. There was really no place to go. Better to beg forgiveness or something like that, right? I unzipped my parka and showed the room the growth on my stomach. "Okay. I'll be honest. I'm fucked up."

"Holy shit!" Tiny said. He stepped back so quickly that he almost tripped over his own feet. Two of the hooded figures grabbed his arms to steady him.

One of the weirdos stepped forward and thrust back her hood, a dark-skinned woman with wild eyes, like those of a television preacher, somebody used to speaking in tongues. "It's beautiful," she said.

The back door banged open. Two Wiseguys came into the kitchen with Frank propped between them.

"What happened, kid?" Tiny said.

Frank didn't answer. He was drooling, one eye toward the ground, his wandering eye frantically trying to look behind him. Shredded sleeves hung loosely over his arms.

"He's drunk, maybe," Mike Infretto said.

"He's not drunk. He's in shock," Billy the Razor said.

Their boss grabbed Frank's face with two fat-fingered hands. Tiny scowled at the man, trying to set him right through sheer force of will.

When that didn't happen, he turned to the strange woman and said, "Doc, I'm real sorry about your merchandise. But the guy with the tumor there has to answer for Frank." Growling at me, Tiny said, "What happened?"

I figured, why not be honest? "We were driving. Then we went someplace else. Or it seemed like we did. It was a dream, maybe. I'm sick, like I said. But it could be we went to hell."

"Hell?" the woman said, pretty interested.

"Hell. There were monsters."

"This is bullshit. Frank!" Tiny pleaded. "Tell me this is bullshit."

Frank wasn't saying anything.

Tiny sighed. He seemed to shrink down. Deflate. He waved at Billy the Razor. "Escort Dr. Bhittani out. Then we're going to talk with this punk right here. I'll get the blowtorch."

Oh, shit. That wasn't good.

Giddy, Dr. Bhittani clapped her hands together. "Wait! Wait! We wanted the brain, and here it is." She leaned forward and poked my tumor experimentally. It pulsed slightly, the many divots of the thing almost winking. "Did it attack you?"

She seemed reasonable, or at least not especially interested in blowtorches, so I answered her. "The brains? I ate them."

The hooded figures gasped as one. Dr. Bhittani screwed up her face. "You ate it?"

"With eggs," I said. "It didn't look like brains."

Dr. Bhittani sighed. "He has no idea." She turned to Tiny. "Mr. Barra, we'd like to keep him."

"He's gotta answer for Frank."

"Couldn't he do that after we have what we need?"

Tiny's grim face considered the woman, then the rest of the figures, then me. He pointed a pinky at Billy the Razor. "Stay with them. When they're done, we're going to give our grillmaster a makeover. Tear him a few new holes and seal up the ones he's already got."

Tiny always did have a way with words.

He and Mike Infretto were helping Frank into the office. Tiny was muttering to the unresponsive man, saying something soothing. Like he was talking to a dog or a small child.

Dr. Bhittani ignored that scene and gestured for her hooded buddies to gather around. "Guys, come here. I've got a great view of the brain. It must be growing inside of him."

No shit. I wrapped my arms over my stomach to try and hide the basketball-sized growth there. It wasn't working. The tuber on my wrist bulged, a smaller version of the one on my stomach. Roots poked from the sleeves of my jacket and hung down my back like a tattered cloak. Thin roots grew with little hairs. Little fibers.

Roots aside, the whole interaction was worrying me. "I've got brains in my stomach? I thought it was quick-cancer. Somebody tell me what's happening."

A hooded woman with red hair barked laughter. "No, dummy. It's not brains. It's a brane. With an E. A brane. As in a membrane."

Dr. Bhittani said, "What you ate was a membrane that stretches across dimensions. Stretches is the wrong word, I suppose. It simply *exists* in multiple dimensions."

I stared at the woman. "You sound crazy."

"You're ignorant. It's okay. I'll explain everything." It didn't sound rude coming from Dr. Bhittani. Fine woman. She had nice, high cheekbones. She said, "Reality is made up of dimensions. It's just a way of measuring the world around us. Okay? It's simple. Like this: in the beginning, there was a single point in space."

"What?" I was lost. Can you blame me?

"A point in empty space," she said.

"Like a meatball," the redhead offered.

"Exactly!" Dr. Bhittani spread her arms wide. "In the beginning, there was just a meatball. That's dimension zero, if you will."

Her last words echoed strangely in my mind.

If you will.

You will.

Will.

The kitchen faded away. I was standing in an empty void. No, not standing. Floating. I tried to touch my face but no longer had hands. Perhaps no face, either.

I know what you're thinking. I should have been terrified. But being faceless and handless in an empty void was only the second or third most horrific thing to happen to me that day.

A voice called from somewhere. "Now, the first dimension is a basic one. A single line. It's like a length of spaghetti stretching between two meatballs in any direction."

The point in space was not a meatball, of course. It was a potato. I knew because I was that potato now. Rough and pitted and buried in the deep dark of the cosmos. My skin opened and my roots burst forth, two lines stretching out into the darkness. The feeling was almost orgasmic.

"And the second dimension is a shape, like a flat square made of spaghetti."

My roots spun around me in a circle, forming a flat shape.

"And the third dimension is like a slice of lasagna! It's a cube. It's got width and depth."

"This is sounding sort of racist," Billy the Razor said from the void. "Like anti-Italian discrimination."

My lumpy form no longer floated but instead balanced itself on some invisible surface. My potato body fell and rolled across the empty void. I had width and depth alright.

"Lasagna. Exactly, Jeremy," Dr. Bhittani said, ignoring Billy the Razor. "For simplicity's sake, let's say we live in the third dimension. We're all three-dimensional beings, right? We have height, width, and depth. Now, here's where it gets tricky. The fourth dimension is time. The timeline of that slice of lasagna. Or people, I guess. We can observe the fourth dimension but can't interact with it. We can see ourselves age but can't move through time at will. Right? We're on a one-way trip."

With eyes not my own, I could see my potato body appearing, growing roots, falling, rolling across the void to where I now lay. It happened again and again, all in one endless loop. A short video clip. It could have been titled: The Potato Falls again.

And again.

And again.

"But the fifth dimension incorporates the entire timeline of that slice of lasagna as well as all possible timelines."

"All possible lasagnas."

"The many-universe theory. Which we can't interact with or observe. Because we're only human."

"Parallel universes," the redhead said. "And the sixth dimension? It gets tricky from there."

"He gets it," Dr. Bhittani said.

I didn't really, but maybe I was starting to. The void was no longer empty. I was surrounded by potatoes of all shapes, sizes, and colors. Parallel potatoes from parallel universes, each unique and connected to one another by forces beyond human comprehension. Connected by a membrane that defied all laws of man's simple sciences. They obeyed only their own kind.

They were glorious.

Dr. Bhittani poked my tumor again, which brought me back from the void and into the kitchen. I gripped the growth protectively, like a pregnant woman holding her belly. The doctor said, "This, my friend, is a membrane that stretches across all possible dimensions. It is a higher being. A more advanced organic form."

I took in the hooded figures, re-orienting myself in time and space. "You're...ummm...math teachers or something?"

"Oh, sweetheart. We come from a school of thought that sees mysticism and physics as one," Dr. Bhittani said. She extended her hand, and one of the hooded figures placed a fat tome there. The book was bigger than a bible. She said, "But I don't understand how you ate it. The brane was secured. Imprisoned, if you will."

"Oh, the box," I said. "I picked the lock."

The hoods muttered amongst themselves. Dr. Bhittani said something too low for me to hear. Then one of them took out a small can while another produced two paintbrushes. Together, they drew white lines on the tile.

"Hey," Billy the Razor said. "Did Tiny say you could paint on his floor?"

They ignored him. They were drawing a white, six-pointed star in what looked like custard or maybe mayonnaise. Around the star, they wrote strange symbols like Chinese or Cyrillic, but I didn't think it was either of those. Then again, what did I know?

I said, "You're a doctor, right? So just tell me. I'm tripping out. I'm seeing things. I'm growing things. Do I have cancer? Or gigantism? Something. I'm dying anyway, right?"

Dr. Bhittani opened her massive book and flipped through the pages, searching. "Oh, no. Not right away, I don't think. You're just becoming one with the brane. One with all possible realities." She beamed up at me. "Don't worry, though. I'll figure out how to separate the two of you."

I gripped my tumor and shuddered. I didn't like the sound of that. Had too much of a blowtorch vibe.

"See? Spells of dissolution and devolution written in a Paste of Unworthy. We got the recipe from the Book of the Unspeakable Horrors." Dr. Bhittani showed me the book, happy to share. "Could you move to the star, please?"

"Is it going to hurt?"

"Oh, I don't know. Probably, yeah."

That was enough. I definitely didn't like where this was going. I pushed myself away from the counter and made for the back door. Billy the Razor grabbed my parka. I struggled, but I wasn't at the top of my game.

"You're not going anywhere until Tiny says you can," Billy said.

I landed a punch across Billy's jaw with all the force of a nerf ball.

"Don't be an ass," Billy the Razor said.

"You're an ass," I muttered.

I tried to push away from Billy the Razor, but the man held me solid. I flopped around, going nowhere, getting angry. I thought of my brief meeting with Tiny and Frank the day before, how they wanted me to play a donkey for the Christmas party. Dominic the Donkey, Santa's Sicilian helper. What assholes. What asses.

"I'm not a donkey," I said. "You're the donkey."

"What did you call me?"

"A donkey," I said. It was true. They all were, all those Outfit guys. Wasn't that true? Dr. Bhittani had gone on and on about dimensions. All possible realities where anything was possible. So somewhere, somehow, there was a different sort of Earth, and all the Outfit guys were donkeys on that Earth. I knew it was true as soon as I thought it up. Giggling, I turned away from the Razor. He wasn't laughing. That was fine.

If I looked hard enough, I could see them. All those donkey-faced Outfit guys kicking around.

Can you see them?

Billy the Razor yelled and gripped his head. Fat, furry ears jutted from the sides of his scalp. His yell devolved into high, nasal braying joined by wet crackling sounds. He doubled over, bones breaking, twisting. Skin greying like old fencing. Teeth jutted from his skull, and his jaw dropped horribly to accommodate them. Clothes tore and pulled apart as different sections of his body shrank and grew. Within seconds, Billy the Razor was kicking at empty air, a donkey in what remained of a leather jacket.

"Jesus!" I crawled onto the prep station to escape the donkey's flailing hooves. The hooded figures raised their hands, chanting excitedly as Billy the Donkey bucked again and ran down the hall. The door to Frank's office burst open, and two more donkeys kicked their way out. One had a fuzzy knit cap stuck over one ear while the other was older and fatter and furious. He snapped at Billy the Donkey's leather jacket. Together, the three rammed their way through the barn doors into the restaurant, where they whined and brayed and stomped through tables.

I giggled. I'll admit it.

The hooded figures regained their composure. Dr. Bhittani said, "Get him!" They came at me, grabbed my arms and jacket and even the roots sticking out of my back. I struggled against the many hands, but it didn't matter. They pulled me to the white star, and I thought this must be what a pig or a lamb felt like right before it was slaughtered.

Thrown to the ground, I didn't have the strength to stand up. I closed my eyes and felt the roots curl around my body protectively. I was weak as a kitten and used that time to second-guess myself. Had I turned the Outfit guys into donkeys? Or was the potato poisoning my body and mind? Was I still back in my apartment, maybe writhing on the kitchen floor? Having a stroke or a seizure or something because of the damned potato?

Dr. Bhittani approached me slowly, her voice full of wonder. "I see you, Elder. And it is as though I have known you my entire life." She raised her dusty, leather-bound book. "Behold the coming of the Elder! The Living Darkness! The Wandering Cosmos!"

What the hell was this, now? Obviously, all those fools in hoods were just as messed up as I was.

Then something happened.

From beyond the kitchen, a new and altogether different voice spoke to me from nowhere and everywhere. My eyes shot open. The sound was like a tuning fork striking my soul. I had no idea what it was saying. The voice spoke in no language I had ever heard. Its whispers were a language human ears could not understand, yet I knew it was talking to me.

"Hello?" I said. But that wasn't quite it. While I was using words, the voice was communicating in some way new and strange.

I tried to push aside the sound and sight of the hooded figures and focus on that voice. I searched for a sound that was not a sound. It was something like trying to fly in a dream. If only I could forget that what I was trying to do was impossible, then maybe I would be able to do it.

There on the ground, I peered into the darkness behind my eyelids. From somewhere deep inside but wholly apart from me, something looked back. Curled on the floor, holding my huge potato-tumor, new roots curling about my body like mother's arms, my mind worked the problem as I would a lock. Carefully. Delicately. I closed my eyes and poked and prodded and found the tumblers, saw how they would line up. And then I saw how the lock could open.

The sensation was like learning how to crawl. Or speak. Or realizing what all that plumbing between my legs was for. It opened up whole new realms of possibility.

In my mind, I unlocked the potato. That's the only way I can describe it. Just lying on the ground, madness all around as I unlocked the potato. I found new locks within myself and forged new keys. The locks were endless.

But I had the keys.

Oh.

Weird.

AFTER SOME TIME, I pushed myself to my knees. I refocused my eyes, but the world was wet paint bleeding together.

Dr. Bhittani was speaking. "The Kansas City Outfit was a big help here."

"While they lasted," the hood named Jeremy said.

The voices were not close. I blinked, and the world congealed in front of me. Dr. Bhittani pulled knives from a drawer on the other side of the kitchen. A cleaver went to one of her followers. A boning knife to another. She handed the redhead a bread slicer.

Interesting. Very interesting.

"We don't need the whole brane. Just a decent chunk of it," Dr. Bhittani said.

"Are you sure?" The redhead asked.

Dr. Bhittani raised the book. "Did you read the last chapter, Helen? Or did I?"

They all turned toward me. I just stood there, looking at my alabaster feet. Wondering how long it took for frostbite to set in. My jacket was torn, shot through with thick roots and bulging tubers. But all those new growths were dwarfed by the one on my stomach.

A man with a beard broke ranks and raised a carving knife. His voice was loud and self-important. "Great Tohrvo Xitalu, I will free you from that vessel of meat."

Couple things caught my attention there. First, the whole idea of freeing something, namely the potato, from a meat vessel, probably my body, while waving a knife. That didn't seem like a good night at the movies.

Second, there was the name. Tohrvo Xitalu. I had never heard it before, but the voice from the potato clued me in. Tohrvo Xitalu, also called the Many-Eyed, the One Who Stretches. Neither god nor demon, but something altogether above and beyond those concepts. Something like a potato.

A potato that was very comfortable living in my stomach. One that felt like it had always been there.

Next...

Hold up.

How can I put this?

Next, the potato's eyes began to open.

The bearded man held the knife upside down like someone who had seen a few movies and taken notes. He snorted through his nose, muttering to himself. Building himself up. Then he stepped over the white line of custard and ran for me.

Roots leapt to life from my side and grabbed the man's arm. He yipped like a struck puppy. The roots twisted his hand around and forced it to sink the carving knife into his own chest. His deep green robe grew black with blood.

I took a shuffling step forward, and the roots pushed the bearded man back. Just Tohrvo Xitalu and I working together. Best friends already.

Helen screamed and launched herself at me, hood back and red hair trailing behind her. All I had to do was put up my hand. She jerked in midair as if worked by some mad puppeteer.

I could feel the forces pulling her weight down, holding her to the Earth. Gravitational forces. Earth's mass latching on to Helen and holding her close. I felt it as sure as I had seen the honey-colored sound wave earlier. Through sheer force of will, I denied the gravitational attraction. The thing on my stomach did not care for silliness such as that. I flicked my wrist, and Helen flew across the room and slammed into a door hard enough to smash it from its hinges. The door crumpled inward with a squealing of metal on tile and breaking bone.

I dropped my swollen hands.

There was so much to see now. At once, I wondered how I could ever make sense of it all. How I had been so blind to the forces surrounding me in the first place. Microwaves and ultraviolet light and tachyon particles bounced between protons. Things I didn't have names for pulsed and streamed in the kitchen, giving weight to reality, giving the future infinite possibilities.

I leaned forward, almost doubling over. Seeing so much took a bit out of me.

Dr. Bhittani's long-bladed chef's knife clattered to the floor. She flipped through her book, flattened a page, and began to read. Something intense. Something aimed at the potato. Her words sparked in the ether, fireworks only I could see. The flames quickly guttered like dying candles.

She was chanting. Casting some sort of spell.

No. I didn't want to hear that. I rubbed my chin thoughtfully as the roots extended from my fingers and massaged my head. Me and old Tohrvo Xitalu, we were really in sync.

With eyes not my own, I saw the doctor.

Tohrvo Xitalu saw the doctor.

Together, we saw the doctor. We saw the doctor as she had once been.

She was, first, a child in a bedroom stuffed with pink and lace, which she didn't care for. Instead, she was on the floor, trying to summon demons with a circle of doll followers. Her first cult.

Cute.

Time moved around us effortlessly. We left the little girl with her dolls.

We saw her next in college, studying string theory and dabbling in psychedelics. She sat amidst textbooks and notes, sweating profusely with pupils so dilated only a faint ring of her nut-brown iris could be seen.

We loomed over her shoulder. Bulbous and misshapen. Heavy with potato. The young occultist saw us. Impossible, maybe, but she actually saw us. We extended our lumpy arms, and she gasped and mirrored our movement. Her lips raced, some incantation or song or prayer. She would talk about the moment for months to come, how she had seen God or a god or something more and had touched enlightenment for just a moment. She would seek to recreate that moment for the rest of her life.

In an instant, we left her. Then we were standing behind her in Frank Acerra's office. She was sitting with Tiny, back when he was a man and not a donkey. She was handing over her life savings, hoping the gangster could help her find an artifact she had only heard whispers of.

Not a brain, she was clarifying, but a brane. A membrane. The gangsters neither understood nor cared. She had money. That was enough.

We laid our hands on her shoulders, and she shuddered with fear and excitement. Our hands dropped. Our roots dropped. Then we were back in the kitchen, watching Dr. Bhittani read.

We felt sorry for her now. We had known her all her life, after all. She was just trying to take control of her destiny, which was what Shawn Allen was trying to do when he stole the dumb potato in the first place.

(No offense, Tohrvo.)

(None taken.)

We wanted to control our destiny. We couldn't blame her for trying to do the same. But she was reading some weird words. Old words. Words we didn't like. Words we had not heard in centuries. Words which turned and twisted and tried to bind us. Words that the pasty white star on the floor knew and responded to in ways we disapproved of. We did not want to hear the end of her prayer, her song, her incantation. We controlled our destiny. After all, today was a new day. The first day of the rest of our life.

We inclined our head slightly and brought her Somewhere Else. The nightmare place was as it was, as it always is. The valley held jagged towers of black and indigo stone. Winged creatures and other, stranger things crawled and slithered. They were horned and toothed, fighting or rutting in the shadows of the great spires.

Dr. Bhittani gasped. She beheld. Her zealot's eyes were full of tears, her book forgotten. She dropped it and fell to her knees in front of us. "Thank you for showing me this beautiful place," she said. Something swooped over us. She recoiled and bit her lip. "But couldn't we go back to the kitchen now?"

Above us, the red sky filled with black shredded wings. The flying dinosaurs had found us, as we knew they would. One swooped low and lashed out with a razored claw, nicking Dr. Bhittani's arm. She yelped and gripped her torn robe. They had tasted her and would be at her now. And she would not be as lucky as Frank had been. We ignored her and thought we should move on.

The part of us that was, and is, and always will be Tohrvo Xitalu was having thoughts too complicated for a human to understand, so we won't confuse you by trying to explain.

The part of us that was Shawn Allen thought, what couldn't he do now? The possibilities were endless. Couldn't he really make something of himself? Couldn't he just step back in time? Just to, say, a year ago? Or five?

Couldn't he fix a thing or two?

He left Dr. Bhittani there, ignoring her as she begged. The echoes of her screams followed him, but only for a moment.

IT WAS cold as hell the day Shawn Allen decided to rip off the Kansas City Outfit. He was hunched over the grill in his worn red Kansas City Chiefs parka. Wind whipped through the coals as they flared from grey to angry red.

We could not quite understand what Shawn wanted. Humans. Who can guess?

At any rate, this wasn't it.

THE DOOR to the closet was crooked in its frame. A yellow rectangle of light cut the black space in front of us. We stared at the thin line of light and caught our breath.

Out in the living room, we could hear Vicky and Devon fighting or rutting.

Shawn shook his head. He didn't want to be there.

That was fine.

We could be anywhere we wanted.

IT WAS FALL, and he was outside. He was laughing, then coughing as he choked on cigarette smoke. Gale was next to him. She was fresh from her shift at Quick Trip, drinking Coke in a bottle and finishing some story about a regular who hid pornographic magazines in the ceiling tiles of a gas station bathroom.

We looked at Gale with all our eyes. We liked her.

SHAWN WAS CUTTING potatoes in the prison kitchen. He was behind, had been late for his shift. Inmates in tan jumpsuits were streaming into the mess hall, wondering where their hash browns were. Why weren't they ready?

A thousand moments became one within us. We chopped furiously, without skill or patience, as potato bits flew. We didn't even stop when we cut off Shawn's middle and index fingers at the bone.

Why were we here? Why relive a life he had already known? A life we already knew?

Blood and starchy flesh flew. Our knife had a mind of its own, cutting man and potato both, making hash of us all.

Breaking us down to our component parts.

Wasn't that better?

We took some time, Shawn Allen and Tohrvo Xitalu, and put ourselves back together.

THE FEW REMAINING cult members were huddled in the corner of the kitchen upon our return. When they were initiated under the tutelage of Dr. Bhittani, they were doing little more than playing dress-up. They were mostly after cheap thrills and rituals involving elaborate sexual acts and psychotropics. The doctor was the true believer of the bunch. The one who did the research. The rest of them had not really reckoned with the enormity of what they were pursuing. They thought they were playing some sort of game.

We could have killed them. Painfully or painlessly, we could have ripped them from reality itself. The idea spoke to our heart, our deepest being. That was the Shawn Allen in us. And Shawn Allen was still reeling from the enormity and entirety of being us.

Even in the nearly empty kitchen, we saw that the world around us was complete. Bursting with unseen forces, matter and antimatter, and stranger forces beyond that. We saw spaces between atoms, and in those spaces, we saw doors to other spaces. Not just Somewhere Else, but an endless multiverse of Somewheres.

Dark things moved through time and space unknowable. Stars flared briefly and collapsed into pits of inescapable gravity no more than faint moonlight filtered through the deepest oceans. Universes expanded until they were stretched as thin as balloon skin that tore and burst and fluttered down into a thousand new universes. We saw it all.

Whatever was still human in Shawn Allen gave himself over to the infinite. It wasn't easy breaking away from his past. Breaking free like that. Pulling himself from the world he had always known, and into the expanse we knew best: the pulsing rhythms of the cosmos. The Kansas City Outfit wanted him to play a donkey. Now he was a god.

This kitchen was nothing, a collection of crude matter against the gleaming towers and castles and metropolises that were the multiverse. We decided to pull it down. Roots smashed through the ceiling tile and found the beams and joists there. Others pierced the drywall and found studs.

Our feet were useless. Our legs were bulbous and bloated, pale green things riddled with lavender divots. Our old body finally betrayed us, and we fell, but our roots caught us and held us up like a strange dark web. What remained of our heart stopped pumping blood to our brain. We did not need such things as blood or bone or starchy flesh. Not anymore.

The roots buried themselves in the grease-stained ceiling. Walls pulled, retracted, and retreated back to our old body with a yawning growl. With them came every stud and beam supporting Jino's Classic Italian Restaurant and Trattoria. The sound was so loud that it filled our dying ears until the thunder of the collapsing building became a long, soothing breath exhaled in a dark room.

The last thought Shawn Allen's dying brain had was this: one day at a time, and today was the day.

Our first thought, having bound ourselves together completely, finite man and infinite Tohrvo Xitalu entwined, was this: all days are one.

GALE FINISHED her shift at Quick Trip and walked down the street to see how clean-up was going. The old Italian restaurant had collapsed a week before, killing numerous employees and customers. That was a shame. The place had been there for like fifty years or something.

It had stopped snowing, but the sidewalk was covered in a thin crust of ice. What remained of the restaurant was blocked off with green privacy fencing.

She had to admit, she would miss the sausages. The funny guy who used to grill them, she would miss him, too. But if she was honest, she might miss the sausages more.

As she passed the restaurant, she glanced at the spot where Shawn used to lean over his grill and smoke and chuckle. Something was sticking out of the snow. It was thin and brown and fibrous.

Grunting, Gale leaned over for a better look. With gloved hands, she pushed the snow away and pulled it up. She stood, lips pursed, examining her find. The brown thing was a long root that led to a strange tuber, pale and sickly green. And it was covered with dozens of tiny lavender eyes.

It looked like a potato, she thought.

VII

Okay, not gonna lie, all this talk about potatoes has made me hungry. I wonder what space vegetables taste like? Is a potato even a vegetable? It's more of a starch, I suppose, though I don't think starch is a food group, so…anybody reading this a nutrition-ist? We got a nutritionist in the house? Yeah, I didn't think so, that sounds way too classy for what I'm putting down here.

Our next story is about a girl; an actress, specifically. And man, lemme tell ya, the trips this chick goes on are literally out of this world; the sort that acid would go on if acid did acid. By the way, did I tell you about the time I snuck into a party at Andy Warhol's? I did?! Damn, sorry about that. There are some serious gaps in this memory of mine. But that's to be expected when you've partied with Andy Warhol like I have. Did I ever tell you about that?

The actress is part of a brand-new show on some channel that's a parody of the CW but isn't. I wonder if CW is regional? Like, certain of you may have no idea what I'm talking about if that's the case. Remember before CW when it was WB, and they had Michigan J. Frog introduce, like, every show? How did that not single-handedly carry that company?! Once upon a time, I'd have told you that frog could sell anything. He once sold my grandfather an insurance policy; saw it with my own two eyes, I did. And this was during those moments when he doesn't even speak English and just croaks like an actual frog. It was one of the more impressive displays of salesmanship I've ever seen, and you're talking to someone who knows a thing or two about jiving for a quick buck.

Now while I sit here and think up more brilliant Get Rich Quick schemes, you go enjoy The Girl who Punched God.

THE GIRL WHO PUNCHED GOD

EMMA JUN

"Q uiet on the set! We're ready to roll."
     The Assistant Director paced alongside the fake ruins of New York.

"Wait," I huffed, adjusting the straps on the ridiculous, porno-looking commando uniform for the millionth time. "Who are these green guys again?" I indicated the man in a ridiculous skintight body-suit. He hunched beside me on top of a collapsed building as if he was having trouble touching his toes. Two white rods with table tennis balls on their ends stretched out of his hands.

"That's Gary from SFX, Mai," said the A.D. I forgot his name. Tim, maybe? From this height, I could almost fail to notice his paunch.

"I know who it *is*. Sorry, Gary."

"No problem. By the way, I loved you in *The Girls.*"

"Not now, Gary," I whispered. Then to Maybe-Tim, "Is he one of the squiggly tentacle guys or the big, goat head one?"

"Page 39, Mai. We haven't got long."

He retreated into the gloom behind the stage lights as if that was an answer.

I was rushed onto the set and hadn't had time to check the script. 90% of my work was to scream and run from things, so I could wing it. However, if possible, I wanted to avoid staring into a goat dude's crotch.

"I'm a tentacle monster," Gary whispered.

"Thank you."

The shot was simple. My role was to retreat to the chopper, which would be CG'd in later, of course, and protect the scientist who was going to save the world. See, Tim? I did know which page.

Gary shook his ball-sticks while advancing, an impressive feat considering he had to shuffle across polystyrene rubble that simulated exploded buildings. I backed off, performing as if trying to hold it together through the terror. "We're not gonna make it!"

One of the scientists replied on cue. "We have to. We're the only ones who know–"

The nerdy, straight, white dude who had been in multiple Oscar-winning period dramas had a ball-stick extended toward him. The squibs in his fluffy, white wig exploded; they'd CG out his head later. He flopped to the rubble. I screamed fake surprise that morphed into fake rage as I whirled my gun around and pulled the trigger. He responded with lolloping flinches.

A civilian cried out behind me. "He was the only one with the formula for dimensional travel."

My gun empty, I threw it down to the rubble. "I'm gonna punch the alien so hard I'll rip a hole through the dimensions!" and pulled back my fist.

"Cut!" Possibly-Tim yelled. "Let's reset and go again."

Again! I thought we were supposed to be rushing this. The dead scientist rose like a classic vampire, triggering laughs from the civilians but receiving an eye roll from me. I unfastened the ammo straps that attempted to part my heavily padded lack-of-breasts.

"What the fuck, Gary?" I eyeballed him. He shrugged his sticks.

Below, two black-suited, middle-aged guys, probably producers, shifted like robots as they approached Possibly-Tim. After a quick exchange, Tim said:

"Take a break. Stay nearby."

"Nobody cares, Tim," I huffed.

I attempted to find my P.A., Mary. Tall, wiry, redheaded Mary. If she wasn't the company-sponsored punching bag for my personal problems....

She waited, holding a coffee that I hoped was more Irish than Dylan Moran.

"I thought this was virus shit."

She handed me the cup. "I heard ratings."

"Ratings? We only aired one show." I sniffed the cup. Nope. Teatotal coffee. A crying shame.

Mary edged her glasses down her nose, probably to dissipate the coffee fog but with the unexpected side effect of having me fall in love with her.

"Two. Last night."

"Are they gonna keep changing the schedule? That's not a good sign. If fans can't find us, this show ain't gonna last."

She flashed a pitying look. "It was Sunday last time."

Stay down, feelings.

I nodded into my coffee. "I knew it was a mistake going head-to-head with the EBO shows. *Game of Bones* and Tom Oliver's *The Week That Was...*" I sipped. "Too much."

"Doesn't matter," she said like it wasn't my career at risk. "It's blowing up."

"I thought you said it was a ratings problem."

"Ratings, yes. Problem, no. Ten bucks says that's what they are talking about."

"A week's wages..." I eyed her to see her reaction and no other reason at all. "You must be confident."

I RETIRED to my trailer to play Spot the Script Changes. Why stand around a cold set when such comfy beanbags waited? Yeah, I know, but I'd had them since kindergarten. Not these particular ones; that would be abhorrent. I set the coffee on the table and collapsed.

"Jesus fu–!" I yanked at the last strap of ammo that just tried to hollow me out and threw it across the room.

Mary stood over me like a scolding parent. I kinda liked that, too.

"The hashtag started trending in week one."

A good buzz? Awful outfits aside, maybe this character would connect with people and net me some influence around here. It was a good show.

I stretched for my phone and logged into Chirper.

"'Another Asian character fulfilling a white man's fantasy?" I quoted. "What is this?"

Mary shrugged. Good buzz for the show, maybe; not so much for the minority lead.

"'Just waiting for that white savior to save her from herself? I am the savior!'"

"It's early days. The twists haven't…" Mary began.

"What do they want? I'm the hero saving the world. There's an authentic backstory in episode one. How could I be any more of a role model?!"

"It's just the critics….and well, the fanbase." She shifted under my most lethal laser-free stare. "You know. It's okay to be a fan, but 'fanbase' is quite the opposite, like an army of gremlins attacking the studio to get what they want." She made the cutest grabbing gesture, like a squirrel biting into a dangling nut. That took the edge off. "But the studio loves that feedback. Helps them with–"

"Ratings." I couldn't help looking at my phone. "Is there anything good about me?"

"Yes. Most critics love it. And you. Lots of positive chirps. The worst are always the most vocal."

"'Die, bitch, die. You should go back to China,'" I read off my phone. "I'm fucking Japanese!"

Mary took the phone and threw it on a beanbag. "You don't need that. The Internet is crazy, and you know it."

I blinked up at her, confused by two totally different, inappropriate thoughts.

"Right. Right. It's early days," I repeated to signal my attentiveness.

"And it gets better."

"And it gets better."

She picked up the coffee and handed it to me.

"On second thought…I'll get you some tea."

Typically, I despised tea. Mary could clearly influence me. "Always looking out."

"Lord knows you don't do it yourself."

Oh yeah? I swore I'd prove her wrong…until evening. I tried to wind down but instead got wound up. More stupid chirps on the hashtag. There was no one to stop me.

Do any of you know how hard it is to find a good job in Hollywood as a minority star, esp. a *woman* in a minority? (1/?)

The show isn't perfect, but we have the best team working on an amazing script, and this "Asian whore" is saving the world. Take that, incels. (2/?)

You can try and take me down but leave the show out of this. Season one will blow your minds! [bloody head explosion gif] #qualia (end).

My phone rang first thing in the morning. "Mom," I croaked. "You know I'm shooting late."

"He's in the hospital again." Her snippy voice preceded a sigh. "It was only a matter of time."

The grief swirled around me like ice-cold water invading a long-tepid bath. We staggered through a short conversation as I held the tears in.

A single thought had aided me through the early days of his illness: there had to be something better. Only now, there wasn't time for that. Through streaming tears, I punched the pillow until fatigue swallowed me.

I couldn't deal with this. The nearest distraction was my phone, and I buried my head in chirps as an off-screen machine gun fired-off notifications. Likes for stuff I didn't recognize, replies to replies to replies, and…fans fighting.

Fuck that.

Instasnap, on the other hand, was always full of love. I reeled in the hearts thanks to the makeup and costume reveal. It was like I'd dipped my modest tits in honey. I ate it up like sherbet and found a sprinkle of happiness again — right before my phone glitched. Never mind. I could get through another day now.

THE NEXT SCENE was earlier in the narrative. I was to rescue a scientist from a gothic, monster-infested laboratory. At least, that's what my script said. When I got there, the set seemed to think it was a spaceship. The walls were white and lustrous, like living in a mePhone.

Picturing what wasn't there was part of the job, but this was like reverse I. I had missed a rewrite; that had to be it. The grey, warehouse-like building of the studio lot hadn't changed, at least.

Gary was chatting with some of the crew. "Still tentacles today?" I asked. He nodded, then returned to his conversation.

Mary waited with my coffee. She looked like a contemporary librarian on the Starship Enterprise. Just imagine, we could travel the stars and hold philosophical discussions about books...

"Did they not dress the set yet, or have I got the wrong page again, Tim?" I yelled across the set.

"It's the same page," said Mary. "Thirty-two. The starship board and rescue." She thrust the coffee in my face. "You shouldn't have sent those chirps. It's aggravated the fanbase."

I nodded guiltily. "I did a me."

"Well, now they've made it a big deal and added another meeting. You have to go."

"That bad?" I whistled for effect.

"After this shoot." Her stare struck deep within me like an arrow at a target. The recording lights clicked on, and people immediately coursed around us. The cameraman swung his bulky machinery around. Just as fast, the studio backlights clicked off. Mary flicked her head in the direction of the set. "Looks like they're ready."

"Page 32, right?"

I secured my weapons in their holsters.

Nobody looked ecstatic when I arrived at the meeting room to find five board members with faces like they had drank from the wrong cup of Christ. The director (was that Tim?), producer Alex (who I knew because he had hit on me five times before I'd even got the part), and a secretary I didn't recognize. She was the typical blonde and ponytailed target of harassment that they brought into places like this, the only one not seated around the glass table. She was ready to record everything I said on her AirBook. I took the seat nearest the door.

"Mai, I know you're busy."

Universal business speak for "you don't work hard enough" from the head of the studio. Suits and deadpan went together like scientists and ethical questions. "Regarding the social media problem, I hope you realize such behavior damages everyone at the studio."

Shields at maximum. Wait your turn, Mai.

"In these incidents, it's standard procedure for us to issue a statement that these are your personal views and not representative of the studio or its employees."

"Of course. That's why it's my Chirper account," I said too soon.

"You must be more careful how your actions reflect on us. More specifically, your comments about lead roles for minority–"

He'd pressed the red button. "How is that your problem? I said you were doing it right."

"If you give a seed to the soil, you get an oak tree." He puffed out his words like a dragon. "Your comment was vague enough that it left the door open for the speculation of the Internet. Which is worldwide. As you would have noticed if you read the thousands of replies and rechirps."

They weren't going to shift blame onto me. Besides, wasn't all publicity good publicity? "I never got the rewrites. Is that some form of punishment for this Chirper thing?" I asked while producing sweaty handprints on the glass table.

The head turned to one of his subordinates and asked, "Have there been any rewrites?"

"We discussed some changes yesterday. However, they aren't due to take place until episode seven."

If I could have eye-rolled my entire head, I would have. "Why has the green screen budget gone up?"

The boss glanced to the side again and noted shaking heads.

He grimaced. "Though it's not my business what you get up to in your trailer, I suggest you keep a clear head if it's affecting your performance."

Something crushed my skull from the eyebrows inward. "What the hell!"

His brow collapsed too. "That's enough. Unless you'd like to be even more of a minority."

The blonde didn't type that last part.

Anger cut me like starvation. The room became a laser grid of stares. I wanted to throw the glass table to the wall. I inhaled the fire and hoped it wouldn't roast my organs.

If Mary had been in the hall to console me with coffee, that would have been perfect. No sign of her, though. Maybe she didn't know me as well as I had hoped. Or perhaps she really was pissed.

Riding the elevator down, I checked the damage on Chirper. Oh boy. The pings of notifications rang like a gunshot in the confined space. The 99+ on the bell icon swelled like a rotten scab about to pop. As I swiped across from the likes to display messages only, the elevator lights flickered.

"Who does she think she is?"

"Just a male fantasy with a woman's skin."

"This show sucks. They haven't made anything good since they canceled *Lanternfly*."

I thrust the phone into my jacket pocket.

Back in my trailer, I collapsed straight into my beanbag and tapped the phone screen before my butt hit beans. "Listen here, you—" I hesitated before deleting the text. "May I reiterate that all chirps are my own and do not reflect the studio or any of its employees." I hit send after attaching a gif of my character shooting an eldritch monstrosity with a deluge of gore. Within seconds there was a ping.

"Her name is Mai, and she started the chirp "may..."" laughing monkey gif.

They didn't even know how to pronounce my name. A few likes. More comments.

"Show us your tits. Oh, that's right, you don't have any cos you're Asian. #KungFlu"

"Cancelled" Coffin lowered gif.

My anger exploded but froze just as quickly when the screen jumped. Texts and images squished into a small space, and I half-expected a hydraulic press animation. Rainbow colors glitched like a unicorn puking on my phone before quickly returning to normal.

The new MePhone was out soon. At least now I had an excuse to buy it.

The lights in my trailer flickered. I would've gotten the tech guys to fix it, but they seemed to hate me, too. Instead, I put my phone on the side cabinet and prepared a cup of tea.

I reached for the electric kettle when something scuttled from behind, too thick to be a spider, too dark to be a rat. It ran off the counter to the beanbag, which I promptly lifted before fear corralled me. Nothing.

I couldn't sleep if I knew there was a spider in the room. Was nothing a relief? It had to be a mouse, moving so fast, but I had only the photo in my mind for reference. I picked up a knife from the kitchenette; it had to have gone to the bed space. My sheets were always a crumpled mess, as though an anthill for bed bugs. The creature could be poised in any curve or crease. I kicked the sheets off with a clumsy sweep of my leg, proving that those martial arts videos had taught me nothing. I found nothing more than breadcrumbs underneath.

A tickle at my ankle became like a bony finger sinking into my skin. I pushed back reflexively with the other leg and toppled over when a bang came at my door.

"Mai? What's wrong? Unlock the door." Mary. Had I screamed? I couldn't remember.

Before me, a black mass writhed like oil seeping out of a hole in space. I couldn't focus on it, but I could *feel* it — one sentient creature in the presence of another. My phone lay next to me, where a notification from Qualia read, "Shipment received." I scrambled to unlock the door, and the inky creature followed when Mary entered. I tried not to look so shaken. She had never seen me in any state other than anger or elation. Fear was something new — for both of us.

She scanned me. "Are you okay?"

"Course. My phone glitched out on me, that's all."

She glared at me. "Just as well if you were on Chirper again. The studio doesn't need your help publicizing the show. They have a team for that."

"Yeah …" I said, forming a plastic smile. My one reassurance was that Mary hadn't freaked out. "Tea?"

I stood by the counter and tried to have a normal conversation, but it seemed impossible. "Sit down," Mary said, watching me fidget. My mind screamed "MONSTER" like it hadn't since childhood. "I'm fine. I need the exercise."

My life had become its own TV show, and I didn't know how to change the channel. I had to follow the script and hope things turned out all right in the end. But I was concerned about the ratings.

EVERY MOMENT IN BED, I lay keenly aware of scuttering in the darkness, waiting for the sensation of sludge on my skin as the only person in the universe. Dawn eventually came and, with it, an early setup for which I had read the script during one of my clearer moments. I had no qualms about the freezer scene. Three soldiers were trapped there by a scientist who didn't trust us yet, and we had to escape after failing to persuade him.

I fought with my military gear and then staggered to make up and collapsed in the chair. I slept there for a while, in the warmth of other people. It felt safe.

"You didn't sleep," I heard Mary say. "Time to go. Espresso?" She thrust a small cup at me. I swigged it down and followed her. I felt like I had a pus-filled ring cinched around my skull. My tunnel vision was worthy of a cross-Atlantic tunnel. "Mary!" I blurted out.

She jumped. "What's wrong with you?"

"You're so far away." Why was the backstage cast dressed like Japanese mascots, all fluffy spheres and exaggerated smiles on bobble-heads? The set itself was a candy-covered nightmarescape.

Mary stopped me in the middle of it all and left. Lights pinned me to the stage. People stared from outside the vignette. I put a hand to my head and realized something was there — a bucket with carpeting around it, like some mascot freak. Whose prank was this?

Thirty screaming kids rampaged the set and clawed at my costume, which was no longer military at all but a cushioned monster suit. I shouted back and kicked at them to escape. "Is this some Last Wish shit no one told me about?" The board's idea of a joke. I fucking hated kids. I wouldn't put it past them.

"Mai," Maybe-Tim called pitilessly. "This is your show. Save the rants for private time. Now do the Goro-Goro dance before the candy set melts."

Were they serious? What would happen if I didn't comply? I hoisted up the nearest brat and, without care for his wiggling legs, dumped him like Internet Explorer, but the tide of kids kept coming. Caring less and less about crushed toes, I lunged for the camera. "You can't do this. Everything I've worked for…"

"This is your job." Maybe-Tim raised his arms, the international symbol for 'what are you gonna do?'

I pushed back from the camera, ignoring the lumps of bodies around me. I looked for Mary, who at least spoke my language, but the situation nosedived as the chaos settled into a sound I couldn't unhear. "Qualia." The kids stopped and chanted, like a video dubbed over with the call of Cthulhu. "Qualia!" Adults joined the chorus, herding me back to center stage as I lumbered blindly for an escape.

This had to be a dream. I'd soon wake up in the trailer with the slime bug on my face, screaming. Until then, I had nothing to fear. I could punt Tim's ugly hipster face into the sun and shit on the producer's desk, and they'd still greet me with fake smiles tomorrow.

"Fuck Qualia!" My battle cry. "Now listen to me, you dick-stunted little shits!" I yelled away the dizziness and fear until they were quiet, then made them wait longer. I punched the nearest man in the face. "Qualia that!"

The crowd erupted. Someone caught the unlucky guy as he toppled, while others ran away. The rest of the mob restrained me, shouting my name as if I were the crazy one. Crazy would have been to stop swinging. I charged after anyone who stood in my way, leaving a sea of snot-nosed brats behind me. After the third or fourth punch, security guards arrived. Maybe there was a weapon — a taser, perhaps — because everything soon went black.

Consciousness discovered me again, but not in my trailer; the chandelier gave it away. I always told people it was crystal, and if they didn't know better, it was.

Ah, my house. I swiveled out of bed. Had I dreamed the whole kid's TV show or was it just that last one? Too much stress had made my dreams anxious again. At least I had some fun with it. But I was home now. Beige I. Minimalist. Joyco Pop collection in the cabinets. The familiar.

Coffee. I stumbled to get myself together, picking up my phone from the bedside table on the way to the kitchen. How was–

Scritch. Scritch.

The phone rang in my hand. "Hello?" I croaked.

"There she is." Mary sounded chipper, further evidence I'd been dreaming. She would not have approved of me punting tiny children across a TV set.

"Where else would I be?" In the kitchen, I fumbled for the coffee jar.

"Obviously not on set. I've been forced to take a holiday because of you."

"Oh?" I paused because *this* made my heart jump. Perhaps I got her in trouble?

"I guess I needed it. Not sure when I last had one."

I breathed again and almost bumped my head on the open cabinet door. "There's a lot of that going around," I muttered. "While I've got you, has the studio announced the changes yet?"

"Changes?" The tone was gentle, but it shrieked in my brain.

"Yeah…the script changes." Hurry up, coffee.

"No. Just a general concern about you fainting on set. They rearranged the shooting schedule to give you a break. They're going to get retakes and B-roll. That's why I called."

Collapsed on set? "That's generous." The water bubbled in the kettle.

"Don't be too forgiving. It's mostly the new virus regulations. They want to be certain you aren't going to spread infection."

I slammed the cabinet door. "It's not the virus. Just a bit foggy. Listen, can you send the latest script over? I'd like to get accustomed to it."

"Sure, I'll bring it over later," she said with a twinkle. Not sure how she managed that over the phone. And then she hung up before I could fuck up what I thought might be flirting.

"Mary. It's shit like that that keeps me guessing." I filled the cup of instant coffee, looked for a spoon, and immediately got a text message. "And stay away from social media, okay?" Stern face emoji, smiley. "Qualia!"

Huh, so the Chirper rants happened, too. At least the jigsaw was clicking into place. I made out with my coffee mug for a few minutes and then danced off to find a suitably oversized hoodie and sweatpants. Duvet days were the best.

I jumped over the back of the sofa and landed on something so cold that I thought I'd become incontinent. On instinct, I wanted to launch it to space. My hand wrapped around a solid lump of dry ice. I immediately wanted to recoil but thought it might tear my skin off. I began to panic. Numbness spread. The world's most hi-tech camera would have had trouble adjusting to the utter darkness of what I held; no way that was a sofa cookie. It lashed out with inky tentacles, and I launched it. Come in, Houston. It squelched to the floor, flipped over, and scrambled away like a metallic slick of oil pulled by a powerful magnet.

A sound like a Halloween grew to a cacophony before countless ebony squids oozed out of cracks in the wall. I broke from my silent terror and dashed for the front door, hoping my feet found space between the growing flood of twitching darkness.

What the fuck was this? An impromptu casting call?

One of the creatures fell from the ceiling to my shoulder. The cold burn caused me to stagger, and it, too, lost balance and flopped to the floor. I yanked the door handle, only it was now a warm hand, one that belonged to Mary. Her body spun into mine like we had just finished a passionate dance. "Oooh, I'm sorry," she cooed. "I lost my balance. You never told me you could dance." She smiled into my confusion, making it doubly so. Her hair was tied up in a loose bun. She wore earrings. A real dress.

"I didn't tell you a lot of things," I said.

We were in a bar. Framed pictures hung alongside tastefully purple décor while wooden shelving displayed various knick-knacks and vinyl sleeves. Lo-fi beats and acoustic guitar notes drifted from the ceiling. Certainly an improvement, but had someone just turned two pages at once? Because color me interested in exactly how we got here.

"What is this place?" I asked.

"Qualia," she said while leading me by the hand to a bar stool. I didn't fight it.

"And then these things started falling from the ceiling..."

She furrowed a brow. "What things? Sounds like renovation problems. Tell me about the movie."

I regarded her like I hadn't already discovered we were dating. She had a fairy glow. "Movie?" I asked, acutely aware of how hard she squeezed my hand. "Or should we get more drinks first?" She glided through the door and left me alone in the bar's side room. My brain blinked. A door swung open. Panic struck. Warmth gushed. The second-floor landing of my house congealed out of spinning platelets of darkness.

Mental note: See a doctor tomorrow.

The ringing of the landline penetrated my brain fog — and my dream. One of the receivers had its own antique table that overlooked the modest entrance.

"Hello?"

No voice. Rasps, maybe. My brain took too long to comprehend. There might have been crying.

"He's gone." Mother's voice croaked.

"Dad?" I gripped the phone. Something vile leaped up my throat. My eyes dissolved.

"He's gone now." The minutes were marked by sobbing.

"Did he ...?"

"His sleep, thank the heavens. He always wanted it so." She paused a moment. In the silence, a scuttling sound. "He's always wanted to go 'round Europe." Her voice was suddenly cheery, something I hadn't heard since his diagnosis. "So, we're going this spring." If I wasn't awake before, I was now. "On a cruise," she continued. "We're going this spring. The virus thing will be over and–"

"Mom!" I screamed at her across the phone. I'd previously encountered guilt trips, but this qualified as trauma. "He's dead."

"That's a terrible thing to say! Especially after his scare last year with the false diagnosis. Aya, why would you say such a thing?"

Finally, my wall of grief was pierced. Sunlight streamed through the bay windows. It banished the witching hour that had haunted me mere moments ago. There was less chance of me crying magic tears than Dad entering remission without aid. Yet here we were. Whatever was wrong, it wasn't me.

The *world* had changed.

"Qualia. I thought you'd like the good news."

"What is Qualia?!" I screamed urgently.

"Get some proper rest. You don't want to drop out of your first movie."

We hung up shortly after, but I stayed curled against the small table as if it were my anchor. Either I had been committed to an asylum long ago, or the changes were real. Not just my TV show; reality. Was there even a TV show? Was I even an actress?

Through sobs and shadows that stretched along the floor, I held on to the idea that I was still me. I would know if I changed. Surely. Someone close to me would know. Mary. She would know. I found my smartphone by the bed. I called her. Two rings, and then a male voice. I clutched the phone.

"Mary?"

"Hi, Mary. Can I help you?" he chirped.

"No. Sorry. I'm looking for Mary." No need to panic. Probably one of the assistants.

"No Mary, here. Wrong number, maybe." He hung up. I checked the number; the exact number I rang every day. She had been home on holiday where no assistant could answer her phone.

Not Mary. They couldn't take her.

I jabbed at the virtual keys on my cell and rang her again. Wait. I'd contacted her parents last spring when her bike had collided with a car. She was terrified of being Jane Doe'd in a hospital bed if it happened again. I dialed, counting the ring tones.

"Hello? Weinstein residence. Susan speaking." Her mother, I felt sure.

"Hello, Mrs. Weinstein," I blurted. "It's…er…Mai from the studio?"

"Mai? I'm sorry, my dear. I didn't think my hair appointment was till Tuesday. I don't—"

"Not a salon studio. The TV studio." She was a lovely old lady, but I was halfway up the walls, and even cats couldn't get me down. "Mary's boss. Friend."

"I'm sorry, I don't know either name. Can I help you?"

"Mary's your daughter," I snapped.

"I don't have a daughter. Have you dialed correctly, miss?"

Don't have a daughter... "Did you... lose her?" I could have choked on my mucus.

"No. Never had children. What is this about?"

"Doesn't matter." I hung up and aimed to get hungover.

But then, why could I remember her?

Steam from a kettle fogged my glasses like a very personal sauna. I let it build. Everything seemed more distant, like a movie. As the kettle clicked off, my glasses cleared like a striptease; that is to say, annoyingly slow. I splashed water into the empty cup before I realized there was no teabag. I reached up to open the top unit where one of those black blobs sat among the jars I never got around to putting home-cooked jam in.

"Oh, it's you again. Bob, is it?"

I had named them long ago to help normalize the cosmic horror of it all. They were all called Bob, and I made a point of checking every time. Don't want to dead-name a shape changer.

"What're you gonna change this time? Purple sky? I like purple. I also wouldn't mind being rich. At the least, I could use some clothes that don't smell like rotten pineapple milk." I pulled at my stained t-shirt.

Bob grew spindle legs, then crawled out of the cupboard to its underside as though gravity was a mere proposition. "Bye, then." I returned to my beverage and hoped I had time to drink the tea before it became a sasquatch.

I sipped and watched more Bobs swarm out of every nook in the kitchen. Then some bored god changed the channel on the TV set I lived in. Qualia.

Ding Dong!

The frickin' doorbell. Last time that rang, a bunch of aliens arrived for a birthday party at my house. Actual aliens. I say birthday party, but I couldn't understand them; it could have been a party for their sixteenth left toe, for all I knew. I hadn't believed they were aliens because of course not. I tried to pull off the 'masks'; luckily, this was interpreted as play and got the party off to a good start. Until they tried to take my face off, anyway. Nicolas Cage, I ain't.

I was halfway down the corridor when the front door burst open. A bunch of black-suited men filled the space as quick as oxygen, guns pointed to clear the room of the threat of me in ripe loungewear.

"Hands up!"

I did as instructed and spilled tea before asking who they were with.

"Be quiet. We're onto you. We apologize if we squash you. Come with us."

I didn't move, so they waved guns from the doorway. "No hand-cuffs?" I asked.

"I'm operating with full restraint. Don't make me shoot you," the agent said.

It was beginning to feel like a Thursday, only slightly better than a Tuesday. The car in my extended driveway was a typical black sedan, except the front was a cat face. As we drove down the road, the siren was turned on to bawl a never-ending "meow." I could only imagine the expression on its face. Definitely a Thursday.

Inside, the car was silent despite my piercing glares. We stopped at a glass office building; I wouldn't have been surprised if a giant hand holding a knife descended from the sky and cut it open to reveal it was cake, but we walked inside to find it pretty normal. Too normal. This was the most normal change in a while.

"If we took the bones out, it wouldn't be crunchy," said one of two businessmen walking past us. Okay, a little weird. The agents got pushy outside the elevator.

"Who do you work for?" I tried, stumbling inside. "So I know who to complain to."

"Only one, ma'am."

This confused me long enough to be dumped in an empty room

behind a desk. Before leaving, one of the agents pulled up a tin of paint from behind a chair and slapped some red on the featureless wall opposite me. Then he followed his coworkers outside. I waited for almost an hour — not that I minded, as I'd learned to enjoy whatever calm came my way. The paint even dried.

Two of the agents returned and gave me an eyeball. I don't know whose eyeball it was, but they laid it on the desk. It rolled a bit and then looked up at me with apparent sentience. "You've been asking the wrong questions," one of the agents said.

"I bet I have," I replied calmly. "I should have been asking you when I can leave."

"Still the wrong question," he said.

The other agent shook his head with his arms crossed. "Not even a question."

"Can I get tea or coffee?" I tried. "I never got to finish mine."

"Yes."

"Great!" I chimed, excited by the progress. "No milk, two sugars."

He swiftly burst this bubble with a cruel twist. "You may not, though." Figures. "Miss, do you know what you've done?"

I gave this considerable thought. If ever there was a loaded question. "I know what I think I've done, and I thought it, so I did it. Right?"

His partner revealed a tiny file from his fingernail, and they each pulled papers out of it. The first one showed me his. "Look, I completed this like I was asked. Check it before I give it to the boss."

"Er, okay," I said.

In neat writing, it seemed to describe how they had been issued a warrant to arrest me for being too close to the truth and how they had me detained because I was a loose cannon. But they were confused about where to put the cannonball.

"Looks great," I told him and handed it back. I hoped this would earn me the tea.

"Thanks."

The other handed me his forms, only it was the centerfold of a porn mag. He had scribbled his case details on top of it in crayon.

"This isn't very good," I said, ignoring that the centerfold was holding a beaver between her legs. It didn't seem particularly happy about it, either.

The second agent burst out crying. "I'm so bad at this!"

The first pushed him aside. "So, you wanna talk now?"

"Not really," I said. "This place is a lot comfier than the Siberian cave I was marooned in for two weeks. I can wait for my tea."

The two agents exchanged shaded glances.

"You aren't getting any tea. And I'm not telling you where the kitchenette is either."

They walked out by way of thunder noises, yet still with the attitude that I had wasted their time. Seconds later, the bad one returned with a tub of blue paint and a brush. He slapped more on the same wall next to the red and glared at me. Then, he vanished.

I told myself to get my head together. Eons had passed; it was time to go out with guns blazing. The door caved in with one kick. The people inside looked like their mothers really had slept with the fishes. Very surprised fishes. The plan was to massacre them before they became angry fish-people. The armed ones, anyway.

Searing beams of energy leaped from my laser rifles into the abandoned kitchen, illuminating it and sending perforated bodies to the floor.

Talk about Friday feeling!

Three bodies went down without a problem. Two more had webbed hands on gun handles. One shoulder vanished in wet chunks, and a torso parted like oil and soap. The last got off a predicted shot before he became holy enough to serve as the Pope. He dropped before the wounds stopped glowing.

Reinforcements clattered behind the far door. I locked it with the transmitter on my wristband, overcharged the power cell of one of my weapons, and lobbed it like a grenade. We had thirty seconds. I leaped onto the table, where the unarmed shark-head sat in its floating chair. Blue light gave its skin a slick appearance in the twilight.

"We've got about twenty seconds until the gun goes boom-boom, so you're going to tell me how to find the evil genius right now," I said

"Who?" they asked with a toothy grin.

My shit was tired of this shit. "You know who I am, so give it up."

It nodded, and water squirted out of its gills. I tried not to flinch. "They say you've lived a thousand lifetimes. All you need worry about is that I've killed worse than you." He snorted. "They are always watching." Its eyes swelled like glistening supernovas; it would have been the cutest thing if not for that needle-filled jaw. I tightened its tie. It gulped.

Sirens in the distance. "Really? You think that's going to scare me after all I've done to get here?" I said.

"They're omnipotent," the shark-head explained. "Whatever you are, you can't contest. At any moment, we could blink out of existence at their whim."

"Like this?" I yanked him out of his chair, and he crashed through the doors and into the street. The crowd, made of all kinds of life in various colors and shapes, didn't hesitate to move around him. The street was lit by microorganisms trapped inside cylindrical worlds that had been molded into advertisement signs. My cybernetic legs propelled me into the sky. The gun exploded with a red flash, vaporizing half the restaurant in a perfect dome. Unfortunately, it formed the base of an infinite vertical complex. The impossible tower groaned like a metallic whale as the streets filled with screams.

I landed on my target: the fishy one. Its guts imploded and sent a ball of visceral innards out of its mouth like a giant sewage meatball. Terrible last words. Even worse smelling.

Above, the tower collided with its neighbors, sending a terrifying thunk across the city. I screamed at the sirens, the fleeing, panicked civilians of this pointless world, and the crashing towers overhead. I pressed the button on my leg to digitize myself for escape. Any later, and they'd lock the routers to prevent it.

An hour later, I was in my favorite bar and slightly drunk on a beverage that tasted like fishy mints. At least the collapsing city hadn't destroyed this place. Purple walls. Fairy lights. Despite the fishy clientele, it resembled a bar in my memory. I hadn't seen Mary since that night, or...it didn't matter. I wasn't sure if any of this was true, and I'd been erring on the side of Nietzsche lately. What I had been experiencing was as real to me as my life was before, so best call a rose a rose.

I downed the drink, thinking about a nice chaser. Who was I

kidding? I doubted I could return to a "Webflix and chill" life anyway. I knew too much. Chiefly, I knew that I knew nothing.

I needed to know what caused all this, a task as simple as reaching inside my DNA and extracting the blueprints of the universe. I had assumed that somehow my actions in the simulation had consequences. Could I grab hold of my creator and convince him to release me? Directors tended to hate actors poking holes in their sets. I guessed I'd be the girl who would punch God in the face. It seemed a pretty universal gesture.

I paid the bar-fish and went to a rented bed-tank that I had requested be drained the previous night. However, despite the blazing sun on this swampy planet and two frogmen (literally) with motel hairdryers, they hadn't managed to completely dry the bed. I lay down with a squish in a space that could have been a closet.

Soon came darkness so cold that life was barely a concept, followed by a groan. Not warm or kind, nor anything my three-dimensional brain could describe beyond "get the fuck outta here."

"Hello?" Yes, I started my conversation with an interdimensional terror using a grand I, but it seemed the thought manifested itself without consideration.

"This is gonna sound funny, but…are you God?"

With its reply, I knew how an ant on a concert speaker felt. It was closer to cosmic resonance than a voice, yet it left the impression of language in my mind.

"Y' certainly hope nafl. Ron ah mgvulgtnah n'ghanglui."

I reeled like I'd taken a powerful punch. "Why am I….here?"

"H's product ot c' l' ah'gotha process hup ymg' lloigg. F' ahuaaah liahe pcs qualia."

"I don't understand." If it was a god, why couldn't it enunciate?

"Qualia is energy," it boomed. "Too lazy to check a dictionary?"

Qualia. Energy. It fed him. A god feeding on my life force? He…it… whatever. It had to be a dude. Just sitting around in this void, letting other people jump through the multiverse to feed him.

Such a dude.

"I'm not doing shit anymore!" I screamed.

"Calm. Have a cup of tea.'"

"No. Listen to me! I'm tired of it. I've jumped on fish-people and seen their innards pop out of their mouths. I've bungee jumped from helicopters on the pubic hairs of sky kangaroos. I've ridden in a screaming cat car to a Matrix-style interrogation written by Monty Python. And I've walked in on a mass orgy where every participant was my 4th-grade homeroom teacher. I'm not afraid of some voice in the dark. So what if you're bigger than the universe? You stop this shit now, or I'll show you what I wanted to do to all my whiney, pain in the ass Chirper followers."

The void was silent for a moment. I had the illusion of being out of breath. Something shifted. "We must generate Qualia to stave off eternity. Your cognition maintains reality."

"I'm making it?"

Silence, then: "Quiet on the set. We're ready to roll."

"He—!"

"Not now, Mai."

The voice resounded. The universe had spoken, but it sounded an awful lot like me. I blinked and suddenly found myself in a tastefully decorated house. Not one that specifically I remembered, but familiarity bled through like I.

"Okay. Not bad," I said. "Having a body and relative dimensions is nice." A wood-paneled hallway opened into a large lounge. I followed it to find men in identical sweaters chugging beers and grabbing each other in drunken expressions of repressed homosexual lust.

The only dude not wearing red was a waiter in white, who hastily dashed around to provide confections. He was a nervous-looking teenager, a freshman. This was a frat house, a recurring nightmare I had experienced for many years. All I managed was a soundless scream, a small mercy in itself, as I caught sight of the yellow and red cheerleader dress I was wearing and retched in disbelief.

This was the exact same nightmare.

"Hey, she's up!" said one of the nearest boys. I forgot retching was their morning chorus. One of them immediately offered me a drink, and I waved it away. This was the part where they got me drunk.

One of them had an exaggerated look of concern. "What's wrong?"

"Maybe your cats will make you feel better," said another. He opened a side door, and a flood of cats came pattering in, meowing for attention. He started collecting cats like they were furry beer cans and thrust one into my arms. It didn't take to the gesture nicely and clawed at my arms until it escaped over my shoulder and dived to the floor with a thud, leaving me with a face full of fur, blowing raspberries to clear my airspace. Something didn't feel right. Lips were too rubbery.

I tried to dash past the crowd to find a mirror, but my legs had swollen joints. Flares of sharp pain kicked their way into my senses. I hobbled to a large mirror at the back wall, where my same outfit now hung off an emaciated and crooked figure. I screamed. This was exactly how my mum had cursed me for my laziness and disinterest in men – to become a decrepit cat lady. I tripped, fell, and smashed my jaw on the ground. My teeth shattered painlessly, leaving me with the awful embarrassment of knowing I would never drink from a cup again.

This was turning into all the recurring dreams I had ever had. Did the god think I liked them because I had them so often? Any minute now, I'd start levitating, only to be chased by government agents who wanted the secret of flight from me. I didn't choose any of this, but perhaps the god handed me the controls.

I rolled over with broken teeth. The frat boys and the cats had gone. Only one figure remained; tall and wiry with long hair in a thin ponytail. She reached out to me, and the hand that reached back was my own.

Mary was bitter, as though I had missed an appointment. But it was her, and that's all that mattered. "You're late," she said.

"Wouldn't surprise me," I said, grinning like a spider monkey.

"And why are you wearing that?"

It seemed I was in control. "Costume change," I said, referring to the cheerleader outfit.

"I've never seen you out of your pants."

"Oh?" I loved double entendres. "Well, who knows what the future holds?"

This was all mine. It had to be. The dreams, the random SF horror concepts, B-movie rubbish; it all mushed together into one. I had a fever, and it was about it break. Or maybe I was having a psychotic break?

Qualia. There was no reality, only our experience of it.

A startled bird flew and gathered with its flock, where they danced in that mesmerizing way that gets hits on ViewTube. Then the mass of them collapsed together.

I experienced a sunset. Cosmic resonance once again washed meaning on the shores of my little island.

"You get it?" Mary asked.

I nodded, squeezed her unnaturally warm hand.

The birds gathered, infinite in number, amassed into a familiar shape. Even though I had never seen him, I knew. Who else would have a face like a lanternfish? If it was anyone else, it was a hell of a special effect.

"You're the tiniest. Hardly any effort to crush you," he said through the briny mass hiding his mouth. The god was ten feet tall and growing. Sickly green muscles bulged in a never-ending contention for space.

"I doubt that," I said.

I let go of Mary's hand. She didn't run, didn't seem to notice him. I didn't want her to, either. If I was wrong about who was in charge, it wouldn't matter. Hell, it might even be better.

He continued to grow until he filled the sky. A green twilight ushered in a new age. The elder god thrust his mighty arm to squash me, and I punched upward to meet it. If this were a dream, it would be ruled by my neuroses. I wouldn't even have made it this far. A reality controlled by an elder god wouldn't give me any control. I'd either be squished or be the queen of my own reality.

The god halted. He turned his wrist over to look at a watch. "This has been great and all, but I've got an appointment at the salon. These tentacles don't take care of themselves, you know." His voice was down to a loudspeaker now.

"Sure thing," I said casually. "I've got...well, infinity, I suppose."

He winked five of his eighteen eyes at me. "You always did, kiddo."

Why was I getting Peter Falk grandfather vibes from a tentacle monster? He turned and stomped away into nothing. I'd maybe invite him back for a game of Go if I got bored. He'd probably be pretty good at rhythm games with all those tentacles ready to press buttons.

Infinity to myself. It would take some getting used to, but then the god was correct. It always had been me. The difference was knowledge.

I imagined a notepad and a pencil, which appeared in my hands. At the top, I wrote: "Project 1: A Perfect World." I underlined it twice. Then, after consideration, I threw it into the void. "Fuck it. No one ever planned a good party."

I walked over to Mary, and she started moving again like nothing had happened.

"You have something on your face," I said like an idiot.

She looked nervous for a moment, as though the veneer had cracked. Before she could ask for a tissue, I kissed her. It was warm, with a faint hint of coffee, but I was scalding hot. She gave me a flick at the corner of my mouth. "Got it."

Clever girl. Just like me. "Now, how about sushi? I know an excellent dimension." With a wave of my hand, I tore a line in the empty air and pulled it open. "We can get some to go," I added.

The hole snapped shut behind us.

IIX

Woah, wasn't that cray-cray! I haven't been jerked around like that since I tried to cancel my cable subscription, which is another joke that feels timely, evergreen, and socially-conscious, all at the same time. I actually had a much more ribald offering but was shot down by the censors aka The Big Guy aka Steve aka THE MOST HYPOCRITICAL PERSONIFICA- TION OF EVIL THIS SIDE OF THE EARTH'S MANTLE! I mean, it's embarrassing. You're supposed to be the ultimate expression of wickedness, and you can't even let a solid masturbation joke slip through the cracks? Psh, unreal. I also had a totally solid ass-crack joke right there and was similarly refused. This place is going to Here.

So, I hear you asking, "Abs, bay-bay, what's this groovy tale about, ya dig?" And rest assured, I do dig and dig hard. See, a lot of these stories have taken us to some pretty wild places, but now it's time to take a little jaunt past the stratosphere and into the deepest realms of the galaxy for hardcore sci-fi action, action, action!

Hey, can I ask you something? Did that triple "action" line just now work for you? It's a little something I've been toying with after spending some time at the motocross, but it feels a little ham-fisted, if I'm being honest. Then again, I do consider my delivery to be naturally porcine — a descriptor I hear all too often — so maybe it jives? I don't know. This intro shit is hard.

The protag's name is Medic, which is funny cause he's an accountant by trade...just kidding, he's a full-on first responder and a damn good one at that. But as you know, Old Lady Space has some serious tricks up her sleeve, and something tells me she's gonna lay it on nice and thick for our man Medic. Sorry if that sounded pornographic.

I'm getting sleepy. I'm gonna lay down for a quick refresher, you folks enjoy Infinity.

INFINITY

BEN MARINER

A tremor rolled through the ship. Medic jerked awake with a start, his eyes immediately narrowing against the bright lights of the med bay. The rumble could mean only one thing: they were coming out of hyperspace.

He'd fallen asleep again, which wasn't uncommon for people like him; it was one of the side effects. As he lurched to his feet, the room spun underneath him; another side-effect.

"Look alive, meat bags." Captain's voice cut through the room. The tinny warble of his timbre was exaggerated by the cheap, third-hand speaker mounted in the corner of the room. "On the shuttle in five."

Medic wasn't prepared. Search and Rescue wasn't something best performed through a groggy haze. Gripping one of the beds to steady himself, he crossed the room to the supply cabinets. Inside was a mess of first aid supplies, plenty to take care of any minor injury. For something more severe, he'd at least be able to patch them up well enough that they could make it to a medical center.

Medic shoveled random odds and ends into a bag beside the supply cabinet. It never hurt to have your own supply on hand and provided the added benefit of making him look more official than he was. Besides, the ship they were looking for had its own medical staff.

He hovered over a box of stimpaks and silently debated whether or not they'd be needed. After making up his mind, he grabbed as many as he could. Most went in the bag, but he slid one into his pants pocket. Just in case.

Their ship wasn't terribly large. A flight deck, crew quarters, med bay, and cargo hold. Nothing to write home about. There were far bigger ships, and this one was beaten half to shit and wouldn't be winning any beauty contests. Still, it was good enough to get from A to B without leaving the crew stranded in the middle of open space. That's all they required.

When Medic stepped into the cargo hold, there was no sign of the rest of his team. They were already on the shuttle, and he was the straggler. No surprise there. He quickly readied his gear and, once suited up, boarded the shuttle and took his usual spot near the boat's rear.

The whole team was there: Captain, Seals, Brock, Johns, the FNG, Johnny Bravo, and, of course, Medic. There was no such thing as a rescue mission without Medic. Some would argue – Medic being chief among them – that he was the most important person on the team; without him, they'd be a group of muscle-bound jarheads good for only pure, unadulterated force. They were blunt instruments used for bashing something to a bloody pulp. Medic was the scalpel that removed the tumor.

One hour prior, a passing frigate picked up the distress call that relayed the signal to Galactic Cruise Lines, who contacted the team. Standard operating procedure, really. Frigates were for hauling space junk, not helping stranded cruise liners. Most frigate med bays had few beds, and the doctors who presided over them were even less adequate. That's why big companies like Galactic Cruise Lines kept rescue teams like Medic's on retainer. When something went wrong, you wanted the best of the best to step in and take over. Mainly to avoid lawsuits; the welfare of passengers was always a distant second.

Once the team was securely onboard, the cargo bay door opened, and Johns piloted the shuttle into open space. Through the cockpit windows, Medic could see the ship they were after. It sat still before them, dead weight in a sea of nothingness.

No one spoke as the shuttle moved closer to the cruise liner. Medic grabbed a nearby datapad and cued the incident report. As far as he could remember, he had never seen a mission report so...incomplete. The only information provided was the passenger count, approximate location, and the ship's name. *Infinity*. There was no accident report, no casualty count, no sitrep. Usually, they came with so much detail it was painful to read; that's where the lawyers came in. It was all a 'cover your ass' move. No one can question liability when every incident is laid out in excruciating detail.

"On your feet, boys!" Captain's voice boomed through the ship. "We're ready for breach in five."

Boots scraped. Guns were cocked. Every member of the team, including the rookie Johnny Bravo, was armed to the teeth. Assault rifles, sidearms, grenades, hand-to-hand weapons. Medic had been on the team for just north of seventy missions, and not once had he actually seen anyone use those overpowered weapons. Still, every time they got called in, the team suited up like they were going to war. Medic, on the other hand, had only a single sidearm (unfired) and his medkit. That was all he'd ever needed and would continue to be so until well into the future.

Outside the starboard side porthole, details of the *Infinity* came into greater focus. It was far more expansive than most ships; at least three extra decks if Medic was counting right. He remembered the slogan from *Infinity*'s maiden voyage several years back. "The biggest and most opulent space cruise liner ever constructed." As their own ship pulled close to the hull, Medic believed it. They were a flea on the haunch of a hound. Hopefully, a frantic paw wasn't about to scrape them away.

"Gimme the Breacher!" shouted Captain. Their ship was up against *Infinity*'s hull with the airlock sealed. Soldiers bounded forward and placed four black nodes in a square large enough for the team to get through.

"3...2...1...breach!" Captain activated the switch on his hip. There was a flash of blinding light as the other ship's hull was phased out, leaving nothing but an intangible blue shield between them and the inside of the *Infinity*.

"Two by two, boys. Medic at the rear," Captain barked in front of the breach. "Just like always." The team formed two lines, shoulder to shoulder, weapons at the ready. Captain and Brock were first, Seals and Johns second, followed by Johnny Bravo and FNG with Medic at the rear. It was the part Medic hated most. In all the missions he'd worked with the team, he'd never quite gotten used to crossing a breach. Something about the science of phasing made him uncomfortable. Never mind that it felt like stepping through a freezing puddle; what scared him was that if the nodes malfunctioned, they would solidify and fuse a person's cells to the hull of the cruise ship. Not something Medic ever wanted to experience.

The groups passed through, and Medic shivered despite crossing the threshold without incident. The smell hit him first; death was unmistakable. Even if the room hadn't been coated in green and red goo, the stench would have told him everything. FNG ripped his helmet off and poured the contents of his stomach onto a patch of carpeting. The rest of the team did their best to keep their own lunches down. As Medic looked around the grand ballroom, he could see small chunks - flesh and bone mostly - clinging to every surface. What he didn't see, though, were bodies. The carnage was unspeakable, but the source was nonexistent. He was suddenly glad he'd brought the additional stimpaks.

"Fuck me," Johns said breathlessly. "What happened here?"

"What's all this green?" Seals wondered aloud. He stuck the toe of his boot in a puddle of putrescence that, when pulled away, brought long, sticky strands with it.

"Stay frosty, boys," Captain hissed. "Heads on a swivel. Whatever did this can still be around."

Medic couldn't help but note that he said *what*ever, not *who*ever. For the first time in his long career, he felt the need for his sidearm. All that blood indicated it might not do much, but he felt better with the pistol's weight in his hands.

The team moved through the ballroom and into the main foyer. 'Opulent' was precisely the word that popped into Medic's head right before the word 'grisly' shoved it out of the way. They stood at the top of a grand marble staircase where highly polished mahogany handrails stretched down either side. The color of marble was a mystery since every last inch was covered in green and red mess.

A gold sign hung over their heads. Typically, it would have directed passengers to this place or that, but the splash of red across the middle made it hard to discern exactly where the arrows led.

"Brock and I will head to the flight deck," Captain said, motioning to the elevator. "Seals, Johns, you two head off to the dining hall and check for survivors. JB and Medic, take FNG down to the med bay and see what you can find. Stay together. I don't want any incidents because one of you decided to go off alone. Got me?"

The team grunted their acknowledgement, none of them confident they'd be able to keep their lunches down if they opened their mouths. As Medic followed Johnny Bravo and FNG across the room to a stairwell, he couldn't help but take one last look at the others. There was a strange feeling in his stomach that he'd never see them again. Not alive, at least.

The stairwell wasn't any different than the foyer or the ballroom, save for its lack of grandeur. It was likely an emergency stairwell only used by staff or in the event of a catastrophe. What made it similar was the sticky green and red stains splattered across the walls. It dripped off the metal handrails and trickled down the walls. Medic felt his hand reach for his pocket when he noticed Johnny Bravo looking in his direction. He pretended to scratch an itch instead.

The team descended six decks, each flight of stairs as treacherous as the next. Slime was congealed over everything. Every landing featured a single door with a simple placard that indicated what floor they were on and any critical locations. The first sign that human life had ever been on the ship appeared at the second door; a severed foot was left between the door and the jamb. Johnny Bravo asked Medic if they should bag and tag it, but Medic declined. There wasn't much good a single foot could do for anyone.

The next door led to the spa. It was hung on a single hinge and was bent nearly in half. Medic said a silent prayer to whatever god might exist that they didn't run into the being that caused such damage.

On the second-to-lowest deck was the infirmary. Companies tended to put them lower on the ship, which always upset Medic. If you required medical attention, the last thing you needed was to search for an elevator or traipse down some stairs. Apparently, the idea of the sick and infirm being near the buffet was worse than those same folks getting timely medical attention.

The door to the deck was undamaged despite its red and green camouflage. FNG opened it at Johnny Bravo's command, who quickly cleared the other side. They were now in a long corridor, with a sign directing them north to the infirmary. Johnny Bravo gave a quick hand gesture for the others to follow.

They moved up the corridor with weapons drawn and ready. Medic caught something out of the corner of his eye that was all too easy to miss. It probably looked like another blood smear to FNG and Johnny Bravo. But that wasn't quite right. Medic bent close and examined the mark.

It had been drawn by a bloody finger, that much was certain. A single inverted V with a circle in the center. It could be literally anything, even just a random mark on the wall. But a sick feeling in Medic's gut said it was much more than that.

"Hey, guys," he said, upright. "Check this out." No response came. Medic turned to look up the corridor and found himself alone. He looked in the other direction. Deserted.

"Hey, JB!" His voice reverberated down the hall. "FNG, you there?" He turned his attention back to the symbol on the wall. How long had he been standing there?

The others couldn't have gotten far. Medic heard the slow, deliberate scrape of a door pushing open from somewhere down the hall. He didn't even think; his hand was in his pocket before he realized what he was doing. He jammed the stimpak into his neck and released its comforting burst of stimulants. Medic felt his senses come alive in an instant. The fix always felt good. And now that his mind was clear, he knew one thing for sure. He did not want to meet whatever was opening that door.

"Shit," FNG hissed. "Medic is gone."

Johnny Bravo spun around. "Where the fuck did he go?"

FNG shrugged. "Maybe back up the stairs?"

Johnny thought about it for a long moment. Captain had told them not to split up; he didn't even know how it happened. The last thing he wanted to do was look for Medic only to have to explain to Captain what was going on.

"Fuck it," Johnny said, making up his mind. "He knows where we're going. He can catch up. If he went back, that's on him. We have a job to do." FNG moved as if to say something but decided against it. He was the team's junior member; it wouldn't do well to argue on his first mission. He followed Johnny Bravo back up the corridor, checking over his shoulder frequently. His brain wanted to believe that Medic had simply broken off from the group, but his instincts told him there was a reason the entire ship was covered in blood; that they were in the territory of whatever had done this.

The med bay wasn't all that dissimilar to their own ship's. FNG would have called it cleaner…except for all the blood splattered across everything. "I am a member of a search and rescue team," Johnny Bravo called out to the empty room. "If anyone is alive, please make yourself known so we can provide you with medical assistance."

How they would do that without Medic was beyond FNG, but he wasn't going to argue. A long moment of tense silence held while they both waited for some sign of life. FNG silently prayed to hear a reply. Finding someone alive would help him salvage what little hope there was.

They waited.

And waited.

And waited.

"Nobody's here," Johnny said, lowering his weapon slightly. "Let's check for supplies. We might need them. Know any first aid?"

"A bit, but—" A large cabinet burst open and caught FNG's words in his throat. A woman in bloodstained scrubs collapsed from her hiding spot onto the floor. Johnny and FNG rushed to her side. "Are you hurt?" Johnny asked frantically. It was difficult to tell with so much gore. Her only response was a moan, a haunting wail that sent a chill down FNG's spine. The two men managed to get her on her back but not without a fight. What they found nearly made FNG jump out of his skin.

Her eyes were gone, replaced by empty, bloody sockets. FNG felt his stomach turn. "Jesus," Johnny said under his breath. "Ma'am, can you hear me? Can you tell me what happened?" All she could do was groan and wail, fear lacing every sound. Johnny pulled her mouth open gently and swore. "Her tongue's gone. Fuck. Go find Medic, now!"

FNG didn't have to be told twice. He hopped up and ran out of the infirmary, taking a sharp right, but only got a few steps down the hall before he stopped. The long corridor they'd just walked up was gone. A conspicuously clean wall stood in its place.

"What the fuck?" he said aloud, letting his gun fall to his side. FNG put a hand on the wall and knocked as if he was sure it was fake. It remained still, implacable. "Hey, JB." FNG turned around. "There's something weird—"

Johnny was there, not more than ten paces away, but he wasn't Johnny anymore. Blood ran down his face in crimson streaks. It was impossible to say whether his eyes were removed like the nurse's; they had been replaced with a vibrant green light that bathed the hallway in its eerie glow.

"JB?" FNG quavered, raising his weapon. Johnny Bravo didn't reply. The nurse they found emerged from the med bay and stood beside Johnny, her eyes lit the same as his. She tossed a soft, bloody mass at FNG's feet; it didn't take long for him to realize it was Johnny's eyes and tongue. FNG disengaged the safety on his weapon and smiled as the corridor filled with gunfire.

SEALS DIDN'T LIKE this one bit. When he heard they were being dispatched to a cruise ship, he thought they'd at least get some decent grub out of the deal. Now that they were in the dining hall, the last thing Seals wanted to do was eat. In fact, his body was seriously considering ejecting anything that happened to be left in his stomach.

The room was grand enough to fit hundreds of passengers. But there wasn't sign of a single living soul. A grandiose crystal chandelier hung overhead, the one object that avoided being covered in green goo. The rest of the room wasn't so lucky. As his eyes scanned the table, Seals was sure he didn't want to meet those present for the meal.

Bits of flesh and bone were scattered across the surface. A lone pinky finger sat so entirely soaked with gore that Seals couldn't tell what color the skin underneath was. Who...no, *whate*ver had feasted did so in a savage frenzy. The idea made Seals' stomach turn again. A storm raged in his gut, a violent hurricane of nausea. It took everything he had to keep it all inside.

"The fuck happened here?" Johns asked, surveying the area.

Seals shook his head. "Don't know if I really want to find out."

"Agreed," Johns said somberly, his eyes rolling over the grisly dining scene. "Let's hit the kitchen and see if there's any grub worth eating."

Seals looked at him, half in confusion, half in disgust. "You want to eat *right now*?"

Johns shrugged. "I'm not *not* going to eat some free food. That would be a crime." He set off towards the kitchen. Seals watched him before jogging to catch up.

"How can your stomach possibly handle food right now," Seals wondered aloud. "Look at where we are."

Johns stopped at the door and looked at his partner. "I've seen worse."

"Fuck you, you have."

Johns opened his mouth to argue when a sound from the kitchen stopped him. Both his and Seals' ears perked up. They were too far away to hear it before, but now that they were close, it was unmistakable. The rhythmic pounding of a knife against a chopping board; the kind of sound someone wouldn't have known they'd recognize until they heard it. Johns brought his weapon up and signaled Seals to do the same.

Guns ready, Seals kicked open the door, allowing Johns to clear the room first. The once-pristine stainless steel of the tables and appliances was awash in crimson and jade. In the middle of the room stood an obese man in a chef's hat, his white coat stained beyond recognition.

"Hands up!" Johns commanded. "Identify yourself!"

The man didn't respond. He continued moving meat onto a chopping block and hacking away at it with a cleaver big enough to remove a man's arm.

"Last chance," Johns warned. "Turn around and identify yourself, or we open fire."

The man continued chopping as if he didn't hear what was happening around him. Johns didn't pull his trigger, and Seals wasn't quick to do so either. There was something odd about the man beyond being the only soul left alive on this carnage cruise. Johns slowly approached with his weapon at the ready when he noticed a green glow covering the table. "Johns—" was all Seals could get out before the man turned and sank the cleaver into Johns' neck. Shock was fresh on his face as his head wobbled against his shoulder. His body remained on its feet momentarily before collapsing to the floor with a sickening thud.

Seals disengaged the safety on his weapon and let the bullets fly. They tore through the chef's flesh, scattering gore across the room. The man was unphased. He watched Seals through green, glowing eyes, waiting for his moment to strike. It didn't take long for the weapon's clip to empty, for the tinkling of hollow shells to fade away. Seals knew he didn't have time to reload, but the chef wasn't moving. He took a step back towards the door. Seals shot his eyes around the room, desperate for some alternate solution. Nothing came to him, so he ran. But when Seals tried to engage his limbs - a moment that felt like two eternities stacked end-to-end - the chef took a step forward, and Seals screamed.

MEDIC NEVER FOUND THE INFIRMARY. He ran up the corridor the same way Johnny Bravo and FNG had gone, but it never stopped. He ran and ran, desperate for a door or even an intersection, something that would put him on a different course. He ran until his lungs burned and his legs ached, until his body protested. The only thing that kept him going was the stimpak coursing through his veins. But that wouldn't last forever, not at this pace.

Almost as if in reply to his thoughts, a door appeared. An exit sign burned brilliantly above it. Medic's heart leaped into his throat, and he made for the door. He didn't get more than two steps before being ground to a halt. The door was five, maybe ten paces away, but on the other side stood a creature unlike anything he'd ever seen, vaguely simian with long front arms to prop itself up. Its skin was tinged with sickly, partially translucent green. Muscles bulged and twitched as the beast snorted great huffs through broad, flat nostrils. Medic's mind flashed to the pistol in his hand, but he knew it would be useless against a creature so massive, so formidable. Its skin stretched thin to reveal a shape underneath; FNG's severed head. His mouth was agape in a ghastly howl of terror.

There were two choices: run or die.

Medic squeezed off two shots almost as a distraction before sprinting for the door. The bullets did nothing; he wasn't even sure they hit their target. The beast charged Medic as he scrambled for the exit; if it was locked, he would be dead. He threw himself at the door, and it burst open. He felt the air behind him ripple as the beast took a swing and missed. Medic fought his way up the stairs as his feet slipped in a congealed mess that seemed adamant about covering the entire surface. He risked a peek over his shoulder and saw the beast easily navigate the staircase. Running suddenly felt as if it was merely a delay of the inevitable.

Medic made it up three decks without being caught. As he passed a sign indicating the security center, a plan entered his mind. It was risky and would require precise timing, but it was all he had. He shot up to the next deck, then rested. The creature took Medic's pause as surrender and leaped forward, jaws wide and hungry. Just before it reached the landing, he put his hands on the metal railing and hopped over, letting himself fall down the narrow space between the stairways. The creature's jagged teeth snapped wildly at its escaping prey.

Medic's arm was nearly ripped out of the socket as he grabbed onto the railing to break his fall, but he'd managed to hold on and pull himself up without losing his bag. There was no way for the beast to follow, as large as it was, but it could backtrack quickly. He had to move fast. Medic scrambled up the railing and hurled himself through the door. The sign pointed to the security station, and he said a silent thank you to the universe that it was just around the corner.

The security center's door was more or less intact. Despite massive dents in the steel, the lock was undamaged. Medic hurried inside and slammed the door behind him, engaging the lock as quickly as possible. The beast was most certainly close behind. After a few long, tense moments, Medic let out an uneasy breath. The pounding he expected at the door never came.

Three banks of monitors were spread out before him along the far wall. Most displayed only static, but several showed horrifying scenes around the ship. Limbs floated in the blood-tinted waters of a swimming pool. A small torso in a cartoon t-shirt leaned against an ice cream machine. Visions Medic knew would haunt him for the rest of his life. However long that happened to be.

A quick scan failed to produce any members of the team; he hoped against hope he wasn't the only one left. The image of FNG's head inside that creature was burned in his memory. He shrugged the bag off his sore shoulder and rummaged around until he found what he was looking for. The cap popped off easily, and Medic jammed the stimpak into his neck. His eyelids fluttered rapidly as his veins sucked up the medicine. His heart rate settled. The fix always felt good.

After giving the drugs a moment to work, he opened his eyes. Most of the equipment was trashed, but a single station appeared operational. A red light blinked on the CPU under the desk. He crossed the room and picked up the nearest chair he could find. Taking a seat, Medic fired up the monitor and saw a notification in the bottom right corner that read: *Flight recorder logs updated. Listen or Send?*

He felt safe for the time being. At the very least, Medic hoped the flight recorder would help him understand what was happening. He chose the listen option and leaned back in his chair.

THREE EMOTIONS WRESTLED each other within Captain; anger, confusion, and fear. The flight deck was abandoned like the rest of the ship but failed to escape the bloodshed. It wasn't illogical that an entire cruise ship worth of passengers could just up and disappear, but it was highly improbable. Even if they had been killed as the blood suggested, a trace would exist, some sign of what happened. So far, all Captain found was gore.

"Fuel cells are at fifty percent," Brock announced from a nearby console. "They didn't run out of gas. They just...*stopped*."

"What about navigation? Life support?" Captain gazed into the abyss beyond the deck.

Brock punched a few keys. "Both operational. This doesn't make sense."

That was for damn sure. The longer they spent on the *Infinity*, the less Captain liked it. Things weren't adding up; that made him nervous. He reached for the radio, his hand over the call button, unsure of what to say. The need for a hasty retreat welled inside him, threatening to break the dam of his resolve. Finally, he pressed the button.

"All teams, report," he said gruffly.

The silence was deafening. He tried again.

"Report, goddammit!"

Brock looked at him uneasily. "What's the call, Cap?"

Captain thought for a long moment. He gazed out at the open space surrounding the *Infinity*, leagues upon leagues of absolutely nothing. They were a long way from help and an even longer way from understanding. It was too much distance for Captain to feel comfortable. He reached up to the radio and pressed the call button again.

"Teams, if you can hear me, get back to the shuttle immediately." He spoke with finality. "Repeat, return to the shuttle. We're getting the fuck off this ship." Silence, to Captain's lack of surprise. He looked at

Brock. "Let's go. We'll regroup and reach out to the cruise line for orders and a report."

"Don't have to tell me twice," Brock said, hopping up eagerly from his chair. Retreat didn't sit right with Captain, though. He'd been on over three hundred Search and Rescue ops, and none proved beyond his capabilities. He was the best at what he did; that's why they used him. Failure stuck in his craw worse than he cared to admit.

This situation was just out of his reach. Evidence was literally splattered over every surface, but none of it helped Captain understand. He jammed his finger into the elevator's call button with more force than necessary. The doors didn't open. He furrowed his brow.

"The car's on deck 3," Brock said, pointing to the digital readout over the doors.

"This is the only elevator that comes up here," replied Captain, readying his weapon. "It doesn't stop at the other decks."

If either one of them thought they'd be fast enough on the trigger for an incoming threat, they were wrong. The elevator doors barely opened when a blur sprang forth, knocking Brock to the floor and pinning him down. The inhuman creature was as bloody as everything else. The Hawaiian shirt it wore was stained dark crimson in stark contrast to the white flowers of the lei around its neck. Glowing, green eyes spoke of something that lived in the mind's darkest recesses.

Brock tried in vain to fight against the creature as it raked his face to shreds with bare hands. Captain kicked out hard, landing his heavy combat boot square in the once-human jaw. A sickening crunch of bone followed, but the creature hardly noticed. Before it could respond, Captain kicked it onto its back, drew his sidearm, stamped one foot down on the creature's head, and emptied the clip into its throat. Green flecks of viscera sprayed up with each shot. By the time Captain was out of bullets, the creature's head was barely attached. A few scraps of skin kept it in place like the last pathetic threads of a worn seam desperately trying to keep a pair of pants from bursting.

The green light in the creature's eyes died out and gave way to empty sockets. Captain reached out to Brock and hauled him to his feet. His face was almost unrecognizable, but Captain could see the grimace of pain through the tattered remnants. Brock sighed, tried to level his heart rate, and looked at Captain with appreciation. At least his eyes were still white, still normal. Still human.

"What the fuck was that thing?" he asked breathlessly.

"I'm guessing that's what's responsible for this mess," Captain replied, kicking the body to make sure it was still dead.

"At least we killed it."

Captain nodded. "Let's get you back to the shuttle. You need Medic."

As if in response, the elevator hunched back to life. Captain watched Brock test his weapon, ensuring it was ready to fire. The doors opened, and their team was waiting.

But it wasn't their team.

Seals, Johnny Bravo, and FNG stood before them with glowing eyes and hungry smiles. Johnny's head hung loosely to one side, resting easily on his left bicep. The stump of his neck was congealed with oozing green effluence.

Captain cocked his gun. "If we're doing this, then let's do it already."

MEDIC SAT BACK in his chair and let out a long, low sigh. "Jesus…" he said, exasperated. The recording explained everything. It all made sense. But there was still a logical part of his mind that simply couldn't accept it. Something that consigned the explanation to the nonsensical ramblings of a madwoman. It was too unbelievable. Too out there. Too… *unreal.*

What follows is a transcript of the final flight recorder transmission of cruise vessel Infinity.

My name is Crewman Dani Adelle, and this is the final flight recording of cruise ship *Infinity*, Earth date November 27, 2714.

[*laughter*]

It's Thanksgiving back home. Not much to give thanks for this year, I suppose.

[*thumping*]

As you can tell from my title, I am not the captain of the *Infinity*. James Edwards is dead. The entire crew is dead. I'm the only one left, and I, too, will be dead soon. Let this act as a record of what happened here.

[*thumping*]

We set sail from Io on November 13, 2714. If I had realized it would be the last time I saw Jupiter or any of its moons, I would have made the departure more celebratory. I didn't even bother to look back, to get one last look at my birthplace. It was supposed to be a routine cruise. Nothing special. Nothing difficult. No big deal, right?

[*thumping*]

There were 1257 souls aboard the ship at departure. It started just like every other cruise. I've completed over thirty trips, and each one has been exactly like the last. Passengers board, Polynesian music plays, we pass out leis while some asshole makes a joke about getting laid...same shit, different day. But if I'd known that was the last dumbass pun I would ever hear, maybe I would have laughed a little harder, given him an extra lei, made a joke myself. I can't even remember what the guy looked like. All I can see now is the blood. The carnage.

[*thumping*]

The first day went well enough. We made good time out to Neptune, and the weather was good enough for the passengers to witness the Ice Giant sculptures. They're beautiful. If you're ever lucky enough to see them, treasure that moment. Pictures don't do them justice. When you see them with your own eyes, even from the lido deck of a cruise ship...magnificent. I pulled picture duty later that day; hundreds of people lined up to get their photo with that sign. 'Now Leaving Earth's Solar System', like it's fucking Vegas or something. I guess if you've never crossed the threshold, it could be considered something special.

[*thumping*]

There was one family I do remember from that day. Two moms, a son, and a daughter. They really weren't remarkable as people, if I'm being honest, but the love they shared for each other was. I've seen a lot of families in this job, and all of them have loved each other...to at least some degree, I'm sure. This family, though, there was something different, something more...genuine about their feelings for each other. They didn't know it, but I sent a picture of them to myself. It had been a long time since I'd felt that kind of love. I wanted to remember it. But I'll never be able to look at that picture again, not after watching what the mother did to her son.

[*thumping*]

We served chicken piccata that first night. Isn't it funny the things you remember? The tiny little details that stick in your brain despite them being so aggressively inconsequential. Chicken piccata on a bed of bucatini in herbed butter sauce, capers, crispy prosciutto, with garlic bread on the side. Marco, the head chef, said he made mine special. It was a little dry, but I didn't have the heart to tell him. He asked me out once, a few trips back. I told him I didn't want to mix work and pleasure...couldn't come up with a more cliched response, I guess. Looking back, I wish I had fucked him just once. Just to know. Just to feel, one last time.

[*thumping*]

The second day was better. They put me at the activity desk, signing people up for deep space excursions. Spacewalks. Speeder bikes. That kind of stuff. Commonplace crap to me, but fantastical to others. I had thought about taking a speeder bike out myself when it all went to hell. They were trashed, though, almost as if they knew. Not that it would have done much good. The range on those things isn't enough. Not to escape.

[*thumping*]

Day three. That's when everything went south. The bridge received an SOS signal that spread through the crew like wildfire. Within fifteen minutes, every last crew member knew. Probably most of the guests, too. Per Earth's interstellar travel laws, we were required to aid any SOS signal we received. Plus, it was right in our path; we wouldn't even have to lose any time changing course. Something tells me they're going to rethink those laws after this.

[*thumping*]

It was a small craft, only big enough for one person. Not one I'd ever seen before, but I'm not exactly a hardened space traveler. It seemed unlikely this was the kind of ship to be so far out on its own; the mere idea raised red flags all around. But I wasn't in a position to make decisions. Captain Edwards didn't see any trouble and brought the ship on board, took the pilot to the med bay. The whole rescue operation took about thirty minutes. Nothing special. Nothing difficult. No big deal, right?

[*thumping*]

If you're still listening, you're probably wondering what that noise is. That incessant pounding. I'm getting to that...

[*thumping*]

I heard rumors after we picked up the stray. He was alive. He was dead. He belonged to one of the rebel factions. He was a member of the Universal Alliance. I don't know what was true; I never saw the guy. Could've been a potato for all I cared. The only news that mattered to me was that he had disappeared. Gone from the med bay in the middle of the night, no trace of him anywhere. Captain Edwards issued an order for a discreet search to be performed. It turned up nothing, of course. His ship was still in the docking bay, but he wasn't. He was a ghost.

[*thumping*]

Day six. We were supposed to turn around and head back to Io. Except we couldn't. The engines were dead. Two state-of-the-art hyperdrive engines that were nothing more than massive paperweights. The engineers and mechanics couldn't figure it out; everything appeared to be in working order. We were dead in the water, so to speak, but told the passengers we were extending the cruise at no cost to them. They were happy...at first.

[*thumping*]

It was late on day seven that the violence began. Space can really mess with a person's brain. When you're out in the vast nothingness of the universe, sometimes you just can't handle it. It wasn't the first time someone had traveled past the limits of the solar system and lost their mind. Violence on cruises isn't uncommon, actually. They aren't generally reported to the public, but there are plenty of sealed records regarding incidents inspired by space dementia. This one was different, though. It sat with me strangely. I couldn't put my finger on it

[*thumping*]

The nurse wigged out. Opened some patient's throat with a scalpel. I heard he came in claiming he had a cold, and she slashed him from ear to ear, smiling the whole time.

[*thumping*]

I want to dissuade you from any opinions you may have of me. I'm not the last surviving member of this cruise because I acted heroically. I did not 'take the fight to them,' as the saying goes. I did not put my life before those of other passengers. I ran. At the first inkling of trouble, I headed for the security station. It's the safest place on the ship, a veritable fortress buried deep within a party mansion. I didn't think they'd let me in, not without clearance. Luckily, I was in good with one of the security technicians. I did go out with him, actually. Once. Right after I first started. It didn't go well, but he always had a soft spot for me.

[*thumping*]

Everything was seen from the security station and the hundreds of cameras scattered across the ship. I witnessed none of the following events first-hand. I certainly wouldn't be making this report right now if I had. I'd be just like the rest of the slaughtered masses.

[*laughter*]

I sat in the safety of the security station with my tech friend and two guards. It was slow at first. We watched the nurse get put in the brig kicking and screaming; watched her rage against the walls of her cell until she beat her own knuckles bloody. Unprompted and unprovoked, the guard on duty pulled out the pistol locked in his desk and emptied the clip into the nurse's chest. Just like that, as if it was the most casual act in the world. The startling part wasn't the cold-blooded nature of the murder. It was her blood splattered against the wall of her cell, neon green and bubbling. Not human blood at all.

[*thumping*]

Another guard entered to investigate the gunshots. The first guard pounced on him and ripped his body to shreds with his bare hands. It was like watching a lion maul a gazelle. Scraps of clothing. Chunks of flesh. All of it flying this way and that. True unmitigated carnage. Worse, though, was when he looked into the camera. It wasn't a closeup, but it was good enough. Good enough to see the green of his eyes. They were not just bright green eyes. They were glowing, luminescent, beaming. Vivid.

[*thumping*]

This mania. This possession. This...fuck, whatever it was. It hopped from screen to screen, massacring everything in its path. Green and red blood blended on the walls, on the floors, on corpses. A grisly Christmas mosaic of slaughtered human effluence.

[*thumping*]

My tech friend and I sat and watched as the ship was overtaken. Every deck. Every stateroom. Every last nook and cranny, all washed in blood. Green or red, it didn't matter; the infection didn't care if it killed its own kind. It only took a day for my friend to tell me he was leaving. I didn't try to stop him. I could see it in his eyes; the futility he felt staying alive, trapped in a room with only a hellscape for entertainment. He accepted it long before I did and chose to meet his end head-on. Didn't even look back as the door swung open and a stream of crimson poured into the room. His footprints are still congealed to the floor.

[*thumping*]

So, I was alone. Stranded in much the same way as the man who started this mess. I'm not even sure he was a man, though; not anymore. The way those eyes glow. The color of the blood. It just seems so fucking...alien. I know I'm not supposed to use that word; honestly, I'm not really worried about being sensitive at this point. Whatever this thing is, it's not human. It doesn't even belong to this solar system. It's something from far beyond. A blight. A cancer.

[*thumping*]

[*laughter*]

Fucking blight. That's as good a name as any for it.

[*erratic pounding*]

Yeah, I'm talking to you, big boy.

[*crash*]

Fuck you!

[*erratic pounding*]

The feast was two days ago. The guests had been gorging themselves on each other for some time, but that was...savage. Wild. This
was different. This was ritualistic. All at once, the violence stopped.
Those left alive — the ones with green eyes — moved as one to the
dining hall and rearranged tables to make a singular place where they
could congregate. They collected the dead; bits and pieces of human
bodies placed atop long, makeshift tables, creating a massive,
grotesque pile. The man at the head of the table stood with a glass of
crimson liquid. He raised it to make a toast. I didn't want to, but I
couldn't stop myself from turning on the sound. Three words. That's
all he said.

[*thumping*]

"To the feast!"

[*thumping*]

I couldn't silence the audio fast enough. The fervor with which they
pulled and tore at the flesh was sickening, sound or no sound. My
stomach turned, thrashed, begged me to look away. But I couldn't. It
was like a derailed train cutting through a metropolitan suburb;
gorgeous destruction that demands your attention even when you
know you shouldn't watch. It pulls you in, lives inside your brain,
pounds blood through your veins.

[*thumping*]

When it was over, nothing was left except bloodied bone. I don't
know what I expected, but it sure as hell wasn't that. I thought they'd
be full, their bloodlust sated. Fuck me, was I wrong. They pounded on
the table and cried out for more. I couldn't hear them, but it was clear
enough. There were at least thirty of them, all with those green eyes.
God, those horrid, green eyes. And then, just like that, the light disappeared from at least half of their eyes. Their faces changed from
ravenous to shocked to terrified. The others, the green-eyed creatures
that remained, turned on them instantly. Ripped them limb from limb.

Then, when those poor bastards died, more green eyes turned white. It kept that way, turning, eating, turning eating, until only one was left. The man at the head of the table. It was just him and me. And you'll never guess who it was staring directly at me through the security monitor.

[*thumping*]

The fucking 'get lei'd' guy.

[*thumping*]

[*laughter*]

[*crash*]

[*laughter*]

[*inaudible shouting*]

[*thumping*]

That's right...the guy trying to beat down the door — the guy trying to eat me, to tear me to shreds, to consume my flesh for his own enjoyment — was the asshole who made the goddamn lei joke.

[*thumping*]

[*laughter*]

[*thumping*]

And that brings us to the present. I could stay here, but the longer he beats at the door, the more likely he is to break it down. Whatever is inside of him, whatever turned his eyes green, won't let him stop. Not until he beats down the door. Not until he gets to me. So, I'm going to open it. I'm going to do what I should have done days ago. Like my tech friend had the sense to do. A single gun was left with me, along with one full clip. At least, I think it's full. I know nothing about guns. Point and pull the trigger. Just go out with a bang.

[*thumping*]

[*thumping*]

[*thumping*]

Before I go, I just want to say I'm sorry. I'm sorry for being a coward. I'm sorry to my mother for not living up to her expectations. I'm sorry to all the friends I've let fall by the wayside. I'm sorry for being a shitty person to good people. I'm sorry for being a good person to shitty people. I never thought about how I'd die, but I definitely didn't expect it to be like this. I hope that in these last few minutes, if there is a God, they'll take pity on me and let it end quickly.

[*thumping*]

[*hiss*]

[*scraping*]

[*inaudible shouting*]

[*gunshots*]

[*screeching*]

[*crash*]

End of Transmission

THERE HE SAT, in the same chair Dani had. Listening to her words. Hearing that pounding, that growling. He'd been chased into this room by a creature he couldn't explain. Nearly killed by something that could only have come from outside his own solar system. Medic stood up and searched the security monitors for his team. Every hall. Every room. Completely empty. The beast was absent, too, but there were too many malfunctioning monitors to be sure it wasn't lurking somewhere out of sight.

If the recording was accurate, none of them had any chance of survival. They'd accepted a suicide mission without realizing it. Medic pulled the pistol from his holster, felt the weight of it in his hand. He checked the chamber and the clip. Plenty of bullets, but all he really needed was one. He slid the clip home, and it snapped into place with overwhelming finality.

Medic had made up his mind.

He turned away from the monitors and went to the door. The lock disengaged easily as if eager to lead him to his death. Medic swung the door open without caring what was on the other side. If the beast was waiting, then so be it.

It wasn't, though. The corridor was deserted. Medic stepped out and scanned the hall. "I'm here! If you want me, come and get me!" There was no response, but he didn't exactly expect one. Medic walked calmly down the hall to the stairwell, then up to the main deck where the team had boarded the ship. The foyer was empty. "Don't be shy now!" His voice bounded off the walls of the empty room. He went to the elevators and pressed the call button. He boarded as the doors opened, then selected the button for the lido deck.

There was a pool, a bar, snack stations, and a burger joint. Would have been quite the party if it hadn't been washed in vermillion and jade. Medic could almost imagine people crowded around the deck, dancing, swimming, drinking, smiling, laughing. Enjoying their cruise.

Poor bastards.

He walked forward and looked up through the glass dome that covered the area, providing a brilliant view of the stars beyond. Medic put the gun to his temple.

"Last chance, asshole!" he called out. "Get it while the getting's good!"

A figure appeared from the shadows across the deck from him. It was a younger man — somewhere in his 30's, Medic guessed — wearing a Hawaiian shirt and a lei, marred with slaughter. Medic looked deep into the glowing, green eyes of the blight and knew this was the guy Dani referred to.

Medic smiled. "You look like a dick," he said, squeezing the trigger gently.

The blight snarled.

You don't want to do that.

The voice was deep, ethereal, driven directly into his mind.

"You think I want you to kill me instead?"

The blight didn't move, but the voice replied. *No. I can see that much. But it makes no difference. Killing yourself won't stop me from using your body.*

Medic huffed. "Then it really doesn't matter."

His finger tightened on the trigger.

I'll let you live.

This gave Medic pause.

"You slaughtered an entire ship's worth of people," he said, easing off the trigger. "Why would you leave me? Some bullshit about wanting me to spread the word about you? Because, if so, you can go fuck yourself."

I can take your body and use it as I wish, but it will require time to acclimate. If you allow me onto your ship and take me to the next planet so I may continue feeding, I will let you live.

"News flash, asshole," Medic said. "You're on a ship right now. What do you need mine for?"

The blight's eyes flashed. *This vessel is too big for one to operate alone; the ones who know how have long since been consumed.*

Medic shrugged. "Sounds like a 'you' problem, amigo." He pulled the trigger, but the darkness didn't come. The blight was on him in the blink of an eye, twisting the gun out of his hand. The bullet lodged harmlessly in a pillar nearby. The blight picked Medic up like a pillow and tossed him across the lido deck. Medic landed hard on a lounge chair that collapsed upon impact. He didn't get up. He didn't try to run. He didn't try to fight. Medic simply rolled over and accepted his fate. There was little else to do. He retrieved one last stimpak and jammed it into his neck.

The fix always felt good.

The blight leaped across the deck and landed on top of Medic. He looked into the glowing, green eyes of death with an unexpected sense of acceptance. The creature opened its mouth, exposing not a tongue but mucus-covered tentacles that snapped hungrily. They crawled over his skin, tickled his nostrils, pulled at his eyelids. The mucus reeked of death and decay. Medic closed his eyes and welcomed the end.

"MEDIC!"

Medic let out a groan.

"Wake the fuck up, Medic. Come on!"

His eyes fluttered open. Johnny Bravo and FNG were standing over him. The new guy looked worried, but Johnny just seemed pissed. Medic scanned his surroundings. He was on the lido deck, stretched out on a lounge chair as if he'd just sat down for a break. There was no sign of the blight. No broken chair nearby. No bullet hole in the wall.

Everything seemed fine.

"Where am I?" he said, his mouth dry as a bone. Classic sign of a stim hangover.

"You tell me, dick," Johnny Bravo said, throwing his hands up. "We were heading down to the infirmary, and you disappeared. Captain said don't split up. We had to find you before he found out and kicked our asses."

Medic stood on wobbly legs. He'd hit the stims too hard this time. He didn't even remember leaving the ship. He strained his mind to remember the breach, boarding the craft, anything. It was all blank. Memory loss, it seemed, was another side effect of heavy stim usage.

"I...uh...fuck," he stammered.

Johnny grabbed him by the flack jacket and pulled him in close, looking deep into his eyes. Medic expected a green glow but couldn't remember why. "Are you stimming again?" JB asked, eyeing Medic's neck where a fresh track mark gleamed like the north star. "Goddamit, get your shit together. Cap's got a survivor in the main foyer. She needs medical attention." He smacked Medic on the side of the head. "You good?"

Medic winced and nodded. "Let's go."

It didn't take long to reach the main foyer. Medic moved on autopilot, barely aware of his surroundings. When they stepped off the elevator, the rest of the team was there, not far away. They formed a circle around a young woman who lay face down, covered in blood.

"Fucking finally," Captain growled. "Get your ass over here, Medic."

Medic rushed forward, his medkit at the ready. Johnny Bravo rolled the woman over after a cursory check for wounds. Medic pulled out his flashlight to check her pupils and was greeted by empty, bloody sockets.

"Shit," FNG hissed, turning his head. Medic thought he would lose his lunch again, but the kid managed to keep it down.

"What's going on?" Captain demanded.

"She's alive," Medic replied, checking vitals. "Something tore out her eyes, though." He eased her mouth open. "And her tongue. We should get her back to the ship."

"Do it," said Captain without hesitation. "Help him, Bravo, and then get your ass back here ASAP."

"Roger that," Johnny Bravo said, positioning himself at the woman's feet.

Medic didn't like it. Moving a trauma victim was dangerous without a stretcher. Who knew what kind of internal injuries she had that could be made worse being hauled around. They didn't have much of a choice, though. The ship was massacred; whatever had done it could burst out of the walls at any moment. It would be just as dangerous to leave her.

Medic was anxious to return to the safety of his own ship. He and Johnny Bravo scooped their arms under the woman's shoulders, lifted her up, and then moved quickly through the ship onto their own. Bravo made sure the woman was secure in the med bay before leaving Medic to his work. That was just fine with Medic; his head was pounding, and he desperately needed another fix. The last thing he wanted to do was work with a thunderstorm raging in his skull. He'd start the preliminaries and then get a new stimpak while the computer was doing its job.

A nametag was clipped to the front of the woman's uniform. Medic wiped away the blood to see her name. Dani. The name rang a bell but was just out of reach of his memory.

"Dani," he said aloud, tasting the word on his tongue. "Let's see who you are." He grabbed the scanner from the side of the bed and used it to read the barcode behind the tag. On the screen to his right, her info appeared. Dani Adele, crewman for Galactic Cruise Lines. Twenty-two. Originally from Io. Single. Nothing special. How she had survived, though, was miraculous.

Medic turned away from Dani in search of a stimpak. As his fingers clasped around familiar plastic, his whole body eased. But he didn't put it to his neck right away. Something was gnawing at the back of his mind, telling him that Dani was more than she appeared. He just couldn't put his finger on why.

Had he been of sound mind, he might have noticed the green glow that had appeared in the room around him for what it was. But the stimpak clouded his brain, making the desire for another shot greater than the danger present in the room. He shrugged, abandoning thoughts of Dani, and turned to check on his patient when a vice grip clamped around his neck. Medic was lifted off the floor, staring at Dani. Her eyes glowed a brilliant green. Medic felt her grip tighten and his windpipe collapse. As the room slowly faded to black, Medic lifted the stimpak in his hand and jammed it into his neck between Dani's cold fingers.

The fix always felt good.

IX

See, stories like that are precisely why I never wanted to be an astronaut growing up. Also, I was dogshit at math. The last thing NASA needs is my dumbass trying to figure out my multiplication tables while a hundred-billion-dollar shuttle actively burns through the atmosphere. Mostly, I'm good at talking while being bad at everything else. That's why I up and joined the circus after high school. College just seemed like more of the same, and I've seen what a Communications degree gets you.

Our next story features more banana-pants-crazy insanity wrapped up in an odd little bow that may or may not actually be a snake; I don't know, things turn into other things, cheese plays a factor, goats are involved…the story plays loosey-goosey with that whole 'reality' concept.

Our protagonist Josh Adams is another one of those average schmucks who just kind of coasts through life and may or may not be on some sort of stimulant, psychedelic, or other mind-altering narcotic. Or maybe he's just weird; I've def known some cats like that over the course of my life. Naturally strange. Soberly odd. Born a little different, to use common parlance. All of this leads to a decision that young Mister Josh must make, one that will have quite the impact on his future, and everyone else's, for that matter. And since you're wondering, yes, it will likely involve goats and/or cheese. (Can it be both? Goat cheese is to DIE for!)

So, while I look for some tasty crackers and delicious cheese, please enjoy All of the Above.

ALL OF THE ABOVE

VANESSA KRAUSS

"Rejoice, for today is the day of judgement!" the disembodied voice boomed. "For you, Josh Adams, are the Chosen One!" A chorus of representatives from the great beyond joined in.

"What an honor."

"Yeeesssss…a great honor."

"Rejoice. Rejoice."

"What choice will he make? I hope he picks mine!"

I blotted my eyes from the harsh glow of the eerie spotlight above. Was this a hostage situation or something else? As tears welled in the corners of my eyes, I winced, unable to gain sight of what I was looking at. Five vaguely discernible shapes towered within a nondescript, formless mist. They vanished in the gloom above, too wide to be trees, too narrow to be buildings.

Squinting strained my eyes, so I let my head drop. The floor was easier to look at, smooth carbon black illuminated by a piercing glow. Neither my hands nor my feet were tied, and I was relieved to find that I was wearing pants. Better yet, dry pants.

Little pat here, little pat there. Pants, shirt, belt—wait! No wallet or cellphone. "You robbed me!" I shouted upwards.

What was red and black and a-lot-of-colors-I-could-not-describe all over? It wasn't a wall attacked by spray paint. For the life of me, I couldn't figure out what it could have been. There were snake tails, octopus tentacles, starfish arms…the list went on and on.

Slowly — v e r y s l o w l y — I ticked my head away from the spot-light to look at anything else. Pillars, the bottom torso of a t-rex, a cloaked shadow with many winking eyeballs, giant Satan legs, and the aforementioned swaying tentacles all gloriously presented themselves. My shoulders relaxed. This was a dream, not an interrogation. I hadn't been knocked out and locked in a holding cell with the FBI demanding to know why I had stolen all those MP3s decades ago.

"Had me for a moment. Okay, I'm going to head this way and see what happens." I gestured toward a scaly pair of crimson goat legs that featured house-sized hooves.

One rule of weird dreams is to blame them on food. What was the last thing I ate? An overstuffed gyro with its slices of seasoned lamb meat nestled in a warm, floury pita filled my mind. Side dish was fried calamari. Note to self: spicy, fried food is bad for the brain. Next time, eat a salad.

As I passed the giant goat legs, one shifted and stopped me from going anywhere—no big deal. Nothing was going to hurt me.

"Come on. Move." I jabbed at the legs, encouraging them to get out of the way. "I want to find the ocean where the calamari came from." Maybe if I was lucky there would be mer-sheep in tacky, shell-shaped bras. What I touched felt scaly, reptilian, and waxy. Oddly real for a lucid dream. I decided to rub it some more and found my assertions were correct. Here be lizard, which meant only one thing. "Aww, come on!!!" Fuck. Not again. "Okay, Darrel. I know you're recording this. Tell you what. Fuck you! When I recover from this, I will hunt you down and murder you! You hear me?!" I was tripping utter balls. Screw my roommate. Screw him with a rusty tire iron straight up his gaping, shit-spraying asshole!

First, it was pot in the brownies. Second time was magic mush-rooms in the pasta sauce. The bastard kept upping his game. Who knows what he'd done this time! I stormed around in a circle, resolute in my determination not to touch anything, lest it be another sex doll or bag of dog shit. "You are *so* dead!"

Who was I kidding? I was probably blubbering nonsense,

screaming into the void of my own mind while drooling in the real world where my body lay prone. "Hur-der-durp-durp. Smeh dinna doo gabba goo." I imitated what Darrel and his horde of habitual hookah hookups must be hearing from my acid-spewing mouth.

"Argh!!!" I raged, then stormed to a spot where nothing was close enough to harm me. "Yep. This is my life. Realities of having a room-mate. Last time I rent a room to someone from Portland." If only my lease had ended sooner. I could have been living with Sarah instead.

"Goats make good roommates," quipped one of the voices.

"No. Good roommates pay their rent on time, and don't poison your coffee with LSD." The voice reminded me of Darrel's buddy, Blake. "Shut up, Blake."

"I am not Blake. I am Billy, like a billy goat." Good, someone under-stood me. Progress.

"Fine, '*Billy.*'" I added air quotes. "What do you want? Why did you drug me?" I looked to where I assumed the heads of the speakers were and let my eyes adjust. While I was no longer fighting back tears, I still couldn't make much out.

A resonating authority spoke. "We have brought you before us, unharmed, to make a decision of great importance."

"Yesss," hissed one of the figures.

"A choice must be made," added another, its voice wispy and soothing.

"Choose!" The last one inflected with a high-pitched whine.

I struggled to physically identify Boomy, Hissy, Whiny, and Wispy. 'Billy' had to be the goat legs behind me; couldn't be anyone else.

The eyeballs that peered from the cloak were unsettling. Blink. Blink. Blink-blink-blink. Blink-blink. Blink. They were cycling in a pattern I thought might be Morse code. Everywhere I looked, my surroundings were dominated by creepy shit I had no capacity to explain. "Look, I'm not playing your game." Darrel, Blake, and whoever else was there could go stuff it.

"The Chosen One does not wish to decide. He does not take us seri-ously." An astute observation by the whispering voice.

"Do whatever you want. Just leave my pants on and don't steal my stuff." I waved them off and returned to my default position of standing with my arms crossed.

The five figures hung around. There was silence, a long, impermeable absence of sound punctuated by my heartbeat. Frankly, it was unnerving. Not even a group of potheads would be so mellow.

A cold chill traveled down my arms. A trickle of sweat tickled my neck. I could hear the sound of my own eyeballs as they blinked. Maybe I was dead? I panicked, ran my fingers through my brown hair and over my chest. There was warmth; I couldn't be dead. I could hear my own thoughts but was deaf to the universe. My Seattle apartment was next to a busy road; I should have been able to hear the traffic humming by. Why wasn't there any noise?

Th-thump. Th-thump. Th-thump. Click.

Dead silence.

Th-thump. Th-thump. Th-thump. Click.

Trapped in an anechoic chamber.

Th-thump. Th-thump. Th-thump. Click.

Let me out!

"Say something!!!"

Just as quickly, sound returned. The eyeballs batted. The tentacles rustled. The mass of appendages faded into the fog, absorbed in their subtle reverberations as they pulsed, writhed, and squirmed around each other. A sickly-sweet aroma of rotting seaweed, fresh lavender, and burnt gasoline penetrated my nostrils as a retreating appendage dragged slime down my cheek.

I had wanted to doubt, to cling to the belief that this was a joke. It wasn't. Fear took over, and I lunged for a space between the goat creature and the pillars of oily marble. Limbs of suckers and teeth and ooze grabbed at my body and dragged me back to the center, where I was deposited as a heap under the great spotlight. My only recourse from insanity was to curl into a fetal position. If I closed my eyes and wished hard enough, the monsters might disappear.

Billy chimed in. "If you were a goat, you could run faster. They can reach speeds of up to 50 kilometers an hour."

If it was trying to comfort me, it was failing. My voice cracked in a pathetic whimper. "I don't want to be here."

"Many would clamber for the position you have been given," countered the whiny voice.

"Then why didn't you pick them instead of me?" I peeked out from my self-imposed hiding place; the five monstrosities were still there. Closing my eyes and hoping they would go away did not work.

"You are the messiah of your species, as described in your moving pictures and flip scrolls. A savior," declared the booming voice. Who was the lead in most TV shows, movies, and books? The classic stereotype of a middle-aged action hero popped into my head, his shirt open, chest glistening, a sexy damsel clinging to his broad biceps. A MAN, in other words.

"Wait, you mean…"

"Yesss!"

"Are you kidding me?" I protested, swiping my arm to the side. "You could have picked a president, a governor, some super-smart science person… and you pick me, a 35-year-old white guy?!" Like, for once, pick the intelligent people and not the meatheads. On the other hand, that gym membership must have been paying off. I flexed my arm; a little hill popped up. Swole.

Billy sulked. "I thought a goat was the sensible choice but was outvoted."

The booming voice enlightened me. "You are the most average of your species, as mentioned in your human lore. As such, you are well poised to determine the outcome that befits all."

My jaw went slack. My ego deflated. I wasn't picked because I was an exemplary action hero, but rather because I was boring. Basic. Average. Just an everyday accountant. No one wanted to be told that their stellar quality, their best characteristic, was that they were in the highest echelon of normality. I slapped my hands into my face and groaned. "Fine. Sure. Whatever. Tell me what I'm agreeing to." At least I'm good at filing tax returns.

THE BOOMING VOICE that I suspected belonged to the ginormous t-rex legs initiated formal proceedings. Nothing says authority like being king of the dinosaurs, except maybe an 8-mile-wide hunk of space rock that would beg to differ.

"You have been chosen to mitigate our dilemma. Only once in an eon do the portals of Végerzom and Earth align. For this hallowed event, five have arrived. It cannot be agreed among us who has the right to dominion over Earth. We have decided to seek the counsel of a representative from your world to select who shall reign."

I was nodding my head along, contemplating their collective predicament. The super-tall scary things with unknown faces from other dimensions wanted to rule Earth. Pretty straightforward.

"And what happens if I don't cooperate?" I smirked, feeling cocky. These idiots could argue for a million years; by then, humanity would be long dead. Economists, futurists, and climatologists alike were betting humans wouldn't make it fifty years before civilization collapsed. There wouldn't be a soul left afterward.

All I had to do was not give them an answer; take one for the team by standing there and ignoring them. Be the real hero. The whiny one countered my logic. "Then we will each share dominion after the planet completes one full rotation."

"Personally, I don't like to share," the goat said. "Goats, however, get along well with many creatures."

I cursed inwardly. Thought I had them there. Instead, I was stuck picking my brain for measly solutions and pulling only crumbs. A more intelligent person could reason their way out of this; I didn't have any other option but to listen and choose. Maybe the tentacle god? Perhaps it just wanted us to stop eating its squid-y children. I crossed my fingers. Please let it be that easy. Please.

"We shall each present our rule." Booming Voice made their proclamation. "Listen and decide."

Up first to plead their case was Billy. "I wish to bring the greatest joy to humanity. A world of fun and frolic. Humans will become the form that expresses the purest delight, bouncing, playing, bleating—"

"Bleating?" I asked. It's goats, isn't it?

"Yes, bleating. And you all shall prance under the warm glow of your star. Families of nannies and Billies, together with their kids, jumping high and low, eating the long grasses, the leaves, the tin cans…"

I tilted my head sideways. My left eye twitched as the contents of my skull tried to fall out of my ear. Yep. The idiot goat god was talking about goats.

"You want to turn people into goats?" I asked with the same deadpan enthusiasm one musters during a surprise colonoscopy.

"Goats are great creatures. They're funny and smart. And loyal. Humanity will enjoy being goats." This, the proposition made by a terrifying space god whose legs looked like they belonged to the devil.

A black-and-white spotted goat once ate my shoelaces at a petting zoo when I was five. Never forgave it; those were my favorite kicks, the bastard. Hellspawn belong in Hell.

"I don't think I'd enjoy being a goat. And if I'm the average person — the representation of everyone — maybe they wouldn't either." Take the hint; stop talking about the source of my five-year-old self's nightmares.

"Many people like goats."

I scowled at the red legs, unconvinced. Whiny Voice spoke next. "Then you may find my reign most amicable, for I am Aazazeel, The Benevolent One. My worshippers offer many praises, for I am generous and kind." The cloak with eyeballs shuddered, the owner of the whiny voice.

Appearances can be deceiving, though. I bobbed my head, a smile across my face. Existing under the watchful care of a selfless deity sounded like what humanity needed, protection from our own stupidity and self-destructive nature.

"For their worship, I give them their hearts' desires: comfort, leisure, entertainment. My children deserve the utmost attention."

Sounding great so far! Skip the other three and sign me up for the cult of Aazazeel!

"They will be rewarded with slaves. Countless slaves. Human slaves."

My face dropped. Of course, there was a catch.

"And they shall do with them as they see fit."

The 'Benevolent One' stopped talking. The several thousand eyeballs from under its cloak pierced me with their gaze. I checked to ensure I was still wearing pants; they were there, but I felt naked regardless. "Umm…thank you. I'll think about it." Think about it a lot. At work. In my dreams. When having sex. Always.

"Very well."

Two down, three to go. Goats suddenly sounded appealing.

Pillar legs that belonged to Wispy Voice shifted, calling attention to their marble veins reflecting oily colors. The process of elimination meant hissing voice had to belong to 'snakes for limbs.'

"Hard choices not made easy," Wispy Voice stated with certainty. "You will be undecided about this one as well. No choice made today will make you happy." Not what I wanted to hear. I gawked upward at the fog. Its shape swayed, a dark blob masked by mist…with legs for days. The voice continued. "The exact nature of my form will remain unknown to you."

The wheels in my head were turning. "How do you know what I want?"

"Goats would be the choice option were it not for past trauma. You liked those shoes." I took a step back, struggled to keep my footing. No way could it do that. No bloody way. "Your suspicions are correct. I see all and know all, including your very thoughts. I am the Lord of All Truths." Its wispy words shifted to a melodic purr.

Can it read my mind? It can read my mind! Oh, shit. Oh, shit. Don't think sexy thoughts, don't think sexy thoughts. Don't think about Sarah. No, idiot, stop thinking about Sarah! Shit! Yes, her ass does look good in that lacy pink underwear. Fuck! Out! Out! Out!

I beat my head with my fists, trying to dislodge the impure thoughts that took residence there.

"Goats also like to headbutt." Billy provided an unhelpful contribution.

The Lord continued. "Sarah does have a nice ass, and you will mate with her and have many children."

Fuck this one the most. I thrust my finger skyward. "Stay the hell out of my head, pervert! How dare you talk about my girlfriend that way! You harm her, and I'll—"

Smack!

"Grrdammit!" I performed a jig of agony as a stop sign popped out of nowhere and bopped me on the nose...and it hurt! The pain, it was real. I looked left, right, up, down; nothing. There for a second and then gone.

What. The. Hell.

"Such insolence," the Lord snarled derisively. If it had arms, they were likely folded in severe judgement.

"Take joy in the information I gave you," the wispy voice cautioned. "I am the Lord of All Truths. Under my dominion, your kind will learn sincerity, the greatest of all virtues." The wagging stop sign reappeared and threatened to discipline me for any further transgressions. It made its point. I rubbed my nose and wished all kinds of misery on it when another monolithic monstrosity attempted an appeal, the one with an army of squiggly appendages.

"I, Sssanassstansss, They Who Givesss, ssshall presssent your raccce with what their ssstomachsss mossst desssire…"

Was it aspirin? I could use some of that.

"Cheeeeessse."

"Wha?" Come again? "Err…cheese?" I was still recovering from being bitch-slapped by a stop sign.

"All the cheeeeessse you could ever desssire. A world of cheeeeessse."

Given how everything was going, I assumed their offer to be literal. Was there a chance we'd be given a board of fine Brie hand-selected by a most discerning cuttlefish? Probably not.

"Yesss."

"Of course," I muttered under my breath, hoping it couldn't hear me lest I receive another stop sign to the face. "And you, lizard legs. What do you have planned?"

"I am Goa'htch'hele."

"Gotcha." Couldn't be bothered to pronounce a name with eight-ish syllables.

"Goa'htch'hele," it repeated, annoyed I wasn't trying to say it correctly. "My demands are simple. I require 100 billion adult humans

— those of the age to comprehend my divinity — to be sacrificed in tribute to my name."

Fifth option, the definite worst: extinction of the human race. No. Just no.

"There are something like 7, maybe 8 billion people on this planet. You can't kill 100 billion people. There haven't been that many alive in Earth's entire history." I glared at the far-off form high above. "I'm not choosing yours."

"We'll see. You have three-quarters of your planet's rotation to decide."

FOR HOURS, I paced. I scrubbed my mind for ideas, tried to identify one that wouldn't doom the entire human race. I gnawed at the inside of my cheek until it grew raw and I tasted metal on my tongue.

Four options. Four exceedingly terrible options. Goats, cheese, the Pinocchio punishment, slavery. Goats, cheese, Pinocchio, slavery. Goat cheese, Pinocchio slavery. Goat cheeses Pinocchio's slavery. Slavery got Pinocchio's goat cheese. My eyes crossed. What was I thinking? Every option was terrible.

From horror to horror, I looked at the feet of these monsters and tried to determine which of their offers was the least worst.

A world of cheese sounded ripe.

A world where every lie resulted in some form of unholy punishment would be nigh impossible to navigate. Didn't the average person lie 30 times a day?

Goats were creepy. They ate everything and acted weird. Plus, those eyes—those glassy eyes with horizontal pupils. I shuddered

Slavery might be okay if I had more context. Better than being a goat.

I tossed my hands through my hair, wracking my brain for solutions. There were none to be found.

"You may ask us for further guidance to help you decide," the Lord of All Truths offered. I struggled to remember what the Lord had said before it read my mind and smacked me around. Blame the latent concussion.

The idiot goat god needed no prompting. "Being a goat is wondrous!" I looked at the deity with Satan legs — with its infatuation with creepy spawn — and grimaced. Yep. I was doing this.

"Tell me. How long does a goat live for?" I sighed in exasperation, the tone of my soul departing my body.

"18 years."

"Does it have to be goats? Can't it be something majestic, like horses?"

I may have offended Billy, then. The crimson legs took a thunderous step backward as the floor rippled under its footfalls.

"Horses? Those chariot pullers of the Friesian fucker? How horrid! I offer a good option for humanity: to become the happiest of animals, not enslaved beasts of burden lacking a sense of humor." Billy spat in disgust; a glob of saliva the size of a kiddie pool slapped the floor. Hint taken.

"So…" I inquired. "Goats and only goats, then?"

"There are over 300 breeds of goat, one for all tastes." The indignation was rife; I could practically hear the idiot goat god pouting. "Horses…hmph!"

"Umm…" I looked at the hissy god with the snake voice made of everything that crawled and slimed and gave me nightmares. "When you said cheese, how much of the world would be cheese?"

"Goat cheese is healthy." Another factoid about the usefulness of goats brought to me by Billy because who else?

"Sssilenccce!" hissed the cheese god.

"I wanted to share—"

"The quessstion isss for me." There were no further remarks from the goat god.

"The ansssswer isss sssimple. The planet. The rocksss, the watersss, the treesss."

"Even the lakes?"

"Yesss."

"And the oceans?"

"Yesss."

"How can the oceans be cheese?"

"There isss liquid cheeeeessse."

My stomach lurched into my throat. A whole ocean full of nacho cheese made me want to puke. I looked away from the deity; anything to clear my thoughts of Limburger hills and Swiss mountains made of actual Swiss.

The other implications were no better. People would starve.

"What about the rain and the water cycle? Also, cheese?" I honestly did not want to know the answer.

"Yesss."

How I wished for a merciful god; this spotlight offered only bleakness. Three days. That is how long people could live without water. After being showered in cheese, every fish, every animal, and every plant would die. I closed my eyes and tried to shut the horrible sight of parmesan blizzards from my mind.

There were still two more.

I skipped over the bloodthirsty deity to 'The Beloved One'— beloved to exactly one alien species and no one else; certainly not me. Slavery sucked; it's why we abolished it. But maybe, just maybe, we could get eighty years of life and some semblance of free will. Domestic servitude was tolerable, no different than being enslaved to the almighty dollar.

"Beloved One," I called out to the cloak of eyeballs blinking in unison. "What are your worshippers like?"

"Ah, yes. My worshippers. They are called the Attebahn. They live on the planet Esk, similar to yours. The Attebahn rise at the morning call to attend worship at my great temples. Following prayer, they carry on with their day of leisure. At the setting of Reez and Reez the Lesser, they attend evening prayer where they dance, feast, and present tribute in honor of me."

What I heard reminded me of Roman society, slaves to a bunch of lazy alien elites at their beck and call. I furrowed my eyebrows. Slavery was only as good as their slaver, and the slavers only as good as the god they served. Aazazeel, with its many eyes and robed cloak of shadows, was piss-worthy.

Saliva slugged down my throat. "What are they like as masters?"

A pause. A long, frightful pause as the light above dimmed. The looming shadow stooped lower and lower, blotting the spotlight as it placed part of itself closer to the ground and to me. There was nowhere to hide from the gigantic multi-colored iris. Its macerated pupil stretched wide as it leaned down close; I could almost reach out and touch the gooey sheen.

"Perfect in my many eyes. They will do to you as they see fit, each action a complement to my great glory. You will slave and serve, feed their bellies, clean their wastes, placate their desires." The pupil shrank to a dot. "They will chase you with implements. Throw you into fires. Drown you in tubs. They will pick you apart particles at a time until you are but dust. They will laugh, and they will sing. They will parade your disemboweled bodies through the streets and dance across your writhing corpses. They will take from you and give their praises to me for the gifts I have given them. I am Beloved."

The great eye pulled away. With its gaze broken, I was released from Aazazeel's hold and collapsed. "I… I can't do this." I wept into my open palms. Each choice was torture. "What do I choose?" Had none of them any empathy? Could they not see my pain? My tears? These weren't choices. The telepath had to feel that I was hurting! I dropped to my knees and begged. "Please."

"Tell me first why you deny my dominion," the Lord of All Truths demanded.

"I…" Okay. That was fair. "I'm afraid of what you will do to people."

"Divine and comedic punishment for lies that are spewed. Each lie is a strike, repeated until your kind learns the ways of divinity. You lie during the day, you lie when it's night…you even lie in your sleep! A child learns its first lie the moment it cries for attention it does not need, to be fed when it does not hunger. You are all born to lie. Strangling the baby in the cot is the merciful end."

I drank it in, my very thoughts repeated back to me. Wetness slipped down my cheek. That was why I did not want to ask; it meant admitting we would not change.

"We are not liars," The Lord spoke. The gods appeared evil yet claimed to be better than humans. Maybe they were right. Maybe we were getting what we deserved. For a species that decimated the world, perhaps starvation, torture, and goats were the best we could ask for.

Tears dripped onto the black floor, breaking the perfect flatness of its surface. "Damned if I do, damned if I don't. These aren't choices," I murmured. "No one would blame me for refusing to decide. We're all going to die horribly and quickly, anyway. Can't you just send me home? Let me say 'hi' to Sarah, and then you can turn our planet into cheese and our people into goats."

My thoughts drifted to Sarah; thinking of her made me smile and cry. What was going to be done to her? To everyone I knew? I would never again see her beautiful smile, hear her joyous laugh, notice how she sometimes snorted when she giggled. I'd never run my hands through her wavy, toffee-colored hair. The engagement ring I purchased two weeks ago would never grace her dainty finger.

Every anguish accumulated in a puddle of sorrow. My mind was consumed with longing. I wished I wasn't there, that I wasn't the one to have to decide the apocalypse. I wanted to spend my last few blissfully ignorant moments with Sarah wrapped in my arms, talking about the future. About how much I loved her and wanted to make a family together.

But instead, these assholes showed up and robbed me of everything.

Damn them! I punctuated my turmoil with a fist to the floor. I wouldn't get to see what we looked like together because we would be goats eaten by a bunch of sadistic aliens who—

'We are not liars.' The Lord of All Truths' words echoed in my memory. It agreed that Sarah had a nice ass and that we would have many children. Not creepy, bug-eyed goat kids; children.

I looked up at the oily marble pillars, then at the dinosaur limbs. "If what the other one said is true, that Sarah and I will have lots of children, then one of these options is survivable." Only two of the five options would encourage human breeding, and one actually depended on it: Gotcha's. My eyes locked onto the dinosaur legs.

"You must have a plan to kill one hundred billion people; otherwise, you'd wipe out the entire human race." It was time for the god of genocide to explain itself.

The deity rumbled a laugh. "You are correct. To reach my goal of eating 100 billion human adults, your species must reproduce. Your planet cannot naturally sustain such numbers. For each excess, I take. Thus, there is balance."

The circuits in my brain fired wildly as a sneer spread across my face. Mother Nature might have had a say, but not if humans beat her to it. Fuck, we're dumb. So was this god. Humanity, with its talent for destruction, was only one nuclear apocalypse away from extinction. The Earth could only support four billion people comfortably. Three billion people outright? A bad deal, but not everyone.

"Three billion or so people off the bat and then some?" I inquired.

Lizard Legs and Leggy Legs turned to each other by a tenth of a degree. There was a stretch of silence. The truthsayer was ratting on me. Crap. Gotcha returned to its position. "I am aware of humanity's fragility and your assumptions that an entity of my grandeur lacks the capacity to mitigate such pitfalls. I assure you and your kind, as Lord over said dominion, I will see to it that the quota is met. A fair trade: protection and sanctuary in exchange for one hundred billion humans."

Billions of people sacrificed for Gotcha's protection. Was I mad? That was more people than had ever lived. The pessimist inside of me liked this argument. It was a good deal. A great deal. One hundred billion human beings would be guaranteed to exist come whatever we and the universe threw at ourselves. And what excess there was would be balanced out by an unscrupulous god.

This was good, even merciful.

One hundred billion people would die, but ninety-three billion humans were guaranteed to survive, more than any futurist could have hoped. Damn the species while also saving it. I rose to my feet, standing tall.

"I have made my decision." The deities stirred and anticipated my choice. "For the next eon, I pick you to hold dominion over Earth." My finger pointed toward the being before me, the owner of the booming voice with the great dinosaur legs. The devourer of mankind. Our protector and savior. "Sacrificing one hundred billion *adult* humans is what I choose. No tricks."

"But goats are much better than people!" Billy whined.

"Noooo," howled the tentacle god.

"Very well," The Beloved said.

"Wise decision," affirmed the Lord of All Truths.

Teeth, rows upon rows of teeth, barred down. Grins upon grins filled the extent of my vision. "Thank you, Chosen One. You have selected well." The deity blew a fetid stench across my face that nearly bowled me over. "Humanity is blessed by Goa'htch'hele."

Or cursed.

The fog descended in a thick blanket that shrouded the five figures in a darkened haze. Before me, I saw the great Cheshire grin of a Lord appeased; the mouth humanity would offer itself to for hundreds of thousands of years to come.

Still better than goats.

X

What a fun romp through temporal planes of alternate realities, eh, kiddos? We're really letting our inter-dimensional freak flag fly now! And I gotta tell ya, I am having just a fantab-ulous time here with you. You kinda hate to see it end! I mean, I know we all have plenty of other responsibili-ties to tend to, and by "we all," I mean "you"; I don't have shit-all going on, and frankly, I'm pretty sure Steve is going to be all over my ass for not cleaning the Iron Maiden yet. I wonder if he'd go easy on me if I turned it into a joke? Like, he goes to inspect the Iron Maiden, and it's dirty but the moment he pulls the door open, Run to the Hills plays right on cue. Might bring a smile to his face.

Our next story is rich in buttery prose, more of a slow-burn Gothic thriller than balls-to-the-wall zaniness. See? I can be an intellectual, too. Not everything has to have cartoon energy, even if that's kind of my brand. Fiction is a rich tapestry of tonality; I am the weaver of dreams. I shall reach deep into my bag of tricks and bestow upon you a bevy of fine literary goods; otherwise, it wouldn't be much a compendium, now, would it?

The protagonist is an old-timey gentleman named Charles, which is not to say that he's necessarily old, just that he comes from a time that doesn't know what Twitter is. He's tasked himself with taking care of something for an old friend, kind of like when I promised my agent I'd pay him right back for that loan but then died 17 years later before I had the chance. Needless to say, creepy shit abounds.

I really should give old Harry a call, so while I rummage through The Big Guy's Rolodex (Seriously, Steve, who still uses a Rolodex?!), you all enjoy In the Yellow House of Birchwood Gale.

IN THE YELLOW HOUSE OF BIRCHWOOD GALE

MT ROBERTS

R ain obscured a rocky shore as the Karen Ann nestled its bow along a wooden pier. A hooded deckhand, brisk in his linen smock, looped a mooring line over one of the bent pilings and held the rolling boat in place. He motioned to Charles, the Karen Ann's only passenger. Charles nodded from under the wheelhouse's awning and flicked his cigarette into the dark eddies of the ship's wake. With a sigh, he shouldered his rucksack and stepped out into the mist.

"You sure you got a place to stay out here?" the deckhand yelled. "Captain says he won't take you any further."

Charles hopped to the pier from the cold gunwale and raised his voice above the weather. "Don't worry about me," he said, "y'all just get on before these swells grow worse."

The deckhand gave a shrug and loosed the mooring line, coiling it from the water as the Karen Ann floated off in a coalescence of steam and brume. Charles watched the vessel labor through the waves, its lamplight a rumor in the fog. Alone, he turned around and wiped the rain from his eyes. The pier ran long and crooked before him, swaying to a side. He popped the collar of his peacoat against the chilling air and checked his watch. It was colder than he'd anticipated—a much gloomier sky than the hour suggested.

Gradually, the pier gave way to a stony charcoal beach where damp sand greeted him. Charles looked around and decided to make for a dark bank of grass just ahead. Already, the odor of salt that clung to the air had weakened. Despite himself, a sensation of contentment had developed. He felt a sense of liberation being here, a path to putting the war behind him, of being something more than a casualty in the eyes of others. Steps fashioned from driftwood had been shoveled into the bank, and as he climbed to more solid ground, the flicker of a lantern from within a copse of madrone trees caught his eye.

An old shack, its frame somewhat depressed, stood back amid the branches, a plume of white smoke piping from its aluminum chimney. Charles hurried under the roof's shallow eave and waited as the rain continued to fall. The window at his left possessed a long crack in its pane, but a drawn curtain beyond gave no indication of what lay inside. He knocked on the door.

"Hello? Excuse me, I've just arrived at the end of your dock down there." He knocked again, gripping the door handle. "My name's Charles Marden...hello?" The rusted handle turned in his palm. Wary, he pushed the door inward. Darkness greeted him; dust and cobwebs; an oppression of mold. The only furniture was a small table set beside a quiet, wood-fire stove. Charles stepped back from the crooked doorway and looked up at the roof, bemused. Had he not just seen white smoke at the chimney?

As if to disprove this, he peeked around the shack's corner, only to find its outdoor lantern hung dormant. Unsure of himself, he moved inside and opened the stove's grated door. A mound of damp ash sat clumped within the firebox and caked along its rusted sides. He dropped his rucksack to the floor, checked the flue, drained whatever water had collected, and looked around for kindling. A stack of spilled newspapers lay in a corner. Charles walked over and grabbed what turned out to be an issue of the Wilkes Harbor Journal—its headline: "Armistice!"

Charles recalled an image of men running beneath a blue sky. Then, those same men dead on the ground, each lumped before a low wall set before a damaged hamlet. Alden came into view.

With a grunt, Charles ripped the year-old paper into pieces and lined the stove. He set his sights on a toppled wooden chair and broke its legs. Then, with a satisfying strike, he ignited his trench lighter, held it to the damp newspaper, and proceeded to blow. Inside the stove, a bead of yellow flame grew. Charles clamped down the cap of his lighter and leaned back on his haunches, rubbing his hands before the fire. His thoughts meandered to his final months in Europe, of the emptiness he'd experienced waiting for demobilization. All those weeks at sea upon a packed civilian vessel headed for New York, the so-called Great War over.

He'd had the chance to catch a train back home to Tupelo, maybe find a job at a creosote mill—but Alden's last words had echoed all too clearly. He felt compelled to return Alden's heirloom to his family. Granted, Wilkes Island was a long way from Tupelo, but there was no one in Tupelo to miss him, and Wilkes Island seemed just as fine a place as any other to settle.

He reached into his pocket and pulled out Alden's old whistle. It was a strange shape and made of what looked to be black marble. Charles put its bit to his mouth and gave it a try. Silence. Alden had used it several times in the war, and for whatever reason, the whistle resisted sounding for anyone except Alden. It had become a minor pastime for them, hunkered together, wondering how Alden did it, what his trick was.

Half an hour passed, and as the fire matured, so did Charles's understanding of what lay around him. From his place on the floor, he could see an attempted Plein Air painting of some old schooner, framed and set above a low bureau. On the bureau sat a coil of fishing line and several lures, as well as pliers and rods and little gears— angler's paraphernalia. Delicate dishware sat in a tin bucket near the closed door, and beyond the frayed table behind him stood a carving, or doll, on the floor. It was hard to make out in the shadows, but it stood out as not altogether belonging.

Charles squinted in the wax and wane of firelight; yes, there was a wooden figurine staring back at him from the far wall. Whatever material had been used to create it possessed an odd glint, as though certain areas were fabricated from a soft metal or greasy alchemical process. Leaving the stove's warmth for a better look, he found that the figurine rose to just above his groin. It was perhaps as thick as his leg, and from its squat base, dense weaves tapered upward into a bulbous knot—the tendrils of dried bull-kelp curled and splayed out to the floor all but suggested this knot as representing a head or skull.

A thin wire led from its back to the floorboards, set tight like a harp string. Charles plucked it for a note with his finger—mute—as the figurine slumped on its side and the wire slackened about the floorboards. As he studied the fallen figure, Charles tried to recall if Alden had ever mentioned anything about an indigenous fetish such as this but drew a blank. Perhaps the Karen Ann's captain had merely dropped him off on a part of the island reserved for tribal land.

After a moment more spent regarding the figurine, Charles lit a cigarette and returned to the stove, where he rearranged a protruding splint of wood and listened to the rainfall on the roof. His watch read midmorning now; if the rain didn't let up, he'd have to get a move-on regardless. It was a Sunday, and an appearance in town prior to church might prove helpful if he wanted to find Alden's uncle.

WILKES ISLAND POSSESSED no main road as far as Charles could tell. Instead, it claimed an assortment of gravel drives and labyrinthine lanes—thruways that led between rolling hills and sparse locks of forest, each a hedged-back path without residence. It wasn't until early afternoon, when the rain stopped, that he noticed a fence with a forlorn kissing gate in a field to his right. Not far away, down a knoll, a conical lighthouse pierced the gray horizon.

Relieved, he eased down the muddy lane he'd been following for the past mile as semblances of a town formed beneath a partition of low clouds. An array of oxen-blue and oxblood timber uprights appeared as if rising from the dark waters of the sound. The port of Wilkes Harbor, old and well past its days as a thriving lime quarry, sat huddled before a stone wharf.

Charles continued down the soggy hill and scanned the rooftops for a white steeple. The church, Alden once said, appeared as a rectangle set to its short side, rising high and straight with a finish as bright as wheat. Charles tugged at the straps of his loose rucksack and focused on a tall hazy building near the water. By far the loftiest of the town's structures, it really did resemble an upright rectangle—from a particular vantage.

At the bottom of the bank, he came to an old stone enclosure set before the town proper. It had the flavor of a more ancient place, really, and reminded him of the villages he'd seen in France. An essence of saltwater again floated on a constant prod of wind. A light mist, transparent as sweating glass, lingered along the built works of each block and avenue as if a layer of preservative glaze had been brushed over their edifice. At the intersection of Avenue B and Stewart Street, Charles took a turn. Here, he saw the semi-monolithic church above the hilly boulevards and made for another corner down Beech Street. As he ascended along a steep cobbled sidewalk, the noise of his steps grew to a relentless din, and the sigh and jangle of his rucksack seemed amplified in the harbor's all-encompassing quiet. There was no birdsong, no ship whistling its arrival at the wharf; not even the leaves of the trimmed cypresses appeared capable of rustling. Charles rubbed at his ears and looked up. The church was only a block away now.

Leaning on a streetlamp in front of a local dentistry, Charles waited, studying the large swath of desiccated lawn that encircled the church. He dropped his cigarette to the sidewalk and crushed it with the toe of his shoe. It was nearing one o'clock, yet there was no sign of service letting out. He gave a moan and stared up at the sky. Between the lingering gray of moving clouds, a hint of blue surfaced. Behind that, an unusual pigment of midnight; a space of lightly brushed-over cerulean black, flecked with tines of throbbing white, star upon star upon—

"Son?"

Charles snapped to attention, gripping the streetlamp. A stout man with a curious gaze stared up at him from the arched street. He'd come from the church; behind him, a throng of people poured out along the building's crescent steps into the dead lawn.

"Excuse me, son?"

Charles cleared his throat and pinched the bridge of his nose. "Hi, yeah, sorry. I was…just…well, I'm looking for someone and…."

The man lowered his hand and grinned. His eyebrows raised as he rubbed the back of his neck. "You shoulda' come on in! We're happy to have guests."

Charles smirked. "I didn't want to disturb—"

"Ohh," the man drawled, "nonsense. Tell me, where do you come from?" He came off the street and stood beside Charles with his palms folded over his belly. "By the looks of that pack, I'd say you was a military man. Am I wrong?"

Charles looked at the man and hoisted his rucksack. "Fismette and Fismes—the Marne, you'd probably call it."

The man gasped. "Ah! You're a hero!" He turned around and waved at the tapering crowd across the street. "Hey! Clarence! Clarence! Yeah! Grab Lloyd! C'mon! Yeah! Get 'im and come over!" He peered at Charles again. "Oh, what a blessing this is. My lord." A sliver of saliva flickered at the corners of his mouth. "What's your name, son?"

"Charles Marden."

"I'm Dr. Pakenam. Yes! Nice to meet you."

"Dr. Pakenam." Charles flexed his fingers in the man's grip, then retreated his cold hand into his pockets. "I came here hoping to pay my respects to the family of a friend of mine. You see—"

"Oh dear," the doctor said. "What was their name?"

"Alden Gale."

Doctor Pakenam looked down; his lips pursed. "Ah, yes," he said, "the Gales."

"So, you know them?"

The doctor removed his hat, held it to his chest, then wiped his brow in the clearing sunlight. "Well…most here know about 'em—the Gales. But only member left I can recall still lives here is old Birchwood. And he's not really a fellow who comes to town."

"Hey, that's great! That's just who I'm looking for. Alden wasn't able to give me much to go on. There really wasn't time…say, there a chance you could tell me where he lives?"

"Now…now hold on there, son. Look, I—"

"Well, what's all the fuss about, Doc?" A pair of men strolled up from the street, dressed in their Sunday best.

Doctor Pakenam turned and flashed a grin at his friends. "Hey there, Clarence. Lloyd. You two like the sermon?"

Clarence and Lloyd were both tall men, perhaps into their mid-forties. Lloyd sucked at his cheek. "Yeah," he said, fidgeting with his collar, "that young Pastor Cal's gonna be a good fit. Organist could loosen up a little, though."

"Who we got here, Doc?" Clarence looked at Charles. His nose and face gave the impression of a molted hawk with sharp, penetrating eyes.

"This is Mr. Marden," Doctor Pakenam said. "He's come to give his respects to Birchwood Gale. Appears young Alden isn't coming home."

"I'm sorry to hear that," Clarence said. "Wow…but no kidding." He looked at Doctor Pakenam and Lloyd, his eyes cold and stony.

Lloyd rubbed his nose. "You got a means to get all the way out there, soldier? Westsound might not be on the furthest point of Wilkes, but it's a hell of a road to get through without a motorcar or horse. Place sits on a spur in the island, you see."

"Actually," Charles said, "Dr. Pakenam here was just about to give me directions. I've no problem walking, but if I can be honest, I'd rather pay for a ride. If it's on anyone's way, of course."

Clarence's gaze honed on Charles momentarily as the other men's heads turned to the sidewalk. "I'll give you a lift," he said. "Got my own Tin Lizzie right over there." Clarence stuck his thumb out down the street. "She's red and rare." He gave a smile. "Who knows. Might be we just end up having ourselves a nice little Sunday drive."

"So how far is it, exactly?"

Clarence cut his red Model T into the street and waved at a passerby. He fixed his side mirror and flashed a smile. "What? Birchwood's? Oh, about an hour, give or take. Why? You got somewhere else to be?" Clarence let out a laugh. "I'm just playing with ya." He grabbed Charles's knee and winked. "Just playing with ya."

Charles lit a cigarette. "I take it you knew Alden as well?"

"Yeah." Clarence snickered. "I knew little Al. Used to see him a lot around the church back there. Always stayed behind with the old pastor on Sundays, God rest his soul. In fact, I gave Al quite a few rides myself most afternoons...me bein' a bit of a cleaner in the janitorial sense back then, staying late too." Clarence's mouth curled into an ugly rictus. "Anyway, that was only when the girls wasn't trying to get him...but Al never did seem too interested in 'em, if you ask me." He slapped the steering wheel as a bug hit the windshield. "That boy had a deep stare..."

Charles flicked the ash off his cherry and closed his eyes to the flapping wind. "Seems you're all very religious here," he said. "I wouldn't have expected that, knowing Alden."

"Yep, yep." Clarence lilted. "Well, the Gales follow something... different. A lot of the folk outside of Wilkes Harbor ain't quite right. So, we tend to stay our separate ways—lot of odd beaches outside of town, weird little totems made of seaweed and stuff. Say...you wanna take the road I used to give Al a ride on? Trust me. It's real long... really nice. You and him almost got the same shade of dark in your peepers. D'you know that?"

Charles focused his attention on the gurgling of the car, the breaks in the tree line. "How've ya'll been getting on with the flu?" he asked.

"Fine, actually! It never reached us all the way out here." Clarence looked over at Charles. "Aw, hey now. C'mon, don't tell me you're getting bored already?" He turned the car down a forested road through strands of sunlight and eased off the clutch. Clarence adjusted himself in the bench seat. "There's a pretty creek right up here. A lot of the kids used to go in there for necking and the like. But not so much nowadays. Place'd be empty if you wanted to stretch your legs a while."

Clarence pulled the car over and yanked on the handbrake. A resonance of wind and bugs played outside. He leaned over and put his hand on Charles's inner thigh. "C'mon now, soldier boy. What do ya say we get you discharged proper?"

Charles turned to face him and gave a small smile. He reached out with his hand, his lit cigarette still between his fingers, and held the side of Clarence's head. With a roll of his digits, Charles slid the burning cigarette into Clarence's ear.

Clarence howled and lurched back; his arms flung about.

"Get out," Charles said. Clarence remained seated, slouched against the driver's side door, his palm over his ear. A contortion of shock and rage had replaced his usual hawkish features. Charles made a fist and struck Clarence in the jaw. "Get out."

Clarence's hand shook as he brought it to his mouth; his sharp eyes glared at the quiet road ahead, welling with tears. He fumbled for the door's latch and popped it ajar to the calm soughing of the forest.

"You pray to whatever God you got that I don't see you again," he said, his jaw tight. "Cause boy, I'm gonna—"

Charles lifted himself up in the seat and kicked the man in the side of his throat, knocking Clarence's head against the upper canopy and spilling him out onto the gravelly road.

THE WINDING LANE seemed intent on losing him. And were it not for the ocean's guiding roar, the numerous interjecting backroads would have undoubtedly returned Charles to Wilkes Harbor. But as he navigated the Model-T through a leaf-strewn hill, a sunlit vista appeared. He let the Ford coast and glanced over the water, where sky and sea met in a flare of radiance. The road straightened, and Charles eased past a row of dead madrones, then descended toward a sparse village on the shore below.

Westsound consisted of only a few buildings, each white and separated by lawns planted with Garry oak and wild beech. A single boat launch tapered into the water beyond, where a truck and trailer sat parked, the glare of the sea bright and hazy. Charles yawned. His movements seemed slow; every gesture and turn of the wheel had to be made with conscious effort. It wasn't long before he pulled the car to a stop beside the local post office and rubbed his eyes.

The rope running along the post office's wooden flagpole whipped about in the breeze, a sporadic conductor keeping time in an otherwise quiet orchestra. Charles got out of the car, felt the wind buffet his body as if searching for some reason to disqualify his presence. He looked around. None of the streets—what few there were—had any markers. But at the foothills, a paved road stretched into obscurity up a dense, wooded rise. He walked around the car and made for the post office. The small building was closed.

Charles squinted against the glass and peered through a window, trying to read the names on the shelving bin behind the counter. No luck. In the corner, near a metal receptacle for paper trash, sat another wooden figurine, this one taller and more manicured, adorned with nine coins along the front of its bulbous head. Palpable dread filled Charles as he returned to the idling car. There, by the hood, he checked his watch and looked over his shoulder at the empty mailing station. It would be dusk soon.

THE GENERAL STORE, like all other buildings in Westsound, stood raised on a series of squat pillars. Charles engaged the parking brake and stepped out onto the gravel lot. A glistering lamp hung above the store's single glass-pane door, barely discernable in the late afternoon. Charles climbed the sinking steps and pulled the door open as a dull bell rang above him.

"Hello there," a raspy voice said. "Oh? Who're you?"

Charles followed the words and saw an old man beside a battered register. He was gaunt and shaky. "Hi, I'm looking for a residence here," Charles said, "the Gale place."

The old man puckered his chin. "Yeah, I know it." He motioned to the goods around him. Charles sighed and strode to a dusty shelf of bottled beer.

"Ah…ah, it's Sunday, boy. Can't be selling you any of that, I'm afraid."

Charles took a deep breath and settled on a packet of chewing gum, laying it on the old man's weathered countertop.

"Let's see." The old man gave a bemused grin. "That'll be five cents. You got that much?"

Charles raised an eyebrow and glared at the old man, flared his nostrils, and dug a dime out of his pocket. He put it on the bruised counter, where the clerk popped the coin in his register and sat back on his stool.

"Birchwood lives up the wooded lane headed out the other end of town. Road only goes one way. He's at the end on top. Might be a little grown over, but it's how it's preferred."

"Thanks." Charles grabbed his gum and left for the door.

"Oh, and young man?"

Charles turned around.

"I know that red Ford outside. Not many made in that color when it was bought. You let Birchwood know who it was gave you a ride, and there might be trouble, you understand? Keep it to yourself and send Clarence on his way." The clerk gave Charles a flinty stare. "Now that's your other five cents right there…don't you come in here again."

THE FORD'S acetylene headlights cast a dim, tawny glow over the narrow road. While driving this strange man's car, a sense of deflation had settled over Charles. He frowned to himself and imagined a life bereft of want or need, of existing without competition between himself and others. Tupelo couldn't offer that, and so far, it seemed neither could Wilkes.

The car bounced as it rolled over a fallen branch. Charles rubbed his eyes and leaned forward in the bench seat as he surveyed the dark road ahead. Past several trails that veered off into unknown recesses, a scrubby patch of dirt, grown over with tall weeds and rotted logs, abruptly halted his trespass. Finding no way over the debris, Charles parked the Ford and kicked some of the malleable wood aside. He leaned against the hood and listened. The engine gurgled within the quiet of the forest; he took a moment and lit a cigarette. Thrashing in the branches brought on by a high wind pulled his gaze skyward. In the canopy of leaves, wavering black limbs pierced the maroon of early evening—and just beyond, ever fleetingly, a smatter of cold stars, far away.

The idling engine's seized cough brought him back. Charles finished his cigarette and went around the car to grab the starting crank. He worked the Ford back to life and wiped his brow as he made for the driver's side door. Behind the wheel, he proceeded slowly up the narrow lane. The dull radiance of the headlights served to broadcast the strangeness of his presence here: in the car, in the woods, on this island. Why did the trees appear to move—and contrary to the wind? Their bodies almost seemed to pivot away from his approach as if disgusted.

While he wound up the road, a crimson sky overtook the forest canopy. Soon, Charles pulled onto a large open lot with an iron gate hanging open at the hinges. A mansion loomed at the other end, set behind a round gravel drive for horse-drawn carriages, its yellow gables and jagged yellow buttresses set bright against the dusk, overlooking the sea.

Charles brought the Ford to a stop and killed the engine. He peered up at the old house; it was too far from town for an electric line, but even so, not a single lamp had been lit. If Alden's uncle had passed, somebody would've mentioned it. Unless, of course, no one knew. Charles got out and lit another cigarette. A cloud raised as he slouched against the car, its steel body cold against his back. There was no getting around his situation—regardless of Birchwood's condition, this is where he would sleep tonight.

Tired and exposed, Charles stepped up to the porch, its floor sunken and warped. He scanned the area, took the brass knocker in his grip, and clapped it over the big door. Its boom reverberated throughout the house, causing the door panel to whine and twang. He jumped back, staring as bats rushed out from the upper eaves and tittered into the night. He honed on a bright planet, low on the ecliptic, then on the waxing moon rising in the south. Charles wiped his face and sucked at his cigarette before casting it on the porch and crushing it under his heel. He knocked again, then considered rounding the house—perhaps Alden's uncle only took to one or two rooms in the back—but dismissed this idea as the wind picked up. Instead, he pushed on the heavy front door. It swung aside in unusual silence.

A thick gloom lingered within. It seemed tangible, melting out in pulsating wisps along the opened doorway, curling up into the porch's rafters. Charles ignited his lighter and held it out as he stepped over the threshold.

"Mr. Gale—" He cut himself off. His ankle was caught on something. Carefully, he knelt and put his flame to the scuffed hardwood flooring. A long metal line had been strung just above the boards, thin and barely detectable. Charles narrowed his eyes against the darkness; the wire's dull sheen ran out of sight to either side of him. He retreated from the pressure at his ankle and heard the wire groan as it settled toward a stationary tension. Vibrations thrummed throughout the house, convulsing through the walls and along the floor, echoing into a place deep and far below him. An odor of seaweed and fish attacked his nose. He proceeded over the wire.

"Mr. Gale…Birchwood? My name's Charles Marden…I was a friend of your nephew's. We fought in the war together." His words echoed as he moved slowly over the floor, his hand stretched out. So far, all he could surmise was that he walked beneath a high ceiling in the mansion's expansive main hall, that each step brought more plucking from beyond.

"Mr. Gale?" Charles came to a wall of tattered wallpaper. He put his hand on the flaky covering and turned his head to an upper window behind him. Revealed from below its murky panes were outlines of a spiral staircase. His first impression of it was the thorax of some giant insect; banister, steps—all of it a tube-shaped exoskeleton with a claret sheen. He clamped his lighter shut to let it cool in his coat pocket. There would be lanterns and candles somewhere inside. For now, he'd follow along the wall and find entry into another room.

As his fingers rasped against the wallpaper, catching and freeing thin furls of it to the floor, his palm made contact with a doorframe.

Charles felt for the knob and eased the door open into a sparse room with tall bay windows, their salt-dyed panels overlooking a dark Pacific. Tastefully set before them on an ugly rug, in the center of the open space, sat an armchair with a small side table holding a dormant oil lamp. Charles entered and felt more vibrations under the floorboards. The sea emitted a violent hum from below as its heavy waves crashed and beat against the cliffside. Charles approached the lamp on the table, saw the fount was half full, removed its glass chimney, and struck his lighter to the wick. A flame sputtered to life, and he delicately turned the knob at the lamp's collar. Soon a bronze glow filled the room to reveal a shallow fireplace at the eastern wall; lumps of charred wood still rested on the grate.

In the armchair, Charles scratched at the stubble on his face and fetched a cigarette. Reclined, he exhaled at the ceiling where he caught a prominent pattern in the woodwork; an outline at first, but then an image—a familiar one. He adjusted himself and tilted his head. Above was an immaculate carving of the same figurines he'd found in the shack and post office, only this wasn't a rendering of bull-kelp and twigs. Here were details, judicious and pointed, flickering between focus and blur, just within reach of the lamp's radiance.

He studied the rises and falls of polished artistry, how thin segments of deep umber crossed over pale placements of curled bar, flowed and diverged upon intersecting squares riven apart by layers of thorn and bramble. A round, bulbous head with nine divots running along its face stared down at him; he couldn't help but think of them as eyes. And what served as a body seemed cut from a single tree trunk, sawed through at the base in a star pattern, with each thick strip tediously bent upward and primed until it resembled something of an outstretched flail. Charles ashed his cigarette over the ugly rug as the wind rapped violently against the windows.

His eyelids grew heavy with the whispering hiss of the lamp. An audible pluck rumbled from the walls while in the bay windows, the reflection of a tall, shrouded man stood at the room's parted doorway, his face white as bone.

"ALDEN! GO!" Charles turned and ran through a battered orchard as bullets sailed past him from behind. Several men fell up the way. Charles ducked and stumbled to his knees, his eyes fixed on the dirt. The chirp of Alden's whistle rang out, and the moment slowed as a leaf hung in the air. All sound ceased. Charles looked up at the blue sky—France was hot in August.

"Charles, get up!" Alden grabbed him by the crook of his arm and lifted him to his feet. The village was only a few yards away, and retaliatory fire from their division was already coming from inside the houses. Charles and Alden moved down a winding street and stuck their backs to the shelter of an abandoned bakery. There they caught their breath.

"The kill-zone...is further in." Charles wheezed. "We need to... meet up with the battalion...find a basement somewhere."

"Right," Alden said. He looked at his friend. "Hey. It's only a few blocks. Huns are still outside. We can make it." He put his hand on Charles's neck and squeezed.

The two gave each other a knowing nod and jogged past the derelict homes. Artillery cracked in the distance, followed by a whirring pitch that cut through the air. A shell hit far to their right, upending wood and stone in a strong clap that rippled over their bodies. Smoldering debris fell from above as more artillery rang out from unseen places. Toward the end of the street, while Charles and Alden strafed between comets of burning timber and a hail of ruined stonework, a group of Doughboys could be seen as they dispersed into the houses and shops.

"There!" Alden cried. "C'mon!"

Charles followed Alden into a wide two-story home, its windows broken by the percussive hits of shellfire. They hurried past toppled chairs and discarded belongings, up a bunched rug on the stairs, and kneeled beside a bedroom window. In the orchard beyond, hundreds of tiny figures in dark gray sprayed bullets into the village. Charles put a cigarette to his lips and motioned to Alden, who tossed him his trench lighter.

"You hear that?" Alden cupped a hand to his ear. "Coming from the north—northwest?"

Charles listened as he watched the damage spread below. Smoke rose in pillars toward the sky. Intermittent shouts raised amid the constant click and snarl of gunfire—through it all, an unmistakable hum, steady and growing.

"Aircraft," Charles whispered.

Alden sniffed. "Right, then. Make for the basement?"

"We'll wait until the Huns get closer. I want to keep an eye on their position for as long as—"

The bedroom wall blew in as a shell landed on a house across the street. Alden's arm and lower body were splintered upon impact as Charles was flung into the doorway.

CHARLES SAT UP. His breath was short. The oil lamp at his side winked and shimmered. He swung his legs to the floor and rubbed his eyes.

"Hello." A tinny voice echoed within the room.

Charles jolted to his feet. A frail man stood at the doorway, his porcelain face bobbing above a dark set of loungewear, markedly out of date. Charles couldn't tell if he'd heard the man's voice from below or behind—a different room, even. He stood up to greet him.

"Forgive me," he said. "I didn't mean to make myself at home. My name's Charles Marden. I'm a friend of Alden's."

The man in the doorway pivoted, his old clothes tapering about loosely. Charles took a step forward, feeling a sense of uncanniness from the man, a kind of aura or antinatural presence. He put his hand out. "Birchwood, right?"

The man glided back into the dark recesses of the main room beyond the doorframe. Squeaks and pops rattled the house.

"Sir?"

The man's white face beamed though his body remained imperceptible.

"I am...proprietor...Birchwood," he said, his unplaceable voice coming off as empty. "Birchwood...Gale. Is...Alden...gone?"

"He is," Charles said. "We were too close to a shell when it landed. Alden passed not long after."

Birchwood remained as only a face, floating like a vision in the pitch.

"I—Alden asked that I come here. I tried removing him from the rubble...but...in his last moments, he was adamant I see you. He made me promise to return this." Charles dug into his pocket and presented Alden's marble whistle. Charles looked down at it with sunken eyes. Its black material absorbed his attention. "Alden always had it on him. It was strange. He...I swear, when he blew into it...it was like he couldn't be hurt. Like the bullets just went around him...right by." Charles inhaled and gave Birchwood a weak smile. "A lot of us had lucky objects out there...little totems from home and whatnot, but this one, Alden's seemed to pause whatever moment we were in—"

"Did...Alden Gale...use it...more than once?"

A cold sweat emerged on Charles's brow. The volume of Birchwood's voice was triggering—so metallic, so mechanical and cold; distant. Charles took a deep breath and stepped back to the armchair as images of smoke and mangled earth crept into his thoughts. The twang and pluck of the house rumbled, and Birchwood appeared in the doorway, his baggy clothes swaying not unlike a drawn curtain. "I...would have you...tell me," he said. "Excess...was not...the indentured...agreement...with Alden...Gale."

Charles held his head, overcome with strange nausea. He lifted his eyes. "Alden's dead—what, what are you talking about? Sir—"

"This...is a house...of Irion," Birchwood said, his words coming out of the walls and floor as if hummed from elsewhere. "You...will return...the device...in Alden's...stead. Or...you may...choose... upon...an optional...indenture."

"I'm not here for a bargain." Charles gnashed his words. "I came to pay my respects! To honor a last request!"

Creaks and bends answered as Birchwood's figure, never any further than the doorway, stood rigid and static.

"Here." Charles put Alden's marble whistle on the side table. He shook the oil lamp, its quivering flame revealing an irregular, broken sheen behind Birchwood—several, in fact.

"You must...put...the device...in here," Birchwood said, his figure pulling back into the main room. "You will...put it...in...here."

Charles sighed and grabbed the whistle as his shoes clacked across the hardwood. He stopped. The room beyond lay still in darkness. His heartbeat quickened as he returned to the armchair and grabbed the lamp.

"You...will   leave...the   flame.   Or...will   you...agree...to an...indenture?"

"I'm afraid I wouldn't be able to see, Mr. Gale. But don't worry. I'm more than happy to leave it by the front door on my way out."

Birchwood slid before him in the main hall's vastness, his clothes dangling just above the floor. Charles went limp and nearly dropped the lamp. Birchwood's pale face teetered side to side, his features little more than a waxen mold. Behind him, from his baggy attire, ran a gleaming array of thin, metal wires. They glistened like an oil streak in the sun, some tight and firm, others slack and drawn as if a hidden puppeteer eased and pulled at them.

"You...will leave...the device...here." The wires at Birchwood's back vibrated, sounding through his clothes, the walls, ceiling, and floor. Shaking, Charles bent down and placed Alden's whistle on the scuffed hardwood.

"What are you," he whispered, his eyes manic, unfocused. "What is this?"

Tweaking and churning. "I...am...and this...is a house...of Irion. Will you...agree...to...an indenture?"

Charles's chest heaved at the sound of pops and twangs; distant gunfire and mortar fall.

"Indentures...left...broken...require...additional...appeasement."

With a moan, Charles stumbled toward the front door as Birchwood's countenance jerked out of reach beyond the lamp's glare—a sound of whining wires and ruffled clothes lingering from above, somewhere at the ceiling. Gasping, Charles clamored over the threshold in a pant, tripped on the wire run low beneath the door, and fell to the porch. The lamp in his hand scattered over the weathered boards and left a trail of glass and kerosene. The acrid fumes enlivened Charles. He scrambled to his feet and lurched down the steps until he came to the Ford's cold hood.

As he caught his breath, a breeze off the night sea caressed the sweat on his neck. Charles turned around, his hand at his throbbing chest. The tall yellow house remained dark, save for a pale, floating face in the doorway. Charles went around the car's body and opened its driver's side door.

"Hey, soldier boy."

Clarence lay in the backseat as if napping, his jawline bruised and swollen like a pulped grapefruit. He sat up and peered at Charles, a ring of crusted blood embellishing his ear. The man's Sunday suit had been ripped and dirtied.

"Guess you never checked the trunk box, huh?" He held a snub-nose revolver in his hand. "Yeah…you young bucks only think halfway through any given day." Clarence cocked the hammer back and pointed the muzzle. Charles retreated and raised his hands as Clarence searched his pants and coat. The man grinned and waved his revolver. "Get on," he said, "you walk to that cliff now."

The crunch of gravel and hard dirt accompanied the pair as Clarence prodded Charles in the back across the wild lawn. "This is good," he whispered. "Real nice view—now you stay facing that water and get on your knees."

Charles stared out over the dark ocean as he heard the man shift his gun. A smear of high clouds obscured the stars.

"I said get on your—"

Charles dropped to the ground in a sweeping motion while his outstretched foot kicked Clarence's legs out from under him. A shot rang out as Clarence fell hard on his side. Charles jumped on him, his hands at Clarence's neck as his knee held the man's grip on the gun. Clarence gasped for air, his teeth clenched together from the strain at his throat. More shots rang out from the weapon as Clarence pivoted his wrist and fired from under Charles's pinning weight.

Pain like molten ore rippled through Charles's torso. He released Clarence and shuffled to his feet. Shaken, he put a hand to his hip and brought it back. Blood dampened his palm. He inhaled and looked up in time to see Clarence rush him.

Beyond the man's impact at his chest, beyond the burning in his hip, he felt a rush of air at his clothes, pulling at his scalp—a thud as he hit the cliff's widening grade. Charles tumbled down the hard earth with Clarence, brushing rocks and shrubs until they slid to a halt on the low, stony shore. Cold sheets of froth whipped at him—a groan from Clarence somewhere.

Wincing, Charles managed to stand. His head was light, and the noise of roaring water only inflated his loss of orientation. Rocks. A thin path of rustling shrubs along the waterside. Heavy winds and cold mist.

He limped against the cliff's angled rise, buffeted by gusts. An odor of seaweed and fish hovered around him, only down here it was more potent and not wholly correct, as though what he'd smelled above in the house was only a layer of heated resin or some superficial hint at an altogether purer substance. His footing slipped as the trail curled and turned. Charles grappled for the cliff, its face nearly vertical. Black ocean roiled below, crawling up the rocks. It was difficult to move. He was losing too much blood—but could he not hear the twang and pull of wires in the distance? Just around this impossible bend? Such twisting and popping, as though some massive finger grazed at myriad open pianos. Craning his neck, he peered around the cliff and caught sight of a bright fulvous haze that illuminated the sea near a cove. If he could just reach around and find a stable hold, he could scuttle across and—

His section of cliff crumbled away, and as Charles hit the ocean, he felt he had exploded apart, his limbs and bones lost within the foam and shock of frigid water; his body catatonic as if he were a child yanked by an unforgiving parent. He broke the turbulent surface and peered up at the cliff as saltwater leaked into his mouth, down his throat. Perched like a ruin, the yellow house of Birchwood Gale stood in silence, old and sinking. Charles, drowsy and fading, followed the descending spine of the cliff with his eyes down to the rocky coast.

There, through the barreling tide, he could see the arched yawn of a sea cave near the path he'd followed—a dark hollow beneath the Gale estate, illuminated from within by a dull crimson glow, a festering cavity in the fevered island.

An involuntary scream escaped him as, in the recesses of the distant cave, nine points of blearing light ignited, each a distant comet caught in stasis. They blinked and swayed in his direction, trailing their brightening light. Eldritch and alive—eyes, mammoth and staring down at him, upon him; nine yellow orbs, each as tall and bright as any lighthouse.

Charles cried in their radiant glory, "Save me! Help! Oh, God!"

But the roaring of waves and hissing of spray towed him further inside the Pacific's yawning mouth; a mouth cold and equivocal, wide and distanced; deep and dark. Charles squinted against the sharp salt-water, floundering against his body's burgeoning acquiescence. His mind a cacophony of images; a view of Alden—then a coldness around his midriff more profound than the water, a pressure at his waist as if in the pinch of two great fingers.

ACRID AIR WOKE him to the dark. An odor of fish. Charles coughed as dripping water from somewhere droned on in a metronome—a wet tattoo. He was against a damp, stone wall with what felt like lines of heat running throughout his slack limbs, chest, and groin. A heavy presence rasped before him; he could sense himself tilting as the sloshing of a stagnant pool obscured the droning water drips. In a revelatory moment, he observed the darkness at his eyes sway to a side; a blue evening, dotted with thick stars and soft, moonless clouds appeared within the jagged frame of a rocky opening. He'd been brought inside the sea cave below the house. But how? By what? Charles willed himself to move but stopped at a heavy disturbance in the water. His skin tingled, unable to imagine the form of the moving, colossal shadow. What giant monstrosity loomed inside this cave with him? Those swirling meteors from before? He could hear whatever it was!

From the evening's light outside, subtle glints of long, bulbous extremities, somehow darker than the cave's own shadow, gave him notions of a mass that seemed to writhe and squirm in such slow deliberation that Charles could barely distinguish what he saw from that of what he heard. A humming far beneath the cave rose up through the bedrock, tickling loose bits of pebble from the cracks and fissures above, each small fragmented chip clattering into the stagnant lagoon. The shadowed entity lifted a trunk-like limb and dabbed at the cave's ceiling. Shining slits of silver wire reflected down as an opening gave way, and the figure of Birchwood Gale descended.

A single, churning orb combusted in the pitch as melting light washed over the cave, blinding Charles. He closed his eyes and moaned. But a rattle and twang of plucked strings drowned him out, followed by a tinny, booming voice.

"You…indenture…so…shall it be…you…are borrowed…as nothing…of mine…do you…wish…to employ. Your debt…imposed…will be…servitude."

In the burning light—the all-around voice—Charles could feel his body lifted into the air. His arms and legs were tugged in all directions. Birchwood remained aloft, his pale face holstered in outstretched clothes intent on enacting a sordid ballet—a pirouette and tourner, one sauter, then a plier and élancer, all adagio amid yards and yards of wire, ablaze in the blistering radiance of that comet hovering about in the cavernous heights. Charles could hear the hiss of water at the walls as it evaporated into mist. He began to laugh and shake his head as the form of Birchwood, dancing and folding like a hollow doll, took on the wavering visage of Alden. Smoke and splintered wood bloomed at his shoulders, brushed by his chiseled, grinning face. Charles let his mouth drop in awe as Alden gave a heavy sigh and spread his arms wide for an embrace.

Tired daylight sank through murky window panes onto an old wooden floor, where leaves from a long distant year lay scuttled and dry. The main room of the Gale mansion had remained untouched for almost two decades, save a hole in the ceiling that had given way at some point. Waves crashing far below filled the empty rooms with a distant, albeit perpetual, sigh; at the eaves, a tell-tale blow from a strengthening wind.

Outside, the rumble of fine-tuned combustion engines infiltrated the home's quiet interior. Vehicles rolled over gravel and came to a stop—their motors cut off. Doors opened and shut as numerous feet scuttled about the lawn.

"You weren't kidding, Leonard. This place is right out of a museum. Look at that old Model T! Damn…and all the way out here."

"Johnny, try and be a little respectful—that goes for all you fellas. We're not supposed to be here."

"Yeah, yeah, but don't forget whose idea this was," Johnny said. "We're only here 'cause you wouldn't shut your mouth about there being something inside that'll help us fight the Japs."

"There is something inside," Leonard murmured, "I've heard stories about this house my whole life. People gone missing. Unnatural sounds. Weird lights. Everyone on the island just pretends it ain't here."

Uneasy shuffles followed—a knock.

"Oh, just open it, will ya?"

The front door creaked ajar, swinging wide and warped as six young men in freshly ironed uniforms stood at the threshold. Each seemed unsure as a cold December breath leaked into the mansion. Leonard, the one in lead, took off his cadet's hat and stepped inside. His nostrils flared.

"It reeks in here—hello?"

His boot caught a low, rusted wire set just within the entrance's parameter; he stumbled forward but regained his composure. The others laughed from the porch.

"Stop! You hear that?" Leonard put his hands out to shush them. "I'm serious! Shut up!"

A twang of rattling wires filled the Gale home, resonating at the walls and floor. It rose in tenor, ultimately overpowering the young men's laughter. A shadow in the rafters passed across the leaf-strewn floor, then shook as it came to a stop, looming like a spider.

"Jesus Christ!" Johnny yelled, taking off into the yard with the others.

Leonard crawled backward as a tall, rattily dressed figure dropped from the ceiling, its body suspended by thin, glistening metal cables. A long, pale face hid within the cave of a hood.

The volitant body jerked as winding shrieks of air from far below pulsed upward throughout the house as though the serpentine pipes of some cyclopean organ were being cleared of thick sediment. A low, thewy voice spoke from everywhere as small black tools fell from the body of clothes to the wooden floor, an oddly shaped whistle among them.

"Hello. I am…proprietor…Charles. Charles Marden. Do you… wish…to enter…an indenture?"

XI

Holy monstrous marionettes, Batman! Another ending coming straight out of left field to secure a victory for the home team. Good showing, indeed! All compliments to the chef.

So here we are again, just two stories left, and who do we have before us but the Eldritch Gods. Always with the Eldritch Gods. I mean, look, don't get me wrong, they're impressive beings and all; it's just that everyone is constantly sucking their tentacles and various enigmatic appendages that don't belong on any creature, living or dead. (Please don't tell them I told you that.) Maybe there are gods of a variety other than Eldritch; did you ever stop to think about that? Perhaps it's time they get shown a little love, as well. You hear us... uh...Protagonitus, God of Fiction-Based Narrative! We behold unto you the gift of short story, in all its glory!

Our next story follows a woman named Kay, 'kay? (Ha! I'm hilarious!) And let me tell you, this chick does not fool around. She has seen some shit, no question, and she carries it with her like a hardened knapsack filled with boulders of tenacity.

Speaking of which, you're not gonna believe this, but that was the name of my punk band in high school, The Hardened Knapsacks. We didn't so much kick ass as suck balls, but the spirit and chutzpah of the genre were there. That, and an inability to play our instruments. I played drums and bass, which is very different than saying I played drum n' bass, which I also enjoyed; I just never got into DJ'ing. Super expensive pursuit, plus I died before it became a thing.

Welp, I'm officially ready to party. I'm gonna find some molly to pop while y'all enjoy Eat the Eldritch.

EAT THE ELDRITCH

NICK DORSEY

The enormous green letters on the side of the building had fallen off years ago, but Kay could still make out the echoes of the words *Holiday Inn* etched in grime and ash. The hotel was across the river from Cincinnati's quiet, nothing-colored ruins. Maybe that's why the idiots made such a racket arguing about beans; they thought there was enough distance between them and that city's terrible new denizens.

They were wrong.

She heard men arguing from blocks away. The safe action to take would be to move on. Kay certainly wasn't going back to the blight of Northern Kentucky in the dark of night. Still, she wasn't going to risk crossing the suspension bridge to the city. Not if she could help it, and certainly not after sunset.

Then she heard them mention beans. Which meant she was going to have to visit the idiots making all that noise after all.

Kay was curious about what kind the men were eating. She had consumed her weight in kidneys and blacks despite being partial to cannellinis. She would've liked red beans, too.

She was a survivor. And she was still human.

Kay walked around the building twice and decided the fire escape was her best way up. She wouldn't have to deal with whatever was still inside the hotel.

Her knees did not thank her.

She was closer to forty than not, with silvery gray hair hacked short. She had been shot twice, stabbed half a dozen times, and even lost a tooth in a particularly violent scuffle. A scar like a treble clef wound around her right thigh, a relic from a previous encounter with one of the smaller beasts. A brand shaped like an ornate 'W' crossed her left shoulder blade; that she did not discuss with anyone. Ever.

Her dusty clothes were full of holes poorly mended. A holster at her belt carried a pistol but no ammunition. She had a single grenade that might or might not work, while a wire garrote twisted around in her pocket in case something more subtle was called for.

With a numerous assortment of knives secured about her person and a small backpack holding little food and less water, Kay wiped her shoes clean. Trail runners, a good size. She cleaned them daily and replaced the laces when she could. And she had enough shoe cement to hold them together until she could find a new pair, though she doubted anyone would ever make running shoes again.

Her parents had been gone long before the world changed. Her brother died in the riots after the monsters came. Her husband died of a fever a year later. She once traveled with a group of civil war re-enactors that had become a sort of militia, and they were mostly dead, too. Arrow wounds.

But Kay survived.

The people on the roof didn't hear her climb over the rail and ease onto the fake wooden decking. They were too busy bickering like siblings. Three of them, near plastic Adirondack chairs. Two men and a woman.

A rusty, portable grill was just starting to smoke. Off to one side was the pool and hot tub combination, now dry, cluttered with leaves and garbage, and who knew what else. Drained for the season before everything went to hell. Or something could have slurped it up. Drunk the whole damn pool, chlorine and all.

"What kind of beans do you have?" Kay said.

The troublemakers stopped talking. The woman, wearing a cowboy hat, froze. The older man with long hair took a step forward while the younger man with an arm full of tattoos stepped back.

Kay's hand dropped to her empty pistol. A showy gesture. Made sure they saw it. Her other hand rested near her thigh, close to a knife with a good weight, should throwing it be needed. She didn't see anything in the way of weapons on the roof besides a few lengths of wood.

Dumber than she thought. Or maybe they were just careful.

"I told you we should have set up a watch," the tattooed kid said.

The woman scoffed. "It's just a person, Sil. Just a person like us."

"They can look like us," the tattooed kid said, and it was true. A few of them could look like humans. But while the monsters might look the part, they acted as strange and otherworldly as their origins and were easy to spot.

"Still," the older man said, turning to Kay, "you look like people."

"If you didn't want company, you should have been quieter," Kay said. "And Sil there is right. You should have kept watch. But I'll tell you what, give me some beans, and I'll help protect you."

The young one said, "What do you think, Jesse?"

The woman in the hat shrugged. "We don't have much. But if it's just one person. And tomorrow…" Her thought was left unfinished.

Kay turned her attention to the older man with long hair and looked into light brown eyes that were not unfriendly. "You alone?" he asked.

"Yeah."

"Come for the meeting? Or just passing through?"

The meeting? Kay was afraid to ask. "I'm just passing through."

A look was exchanged between the three of them.

"I guess we have a little to spare," the older man said.

While her hands eased away from her weapons, her eyes narrowed. Kay had been overly focused on the beans, that much she could admit. The hair on her neck stood tall.

These three were too friendly. Caution was forgotten, along with that world they all lived in.

Still, Kay stayed.

Jesse told her they had red beans as they encircled the grill with the Adirondack chairs. Between the four, they shared a dinner consisting of one can of beans and another can of tomatoes. There was also a salad of greens Sil had foraged that looked to be primarily weeds, but both Jesse and the older man, Farek, said they would be safe to eat.

Jesse and Farek came from Louisville and had been together for five years when Sil joined them only last month. Before that, Sil had lived his life on the road. A hard way to live, Kay knew.

Farek grunted as, from his orange backpack, he pulled a slightly dented but exceptionally clean can of peaches. Jesse and the young man didn't say anything. Kay heard herself gasp. When was the last time she had fruit? The sudden display of wealth made her uncomfortable. Red beans and now peaches. She felt energy like a gathering storm settle over the three. Something was coming, she knew. Maybe some awkward conversation or request. Farek spooned portions of the delicacy into tin dishes.

They ate, and it was fine. Kay waited until they were ready.

The sun was setting behind the hotel when Jesse finally worked up the nerve. "You should come to the meeting tomorrow."

There it was.

The peaches were no temperature at all. Soft and slick and sweeter than Kay imagined. She decided to humor them. "What meeting?" Juice dripped down her chin that she caught with a finger.

"More of a protest," Farek said. "To get some attention."

Kay snorted. "Protest somewhere else. Cincinnati is crawling with big ones. Named ones, you know."

Not all of the creatures that ruled the world had names. Some came as unthinking as army ants; dull, cruel beasts. Others were wholly unique, equipped with terrible intelligence, with names like Torvo the Eye. Like Ferri the Sunken Root. Dun'praya the Many Tongued. They controlled men and territory, fed on flesh, screams, and fear. Kay did not know if the creatures had risen from hell or descended from the stars, only that they now reigned supreme.

Kay had long ago adapted to life under their rule.

"We know there are named ones here," Sil said. "That's why we've come."

Kay didn't get it. She said so.

"Because they'll understand," Jesse said as she slurped peach slime from her plate. "I mean, we've all got to live in this world, don't we? Live together?"

This sounded both obvious and insane.

"We're going to protest them. We're just going to make our feelings known," Farek said. He grabbed a length of wood, which was not a weapon but the handle of a picket sign. "SHARE THE WORLD" was printed on thick paper in a childish script. He pulled another that read "EARTH FOR EVERYONE." The handwriting was better, at least.

Kay let out a deep, peachy breath. Protestors. Looking for attention. Which was precisely what most sane people had been avoiding for the past decade. Don't make a spectacle of yourself. Keep your head down. That's how you survived.

Now, this. With each passing year, folks found brand new ways to act foolishly. They thought they could reason with monsters, the same ones that turned the world upside down. But people have always been a little crazy.

"They don't care, you know," Kay said. "They might have followers. Some desperate people might have started religions around them, started calling them the old gods. But the creatures themselves don't care."

"They'll listen to reason," Farek said.

Kay spat at the base of the grill. "I've seen 'em up close. They are, at best, unreasonable." She didn't like to think about her closest encounter. Gorbunew the Boar. Called that because it looked like a giant pig, only with more tusks and legs and eyes. Kay and a few dozen others tried to fight it, guns blazing. When that didn't work, they ran. When that didn't work, they died.

Most of them, anyway.

"We have to try," Jesse said. Her face was full of passion.

Joylessly, Kay said, "It's gonna be like talking to a rock. Arguing with a thunderstorm. Like ants lecturing a kid with a magnifying glass, and you're the ants. It's not going to end well."

"There's going to be plenty of us," Sil said, sounding almost noble. He was leaning on the edge of the roof. "They're crossing the Roebling now. Getting set up."

"The what?"

"The bridge."

Kay found a pair of binoculars in her backpack. One lens was cracked, but they otherwise worked well. She looked along the length of the massive suspension bridge that spanned the Ohio River and led into Cincinnati proper. She could see the silhouette of people against the purpling dusk.

They were now making their way into the city, legs bowed under heavy backpacks. Somebody once told Kay the refineries in the South were still churning out gasoline but that none of the stuff made it this far north. Even bicycle tires were hard to come by. Most of the horses had been eaten years ago; she had to admit that humanity might have jumped the gun in that regard. They weren't as hungry as they thought then. But it was the early days.

Who knew what was to come?

Flashlights lit up the bridge while others carried torches. And those people carried signs; placards.

EARTH FOR EVERYONE.

NOBODY IS A MONSTER.

COEXIST.

More delusional individuals, like her hosts. There were other signs, though they did not express the same sentiments.

OLD GODS, OLD IDEAS.

I AM HUMAN, HEAR ME ROAR.

EAT THE ELDRITCH.

Kay found she did have a favorite sign:

WHICH SIDE ARE YOU ON?

As though the monsters were willing to welcome anyone to their side. As though they even had a discernible side. "Some don't look like they want to reason with anybody. They want a fight."

Sil said, "We don't associate with them. They're violently anti-bomo."

"Anti-bomo?" Kay didn't like the sound of that.

"Anti-behemoth."

Oh, Christ. Just like the before times, there was no cause too stupid, no mission so hopeless that it did not need a ridiculous-sounding name.

Kay set her binoculars on one knee. "They think those things are going to read the signs and, what, appreciate their wit?"

"I know," Jesse scoffed. "So antagonistic."

"You don't know. Those monsters are going to eat the world. *Are* eating the world. Have eaten most of it already, even. It's over. We're done. Signs and posters and shit? Are you joking? Work with them? Fight against them? It doesn't matter. Just make it to tomorrow. That's the name of the game, now."

As Kay went on, two separate factions — the anti-bomo squad and the coexistence folks — met below the bridge and traded strong words. Loud words. The city beyond the bridge remained dark and still, but Kay didn't think that would last. The creatures would take notice eventually.

Her three hosts leaned over the railing and watched the crowd throb below.

Strong words quickly became blows. Signs became shillelaghs. The whole bridge erupted into the sort of riot Kay had not seen since the world was only recently thrown into complete turmoil.

Kay's hosts quickly gathered their things. Farek pulled on his orange backpack, muttering something about showing those jerks that the planet was meant for everyone.

"Come on," Jesse said to Kay. "We're going to straighten them out."

"No," Kay said. "I don't think you will." But they were already walking to a door labeled 'staircase', which would take them through the building. The dark, abandoned building.

There was no end to their bad ideas.

Kay waited until they had been gone a full three minutes, then searched the roof for anything they might have left behind but found nothing. For that, at least, she gave the idiots credit.

She squinted through her binoculars and watched her former hosts cross the street, Farek's orange pack dipping in and out of shadow until they melted into the protest-turned-riot. A man hit Farek with a metal pipe or an aluminum bat, and then it was all chaos. Kay lost track of her hosts. She had tried to warn them. Now they were lost. She didn't feel too sentimental about it.

She felt differently about Farek's orange bag, though. That was still lying on the bridge, full of peaches or beans or who knew what. She threw her binoculars back into her dusty pack and sat in a plastic Adirondack chair. She chewed her lip. Those three had made their choices, and they would live with them. Or not. All things considered, she didn't feel any way at all about the matter.

But the bag, forgotten in the madness on the bridge, didn't sit right with her. If there was something she could use in there, she was duty-bound to claim it before someone else did.

There was only a violent mob and soon-to-be-awoken nightmare fuel between her and a backpack full of delicacies.

"Screw it," Kay said. She used the fire escape and made her way down to the street.

The steel and concrete bridge was on fire. Maybe somebody lost control of a homemade Molotov? Screams of anger and fear combined with sharp grunts of pain that faded to white noise. As she approached the bridge, she couldn't tell who was on whose side, only that nobody was winning. But there, only a few yards down the bridge, was Farek's pack.

Kay picked up a discarded placard and waved it in front of her, trying to keep to the fringes of the brawl. She quickly scooped up the bag and threw it over her shoulder, then turned to find herself face to face with a snarling woman. "Earth is for everyone!" the woman screamed as she shot a fist across Kay's cheek.

Kay had the presence of mind to club the woman with her sign, and the woman went down howling.

Except.

That wasn't a woman. That was something else. Something that howled in a way that made Kay's heart pound and her bowels relax. She joined the rioters looking across the bridge at the ruins of Cincinnati. Against the purple sky was the baseball stadium with its tall lights shaped like toothbrushes for reasons Kay couldn't remember or had possibly never known.

A massive tentacle wrapped itself around one of the lights while, separately, another tentacle did the same. Together, they hoisted a mass of corrupted tissue into the air. Kay couldn't see the creature's eyes, but she knew it was looking at the bridge, regardless.

Some protestors dropped their signs and ran. The smart ones, at least. The dumb ones started arguing, blaming others for waking up the monster. They didn't even notice the sound of a hundred boots marching across the bridge.

Men and women clad in black marched in waves from the city and stretched across the bridge's entrance. The protestors were surrounded by newcomers who wore steel-toe boots and riot shields and carried batons. Not even they could afford guns and ammunition.

Kay had seen people like this before. Like any giant beast, the otherworldly monsters attracted parasites. Devotees, they said, or worshippers or cultists. They pretended to understand the wants and needs of the monsters, and the monsters did whatever they wanted and let the idiots in robes scour their actions for signs. For meaning. For prophecy.

All nonsense. All madness.

Now the cultists were militarized and tactically deployed. Forewarned or not, they were here, and they were angry. The howling from the baseball stadium wasn't calming matters down, either.

From the mouth of the bridge, they charged, barking some war cry. Kay decided that perhaps there was a particular safety in numbers. For her, at least. Not the numbers. She ensured her pack and Farek's orange bag were secure, then waded into the sea of rioters, knocking heads with her protest sign.

She let the first wave of armed cultists smash into the protestors behind her, moving deliberately while everyone else panicked. But not Kay. She would not allow herself to panic. She grit her teeth, cut her eyes, and gripped the wooden post of her picket sign so tight her knuckles stood out as pale dots in the night.

The thought crossed her mind that this was the closest she had been to a group of human beings in years. Before, she might have seen crowds at parties, football games, or even a mall. Not any longer.

Kay did not relish the last time she had seen so many people. She had been more naive then, lingering with a crowd of scavengers in front of Advocate Trinity Hospital in Chicago. Everyone near the hospital was unwashed, afraid, and starving, waiting for a supply drop from the then-still operational Canadian Relief Force. When the pallets parachuted down from three passing helicopters, everyone waited patiently for them to land, even organizing themselves into a makeshift queue.

Then the gangs made themselves known.

Two rival forces, each claiming the Heights as their territory, bullied through the crowd and tried to take the lion's share of supplies. But the others were starving, and hunger often outweighs fear.

Kay was caught in the middle of it all, alone, unsure if she should be more concerned with the rude, angry people in the crowd or the emotionless, unholy creatures rumored to be nesting within earshot. She had two bottles of water, a 9mm pistol finished in pink, and a box of ammunition to her name.

When the crowd turned, she decided her best bet was to get to Lake Michigan. Get out of town. Skirt the city entirely. Scared, nervous, and angry, she picked a direction, hauled up her pink pistol, and started shooting.

She made it to the water. When the sun finally set behind the smoking city, she was not the person she had been when it rose that morning.

By the light of the torches and the burning bridge, Kay tried to forget the Chicago of years past. She needed a way through the violence. Protestors cursed and beat one another with picket signs while cultists clubbed and pushed against them with riot shields. Kay waited until a few black-clad bruisers were separated from the throng. A man of middling height who had lost his baton gestured with his shield half-heartedly, already tired. He would be her mark.

She crouched down and wove through the rioters when a cultist smashed his nose into the end of Kay's protest sign. Kay turned to her mark and tackled him, tore the hood and shield from his body, donned her new gear for herself, and left him at the mercy of the others. Then, she cursed. The way forward was now a solid wall of rioters. But it was the only way off the bridge, it seemed.

She had no choice. She pushed her way into the city.

To her left was a dark, empty football stadium. To her right was the baseball stadium, complete with tentacled monstrosity within. So, she would go left. But just as she moved from the pavement and set foot in the overgrown median, someone yelled out.

"Hey! You're going the wrong way."

Kay ignored the comment and walked quickly into the waist-high brush. Footsteps followed her. "Hey! You! Get back on the bridge! Great Gnu-Val commands it!"

She stopped. She didn't want to, but she didn't want the man raising any sort of alarm, either. A purple-clad figure appeared behind her, sporting a long goatee and a pug nose. He looked like the only person on the planet to never miss a meal. Taller than Kay liked, too. He put two meaty fists on his hips and barked.

"Gnu-Val commands it!"

Kay set the edge of her shield on the ground and tried to come up with some excuse but wound up throat-punching him instead. He looked surprised, then worried as he fell to his knees, gasping for air. That should have settled the matter, but he was able to grip her ankle and hold fast, even as he was hacking and trying to breathe.

The thing in the baseball stadium let loose a sound that Kay felt in her sinuses. She froze. The cultist in purple froze. The rioters on the bridge probably froze, too. Kay momentarily regretted punching the guy in purple. For the first time, she was willing to accept that maybe the cult leader might actually have some sort of relationship with the monster.

Kay pulled one of her knives and rolled over to the gasping man, where she pinned his body under her shield. She spoke quietly. "Tell that thing to let me go, and I'll just go. No harm, no foul." She wiggled the rusty Ka-Bar blade toward his eye. "Deal?"

The man snorted and managed to draw in a breath. "Tell Gnu-Val?"

"Yes. However you do it, do it!"

The man nodded. Kay let him up. He laid back in the tall grass and made a slight sound, almost like a laugh. Then he yelled. "Great Gnu-Val, save your loyal servant!"

The monster in the baseball stadium roared again, a sound like a hundred babies being pureed in a giant blender and that blender being run over by a garbage truck being driven by a trumpeting elephant. Tentacles slapped the side of the stadium and pulled the creature over its walls. The whole bloated thing fell onto the street below like some cancer-riddled cephalopod.

The teardrop-shaped body rose on many legs and turned to the bridge, where the creature opened its lone, giant eye. The milky white orb possessed a cat's vertical pupil that stretched ten feet high. Kay could not find the breath to curse. She could not believe the monster would obey this grinning idiot in purple.

The cyclopean beast crept across the parking lot at shocking speed and was soon wading through the Ohio river, wrapping those massive tentacles around the Roebling Bridge and pulling itself up. Kay expected the rioters and cultists to run for their lives, but they were oddly silent. They weren't even fighting.

A mouth appeared along the bottom of the beast, making it look like an upside-down pistachio. Then it began to feed.

Kay cracked her knuckles. She wasn't frozen. She wasn't hypno-tized the way she assumed the other must be. She leaned over and punched a cultist in the stomach to test her theory. He gasped and rolled onto his side.

"Save your loyal servant, right?" Kay punched him again, this time in the general vicinity of his kidneys. "That thing isn't listening to you, is it?"

"Gnu-Val!" the man croaked.

Kay just shook her head as the man rolled away and sighed. He shrugged helplessly, a child realizing he had no power in the world. "I can't control them. The people I can order around, but them? I don't know."

"Shit," Kay said. She *had* been right before. Of course those idiots didn't control the beasts. The monsters simply did what they did.

The beast on the bridge was moving slowly through the crowd, gobbling protestors and cultists as crows do worms.

"It's eating your people," Kay said.

The man sighed. "Yeah. Shit."

Kay stood and leaned on her shield, watching the carnage. The man explained that he and his kind had summoned the creatures. It was a popular theory, of course, but not one she ever really believed. She always thought there had been some explosion that tore the fabric of reality and allowed the beasts to come to Earth. A large hadron collider or someone testing out a new hydrogen bomb. Maybe one country or another was working through some theoretical quantum mechanics nonsense in space, just past Mars. She could see that.

But now this guy was saying they were summoned. Invited.

Yeah. People had always been a little crazy.

"What's your name?" Kay asked.

It took him a moment to answer. "High Priest Turok."

Kay glanced at him sideways but didn't challenge the ridiculous name. She suspected he had given himself the title of High Priest, too.

"Okay, Turok. You can't control them. But you summoned them? Personally?"

"A group of us."

Kay didn't know how much she believed. She knew she should probably get as far from the monster as possible. Then again, what better guide to the fallen city of Cincinnati than the High Priest? She pointed her knife at the man. "Show me how."

He protested and snarled about sacred texts and ancient rites.

But Kay had all the knives.

They went through a half dozen side streets, away from the bridge, and into a darkness that Kay did not appreciate. Turok said it was the best way. "Gnu-Val will probably be busy for a while. It's best to give him a wide berth when he's hungry."

She agreed with that, at least.

After a few blocks, she realized Turok was taking her to the baseball stadium. This whole thing had been a bad idea, she knew. And getting worse all the time.

Turok told her that he and the other cult members lived in the box seats and restaurants and various tunnels and breezeways below the baseball stadium. The beast mostly slept in the center of the field. Mostly.

They entered the stadium and passed a bronze statue of a man with a giant baseball for a head. The baseball head even had a large, curling mustache. He seemed to be no less a monster than the other things crawling about the city. Turok sighed. "Most everybody I knew was up there. This place is going to feel pretty empty."

"I'm sorry for your loss," Kay said, and they both knew she didn't mean it.

He led her through a maze of concrete tunnels that smelled of vinegar and something earthy and warm. The smell was so overpowering that Kay had to place a hand against the concrete wall to let her stomach settle.

"You get used to it," Turok said, pushing back his hood. He was older than Kay, with grey eyes and an unreasonably calm disposition. He stepped onto a landing lit by the moon, beyond which the stadium seats sloped downward toward a baseball diamond now concealed in black.

The smell was strongest here. The monster's nest was hidden in the darkness below.

Turok moved from the landing to an expansive room that was once a merchandise store. Everything was gone now, save for broken glass and stains of undetermined origin. Kay's trail runners whispered against the concrete floor as she looked for signs of life but found none.

Turok shouldered open a door that led to some sort of storage room. The strange vinegar odor was gone, replaced by the human smells of unwashed bodies and cooked food.

She pointed the blade of her Ka-Bar at Turok. "There's nobody else here?"

"Why would there be?" he said, sounding so forlorn that Kay believed him.

There was no one. Only a few sleeping bags and a cold camp stove. Red pentagrams adorned the wall like the room of a teenage witchcraft enthusiast. The cultists were not living in luxury, it seemed.

Turok told her the high priests slept here. In contrast, the other members — the goons with the shields and clubs — slept at different points around the stadium. They wanted to surveil the creature but also remain hidden if Gnu-Val started hunting for a midnight snack.

"We set up an altar in the owner's box," Turok said. "But we keep the sacred texts here." He shoved a few dirty blankets out of the way, unearthed a dented firebox, and fumbled for the key. The only sacred text inside the metal box was a book. Not an illuminated manuscript bound in leather, but a simple book. An airport paperback with a plain blue cover nestled in a black silk cloth. Turok used this cloth to hold the book as he pulled it from the firebox.

He gasped when Kay snatched the book with her bare hands. The cover was blank. There was no title page, no copyright. No chapters. Just walls of text. Page after page of it. One page would be a paragraph of something in the English alphabet but decidedly not in English, and opposite that would be lines and lines of something like Mandarin. She didn't think it was, though. There were strange symbols mixed throughout, rune-like markings that resembled Nordic script.

"You've had this the whole time," Kay said, flipping through the book. "Did you ever try to use it to send them back?"

Turok shrugged.

Of course not. Why would they want to banish their gods? Kay decided to try some of the English. "Jock-li, branp, brangu werg. Brangu werg." She made a face. "Doesn't feel good to say." She meant it physically. The words seemed to either curdle in the back of her throat or turn to cotton on her tongue. "What does it mean?"

Turok shrugged slightly. "It's the language of the old gods."

"Yeah, but what does it mean?"

Outside the stadium, the monster roared again, in triumph or boredom. Turok hid his face in his hands. "Gnu-Val has fed."

Kay slapped the book shut. "Yeah." She studied the high priest. She had known her fair share of con men and charlatans, and she didn't see much difference between them and the man before her. "You can't read this nonsense, can you?"

After a hesitant moment, he waved his hands in surrender and sat down on the dirty blankets. "No. We know nothing."

"So you guys didn't summon them?"

"I didn't. But we did," he admitted. "The royal we, I mean. Some members of our sect."

Kay sighed. "So, who then?"

"Whoever was here before me."

Kay flipped through the book. She had possibly found an ancient text, a gateway to an unimaginable world home to monsters. Here was the reason the world had gone wrong, the reason so many had died or been driven to madness. Here was, possibly, a way to communicate with the monsters. A way to send them back to their own world, even.

Or it was entirely possible that the high priest was full of shit. The book could've been full of recipes or erotic tales written in a language she had never seen. Still, there was a chance. She could take the book and look for someone who did know. This thin, blue book could be the key to humanity's future. A return to civilization. A return to grocery stores and movie theaters. Churches and libraries. Highways and cars. Gasoline. The whole oil industry could come back. The forty-hour work week, too. And the suburbs along with it. Homeowners Associations. Traffic jams. Talk radio. Endless advertisements for pills and tinctures and tonics. Taxes and the IRS. Police and police brutality. Licenses and registrations. Social security numbers and credit scores.

They could all come back.

Kay wrinkled her nose.

She looked at the sad man calling himself a high priest and tossed the book to him. He fumbled briefly, then carefully folded the silk cloth around the object.

"You really think that's the book? That right there?" she asked.

"I do."

Kay decided it was better safe than sorry. She popped the pin out of her grenade and tossed it into the blankets at Turok's feet. He managed to say something, but Kay didn't hear. She pushed through a nearby door and slammed it behind her.

For an unnerving few seconds, she thought the grenade might have been a dud. Then it proved to be live. The explosion popped the door from its hinges and sent her sprawling into the empty store. The storage room burped smoke. Flames crawled out of the doorway, searching in vain for something else to consume.

Kay dusted herself off, made sure the baseball diamond was still empty, and found her way back to the ground floor. The stadium and the city beyond were eerily quiet. At the statue of the man with a baseball for a head, she sat on a bench and finally inspected Farek's orange backpack.

Two cans of red beans, one of artichokes, one of peas, and four cans of peaches. Kay was a rich woman.

There was no sign of the monster Gnu-Val on the Roebling Bridge, so Kay thought it was safe to cross. She did so at a light jog. Better safe than sorry. She slowed to a steady walk on the Kentucky side of the river to conserve her energy.

The fallen world had made Kay what she was, and she would be ready for whatever it might hold.

Kay was a survivor.

XII

Once again, those Eldritch Gods can't help but show off their gigantic, monstrous forms to remind the rest of us how minuscule we really are. You'd think being so mighty and all-powerful that they wouldn't have to be such dicks about it, but here we are. Elitist douchebags.

Wait, is this seriously the last story? Already? Man, I was having so much fun I didn't even realize! Wow, I mean, that might be kind of a bummer if we didn't have such an awesomely strange story to go out on, but thankfully we do! It's about this keeper of all the universe's knowledge that happens to be a slug, and he keeps said knowledge housed within teeth that he will only provide in exchange for animal bones. You know, that old story.

I remember when I had bones. Dynamite bones, they were, never broke once, not even the time that carnie had his elephant kick me in the ribs on account of sleeping with his lady, who, in my defense, I thought was his mom. Like I said, dynamite bones, which is also a great name for an action hero.

The story features a nameless protagonist, which means it really

281

could be anyone's story, even yours. Have you ever spent time at the bottom of the sea in search of bones to exchange for knowledge teeth? If so, please don't sue us for telling your story without the proper authorizations and clearances, just hit me up and I'll be happy to split the profits from this book with you. (Joke's on you, my books never turn a profit! I does it for da art, son.)

So, while I run off and cry in a corner because of how much I'm gonna miss you guys, I invite each and every one of you, for the last time, to sit back, relax, and enjoy Teeth for Trade.

TEETH FOR TRADE

CHRIS WOOLSEY

THE DAY I MET THE KNOWLEDGE KEEPER

Today marks a monumental event in my life story: I have made it to the bottom of the ocean. I created a small habitat using my oxygen supply and a spot of amateur craftsmanship, which, while uncomfortable, provides a dry haven from the dark sea. Among my possessions are batteries for various pieces of equipment, oxygen tanks, a dehydrator, lumber that has grown swollen from the trip, ink, a pen, some books, and a bedroll. I have built a desk where I can write down my exploration of the ocean floor, as well as my dealings with The Knowledge Keeper.

There is only one thing I seek: A higher understanding.

When I was first told about the Knowledge Keeper, I had assumed the reason for my informant's ambiguity was to keep their identity anonymous. They refused to speak about features or gender, said I would know them when I saw them. As it turned out, the purpose for their secrecy was, in my estimation, to simply avoid sounding like an unbelievable lunatic – for the Knowledge Keeper was not human.

Rather, it was an oversized slug, just shorter than myself at five foot seven. It stuck to the ocean floor by secreting mucus and sat upon a trench cliff, tail hung off the side. If it weren't for its mannerisms, I never would have guessed it was anything more than a large, dumb creature, let alone capable of complex thought.

Two studious eyes sat atop wavy stalks on its cranium. The Knowledge Keeper accepted me with a terrifying smile that would be a source of anxiety for the rest of my life. Rows behind rows of human teeth gave it a threatening expression. "You have come for knowledge." It was direct, skipping the niceties so typical among humans. Instead, the slug's greeting was a statement. It knew precisely why I had come.

To describe the conversation in exact detail would do the interaction injustice. Strangely, words were never formally uttered. Though its mouth moved, the voice was heard directly in my head, the movement of the slug's mouth merely an imitation, perhaps to make me feel comfortable. Suffice it to say, it was an unsettling experience. And a disappointing one. I had envisioned a wise man ready to deliver impartial wisdom, not the gross, slippery monster I now know.

And, of course, there was a catch. The Knowledge Keeper wouldn't just hand out its wisdom for free. Furthermore, the knowledge I seek doesn't come from lectures, mind-to-mind transferal, or anything of that nature. No, knowledge, according to this strange slug, comes from teeth.

The creature explained that human memories lived in our teeth long after death had claimed us, and the enamel had rotted away. The memories were not easy to extract, but as my colleague promised, the slug had the secrets to gaining such knowledge. Through the many teeth it had acquired over the years, I would live the lives of other men and know their truths, their secrets. However, these secrets would remain so unless I could provide the slug's one genuine desire in exchange: human bones.

So, in short: teeth for bone.

"Where am I supposed to get bones?" I inquired, but the slug gave me nothing more. Perhaps it was a silly question.

THE DAY I STARTED MY SEARCH

Unfortunately, the process has proven to be more complicated than I had hoped. Had I known what the Knowledge Keeper was going to ask before I arrived, I would have brought as many bones as I could travel with. I will be sure to chide my colleague for that upon my return.

The first issue I am facing is the sheer darkness of the ocean depths. It is hard to see much further than twenty feet out, even with heavy-grade lights, and after a few hours of fruitless searching, I've found myself frustrated. It's upsetting to think about how much money I spent on equipment that barely works and the exorbitant amount of time it took to make this trip possible. It makes more sense to search for bones on land than it does down here, but I don't have that sort of time! Furthermore, why on earth does the goddamned slug need bones? It is absolutely ridiculous that it would hold back the world's greatest treasures over something as worthless as rotting skeletons.

Secondly, there is a distinct lack of life in the abysmal crater that is the bottom of the sea. I've seen fish, sharks, and plenty of coral, but not much else. No matter where I look, there is no dead sea life. I have no idea if I am merely unlucky or if predators are as desperate to consume as I am to learn. It feels like I'm the late bird, and all the worms have already been eaten.

Finally, and most disconcerting, is a return to old, bad habits. I have a small gap between my two front teeth, resulting from poor choices in my youth. This led to a disgusting comfort of restlessly tonguing the hole to debase boredom. Every time I feel the gap, it reminds me that I still have no knowledge from the Keeper of Teeth.

THE DAY I LEARNED ABOUT THE HISTORIES OF ANCIENT CIVILIZATIONS

This is absolutely remarkable. Day after day, I have searched the ocean's depths for bones to no avail. Yet today, success was delivered by way of a laughable cliché: an underwater shipwreck. The ship's decrepit remains were a muddled labyrinth of moss, old wood, and barnacles. The search began as it always does, fruitless and challenging. I considered that my discovery had been explored by predecessors; if there were any human remains, they'd have likely been pillaged.

Ransacked or not, it was the best option I had. I meticulously examined every corner of the ship over two days. If wood was light enough to move or break, I searched it. If there was a hole large enough to fit me, I squeezed through it. I even swept up debris with my bare hands.

Then, after thirty-five recorded hours of careful search, I found my bounty. A single human finger underneath a patch of seaweed that had tried to claim the ship as its home. To say that I was excited is an understatement. I was ecstatic! It was finally time for me to claim what I had come for.

The slug waited in its usual spot, motionless save for its wiggling eye stalks. I considered making small talk but opted to get right to the point. I wanted knowledge and was willing to take anything as a reward. I practically threw the pilfered finger at the beast, as much as one can underwater. Over the last week, my ego had suffered the depressive effects of failure. I felt justified in this tiny gesture of pride.

Excellent bone. Wonderful joint. Thank you.

What on earth did this beast want with bone anyway?

Remove your mask.

I'm pretty good at holding my breath, so I obliged.

For you.

A stalk on the Knowledge Keeper's head reached into its seemingly infinite black hole of a mouth and presented a dislodged tooth. The free eye stalk crept toward me, then quickly removed one of my molars without warning. Sharp, welcome pain teased my mouth as my new molar found its home.

Memories snapped to the forefront of my mind. I saw myself standing among peers in a well-lit chamber filled to the brim with exotic niceties. Pottery, art, and hunting trophies decorated the room. We had just returned from an excursion of thievery, reveling in the price of our score. It was a snapshot of another life. One that felt entirely my own, though I knew that to be impossible.

I returned to myself, snapped my helmet onto my suit, expelled the water, and took a deep breath of oxygen.

"This…this is remarkable," I said to the slug. With this tooth, I had gained the memories of a man one thousand years dead. I now know massive international secrets and conspiracies. Through his memories, I've become enlightened to many mistakes in our current under-standing of history.

More bones.

"I know so many secrets."

More secrets.

"Yes, more secrets."

More bones.

THE DAY I MET JESUS

I met Jesus this morning. Rather, I should say, I met his corpse. I had initially imagined the flood of information from the molar would represent all the knowledge there was to gain, but the more time I spend pondering its contents only begets more questions.

Accessing the memory of the thief's tooth was more akin to a process than a single incident. Fishel, the original owner, was a wildly successful yet unknown swindler who lived by the idea that "notoriety and success cannot coexist among thieves." He was never appre-hended, opting for a fake name and title when hired, and died of old age with a wife and children. During his latter days, he lived under disguise as one of the wealthiest merchants in the promised land.

He had plundered many a man of his wealth and had taken more contracts than a mule collected flies. But perhaps his most influential heist was that of the Messiah of Israel: Jesus Christ. In short, Fishel was hired to sneak into the tomb of Christ and remove the body. I'd prefer not to go into specifics of what was done afterward. It is well enough to note that every gruesome detail was transferred from the recesses of this tooth to me.

I am the reason He was believed to have risen. Or rather, Fishel, who is now a part of me, is the reason. This enlightenment perturbs me greatly. How do I now follow what I know to be a forged God? Despite my eagerness to receive such knowledge, I have already considered the possibility of its reversal.

If I remove the tooth, will the memories leave or stay?

Fishel's personality has also snuck into my own, like tea leaves to water. He welcomes the revelation that there are no Gods to fear. Without a master to obey, he says I have no need for guilt or shame.

I believe him to be wrong.

Nonetheless, other than this particularly contemplative set of memories, the thief's tooth has also yielded a bounty of practical knowledge. The most profitable bit is that treasures are often buried. So, I returned to the shipwreck on the hunch of a treasure hunter and professional thief. Reading its angles and the flow of the sea, I chose a spot and dug. The ground yielded many bounties. Some short hours of labor later, I had a decent selection of bones. I intend to take them to the Keeper for even more knowledge.

A sunken ship and now buried treasure. How silly to think my journal is starting to sound like an 1800s pirate novel.

THE DAY THE KEEPER PREACHED TO ME

"If God doesn't exist, I don't know why I should strive for anything in life."

Determination comes from the roots, not from above.

"Tell me, Keeper, did you ever believe in God?"

No response.

"I'll take that as a no. Well, I did, Keeper. I'd like to think that I still do, but the truth you have given me is far too cumbersome to ignore. Would you find it superficial to believe in something for the sake of belief alone? For the entirety of my life, I've comforted myself with tradition and reverence for the man above. Though I know this to be faulty, I do not wish to give it up. It sounds foolish, but I consider it human to want something to believe in, something bigger than myself.

"I think I will hold on to my faith and keep this knowledge to myself. I doubt anyone would believe me anyway. Fishel's person isn't recorded anywhere in history. How ironic that a thief happens to be the greatest prophet of all time. Keeper, does he know that he is with me now? Or is he ignorant to the claim he has made upon me? Does he fight for my consciousness without knowing? Are these teeth of knowledge sentient, or is this just the side effect of humans tampering with celestial powers?"

The slug watched lazily, its body hanging over the edge of the dark trench, its tail hidden from my human eye.

"No matter. I have brought more bones. I believe this to be a femur, and these are from a foot."

The Knowledge Keeper repeated the transferal process, gifting me the knowledge of a master engineer. I turned to leave.

The Gods do exist.

"Who are the Gods? Where are they? Did they create you?"

I created myself.

"Are you a God?"

One of his eyes looked back as if bored. If he is a God, he's a silent one.

THE DAY I LEARNED HOW TO RIDE A HORSE

Since my last entry, I have learned astrology, hunting, biology, robotics, botany, and myriad Turkish government secrets.

Today, I learned how to ride a goddamned horse.

Not every tooth is equal. Nor is every bone.

Part of me wanted to reach into the slug's mouth and rip out his teeth just so I could understand what he was saying to me. I argued with the creature. "You delivered the tooth of a physicist for a single bone! Now, I deliver a haul of ribs, and you teach me how to ride a fucking horse?"

His right eye drifted lazily to the side, staring apathetically at a school of fish. At this point, I should know better than to argue. The Keeper has the same conversation skills as the coral it makes its bed upon.

In a crude gesture of frustration, I reached back into my mouth and yanked the tooth away. Blood and shredded bits of gum leaked from my mouth into the dark ocean. I dropped the useless tooth and let it sink slowly to the floor, watching as the slug's eyes followed it to the bottom. After it struck sand, the Keeper's eyes retreated into its body.

Though I prompted further conversation, the slug never released itself from its retracted state. I immediately regretted my decision. With each additional tooth in my skull, I feel a further sense of escape, a firmer grasp of what I want to make of reality. As with Fishel, each tooth came with a particular set of skills, memories, and character. I initially felt that each personality I gained had been melded to my own psyche, but after over a dozen teeth – lives – I've determined that is incorrect. I am not combining the personalities of others with my own but instead inviting each guest to rip a piece of me away and take a permanent stake of ownership. I am eighteen parts myself and four-teen parts other, now. Each personality holds a small claim over me.

Lethargy is a trait I have been fortunate enough to avoid. I've always prided myself on my propensity to stay focused, ambitious. As of late, though, I've felt more like sleeping than anything else. I've managed to fight the procrastinator's urges, but I think that soon I may need to give in to a day of slumber to appease this 1/32nd portion of myself.

I wonder if the Keeper sleeps? I do hope that I have not managed to permanently offend it. After all this time, I still know so little about the creature.

THE DAY I GOT INTO AN ACCIDENT

The sun has finally retired after a tiresome day; at least, I suppose it has. I live too far underneath the water to tell. Still, according to the watch I built and my understanding of the solar schedule, it has just now dipped below the horizon.

The majority of my day was spent wallowing in waste and self-pity. As I feared, I have created an enemy of the Knowledge Keeper. Since the horse incident, as I've decided to call it, the slug has refused to see me. I have brought bounties of bones, yet the beast continues to elude me, its eyes forever retreated into its massive body. I noticed it slowly sliding backward over the cliff face as if to hide from me.

The horse tooth, however, was no longer in the ground. Whether it has found its way back into the Keeper's void or some other creature has claimed its prize, I do not know. The rational part of me, Radhika, felt I was too quick to discard it and that perhaps I could have gained something valuable in its exchange. I shrugged her – my – thoughts away. Radhika, unlike myself, was used to subservience. A quiet, patient way of living. Her ideas were worth considering, but I still had my own aspirations. They didn't align with her recommendation of a subtle touch.

I stalked away slowly, looking back often in case the Keeper's eyes reemerged. But my caution was in vain. The slug would outlast me no matter how patient I pretended to be. I spent the rest of my day exploring familiar territories near the sunken ship. A rocky cliff face was about a quarter of a nautical mile from the boat. Early in my adventure — thanks to Fishel's keen eye for plunder — I happened upon a shin bone stuck between two rocks. I assumed the body had been carried over by a predator but declined to investigate further. Then, throwing caution to the wind – or I suppose the currents – I decided to try my luck. I needed something that would please the Keeper.

Radhika urged caution. Adam shared indifference. Fishel encouraged me to continue. I listened to my longest-standing friend and shimmied through tight spaces, rotating large rocks as I explored the labyrinthian tomb. They were – *I was* – right, in their own ways. I found treasure and also tragedy. But I didn't care. The prize I found was worth the sacrifice.

Was it worth our hand? You think your prize is so critical as to discard the body Brahman gave us? You have made me an abomination. You have tossed my humanity aside with your new pet tooth. You hold us back from our eternities only to curse us with this molestation of the human body. That is selfish of you. I told you to heed caution, but you chose not to listen.

I chose knowledge, Radhika, as I always have. Furthermore, this body is mine, not ours. Perhaps you would learn well from Fishel to act as an ally instead of the uninvited torrent you have become...lest I pluck you out!

Selfish!

Enough! Writing is hard enough without you fighting for the pen. Cease your transcription!

THE PRIZE I found was worth the sacrifice that would come, for it would prove to be my solution to the wanton relationship with the Keeper, albeit a tragic one. I discovered a skull lodged underneath two massive stones. It had managed to stay unscathed other than a minor crack or two. With both hands, I pulled on the smaller of the rocks, both feet planted, heaving as hard as I could. After several minutes, the stone came loose. It fell away from the skull and onto my left hand, pinning it down but not before tearing my suit.

I instantly lost my ability to breathe. Air bubbles taunted me during their ascent to the surface. Water filled my suit with a terrifying quickness. I knew I had ten minutes at most and began to panic. I needed to find a solution quickly. All the knowledge in the world couldn't save me from a watery grave, a fate that would have been yet another cliché in my story. Oxygen and tools were back at camp, but it was too far away. I should have been carrying emergency equipment, but it hardly matters now. I no longer have any need for my suit.

The only tool at my disposal was a serrated knife. Naturally, I did not want to do what needed to be done. My heart beat fast, racing against the passing moments as my oxygen supply diminished. I held the jagged tool against my forearm, then pulled away and slowly returned the knife multiple times. I began to cut where the bones had broken. Blood seeped into the water, clouding my vision. Urgently, I cut quicker. I bit my tongue, tearing the mucosa and filling my mouth with even more blood. I yanked as I cut, hoping to dislodge myself quicker as each passing moment deepened the intensity of my terror. My chest rose and fell with dread. My stomach devolved into a rolling jumble of nausea and anxiety until, finally, I was released from the rocks' grasp.

I swam clear of the blood cloud and not a moment too soon, for just as I regained sight, a shark barreled through, twisting violently towards me. Glazed, ghostly eyes stared through me. Teeth angled outwards, sharp and jagged. With the instincts of a thief, I used the knife in my hand to puncture the shark's belly. The creature tried to escape, but I used my free arm to hug its body close to mine as I dug the knife deeper and rotated the blade. Soon, it stopped thrashing. Its blood joined my own in a dark, hazy cloud.

I had survived the attack but had no way of getting oxygen. I felt myself fading away and did the only thing I could think of, the only option I had. I shoved my hand into the beast's mouth, ripped out one of its teeth, and then jammed it into my own. Sweet air instantly filled my lungs, or whatever it is that sharks use to breathe underwater. I floated there for a moment in silent reflection, ignoring the myriad voices fighting for attention as I felt a new one join the mass, one obviously not human. I instantly acquired an affinity for fish and blood. But, more importantly, I learned I didn't need the slug to gain knowledge.

All I needed were the teeth.

I looked at the skull, recently freed from the oversized rocks. A head full of teeth. I fetched it along with my detached hand and made my way back to the undersea camp. Warm water covered the cave's entrance, likely brought on by a welcome current. Remarkably, I have not developed any new physical features. I can now breathe underwater. My actions are strictly mind over matter, or rather tooth over matter. It is a surreal experience.

What use is logic in my state? I have the knowledge of many lifetimes of dedicated study, and my body now transcends the bounds of celestial intent. I am freer than I have ever been. Fishel was right. I've no need for Gods when I can become one myself.

My dead hand lies preserved in a plastic bag. Without ice, I've resorted to tying off the bag and dangling it into the water at the edge of my cave floor. Hopefully, the cold will return soon to better preserve it. Only an amateur-grade tourniquet keeps me from bleeding out. I've searched the knowledge in my teeth for related medical skills but found nothing. I can only hope the skull delivers the prize I require.

After examining the cranium further, I've discovered that the teeth inside are unnatural. As in, they are all different sizes. None of them match. This skull belonged to another knowledge seeker. Someone like me, but whose fate had turned grisly. I consider myself lucky to have only lost a hand and not my life.

Our lives.

Silence! I'm beginning to grow lightheaded and must attend to myself now. Tonight, I shall sleep, and tomorrow I will explore this new skull.

THE DAY I OVERSLEPT

This morning, I woke up extremely groggy, with my head pounding. I sat up in bed and blinked wearily as I tried to piece together my surroundings. Yellow sheets, tan comforter, dirty carpet, a half-empty pizza box. A clock I didn't recognize said 1:03 on an equally foreign nightstand.

I should quit drinking so heavily.

I crawled out of the messy bedspread and dressed in some clothes lying on the ground. Soon, I was outside my apartment. A quick glance at the numbers told me I was on the 44th floor. My stomach grumbled. Time for lunch. The elevator button clicked, but the mechanism didn't respond.

While little felt familiar, I hadn't completely forgotten who I was. I knew I spoke Mandarin, my name was LiBao, and I lived in Shanghai. I was really good at making terrible choices and made a comfortable living selling pirated media. I just couldn't remember yesterday. Or the last week. The long journey down the stairs gave me time to ponder the many gaps in my memory, which turned out to be a lot. One memory was something about swimming. No, hunting? Did I watch some weird American movie again? Had I always had these gaps? I needed to talk to Ma but was already late.

I grabbed a hot bowl of street noodles before heading to work. When I pulled out my wallet, I realized it wasn't mine. Thankfully, the guy had just enough yuan to buy my lunch. Shit, where was *my* wallet? I wanted to reflect on last night, but my hangover hurt too much. I hadn't had enough water. With a steaming pile of noodles, I strolled into MEGA COMPUTER two hours late.

"LiBao!" one of the stock boys yelled. "Where the fuck have you been? Out fucking your hand again? Get in the backroom now! You're in trouble." I hadn't bothered learning the guy's name.

"Yeah, yeah, I got it." I walked to the back of the computer store and opened the 'employees only' door. It's not really for employees; it's just a front. Behind the locked door is where we sell our contraband. The boss was in the room, illuminated by a single light that hung on a thin cord. He was fat and angry, which was nothing new. "I thought you said you were bringing in customers today!" Some of his spit fell onto cases of shoddily printed DVD labels of odd-looking American cartoons. One was labeled "Tom and Jerry," and the other "Birdman." I watched an American cartoon once but didn't understand the humor. Lots of mallets over the heads and falling off cliffs.

"Sorry, I overslept. I'll get customers tomorrow."

"No, you're handing out pamphlets today," he argued. The boss leaned back in his chair with pouty, folded arms. I've never liked him much. Such crooked and ugly teeth.

"Boss, you aren't really going to make me go outside, are you?! Come on, let me rip today. You know I'm fast on the PC."

"No!"

I continued to plead my case when one of my other coworkers, the cute new girl who started in Legal last week, poked her head into the room. "LiBao, you need to come out front. We have a problem." Her voice was soft, shy, and apologetic.

I looked at the boss. He grunted and waved me off dismissively. "Hurry up. This doesn't get you out of pamphlet duty!"

When I stepped onto the main floor, a pissed-off man was standing at the counter, though he seemed to not be buying anything. Some customers waited behind him. "Is that him?" asked the man, pointing at me.

My wallet and identification card sat on the counter before my coworker. By the looks of it, the enraged man was with 14K, one of the triad gangs.

What did I do to piss him off?

"You! Get your ass over here now!" I don't know why he yelled that because instead of waiting, he sprinted after me like an angry dog chasing a wounded fox. I was halfway out of the 'employees only' door when I ducked back inside and jumped over the table the boss was working at, knocking over the stacks of DVDs he'd just organized. Birdman took flight. The door was swinging closed as the angry man yanked it open, loosening it from its hinges. Cheap, like most everything else in the store.

"Sorry, boss, I'll be back!" Like most that sell contraband, our store has a hidden exit in the back. I burst into the alleyway behind MEGA COMPUTER when, as was my luck, two men happened to be smoking. Instead of a clean getaway, I crashed into them and fell to the ground. They yelled, and one of them spit on me. His teeth were gross and yellow like most smokers' are. I crawled back into the alley wall, apologizing, then pushed myself up and ran as fast as possible. Even with my head start, the man didn't take long to catch up. He tackled me from behind, throwing me into the concrete, then sat on my back and launched punches while yelling something about not messing with 14K.

Somehow, amidst the barrage of fists, I rolled onto my back, dizzy, like I might throw up. I'm pretty sure I pissed myself. Somehow, I managed to jerk my head to the side just in time to miss his punch and let the ground take it. He hissed as his hand crunched into the ground.

I only had a moment to act. My hand wrapped around his head and pulled it close to mine. I smashed his nose with my skull. He fell back, and I was free.

I looked for something I could use as a weapon. If I could keep the guy down, maybe I could get away. A couple of bricks sat by one of the alley doors. I grabbed one and, with the strongest swing I could manage, broke the man's face. My senses sharpened. Time slowed down. A tooth dislodged itself from the man's mouth and skittered across the piss-and-blood-covered battleground. I watched it skip from one puddle of muck to another.

Then, something. A pull that felt familiar, irresistible. I dove to the ground hungrily, desperate for the tooth that waited patiently to be claimed. I stared, thinking it must have wanted me as badly as I wanted it.

Something wasn't right.

But it was right. Everything was right.

I opened my mouth and fished around with my tongue for a gap but couldn't find one, so I pressed the root of the tooth against the roof of my mouth and forced the matter. Pain shot through my jaw and into my eyes.

Then, the high came.

My lungs filled.

Teeth jittered.

Eyes dilated.

I was in my prime.

Memories floated.

A sick child.

Tireless nights.

Working late.

Finding opportunities.

Criminal organizations.

Hating myself.

"How?" I raised my hands to find them covered in blood. My own blood? No, his blood. Who's blood? I couldn't tell. I look down upon myself, a pitiful, scared child covered in piss. Is this really what I looked like? Pathetic. I could taste blood trickling out of my mouth and onto the pavement. Was it my blood? I looked up at him – me, the other me – with tears falling from my swollen eyes. "I'm sorry."

He – I – stomped over, fists ready to finish the job. "I know."

THE DAY I WENT SWIMMING

Something happened yesterday. Somehow, I left the ocean without ever leaving my cave. I felt more than just the thoughts of another; I lived their life. There is also a gap in my memory. According to my instruments, my most recent entry was three days ago. Yet, another was penned last night, one not in my handwriting.

I've concluded that somehow, LiBao had taken over. LiBao, one of eight teeth I'd extracted from the skull. Considering that a tooth from a shark gave me the ability to breathe underwater, it hardly seems a stretch that this man's memories allowed him to write through me. I've spent the morning transcribing the pages.

I know that while in control of my body, LiBao did not actually travel to the surface. So, the question I raise now is: what did he do while I was living his memories? I have prompted him, but unlike the others, he remains silent.

I wonder if my colleague who told me about this secret has similar interactions with his teeth? I do not remember his smile ever looking different than before. Perhaps he has only taken a tooth or two towards the back of his mouth?

My grin, on the other hand, is an amalgamation of dentistry nightmares. I doubt anyone would find my smile attractive, what with the interspecies mixing and all. I wonder if my colleague has supernatural abilities or if I am unique in this trait?

I've considered the Keeper for a while now. It was a creature of such few words that everything it said felt important. *The Gods exist*, it told me. What Gods did it refer to? And how was it so sure? It must have had enough knowledge to know that every religion was a sham – a concept I once zealously fought against but have since grown to accept, despite Radhika's protest. What would the slug gain from preaching false prophets? And why tell me? What was it these Gods controlled? Why did the Keeper believe what I had lost faith in?

I also have a hard time understanding its propensity toward offense. It claimed to be a God itself, but a God wouldn't recoil at the actions and words of a mortal. Would it? The slug was too gentle and simply could not be a God. But it did have secrets. Secrets I wanted to learn. Secrets I had to learn.

LiBao, you were an anomaly. A lucky coincidence. I will take caution not to repeat my mistakes, and you, like the others, will watch as I continue to pilot my body.

I will be extracting more teeth from the skull tonight.

THE DAY I HUNTED

Which was before I took a vacation to the Saharan desert, but after I got my carpenters' license.

I don't remember when I picked up smoking, but I know that it's the one love in my life that's always been there. My only constant. Sure, it's taken my lungs, reduced my life, and given me a chronic cough, but it's sure as hell a lot less damage than my ex-wife caused. The smell of smoke soothes me. It calms my nerves. Helps me on my hunts.

Cold Russian air bit at my skin, a cold I could feel in my bones. In my teeth. Cigarette smoke drifted lazily before me where, habitually for the next three hours, I hunkered in a larch tree and checked my rifle. I ensured the safety was off, the scope was aligned, and the ammo was loaded. Everything was how it should've been. I am an expert with weaponry, never had a jammed weapon or a missed shot. I am not a man of blunder. Perfection is all I allow. The day I'm imperfect will be the day I turn the rifle around.

A single snowflake fell from the sky, just close enough for me to reach my hand out and catch it. Though the rest of me was bundled up to fight the chill, I ignored gloves to better handle my weapon. When I claimed my hunt, my hands would become warm. Never sooner. The snowflake landed on my palm. My skin — a splotchy mix of cold blue and irritated red — preserved the flake's shape. Every snowflake is unique, with a construction all its own. That makes them more impressive than my human brethren. With a dry and puffy tongue, I licked the snowflake. I hadn't drunk alcohol since the previous day, but the taste of vodka lingered in my tonsils. I relished the sensation and spared myself a moment to close my eyes. Patience is a virtue I have plenty of. Mama used to always tell me, "Ride slower, Samuil; you'll get farther." It didn't make much sense to me when I was younger, but I understand these days, on my hunts. Good things only come to those willing to wait for them. Even still, my tongue twitched in anticipation, fingers aching to squeeze my rifle's trigger.

The sun would be up soon, but my prey would arise before then. I'd been studying this mark for months. Every day, an hour before sunrise, she would come to her back porch, light a small fire pit, and drink her morning coffee. The light in her bedroom turned on, ten minutes later than expected but still relatively on time. The woman, a subject I'd obsessed over for quite a while, took her time. I watched the house light up room by room as she went about her routine, ending in the kitchen.

I extinguished the cigarette against my palm and winced mildly at the cinders. With the hunt in sight, my tongue moistened. It felt like I'd waited an eternity, and now, mere moments away from the shot, my breath hastened. Each inhalation brought the staunch taste of smoke and alcohol. Every exhalation stirred the hunger within me.

Ride slower, Samuil; you'll get farther.

The back door opened, and a wave of anticipation flooded through my blood. My prey stepped onto the back porch in warm pajamas, coffee in hand, progressing toward the fire pit alone. It was another reason I chose her. There would be no witnesses. No animals to quiet. No distraction. Finally, my prey sensed that something was wrong. She sniffed the air, trying to discover the source of cigarette smoke, coffee in hand, as she journeyed into the frozen yard. I counted her steps.

Один, два, три...

I followed her with my eyes, waiting until she stood directly below me. Finally, she looked up. I relished the sight of panic in her eyes. The muscles in her neck tensed, a tension released when the heavy tranquilizer shot out from my rifle and dug into her breast. She flopped to the ground like snow melting off a shingle.

I made my way down the larch and dropped onto fresh morning snow. She lay on the ground, body twitching softly, trying to fight the drugs injected into her bloodstream to no avail. My gaze lingered on her soft mouth. Eagerly, I reached down and relished the smooth texture of saliva on her squirming tongue. She tried to bite down but couldn't draw the strength. The backs of my hands faced each other as I wrapped my palms across her jaws and unhinged them with a satisfying snap. The slightest whisper of a wheeze escaped her throat. She would die soon, which meant I only had so long to get what I needed. With a set of clean pliers retrieved from my coat pocket, I grabbed hold of the most succulent-looking tooth I could find.

Tender care. A soft wiggle. The easy loosening of gums.

Then, a jolt of release, a pull that unrooted the enamel. My free hand felt inside her mouth, graciously accepting the warm respite from the cold to take her tooth in my bloody palm. She began to choke, so I rolled her onto her side. The snow was dyed a beautiful black as her blood mixed with the spilled coffee. My bloody hand — the one with the tooth — rose ceremoniously toward my eager mouth, tongue dripping with glee. Like candy, I popped the tooth into my mouth and sucked. I inhaled deeply, swallowing the blood and saliva, grinding the woman's tooth against my own. My prey's life is fleeting; I have to take advantage of the time when they are fresh. I spat the tooth into my hand and stored it in my pocket.

The next of many teeth is ripped out, this one a canine. I took a little extra time scraping my tongue against its sharp edges.

One after another, I suckled her teeth.

Delicious, delicious teeth.

THE DAY I SCREAMED

WHO
    AM
    I
    I
    CAN'T
    WRITE
    I
    CAN'T
    THINK
    WHO
    IS
    HE

THE DAY I FORGOT MY OWN TEETH

Samuil has trapped me. Once again, as with LiBao, I have fallen into a lethargic trance. My suit's timekeeper has broken, and I cannot tell how many days it's been since I last claimed lucidity. My body is malnourished and famished. I have not been in control for some time.

The other personalities are more prevalent as well. I explained before that it was like voices, but that is incorrect. Having the others in my mind is like having split thoughts. One moment I think like myself, and then the next, like LiBao, Radhika, Fishel. Their memories are old, eternal. They are just as much a part of me as I am.

Sometimes I feel as though I don't know who I am anymore. The memories of my life are fleeting, and I fear they will soon be forgotten as those of the others take over. I have given up the notion of returning to an everyday life. Too much time has passed, and I know my job is no longer waiting for me. Besides, my appetite for treasure has become all-engrossing, and the concept of a mundane, stable life sounds more terrible than death.

The surface is still a possibility, but my old existence is a thought of the past. One of my pasts. Besides, I have a mouth full of teeth and the mind of forty men. It would be a crime if I devoted my ambitions to capitalism alone. Imagine what I could do for this world. Except, I cannot return with Samuil. He must be rooted from me at any cost. His death should have remained permanent. All I need to do is extract his tooth, and then I'll be safe to return to the surface once again, monstrous appearance or not.

Therein lies the trap. Somehow Samuil has hidden knowledge from me; the truth of which tooth is which. I could start pulling teeth randomly, hoping to draw him out, but the same risk exists that I would remove myself, which is what he wants. I have only kept two of my original teeth so as to maintain control over the others. If I remove one of my own, I will no longer hold that power.

MY HAND IS MISSING. HAS IT ALWAYS BEEN MISSING? WHERE IS MY HAND?

Which is the day I ground teeth and drank them.

My head hurts, and my mouth pulses with pain. My jaw is stiff as if I've been clenching. I'm dehydrated. At least I remember who I am. I need to find food, water, fresh air to breathe. Maybe I should consider returning to the surface before this nightmare becomes a terror? Except that there is still something I must do. Samuil has trapped me, locked me away from myself. I fear that my own memories are fleeting while others take over. I must remove him before I return to the surface.

I…

I have written this before. I have thought these thoughts before. I need to find the Keeper.

THE DAY I SOUGHT THE KEEPER

I can see myself now. Not metaphorically. I can actually see myself, sometimes right in front of me. Other times I'm in the corner of my vision or behind a rock. Sometimes I'm behind myself. I realized today that I had control of myself for the first time in a while. Complete lucidity. I used this advantage to visit the Keeper to see if perhaps he could help identify my teeth. However, when I arrived at the slug's usual spot, I was met with an empty indent on a bed of seaweed and corral. I recalled my last visit when the slug had slid backward over the drop. I swam forward and peered into the dark abyss, hoping to find clues to the Keeper's whereabouts.

At a distance, I saw an enormous, hulking mass. At first, I considered a whale, but my extensive knowledge of marine biology argued that none would be this deep. Then, my knowledge of history and mythology tickled the imagination, considering the fabled Kraken or perhaps a giant squid. Curiosity drove me forward. The hunt fueled my ambition. For a moment, I forgot my initial mission.

Upon closer inspection, the mass was a collection of sinew and skin. It had the familiar look of the bottom half of an octopus but the confusing design of an overgrown forest. Some of it floated, but most lay upon the ocean floor. The mass was entirely still, aside from a constant, pulsing breath. Something inside me felt an immediate and innate understanding of horror. A small, almost translucent creature crawled along the mass. Curiously, I swam closer, only to realize the animal was the familiar vision of myself. It scaled along the mass, finding a satisfactory location before tearing at it with its many teeth. I watched the projection of myself as I struggled to rip the skin to shreds until I slowly faded out of sight.

"Eat it," Samuil demanded.

More than anyone, Samuil frightened me. Despite the ever-present dread that consumed my thoughts, I decided to comply with his request. I swam to the mass and began crawling along it. The skin felt tough and impenetrable, so I kept crawling until I found a soft spot. Some paranoid facet of my mind felt like I was being watched; I obediently latched onto the monster's skin with my teeth. After a few attempts, the skin finally gave out. I had expected blood to fill the water; instead, the skin peeled back like rolled paper. It took a moment to realize what I was looking at, but after clicking my teeth together, I understood.

They were bones. Bones linked with bones inside the egregiously stretched skin of what I thought was a much smaller creature. The Knowledge Keeper was an amalgamation of bones. A gigantic sack of desecrated remains. What I had communicated with was only a tiny portion of what lived in the crust of this earth.

I have yet to understand what this discovery should teach me. The mass continues for some distance, and I know I will find its head if I follow it. I will be making my return hastily with an offering the slug will not be able to refuse.

My own bones.

SAMUIL HAS TRAPPED ME

Samuil has trapped me. Samuil has trapped me. Samuil has trapped me. Samuil has trapped me. Samuil has trapped me. Samuil has trapped me. Samuil has trapped me. Samuil has trapped me. Samuil has trapped me. Samuil has trapped me. Samuil has trapped me. Samuil has trapped me. Samuil has trapped me. Samuil has trapped me. Samuil has trapped me. Samuil has trapped me. Samuil has trapped me. Samuil has trapped me. Samuil has trapped me. Samuil has trapped me.

THE DAY MY HAND WENT MISSING

I discovered today that my hand is missing. Not just from my body but from my home. Fishel, did you hide it? I have a vague memory of it being buried. There are fifty-one of us now. Six at the helm, though it could be more. My mouth is full. The roof has no space. This is absurd.

I FOUND YOU

I made a mistake. I assumed Samuil's entry into our collective mind indicated we were fighting a common enemy; that we would all agree his removal was more important than personal desires. After all, the sins the man had committed were beyond atrocious.

Fishel, that thieving bastard, thought otherwise.

While Samuil was able to hide the identities of the teeth, Fishel convinced me that he knew which was Samuil's and prompted me to pluck it out.

It was my own tooth.

Immediately, I lost command over the others and was thrust into a muddled pool of thoughts. If I felt overburdened with ideas before, this was genuine hellish confusion. However, I was also able to access their secrets. Until that moment, I was unaware they had secrets. I learned that the most significant figures in my head — the strongest personalities — had made a pact to share control. Fishel swam to the location where my hand was hidden. The ocean current had always been a comfort to me, but now, hidden behind a wall in my body, it felt hollow.

The second of my teeth was hidden in a cave. If I could only gain control of my body for a while, I could retrieve the tooth and jam it back in my mouth. I fought desperately to retake control of my faculties but quickly learned it was a foolish battle. The minds were too well bonded together. There was nothing I could do to cut through them.

Eventually, I pulled myself to the furthest reaches of my own consciousness, a frightened observer of what used to be mine but no longer was. The personalities traded places as they tracked monstrous tendrils to the well-known head and mouthpiece of the Knowledge Keeper. My body stopped moving. LiBao, who currently fronted me, stood frightened. He'd never seen the slug before, and it terrified him. Every part of him wanted to run, to bury himself in a hole and hide for the rest of his days. Surprisingly, it was Radhika who soothed him. "It's just like my plants," she said. "They shy from love when they need it most." With a pat on his back and a kiss on his cheek, LiBao felt comforted enough to continue. He stepped forward, holding my offering with our one good hand. The creature maintained its retreated stance. But after a moment, its eyestalks made an appearance.

These are your bones.

"I brought them for you." LiBao spoke hesitantly, scared but committed.

You are the first human to truly understand.

Teeth flashed behind a lipless mouth with every word the slug mimicked. How could the Keeper not see who was really behind those eyes? I had assumed the Keeper was intelligent and all-knowing, yet he could not see past this compulsive coward of a druggy?

"Understand what?" LiBao almost said before Radhika placed a spiritual hand on his shoulder.

"Keep that to yourself. It may be better if it thinks we know something we don't."

"Perhaps we do know it within one of our teeth."

"Ask about Samuil!" I yelled at LiBao, hoping to somehow urge him to reason. "Let me take control!" He couldn't hear me. The Knowledge Keeper retracted an eye as it had many times before, but instead of emerging with a tooth, it held a single sacrum. Fishel grasped it in his hands and held it close. He gazed at the piece as if, after everything in his life, this was the greatest treasure he'd ever plundered. Perhaps it was.

I was confused. The Keeper had trusted us with a secret, but as to what it meant, I didn't know. Nor did the others. Fishel swam off without even a platitude or polite nod. It was not the reunion with the Keeper I had hoped for; I longed to speak to the slug. I had questions I needed to ask. I tried to push the others back towards the Keeper, but they fought me and ignored my pleas as they made their way back to my cave.

"This bone is the ultimate truth from the slug. It can free us," Radhika said.

"It scares me," Li prompted in response.

"Tooth is truth," Samuil butted in, angry at the shift in focus.

"Shush! All of you!" Fishel urged.

Once in my younger years, I had a nightmare that someone had broken into my room and wished to hurt me. The terror from that dream woke me, yet my body remained in slumber. I was in sleep paralysis, unable to move. Someone was with me; unless I could urge myself awake, I would perish. That sense of terror was what I felt at this moment, except the aggressor lived within me, and I had invited them in. Back then, a tiny bite of my tongue allowed me to shake off the coils of slumber. Perhaps I could make it happen again with a small amount of control?

I searched through the emotions, thoughts, and personalities within my mind, each a complicated tomb of history rich with personalized detail. One, however, stood out from the rest. One that lacked flare; lacked the color and pride of an individual. A personality concerned with nothing but survival and hunger.

I found the shark.

Urging the beast, I was able to close my own mouth. The jaw snapped shut, surprising Fishel as the shark's tooth cut into the soft side of my own cheek. I couldn't feel pain, but I knew he could. The brief shock allowed just enough time to take my body back. Fishel and the others screamed in anguish as they lost control. They aggressively pounded the walls of my psyche in a desperate attempt at control.

My cave, the only location of solace during my time in the ocean, was only about a minute's swim away. My plan was to swim back, reacquire my second tooth, and thrust it back in my mouth, thus reclaiming my advantage over the others.

That quickly proved impossible.

With no advantage over my psychic pursuers, it would be a matter of seconds before I lost control to someone again. The sacrum was the key. Without considering the consequences, I grabbed it and thrust it into the gap in my mouth. As usual, an immediate swell of knowledge pooled within me. Except that this time, I did not feel the benefits in my mind.

I felt it in my soul.

The innermost part of me that had been all but abandoned. My true self, completely forgotten until now. The sacrum gave me complete control, not only of my own body but of my spirit. I could see myself outside my body as before, but now I willed it to be so. I could think of every thought I'd ever had at once.

I became a God.

Fishel, you fool. It was your caution that felled you in the end. Now I will do what you should have done while you held claim to my body.

I will eat the slug.

THE DAY I TOLD YOU ABOUT ME

When my deeds of spreading divine knowledge were discovered, I was removed from my own world and placed here. Millenia passed while I wore the crust of your planet as my shell, long before your kind showed up and were capable of any form of intellect. In my imprisoned state, I could no longer meddle in lesser beings' affairs. Until the day I was discovered.

A marine biologist assumed I was an evolutionary marvel and wanted to keep me secret until she could determine what I was. I dug into her mind like I did yours, and upon revealing my true nature, she traded me her teeth in exchange for secrecy. She returned to the surface a gum-mouthed lunatic.

I then learned that I could utilize the human body for my own passions. Once again, I had a playground. Human after human would arrive, only knowing of my existence through a closely held secret. Each regarded me as their greatest treasure. Zelamet, The Crust God, The Embellishing One, The Blessing to their creed. Proof that they were the chosen people. In truth, this was nothing more than a game to satiate life in exile. Without any understanding, you came to me with a desire rivaling any human I had seen before. You were still weak and pathetic but were the first to dare reject my gifts. Other Gods rewarded your kind with destruction, confusion, and terror, yet you, an insignificant being, spat upon the ground that I had made holy in my presence.

None of the teeth were special. Not until I made them so. It was the bones that you so willingly gave that held the true wonders of your universe. I am not the only God that collects them, but I am the only one who offers something in return. You weren't supposed to acquire knowledge by yourself, yet you did. This is what impressed me most and why I was banished to this world after all. Sharing Greater knowledge with lesser beings. Yet, because of cosmic celestial boredom only a vast emptiness can conjure, I betrayed my kind again.

I thought you had learned the secret. I was wrong.

Even Gods make mistakes. That is how humans came to be, after all. Bones are like teeth, tools created within a pathetic body to accomplish menial tasks on an insignificant planet. The difference with bone is that it can regenerate, which allowed me to forge it as a vessel of never-ending knowledge. Had you taken the sacrum and its truths with you, you could have one day assumed power far beyond any human's comprehension. You feared the knowledge I gave you. You looked for monsters at the bottom of the ocean when there were none. In truth, the most dangerous tooth of all was your own. You harbored an insatiable hunger for knowledge that drove you further than any other human before you. In a world with secret terrors and hidden Gods, you truly were a monster.

When you finally attained what you came for — the ultimate knowledge above anything a human had ever truly known — you turned your eyes on me. I could have stopped you. I could have crushed you as you scaled my body, smothered you as you crawled inside me through the hole you chewed. I could have removed your soul entirely. I did none of that. I let you crawl all the way to my skull from inside and waited silently as you stretched your jaw around my mind. Now I watch as you squirm in agony on a scale more incredible than the many universes that surround us.

You, like me, are a prisoner. You wear me, just how I wear your planet in exile. The Greater are not forgiving, and though I would spare your inconsequential soul for my own peace, I cannot. You will join me for eternity, experiencing the pain that only a God should experience.

You should have left when you had the chance.

THAT'S ALL, FOLKS!

And that wraps it up, kiddos! I can't believe what a long, strange trip it's been. By the way, did you know that I coined that phrase long before Jerry Garcia and the rest of those crazy cats ever did? Stole it from me, just like the melody to Casey Jones, who was a real guy I actually partied with back in the day, and I can confirm that, yes, the dude did love himself both trains and blow.

From the bottom of what used to be my heart and is now just an amalgam of black sludge and vinegar, I want to thank you for joining me on this trip, which I think is the perfect word to describe the journey we just undertook together. We zagged our way through twelve weird, wonderful tales, and I, for one, could have gone for another dozen, but The Big Guy is telling me we have to save those for the sequel. (Assuming this collection does well, so, tell your friends! Or just give them this copy to read; like I said, I'm used to losing money. Besides, what good is cash in Hell, anyway? It always burns up before you have a chance to use it. Same as it did on Earth)

If you enjoyed any specific stories, be sure to reach out to the authors and let them know; you'll find their contact info on the following pages. Or who knows, maybe by the time the next book hits, they'll be down here with me already, narrating that collection and the plenty of others that will inevitably follow? A bit macabre, perhaps, but only time will truly tell. (mwah-Ha-HAAA!)

For myself, all of the authors, and yes, even Steve (you hear me, Big Guy! I'm even doing your shout-outs for you now, ya lazy bastard!), thank you for joining us here at:

ABOUT THE AUTHORS

Jason Peters is your quintessential jack of all trades, master of none. In addition to writing the novel Preconscious and multiple short stories, he has written several screenplays, edited several dozen books and short stories, directed a feature length comedy, and continues to host a film analysis podcast. He lives in Los Angeles with his wife, daughter, and cats.

- E-Mail: jasonaberrant@yahoo.com
- Twitter: @jasonaberrant
- Instagram: @jasonaberrant
- Web: aberrantliterature.com & esotericacinema.com

Daniel Kurland is a writer, entertainment journalist, and surrealist who enjoys experimenting with form and the limits of abstraction. His work can be read on Vulture, Bloody Disgusting, Den of Geek, and across the Internet. Daniel knows that "Psycho II" is better than the original and that "Hannibal" is the greatest love story ever told. The owls are not what they seem.

- E-Mail: danielkurland1@gmail.com
- Twitter: @danielkurlansky

Ashton Macaulay is a fiction writer living in Seattle Washington. His other works include *The Nick Ventner Adventures*, tales of a drunken monster hunter traveling around the world in search of creatures that shouldn't exist, and *The First Ambassador to Crustacea*, the world's premier crab-based, science fiction, political comedy novella.

- E-Mail: ashtondmacaulay@gmail.com
- Twitter: @RealMacAshton
- Instagram: @Mac_Ashton
- Web: MacAshton.com

Vanessa Krauss is a Vancouver, Canada resident who loves creating characters and worlds through art and literature. Published works include One Aon Fatality, Thin, and multiple short stories. Vanessa's overall brand is weird, speculative, and SPAAACE!!! Sanity is never guaranteed. Visit her web site for art and literary updates, or join her in the Twitter void!

- E-Mail: vlk249@hotmail.com
- Twitter: @bubbleybrain
- Web: vlk249.com

M. T. Roberts grew up in the Deep South, where he developed an affinity for gothic literature and horror. He currently resides in the Puget Northwest and gets around on an old Enfield motorcycle. An author of several short stories and the novel *The Ghost in The Grass,* his works have been featured in various anthologies.

- E-Mail: tmtrp@hotmail.com
- Twitter: @realmtroberts
- Web: mtroberts.com

Nick Dorsey lives in Austin, Texas with his wife and their ever-growing menagerie. His most recent novel, The Immortal Phineas Gage, is available on Amazon.

- E-Mail: nickdorseyofnola@gmail.com
- Twitter: @real_nickdorsey

Emma Jun grew up in England and now lives in Japan, yet continues to write in English because its complicated, okay, don't ask. She loves long hair and tentacles, sapphic romance and soft MCs who go badass and stabby when their LO is in danger. She writes literary comic books and wacky cosmic horror, or at least that's how she brands the random ideas that come to her, one's that generally point out the futile, unforgiving nature of life, the universe and everything, but with laughs and cool fight scenes. She thinks 42 means the number of books she has to write.

- E-Mail: imagineemmajun@gmail.com
- Twitter: @EmmaJuned

Ben Mariner - authorbenmariner@gmail.com

Chris Woolsey is a Search and Rescue Swimmer for the United States Navy. When he's not swimming, he enjoys pursuing his passion for literature. He writes in a style inspired by authors including H. P. Lovecraft, Jorge Borges, and Haruki Murakami, and currently lives in Japan with his wife, daughter, and dog, where he spends his free time writing stories about strange, mundane, and horrific events.

- E-Mail: coolsey137@gmail.com
- Instagram: @yigthewriter

Aberrant Tales is a collection unlike any other. Within this book are a variety of tales bursting at the seams with creativity and wonder. Tales of corporations that allow you to see into your own future. Tales of creatures that dwell within our dreams and nightmares. Tales of gallant knights battling through surreal, gothic landscapes to rescue the ones they love. These are stories that dare to be unique, to have a different point of view. Stories that entertain while conjuring up emotions of fear, excitement, and curiosity.

Aberrant Tales embraces a variety of narratives from the realms of science fiction, fantasy, and horror, and weaves them into one satisfying, eclectic package. Featuring twelve unique tales, *Aberrant Tales* will keep you on your toes as you experience the thrill of careening from one genre to another.

With *Aberrant Tales*, you truly never know what type of story you will encounter next. So prepare to fully immerse yourself in this collection of twelve fascinating tales filled with suspense, intrigue, and imagination. You'll find it to be one hell of a ride.

Jim awakens in an unknown room, drenched in sweat and newly amnesiac. As he ventures out to explore the apartment complex, he meets Skeeter, a genial, elderly man who holds the key to unlocking his memory.

Skeeter sends Jim on a metaphysical journey through time and space, with the apartments acting as unique wormholes to fantastic worlds and altered states of being that will ultimately reveal the truth of who he is.

Featuring boundless imagination and colorful, effective prose, *Preconscious* is a fast-paced, surreal journey that will leave you relentlessly turning the pages until it's mind-bending finale.

Aberrant Literature Presents

THE GHOST IN THE GRASS

a novel

MT ROBERTS

After receiving a letter from a once dear but now estranged colleague, Dr. Mannswell travels to the Karoo of South Africa. With scars of the Boer War still evident and his colleague missing, Mannswell is plummeted into a world of bureaucracy and decay.

As a series of unnerving clues and coincidences point to a centuries-old conspiracy, Mannswell is compelled to descend a mysterious gaping hole in pursuit of his sanity.

Featuring lyrical prose and a captivating alternate view of history, *The Ghost in the Grass* is a unique, slow-burn of a novel that deftly weaves history, suspense, and literary flair.

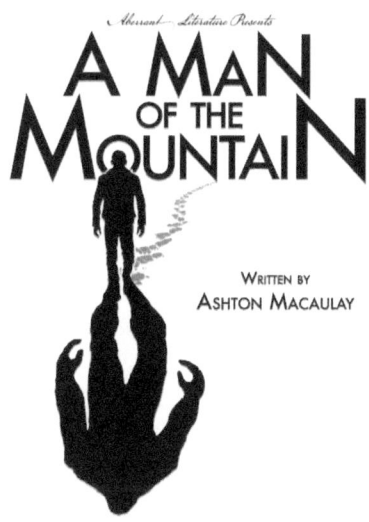

Aberrant Literature Presents

A MAN OF THE MOUNTAIN

WRITTEN BY
ASHTON MACAULAY

Jonas is a recluse. He lives in the mountains alone, appreciative of the peace and solitude the wilderness has to offer. It also enables him to keep his unusual line of work a secret.

At the behest of mysterious employers, Jonas has been instructed to wear a fur-covered suit and terrorize hikers at a local mountain range, all in an effort to maintain the mythical legend of Bigfoot. While typically uneventful, there are times when a hiker gets too close and the situation becomes...messy. Jonas may not be bloodthirsty, but he always does what's necessary to uphold a certain level of discretion.

After several high-profile 'accidents' are written off by authorities as bear attacks, tabloid reporter Shirley Codwell notices a pattern and sets out to unravel the truth. Convinced that the killings are the work of a legendary beast, she calls upon the monster hunting community for assistance. The events that transpire are like nothing she could have expected...and will send Jonas running for his life.

Set in the Whiteout universe, *A Man of the Mountain* is a thrilling dark-comic adventure that will keep you turning the pages right through to it's incredible, shocking conclusion.

Nick Ventner is a drunk with a blatant disregard for others. He's also damned good at hunting creatures that aren't supposed to exist. From amateur necromancers in the bayou to Sasquatch impersonators in the Pacific Northwest, Nick's seen it all. Even if some of the details might be a little fuzzy.

In *Whiteout*, Nick faces his greatest challenge to date. Accompanied by his trusty mountain guide, Lopsang, and his testy apprentice, James, Nick journeys into the Himalayas to settle a matter of pride and payouts, as he searches for the lost riches of Shangri-La rumored to lie within the mountain's peak.

However, the sudden arrival of Nick's greatest adversary, Manchester, complicates matters, and pits the two in a race towards the top, and both soon find that they have not just one another to contend with, but also a mythical and elusive yeti that has been terrorizing the mountain.

Featuring death-defying obstacles, hair-raising encounters with creatures from beyond, and a heavy dose of sarcasm along the way, *Whiteout* is sure to satisfy anyone looking for a fast-paced adventure novel brimming with action, suspense, and imagination. Not to mention the occasional whiskey on the rocks.

ABERRANT LITERATURE